THE GRANNY DIARIES

Hazel May Lebrun

Ant-Ken Books

Copyright © 2022 Hazel May Lebrun

All rights reserved

The characters and events portrayed in this book are fictitious. Any similarity to real persons, living or dead, is coincidental and not intended by the author.

No part of this book may be reproduced, or stored in a retrieval system, or transmitted in any form or by any means, electronic, mechanical, photocopying, recording, or otherwise, without express written permission of the publisher.

Ant-Ken Books, hazelmay64@gmail.com

ISBN-9798842342839

To my parents, Clarence Lebrun, who could not read a word that I wrote, but gave me more of an education than any institution ever could, and Ella May Lebrun, the woman who loved to write, and whose gift lives on in me.

Also, thank you, Mrs. McEwen, who scolded me (and I deserved it) in grade 6 and told me, quote, "You use that God-given talent for good." I hope I have done that every day since then. A wise teacher is a treasure.

"Friends are the siblings God never gave us."

                                        MENCIUS

INTRODUCTION

I have met pieces of Gladys Peachy, Ethel MacNarland, Tallulah Pratt and Dawn Kehoe at various places and times in my life. While I was working on "The Granny Diaries," there were times when I would be on a transit bus, in a cafe or mall, and suddenly, my mouth would drop open and I would literally see someone who would be perfect to play one of these characters in a film.

Gladys is a composite of a number of pastors' wives that I have met throughout my life. Though technically, she is a pastor's daughter-in-law, I drew on a lifetime of church women whom I admire to write her, and I grew to love her more as the pages kept turning.

Ethel is a composite of a number of neighbours I grew up close to, older women who would get me to run errands for them or would invite me in for tea and cookies.

Tallulah is also based on a few older women I have known, the ones who seemed to defy the physical aspects of their age. They could be identified as older, but they were still spry, lively and wonderfully vivacious and unapologetic. Who has time to apologize for stepping over social norms in your 70s? That certainly won't be me!

Dawn, a.k.a. Donkey, are those women who are starting to lose touch with the world, but are so beautiful and spunky and fun, you can't help but adore them. It's bittersweet to spend time with them because you know their sun is setting, and you mourn them even before they are really gone.

I hope you enjoy the adventures and the characters of Tranquil Meadows Seniors Villa as much as I did bringing them to life. Joy, pain, laughter, tears, fun, problems, relationships... these don't end after retirement. Don't believe me? Pop in to Tranquil Meadows and you'll find out, Dear Heart.

If you enjoy this book, feel free to drop the author a line...

hazelmay64@gmail.com

Kind regards,

Hazel May Lebrun

THE GRANNY DIARIES

Chapter One

Gladys Peachy

Why am I still alive? I ask myself the same question every morning when I awaken about a half hour before the sun's eye peers over the grove of white pine trees that line the Eastern boundary of the grounds at Tranquil Meadows Seniors' Villa. I live in Ottawa, Canada's capital city, although I spent most of my life in smaller towns around Ontario, colourful patches of farmland spreading out around me like a giant quilt.

My name is Gladys Peachy. It wasn't always. I was born Gladys Early, two whole months before my parents expected me to arrive. They thought I wouldn't make it, but what a plucky duck I proved to be, surprising the doctor and my parents and Great Aunt Mabel who said that her tea leaves predicted my certain demise. So much for porcelain prophecies.

My father made a joke out of it. He would say, "You're always early, Gladys Early!" And then, his pale green eyes would beam down on me as if Heaven's love were flowing through him into my soul. How I miss him! I see his eyes staring back at me when I look in the mirror, and my mother's curls, grey now, though they once were a rich, dark brown.

I like to sit at the window and watch the darkness retreat before the superior power of the light. There is no purer moment than this for me. I smile and think about the day I met Paul Peachy, son of the Reverend John Peachy, a firebrand and a revivalist; the type of man who seemed to hold life and death in his mouth. He traveled the circuit in his younger years, pitching tents from place to place, drawing in crowds like Billy Graham or AA Allen did. They claimed the Reverend Peachy was a good man. They may have been right, but I was as terrified of him as a child might be of an imaginary monster in the closet.

Paul was a good man. He had the same devout faith as his father, but a softness that drew me to his side like a moth to a flame. I was attracted to his virtue and his smarts. Paul planned to be a school teacher. Of course, it didn't hurt that he had eyes as blue as a peaceful lagoon.

"My father and Paul were guiding lights. I have been blessed with a luminous life." I whisper this to the air, breathe in the smell of the *Morning Glory* perfume I dab on my wrist every day. It masks the odor of disinfectant in this place. I know they have to keep it clean and germ-free, but the house I spent 40 years in over on Dunfield Crescent always smelled fresh without the scent of chemicals hanging over everything.

I raise a bony hand to my mouth and cough.

Tap tap tap.

A light knocking interrupts my thoughts and I hear the timorous whinge of the door as it opens and a pair of brown, deep set eyes appear.

"Good morning, Gladys."

"Good morning, Donkey. What time is it?"

She enters and glances at her wrist, looking at a watch that isn't there. "Half past a freckle." She laughs at a joke that isn't funny.

I humour her with a grin. "You're not quite dressed for the day." I notice she's still in a white cotton nightie; silver, short hair disheveled.

"No. Not yet, but I'm hungry. Is it time for breakfast?"

I pat my unmade bed and invite her to come and sit. "Soon." I open the drawer to my night table and produce a package of oatmeal cookies. "You can have these if you want."

Snatch!

She grabs the cookies as if she hasn't eaten in years. I know she had a sandwich before bed last night. She wore half of it and Ethel, Lula and I helped to clean it off of her face.

"I wonder if they'll give us bacon." Donkey smiles. "I would love that."

I know they won't serve us bacon. We're all in the autumn years of life, but they keep feeding us what they call 'healthy food', as if we're all eager to live to be 200.

"What's that? Did you hurt yourself?" I pass a finger over the back of her wrist.

"I don't know." She winces and pulls her hand away.

I'll have to ask the staff about it later. I see a bruise.

The cookie packet is empty now, my bed christened with a sparse layer of crumbs. "There now. Did that hit the spot?" I indicate the waste basket beside the bed. She puts the wrapper in it.

She nods. "They're good. Now we go for breakfast?"

I grin. "It's not quite time. Just a little while longer, Donkey."

Her name isn't really Donkey. It's Dawn Kehoe, but the way the syllables flow along, as in Don-Key-Hoe, made it easy to string them together, lop off the 'hoe' and call her Donkey. She accepted it as our pet name for her and we've been using it for the past two years, since her arrival as one of the residents at Tranquil Meadows.

Ethel MacNarland

Where did I put my glasses? Where where where? I've been

looking for them for ten minutes. I have a mad urge to go to the bathroom, but I'm blind as a bat. I squeeze my legs together to stop my bladder from baptizing my legs in hot pee. Ha! That's a good one. I'll have to tell the girls at breakfast.

My damned glasses! Where are they? Oh… I really have to go. Come on, Bladder. Can't you just keep it together for a few more minutes?

Dance… prance… dance… prance. I'm making my way to the blurry bathroom now, looking like some spindly-legged bird doing a courting ritual. That's a funny one. Everybody says I have a way with words.

Hurry up, Ethel MacNarland! You're going to leave a trail of pee all the way to the damned toilet! No no no! They'll make me wear diapers! Tranquil Meadows isn't happy when they find out you've got bladder control problems. They're the adult diaper police! *Heaven help me! Not going to pee not going to pee NOTGOINGTOPEE!*

Ahhh… there. I'm sitting down. You stupid bladder! Go ahead and make like Niagara Falls. That feels better. Now… where's the sink? There it is.

And where, for the love of Pete, are my glasses?

I want to write in my journal before breakfast. It was Mother's Day yesterday. I am going to wear the new clothes that Marianne and my granddaughters gave me. I remember those Sunday mornings when my two girls, Marianne and Meg would come up the stairs all a-twitter, trying to be quiet, but their whispers met my ears long before they pushed open the door to the bedroom.

There they would be, standing with a tray, their little brother Tim grinning behind them, cheeks full of dimples and roses. I was never so happy eating burnt toast and runny eggs. I'd trade all of this in a heartbeat to be back there, just for one day, back where they were young and still believed I was wise and could teach them something. When did things change? When did I become someone who couldn't live without them telling me what to do? How do they think I survived before I had them?

Where are my glasses? Where is my journal? I know. I'm primitive. All the young ones are blogging these days -- and vlogging! That sounds almost naughty, doesn't it? Oh, where is the stupid thing? I want to write my thoughts down on paper before I forget. I'm always most creative in the morning.

Tallulah Pratt (Lula)

It's been five years today since I lost my Tom. I can't complain. We had 45 years together. They were good years. Well, to be honest, some of them were horrid. There was that time our little Sarah got scarlet fever. The beautiful little thing. Neither one of us slept for days. Doctors. Medicine. Cold compresses. The poor child was delirious. She thought she saw angels, devils, Santa Claus. That was one of my most fearful times. Thank God we didn't lose her, but raising a deaf child wasn't easy.

"You were a good father, Tom." I smile, sweeping a stray strand of still carrot-coloured hair out of my eyes. I don't use dye either. The grey hair fairy hasn't landed on me yet, even though I am 72 years old. "I miss the way you laughed, those stupid jokes you told over and over again." I frown. "I forgive you."

There was much to forgive. The life of a traveling salesman took my husband away from home for weeks at a time. I didn't resent it. Sometimes, I thought it made our marriage stronger.

I sigh.

"I wonder if **she** forgives you too."

I don't care if she does. Beulah Brantford deserved what she got. She deserved to lose the man she had an affair with for ten years. What kind of woman does that? It's like emotional cannibalism. That's what Ethel says. She has such a way with words.

What time is it? I check my watch. I'm pretty sure it says 7:30. Not because I can see these numbers. Why do they have to make them so small? Thank goodness the hands are thick and black and I can tell that the little one is at the position where the 7 should be and the big one is pointing straight down.

Maybe I should listen to Ethel. She says I should let the eye doctor check me over and prescribe a pair of glasses. Well, that's easy for her to say. She's used to wearing glasses. I have always had near perfect vision. It's only lately that my eyes have gone a bit funny. I don't want some contraption covering my face like that. It's fine for her. She's not exactly a looker, but me? Why, I have the bluest eyes this side of Heaven. At least that's what Tom used to say.

Of course, for all his raving about my eyes, his philandering peepers still wandered until they found that ugly troll he strung along for ten years until I found out and then, in the end, he chose to dump her like an old pair of loafers. That's all she was good for too, walking on. What a dolt! Couldn't she get a man of her own?

Oh, I don't want to think about that anymore. It's almost time for breakfast. I think I'll head down to the dining room and see if Gladdy, Ethel and Donkey are there yet.

Wait. Let me check myself out in the mirror. "Tallulah Pratt. You don't look half bad for an old bird. Oh go on, Lula. No. I mean it. Go on and on and on."

Dawn Kehoe (Donkey)

I'm hungry. That's what I noticed first when I woke up. My stomach kept growling like I had a wild dog living inside me. They'll have to call me Doggy instead of Donkey.

The sun is up and the sky is turning the same shade of blue as a baby boy's blanket. I remember my Gabe. What a beautiful child! The nurses said he looked like an angel and that is why I called him Gabriel. It was the perfect name for him because when he sings, people think they died and went to Heaven.

I miss Gabe. I haven't seen him in a long time. I wonder when he's going to come and visit. I hope he brings my grandsons, Connor and Tyler, with him.

I'm so hungry. I can't believe it. It must be close to breakfast time. I haven't eaten anything since... I think it was Saturday. I don't like it here.

Look! Gladys is sitting right there. I don't remember her coming to my room. Wait a minute. This isn't my room. I have a pink and white crocheted afghan at the end of my bed. I won it in a raffle... I'm pretty sure I did.

Gladys is pointing to the trashcan beside her bed. I've got a cookie wrapper in my hand. When did I eat cookies? Maybe she ate them. Look at all the crumbs on her bed. It must have been her.

"It's not quite time. Just a little while longer, Donkey." Gladys says.

My hand is sore. Where did I get that bruise?

"I saw Gabe yesterday." Gladys says. "He said that he sang the national anthem before the Stanley Cup playoff game last Thursday night. He was on television in front of the whole country. You must be so proud."

I nod. "I'm proud of my son. I just wish he would visit. He hasn't been here in such a long time. Ungrateful is what he is! I worked so hard when he was growing up. I tried to give him the best of everything."

Gladys shakes her head. "He was here yesterday, Donkey. Don't you remember?"

I think... hard. Today is... Monday. It's the month of April. No. It's May. Yesterday was Mother's Day. Gabe came to visit with Connor and Tyler and they gave me... "They brought me flowers."

"That's right. Beautiful carnations. Pink. Your favourite colour."

I smile. "Such good boys. They remembered."

"Come on." Gladys leads me toward the door. "Let's go to your room and help you get ready for breakfast."

"Breakfast?" I cock my head to one side. "Is it morning?"

"Yes it is."

We walk down the hallway, voices and cling-clang echoing around us. I hear a familiar melody. I know who that is. It's Guy, the janitor who whistles show tunes while he works. "That's *Some Enchanted Evening*."

"Yes, Donkey."

"And it's Monday." I say, but not with much confidence.

"All day."

The nurse that came with me helps me to pick out clothes and she combs my hair. Wait. That is not a nurse. That's... that's... I think hard. Her name is Gladys Peachy. She's my best friend.

Chapter Two

Gladys Peachy

I couldn't convince Donkey that orange and purple clash. I feel embarrassed for her. She's in the dining room devouring poached eggs and toast. She's wearing a bright orange blouse. It's almost neon. Bright colours can be pretty, but her pants are the same shade of purple as an Easter egg. If Donkey goes outside, she'll be visible from the space station.

"Would you like some strawberry jam for your toast?" I ask, holding up the little packets that always come with our meals. I don't think the staff trust us to open jars.

"Yes, please." She takes the packet before I can open it for her.

"Be careful." I don't know why I bother to say that. It doesn't take long before Donkey has half the jam on her toast and half on the neon blouse.

"Oh, Lordy." Lula grabs a napkin to help clean up the splotch on Donkey's chest. "We should have grabbed one of those bibs."

"She won't wear it." I roll my eyes. "Says it makes her feel like a baby."

"It does. I'm 78, Gladys. I don't want to wear a bib or sit in a high chair."

"But... tsk tsk tsk... your beautiful blouse." Lula dabs at the stain.

"I think you should get glasses, Lula." I say.

Ethel takes off her specs. "Here. Want to try mine?"

"Keep those on." Lula giggles. "It took you half an hour to find them this morning."

"And they were on top of my head. I slept with them there." Ethel takes a bite of toast. "Then it took me another ten minutes to find my hearing aid."

Lula gives up. "There. That's the best I can do. You're going to have a red blotch in the middle of your blouse all day unless you change it."

Great! Now the space station will have a bulls-eye if they decide to shoot that orange and purple thing they're looking at from up there. Maybe we can persuade Donkey to change to a more suitable colour after breakfast.

Ethel MacNarland

I want another cup of tea. I don't dare. I pee an ocean as it is.

There are days when I think I should move my bed, my desk, my television and my bookshelf into the bathroom. If I just sit permanently on the toilet, I won't spend so much time fretting and crossing my legs, or maybe I should surrender and wear bladder control underwear. I don't want to, but if Tranquil Meadows finds out I can't hold my water, that will mean trouble.

"Is that the blouse you got from Marianne and the girls?" Lula points to my pale blue top with the daisy pattern. "It looks lovely on you. Really brings out your features."

"Yes yes. They brought it yesterday along with a box of chocolates and a pretty homemade card that Savannah made at school. That girl has a flair for drawing." I adjust the napkin that I am using as a makeshift bib. Unlike Donkey, I don't care if I look like a baby. "They brought me a gift card from Meg. She's still traipsing about Europe, and Tim and the children brought me flowers."

"I saw those flowers." Lula's hands flounce. "Orchids! My! They are the most gorgeous things!"

"Savannah is such a lovely girl." Gladys dabs her mouth with her napkin. "I love her long blond hair. Marianne takes good care of those children."

"Yes. She does." I smirk. "It's a miracle. When she was young, I don't know how many hamsters we had. She kept forgetting to close the cage door and they would go AWOL. I found one in the dryer. I found one in the mouse trap that I kept behind the fridge in case of unexpected rodents. I never meant to catch the family pet."

Lula covers her mouth and laughs. "Oh! That's awful."

"I know. Marianne and Jim were married almost 9 years without children. I thought she had just decided she didn't want any, but then one day, she comes over to the house and tells me she's expecting. Let me tell you. I had nightmares of finding a toddler in the dryer and trapped behind the fridge!"

"Ethel!" Gladys chuckles. "It couldn't be that bad."

"I had serious misgivings. Fortunately, Savannah and Lacy are both happy, well-adjusted girls. We don't have to go on Dr. Phil after all." I raise my head high. "I don't know what all the fuss is over that man. His show is like Jerry Springer – Texas style."

"Oh!" Gladys stifles a giggle. "I never thought of it that way, but I suppose he has the same kind of guests on."

"Sure." I sip my tea. "They don't throw chairs or pull hair, but it's the same thing. My kids are freaks. My husband's a cheater. I can't stop shoplifting at Walmart."

Gladys and I are laughing. Donkey keeps on filling her face with eggs and toast and part of Gladys' plate too. Lula sits there with a funny expression. Her face is funny at the best of times what with all those freckles sprinkled across her nose, the darker age spots above her left eye, that wild fiery hair framing her features. I have to say, though, Lula has the prettiest blue eyes you ever did see. Did God put sapphires in her face? I'd better stop thinking about that because it strikes me funny and Lula isn't laughing right now. She looks like she wants to swat me.

Tallulah Pratt (Lula)

That Ethel MacNarland should learn to keep her big mouth shut! Insensitive! That's what she is, and after I made such a compliment about the ugly blouse she got for Mother's Day. Where did Marianne pick that gem up? Gaudy Clothes Emporium?

Why am I so angry with Ethel? She didn't mean any harm. Still, doesn't she realize? She probably doesn't. I need to stop this nonsense!

I can't help it. I've been out of sorts ever since I opened my eyes this morning. First, I spent a while thinking about Tom. Oh Lord, I miss that man! Not all the time. Some days, he doesn't even cross my mind anymore, but it's been five years today since I lost him.

Ethel, how could you make a wise crack like that about going on Dr. Phil with your cheater husband? I belong on that show. Just call it, "I was a naïve fool for ten years, believing that two-timing jackass when he said he was going on another sales run." Have you got any episodes called that, Dr. Phil?!

"Lula. Is everything all right? You look cross. Did somebody pee in your tea?" Ethel grins.

I could slap it off of her face. I need to calm myself. My philandering husband isn't Ethel's fault. I'm just looking for someplace to spend my anger and, right now, Ethel looks like a great place to do it, but she's my friend. Whatever else happens and her daughter's awful taste in blouses notwithstanding, Ethel is a dear friend.

"Lula?" Gladys touches my arm like the gentle soul that she is. "What's the matter, Dear Heart?"

Everyone is surprised when the tears appear, myself included. How did they get there?

"Oh! Merciful Jesus!" Gladys grabs one of the few clean napkins that we didn't use on Donkey.

"Oh dear! I... I'm sorry..." I take the napkin and raise it to my eyes like a white flag. "I didn't think it was bothering me so much."

Dawn Kehoe (Donkey)

Breakfast tastes so good. I like coming to this place. Gladys, Ethel and Lula must like it too. We meet here a lot. That's what friendship is all about.

Gladys shared some of her food with me. She doesn't eat enough. Sometimes, I worry about her.

Look at all the people here. It's a popular joint. Either they have great advertising or word on the street is the food at Denny's is awesome.

Well, would you look at that? Who spilled jam all over my blouse?

"Lula? What are you doing?" I ask.

She's helping me wipe it off. She must have done it. For Pete's sake, can't she be more careful?

Strawberry jam will be a bit-. Oops! What's wrong with me? That was nearly a swear. I hope I remembered to pick up some *Shout* stain remover when I went grocery shopping.

Gabe makes it hard to shop. He's always fussing and whining in the shopping cart. He wants Frosted Flakes. He wants a candy. He wants to touch everything. They say those army men experience war and trauma, but it's mothers in the grocery store checkout line who go through war! This child won't stop shrieking. All the mothers stare at me like I'm a failure. *Shut up, Gabe! I'm doing the best I can!*

Wait. Gabe isn't crying. He's not even here. That's not him. I'm not in a store. I'm... I think hard. I'm at the breakfast table with my best friends, Gladys, Ethel and... oh my goodness! It's Lula! "Oh! Lula, Dear! What's the matter? Let me help you."

Lula has a tissue. She dabs at her lovely blue eyes. Gladys and Ethel are on either side, consoling and speaking comfort.

And what are you doing, Dawn Kehoe? Filling your stupid face with... what did I just eat? Eggs and toast. What kind of friend does that?

"You know I love you, Lula. With all of my heart." I offer my best smile.

Lula manages to smile back. "Thank you, Donkey." She reaches a hand across to touch mine. "You're wonderful friends. All of you."

I wince. Why does Lula's touch hurt? I look down. She gave me a nasty bruise.

"But, what's bothering you?" I really want to know.

"It's foolish, really. Today is the fifth anniversary of the day I lost my husband."

"I know how you feel." I reassure her. "I still cry over losing my husband. I miss him so."

Lula and Gladys exchange glances before Lula says. "But, you lost Lowell 45 years ago. Do you mean to tell me, you're still not over it?"

"What are you talking about? Who is Lowell? It wasn't long ago at all. It was such a tragedy too. He was mown down in the prime of his life by a careless pilot that swooped down low over the field where he was walking. I'll never forgive that awful man! I remember how handsome my husband was. A real humdinger!"

Gladys pokes Lula in the arm. "North by Northwest was playing on the TV in the activity room last night."

"Who were you married to, Cary Grant?" Ethel bursts out laughing.

I don't know what there is to laugh about.

"Ethel. Don't even go there. It's Cary Grant today and it will be Errol Flynn tomorrow." Gladys takes another sip of her tea.

The girls all laugh. I don't know what for, but at least Lula isn't crying and moaning about her husband anymore. I return to my breakfast and take another bite of toast. It's getting cold.

Chapter Three

Gladys Peachy

I am standing in my kitchen at 45 Dunfield Crescent in the small town of Goodrich. How I love this room! It has so many counters and cupboards and fanciful swirly mouldings. The wood swoops gently like waves that rise and then fall in the middle, a heart perched over the mid-section like a crown.

The large maple table that my father made for us is like the hub of the wheel of my life. I serve meals, hold hands and spend time with my Paul. Friends come over for tea. I make grocery lists and cut coupons and solve crosswords. Sometimes I sit in the chair closest to the window that faces the back porch, elbows resting on the white linen tablecloth, fingers intertwined as I hand over my fears and cares to God.

I am painting the walls to match the daffodils in the front yard. Bright yellow is like sunshine. It lifts you up, warms your insides, and whispers that everything will be all right in the morning.

I smile and look down at my belly, the telling protrusion that lets everyone around me know that I, Gladys Peachy, am incubating one of God's miracles. "Just two and a half months, Little One, and you'll be here with us. One plus one equals three!" I bite back a happy tear.

Oh, my back! How it aches and moans at me! Am I getting old? I laugh at the thought. I'm only 27.

"Gladdy, My Love. You should let me finish that." Paul emerges from his study where he has been preparing lessons for the grade seven class that he teaches over at Stuart Morrison Public School.

"It's all right." I set the brush on top of the paint can lid and wash my dirty hands. "I'm being careful. Dr. Carter says I can do normal activities. Just no heavy lifting. I promise to leave all the tough stuff for you." I pull the smock over my head and now I am back to my red maternity dress with the tiny white lambs scattered over it.

Paul reaches for me and I relish his embrace. It's a little awkward with our little Mister or Miss between us, but we manage. I lift my face to receive his kiss, enveloped in the unshakeable knowledge that I am loved. I belong. God has rained down blessings on me.

I pull away. Check the pork chops that I started baking almost an hour ago. I click off the oven, turn to Paul and smile, and then…

A knife pierces me through. Razor sharp and ruthless. I cry in horror. Paul reaches out to steady me, but I have no strength. It's fierce, this stabbing pain. I look into the peaceful blue of Paul's eyes, but all I see is my own face in the middle of the ocean, flailing, head bobbing barely above the water, mouth agape, sinking beyond his reach.

I start and awaken. Where am I? I am in a recliner in the big activity room at Tranquil Meadows Seniors' Villa. I must have nodded off. The images from my dreams linger in my mind's eye even as the rest of the room seems riveted to some movie on the TV. What are they watching? Is that Dick Van Dyke on the screen? They're watching *Mary Poppins*.

"You're always early, Gladys Early." How many times had my father said those words to me?

Even as the pangs of premature labour overtook me all those years ago, I had hope. I expected our beautiful Johnny to live. I made it, and believe me, that little bundle was every bit as feisty as I was, maybe more so.

Paul and I were permitted to hold John Paul Peachy when the doctor realized that our son was slipping away. I sat in a wooden rocking chair in my nightgown and rocked him while Paul, a much better singer than I, sang "*All night, all day, angels watching over me, my Lord. All night, all day, angels watching over me.*"

"Oh, Paul. It was all my fault."

"What was all your fault, Gladdy?" Lula looks up from the sofa beside me, where she has been busy crocheting squares for a new afghan.

"Nothing. I was just thinking out loud."

"Hogwash." Lula grins. "But, if you don't feel like talking about it, that's all right with me."

"To be honest, I'd rather forget."

"Oh you'll forget all right." She points to the large, round-faced clock above the door, the ugly white one with the big black hands. "The choir from St. Bart's is coming in about ten minutes."

I grimace. "You're kidding."

"I wish I was."

"They sing off key."

"I know."

"They were here last month."

"Yes, and they're going to punish us again. You'll forget all about your troubles." Lula sighs. "And so will I."

Ethel MacNarland

THE GRANNY DIARIES

We have several activity rooms at Tranquil Meadows. I am sitting in the biggest one. It's not the one where we play cards. It's the TV area, a bright rectangular space with tall side by side windows, cheery peach walls and Norman Rockwell prints that are supposed to remind us of the good old days. There are recliners, armchairs and sofas as well as hard-backed cushioned chairs, for those of us who don't care about comfort.

I am in a recliner beside the uncomfortable cushioned chairs. Gladys and Lula are across the way, sleeping and crocheting, but not at the same time. Haha! That's a funny thought.

Donkey is on a light brown, floral-patterned sofa with Dinah Gillespie and Agnes Holmes. Dinah is almost as dotty as Donkey, but Agnes is still spry and remarkably fit for her age. She was a professional dance instructor once and her limbs are still supple. Sometimes, when the dancers from the Fred Astaire studios drop by, Agnes demonstrates ballroom dancing with one of the dashing young men. Did I say young? I meant younger. That handsome Italian. Mario, still sports a full head of black hair and he's in his early forties.

Mary Poppins is on the floor model TV. Why don't they get us one of those big screens? Not that the screen is small on this one, but it's obviously old. My daughter Marianne has one of those flat screen models. The colours are rich and bright. When I go to visit, she puts on the shows I like and I can see everything much clearer than I can on this old relic.

Tim, my youngest, also has one of those TVs, but I don't visit there often. He chain smokes and all I can smell from the sofa, the curtains and the carpet is the stale aroma of tobacco. Revolting! It's better for my health if I let him bring his kids around to visit me here. Little Laird and Erin get a break from the stinky house too that way. Grandma is a smart old bird!

I grin as I watch Dick Van Dyke sing and dance. I won't be

19

surprised if Donkey's husband is a chimney sweep sometime today. Died tragically falling down the flue. The poor old gal. She's lovely, but she lives in two worlds. Maybe she's the lucky one. Maybe her world is better than ours.

Gladys is awake. She's chatting it up with Lula. It's just as well. I don't want to hear any more about Lula's dead husband. I, for one, am just as happy being a widow. I'm sure that some marriages are all sunshine and lollipops, but I felt like a canary in a cage. *Laird MacNarland. You were a harsh taskmaster.* I thought I was going to lose my marbles. All those silly questions. *Where have you been? Who were you with? What's for supper?* I frown. *You can just make it yourself, you mean-spirited ogre!* Why did I marry him? I think I loved him once. It's hard to remember. It was half a century ago and Laird has been nothing more than a ghost in my memory for nearly 15 years.

I may not be living the high life at Tranquil Meadows, but it's amazing how I can do all the simple things that people take for granted. For instance, I can inhale and exhale... inhale and exhale... I don't even have to ask permission first.

Who's that in the hallway? I know that face. *Think, Ethel.* Oh no! It's the Reverend Bellows from St. Bart's Anglican church. He's not here on visitation. He brought the Hell Choir! I envy Donkey. She'll never remember this concert. I turn toward Gladys and Lula. Their facial expressions tell me that they're as underwhelmed as I am. Can we escape? Can we just go back to our rooms and hide?

The activity room is filling up. I guess we're stuck here. It would be rude to just walk away now that the choir is standing right there, waiting to come in and torture us.

Tallulah Pratt (Lula)

Gladys doesn't want to tell me what's on her mind. I know it's something painful. She feels guilty. At our age, there are bound to be some regrets, some memories that we wish we could change, or at least forget.

Bless Donkey. She has the bliss of ignorance on her side. Not all the time. Sometimes she has extended periods of sharp and jarring lucidity. So much so, in fact, that I used to think she was faking it when she went off on one of her mind excursions. Look at her over there, watching *Mary Poppins.* She probably thinks Julie Andrews can really fly with an umbrella.

I smile and bite my lip. *I love you, Donkey. You weren't like this when you arrived here. What's happening inside that brain of yours?* My smile fades. *Will that happen to me?*

"Good afternoon, Ladies." Emmett Muggeridge doffs his fedora as he walks past, grinning at me in that way he always does.

He makes me uncomfortable. I haven't had that kind of attention from a man in years and I don't trust a man who smiles too much.

"Lovely afternoon ain't it?" Emmett chooses a seat on the white sofa with the blue paisley pattern.

Why does he have to sit there? I'm sitting on it. Well, I don't own the whole thing, but there are perfectly good recliners and sofas. I look around the room and realize that he has to sit there. The other seats are filling up fast. It must be almost time for St. Bart's.

"It's a beautiful day." I respond. It would be rude to say nothing. "I'm thinking of taking a stroll in the gardens after the performance."

Emmett nods. "It's a fine day for that. Maybe you should have some company."

Mercy! Tallulah! You walked right into that one. What is wrong with you? Emmett Muggeridge has been after you for a date for half a year. You should be wise to his advances by now, but even at 73, Emmett has most of his hair, salt and pepper coloured. His hazel eyes twinkle when he smiles and I can see that he must have been a lady-killer in his youth. He disarms me too easily and I smile, but, Lordy, that sends him the wrong message!

A thought runs through my mind. *Is that how Tom did it? Is that how he lured Beulah Brantford to be his mistress? Did he flash those baby blues at her? Smile? Charm her?*

I am spared the pain of having to decline Emmett's offer as Pete Marsden walks by and plunks himself on the sofa between us.

"Hello Pete." I greet him as if he were my saviour. "It's nice to see you. You're looking much better after that bout with shingles."

"Pardon me?" Pete hesitates, pulls the hearing aid out of his ear and adjusts the volume before shoving it back in again.

"I said it's nice to see you. You look much better now that you're over the shingles."

He smiles at me and nods, his silver comb-over not fooling anyone. He's as bare as a baby's bottom up top, although he still has hair on either side and at the back. "Hello Tallulah. Thank you kindly. I'm feeling much better too. I'll tell you. I don't wish those shingles on my worst enemy. I think that's the most painful thing I ever had… except maybe that time I had the car accident and broke two ribs and an arm."

Emmett jabs Pete in the ribs. "Was it that side that you broke the ribs on?"

"Ow! Yes, it was. What did you do that for?"

"Just checking."

Pete scowls. "Next time, don't check so hard."

Emmett points across the room. "Looky there, Pete. There's Ethel sitting in a recliner. Wouldn't you like to sit a little closer to her?"

I didn't know Pete was sweet on Ethel. Really?

Pete shrugs. "Where? There's no chair over there except one of those ones that make my backside hurt."

Emmett doesn't miss a beat. "Ethel told me that she likes to dance. She was hoping you would ask to be her escort to the spring social."

Pete's eyes widen. "She told you that?"

Emmett nods. "Surely did. You'd better hurry up too. I hear Nino Fabrini wants to ask her. He might beat you to it. You know those Italians. They've got a way with the ladies..."

Up Pete jumps, literally, and marches over to one of the cushioned chairs that everybody avoids. It has a great location though and now he is seated right beside the recliner where Ethel is watching TV. Did Ethel really say she wanted to go to the social with Pete? She never mentioned it to me. What a bit of cheek!

Here comes the Reverend Bellows and the *Screeching Cat Choir*. Ethel calls them the *Hell Choir*. That's funny, but I can't go that far. I might even enjoy their music if... well... do they actually practise?

Dawn Kehoe (Donkey)

Dinah Gillespie came and sat beside me. I never said she could sit there. She's half crazy. Do you know she thinks she's related to the Queen of England? If that's true, then I'm the Prime Minister's third cousin twice removed. I wish she would go sit someplace else. I don't like people who tell me lies.

I'll tell you what. Guess who's sitting at the other end of the couch. It's Ginger Rogers; the famous dancer who used to glide across the floor with Fred Astaire in the movies. She's lovely. Look at her beautiful hair all twirled up in a bun. I wish my hair could do that. It's too short. I used to have long, bone straight hair, dark as charcoal, which hung down almost to my waist. I don't know when I decided on this stupid haircut. I don't like it. Maybe I'll grow my hair out again. If Ginger can have long hair, so can I.

Gee… what's that music playing? I know this song. I'm sure I've heard it before. Something about a chim-chiminey, chim-chiminey…

Look at the room filling up with people!

"Dinah. Are we going to have a party?" I ask, curious. She just stares off into space like the drippy dame that she is. "Dinah? Why are all these people cramming in here?"

She shrugs her droopy shoulders and shakes her head. "It's your house. You tell me."

"My house?" I look around. "This doesn't look like my house."

My husband and I lived in a house with white siding and blue shuttered windows. It had two stories plus a cluttered basement and a creepy attic. I was always scared to go up there even though all the contents of that room were mine and I certainly didn't store any skeletons or corpses anywhere. What a thought!

I was afraid of ghosts. My sister insisted that the place was haunted. Silly Eve. She believed all kinds of nonsense like that. I told her it was foolish. I still wouldn't climb up those steps alone. I guess I was just as yellow as she was.

"It's a concert." Dinah points to a group of people in regal burgundy gowns. They are filing in, songbooks in hand. "Are we having the Mormon Tabernacle Choir?"

I throw my hands out. "Must be, but... I thought there would be more of them."

Chapter Four

Gladys Peachy

What a friend we have in Jesus
All our sins and griefs to bear
What a privilege to carry
Everything to God in prayer

That used to be my favourite hymn. It's a pity the choir from St. Bart's is murdering it.

We used to sing *What a Friend We Have in Jesus at* those wild revival camp meetings when I was a teenager. Reverend Peachy would set up a tent and the posters would go up on the lamp posts, ads in the newspaper, word of mouth spreading like a brush fire through town.

I was a rosy-cheeked 16 year old the first time my parents took me to a Peachy Revival meeting. The dog days of August made it feel like we were in an oven, at least until the sun went down and the cooler night air began to roll in on the breeze. We all sang at the top of our lungs. Hymns. Choruses. How I loved the songs! I wasn't a good singer. I wasn't horrid, but there was nothing remarkable about my voice.

Maybe that is why I noticed it. All the voices raised in unisonous worship, blending and merging until it was nearly impossible to tell one from another. What song were we singing? I think it was... yes it was... *There is power power wonder working power in the blood of the lamb...* I heard something behind me. It could have been the voice of an angel. I had to risk the wrath of my mother and crane my neck around to see what it was. I wouldn't have been surprised if I had seen an angelic being, wings and all, but what I saw was a handsome young man with waves of honey-coloured hair and tropical blue eyes. He smiled at me and a firework bud burst open in my heart. That was my first encounter with Paul Peachy.

I was so dazzled by the preacher's son that I didn't even think it so glorious when Lillian Forsythe got up out of her wheelchair and began to dance about the stage. I mean, she had been in that contraption since before I was born. I should have been gobsmacked. I was, but I feel guilty for admitting, it wasn't God's miracle that made me that way. Of course, a good marriage is like a miracle, isn't it? I've heard plenty of horror stories. Maybe meeting Paul was just as much a miracle from Heaven as Lillian Forsythe's ample body jitterbugging in front of the whole camp meeting.

I don't remember much of Reverend Peachy's sermon that night. I have vague recollections of his broad, imposing frame hopping up and down to intensify the meaning of his words, but the eyes of the younger, longer and leaner Peachy seemed to drill through the back of my head as if his gaze had an electrical charge. I had had a crush on a boy once in grade school. Jimmy Whitmore. I drew hearts and put *Jimmy + Gladys Forever* inside them. The affection had blown away as easily as dandelion seeds by the end of the school year.

This feeling had some elements of that first infatuation, but it didn't feel like Cupid's arrow. It felt like Cupid's sword impaled me clear through. I had been a complete person yesterday. Now, I was severed in half and the rest of me was sitting not five feet away, though it could have been a thousand miles.

A hush settled over the crowd. Reverend Peachy came out from behind his pulpit and stood front and center, face condensed into a look of intense concentration.

"My friends. John 3:16 says that God... the God who made everything... He loved this world so much... and you can insert your name there. For God so loved Johnny or Susie or Mary or

Jim. Put your name in that verse, for God so loved you and I that He gave his only Son that whosoever... put your name in there again... God gave his only son that if Johnny or Susie or Mary or Jim... believe in him, then they will not perish. That's you again. You will not perish. You will have everlasting life. You will spend eternity in the beautiful place that is being prepared for you right now.

"My friends, do not hesitate to accept this wondrous gift. The opportunity may not come again. None of us know when our moment may arrive and death may require our souls of us. Please... say yes to Jesus. Say yes to living forever. Say it today. Make a decision and, if you are wise enough to make that decision today, then jump to your feet right now, make your way down this aisle and stand here with me while we pray you into God's Kingdom. Hallelujah!"

He told me not to hesitate. I did. I mean, I had prayed for Jesus to come into my heart in Sunday School at the ripe age of four and a half, but I thought it couldn't do any harm to pray again... just in case God forgot. I was going to step into the aisle, but my feet were glued to the ground. That is, until...

"Do you know Jesus as your Lord and Saviour?" The same angelic voice that had captured my heart when we were singing now asked me this question. His strong, unblemished hand was stretched toward me, beckoning me, offering to escort me to the front of the tent.

"Thank you, Jesus." I said as I reached out and took his hand. He thought I was thankful for salvation. I guess I was, but I felt more blessed than anybody in the tent. Divine providence had given me the opportunity to stand beside this beautiful young man. I had no idea that soon, we would choose to stand beside each other for life.

Oh dear! Is the choir still singing? I zoned out. It's just as well. Now they're screeching *Oh How I Love Jesus because he first loved me.* I've never thought of hymns as unpleasant before, but... how can I stand one more second of this?

I look over at Lula. She's just as upset as I am. Emmett Muggeridge too. I shrug at them. Emmett smiles at me, though not the way he smiles at Lula. Friendly like. He's a sweet old gentleman. I don't know why Lula won't let him court her.

I look across the room at the other people. Some of them have the same pained expressions as us, but some of them are smiling so sweetly. Donkey is, though she does that at the best of times. Ethel is smiling! So is Pete Marsden and Agnes Holmes! Are they actually enjoying this? I don't believe it. Maybe I'm the problem. Are they not really the worst choir in the history of music?

Ethel MacNarland

How I dread sitting through an hour with the Hell Choir. I honestly wonder how I can keep a straight face through it. Here I am, wishing that the urge to pee would take over and give me a valid excuse to just up and leave the activity room, but no. When I need my bladder to save me, where is it?

Wouldn't this be a good time for Jenny Logan to take one of her fainting spells? There she is, sitting dressed to the nines on the old plaid sofa closest to the bookshelves. Where does she think she's going? High tea? A meeting with the Prime Minister? Her mauve dress is fitted and she wears gloves and a hat to match, with low heels and a purse to complete the ensemble. She isn't fooling me. I know that underneath that prim exterior, she's wearing Depends. So much for airs and graces.

"Good afternoon Ethel." Pete Marsden takes one of those uncomfortable seats beside me.

"It's a lovely day." I smile. "Are you sure you want to take that seat? I'm sure they use those chairs to torture prisoners of war."

Pete laughs. "I don't mind. Ever since the doctor gave me pills for my back, I don't feel it so much. Besides..." He tosses a quick glance Lula's way. "I think Emmett wanted me to give him a chance to sweet talk Lula."

"She'll be less than impressed with that. She complains about it an awful lot and today... well, I probably shouldn't mention this, but Lula lost her husband five years ago. I'm not so sure she wants Emmett to..."

"She complains a lot, does she?"

"Quite a bit, yes."

He grins and nods. "Don't you think that perhaps she doth protest too much?"

I hadn't thought of it that way. "Perhaps she does. Gladys doesn't understand it either. She keeps telling her there's no harm in sharing a meal with Emmett."

Pete's smile softens. "Or maybe even dancing?"

"That would be fine too. The spring social is coming up." I frown. "My husband Laird wasn't a great dancer. The only thing he could do now and then was a stupid highland fling."

Pete raises a bushy eyebrow. "That would be hard to do with a lady."

"Yes. It would."

"Do you like to dance?"

"I suppose I do. Oh... but I'm not very good at it." Why is Pete looking at me like that? Is he a man or a puppy? His grey eyes have gone all soft and droopy.

"I'm no Fred Astaire." He shrugs. "But you and me... we could dance badly together at the spring social. I mean, if you were so inclined to let me escort you. Would you?"

Now, that came out of the blue! Pete Marsden is asking me on a date. What do I say? I don't want a date... do I? I open my mouth to answer, but that is when the Hell Choir decides to make their entrance.

"Oh-oh." Pete takes his hearing aid out, fiddling with the volume button. "You should do this too, Ethel..." He snorts. "... unless you want to actually hear them."

"You're turning the volume so low." I shake my head. "You won't be able to hear a thing!"

"Pardon me?" He looks up, squinting.

I raise my voice. "You can't hear!"

"Exactly." He pops the device back in his ear and the grin on his face would make the Cheshire cat from *Alice in Wonderland* jealous.

I look at the assembling choir. I look at Pete. I look around the room and notice that Agnes Holmes has her hearing aid out too as do several others within my scope of vision. I giggle and bite my lip. I feel like a child who has just discovered a naughty secret. Out comes my hearing aid. Down goes the volume.

Reverend Bellows introduces the choir, but all I perceive are his lips moving. He could be telling me about a sale on melons at Loblaws for all I know. Ha! Wait until I tell the girls later!

As the singers open their mouths to begin, in my mind, at first, I insert whatever I want to an imaginary tune. How about... *Hello my Baby. Hello my Honey. Hello my ragtime gal...* I have to stop that though because it makes me want to laugh and I don't think the choir from St. Bart's would appreciate that.

Tallulah Pratt (Lula)

Emmett Muggeridge can keep his roaming hands to himself. The gall! What does he think I am? Some cheap little floozy he picked up at a house of ill repute? Does he think my name is Beulah Brantford and he can sweep me off my feet and make me into a would-be home wrecker? Ha! The joke was on her, wasn't it?

And you should have seen Beulah. I don't know what the fuss was about. Five foot two, dull grey eyes, ugly brown bowl cut. All right. Maybe it wasn't a bowl... a page boy. Still, it didn't suit her. She tried desperately to colour over the grey, but no matter what she did, it turned out like a Neapolitan ice cream cone; part vanilla, part chocolate and part whatever that god-awful colour was.

Enough about Beulah, the troll of my life. Emmett is the problem now. I don't want to hold hands. It doesn't matter how sweetly that man smiles at me. I don't trust him! Did he cheat on his wife? What was her name again? Lois? Louise? Lorna! I remember. It was Lorna. He says that she could steal any man's heart with one taste of her cooking and one wink of her eye. Hmm... well... that is a nice thing to say. I suppose Emmett's not a bad sort. He can be cheeky though. What will people think if I just up and hold hands in the middle of the activity room during an earful assault by the world's worst choir?

"We don't have to explain ourselves at our age." He says.

Well, I do! Imagine if the girls saw him slide his large, surprisingly still strong hand over mine. Would I ever hear the end of it? That is why I pulled my hand away and folded them both in front of me on the afghan I'm working on. Then, when he sidled even closer and tried it again, I moved my hands and sat on them.

Now I'm sitting here, full weight on my hands, and it's getting uncomfortable and they're starting to fall asleep. So are a few of the residents. In between hymns, I can hear Dinah Gillespie's snoring and her chin has dropped down against her chest.

When will this be over? Haven't we heard enough? Maybe somebody should politely tell these well-meaning twits that they weren't cut out for this.

What's the deal with all the smiling faces in here? I see scowls, some blank stares, a few sleepers, and then all these happy, smiling idiots. Even Ethel! What is there to smile about? These people can't sing! How are they managing to look so serene? I'd like to know because I sure can't keep a peaceful look on my face while St. Bart's is butchering *In the Sweet By and By*.

I look at the clock. It's been almost 40 minutes. That means we're stuck here for at least another 20. I start wondering if I can make a graceful (or ungraceful) exit. Make up a coughing fit. Pretend I have to be sick. Wave my hand in front of my face and exclaim, *"Lordy, I've got the vapours!"*

I turn toward Emmett who is still patiently sitting beside me, suffering my coldness to his warm advances. He must have gotten an A in persistence. I smile, escaping into the warmth of his welcoming eyes for a few seconds. It helps me forget the horrible music. I almost hear another tune in my head; something happy and snappy and old.

Wait a second. That's not in my head. I'm really hearing… my mouth drops open even before I turn my neck to see what is transpiring in the middle of St. Bart's concert of horrors.

"Supercalifragilisticexpialidocious…"

"Donkey! No!" I am about to leap to my feet, but Emmett taps my shoulder and shakes his head.

"She's our salvation."

"What?"

Emmett grins.

I look over at Gladys who is on her feet, but also stifling giggles. She glances over at my befuddled face and mouths, "We shouldn't have let her watch Mary Poppins."

I turn back toward Donkey and notice Ethel hurriedly yanking the hearing aid from her ear and adjusting the volume up. Well, that explains her silly smile. Now what are we going to do about Donkey? She is having a mini concert of her own. She is up off the sofa, singing, dancing, giving her best stage performance. I have to admit that her singing voice is better than the members of that choir. So that's where Gabe got it from.

"What do we do?" I tap Gladys on the arm.

"We have to redirect her somehow."

Now I get up, despite Emmett's protests and cross the floor with Gladys. We meet Ethel and the three of us just stand there for a moment, mesmerized, taken aback at Donkey's dedication and agility as she continues.

"It's nuts." Ethel says. "It's absolutely nuts."

"Singing Mary Poppins in the middle of the floor? I guess so." I shrug. "She got a hold of Dinah Gillespie's cane and now it's a prop."

I hope Emmett keeps an eye on his fedora. She'll be grabbing for it next.

Gladys takes a step forward, then changes her mind. "I hate to stop her. Look! She's got the whole room singing along, even the choir."

"Oh Lordy. Not them." I cringe.

"She probably really thinks she's Julie Andrews." Gladys' eyes mist over.

Gladys is right. Donkey may have gone off to la-la land, but she's working some kind of spell over the residents who have been suffering through badly sung hymns for more than half an hour. Something amazing is happening. It's almost inspiring to watch. Almost every mouth, those who are awake at least, is moving and singing along with our dotty friend as she smiles, waves her hands, nods and encourages them to join in her cheerful rebellion.

I glance over at the choir. They look dumbfounded, although a few of the members have abandoned *I'll Fly Away* and are now singing with Donkey. Reverend Bellows purses his lips together as if he just put a lemon in his mouth.

"Wowie." Ethel puts a hand beneath her chin. "Donkey can't remember what day it is, what time it is, who she saw today or what she ate, but she knows every single word to *Supercalifragilisticexpialidocious*."

I can't take it anymore. I double over and start to belly laugh.

Dawn Kehoe (Donkey)

Who are these people? I thought they were The Mormon Tabernacle Choir, but they can't be. Not unless they've gone seriously downhill.

Somebody in that group is tone deaf.

I know it isn't me.

When I was a young girl, I was admitted to a prestigious school called the Jean Montgomery Institute of Music. Eve, my older sister, and I both auditioned to go, but I was the only one that was accepted. Eve was madder than a wet hen when I got in and she didn't. I don't know if she has ever forgiven me.

That is how I know that these singers aren't doing it right. Are they singing badly on purpose? Is it some new fashion to be out of tune?

Look at that! Ginger Rogers is smiling. She seems to like it. Ethel is smiling too. I don't understand it. I can't be the only one with perfect pitch in the room. That's what Miss Montgomery said my first week at her music school. *"Dawn Gardiner. You have a gift. Many musicians would give their eye teeth for perfect pitch."* I don't want anyone giving me teeth, and right now, listening to these awful vocalists, I don't know if it's truly a gift. It did get me a lead role in our annual recital though, and today is the day!

I look out over the audience. So many smiling faces. Every chair filled in the big auditorium. My mother, my father, my brother and Eve take their seats in the second row from the front. I want to make them proud of me. All of those lessons, the hours and hours of rehearsal, they will pay off when the curtain opens and I am front and center.

I've practised every line, every step, every part. I could do my own part and most of the others if I had to. That's how much I paid attention to my instructors. This is the most important moment of my life, the day I step out from under the shadow of Eve and become a formidable girl, maybe even a woman, in my own right. I hope I don't make any mistakes. I couldn't bear to see that look my mother gets when I've disappointed her again.

A hush falls over the crowd as the curtain rises. The music begins. There is my cue...

"Supercalifragilisticexpialidocious..."

I am singing. I am dancing. I am inciting the audience to

participate. Miss Montgomery says that a true entertainer engages the audience to the point where they temporarily forget their own lives and willingly go on a journey with you wherever you decide to take them. First, you've got to grab their attention and get them in the door. Then, once they're there, you'd better have a wonderful place to bring them so their focus doesn't wander. If they start thinking about their shopping lists, their jobs or their troubles while you're performing, your boat is sunk.

I'm giving it my all. I'm working the room, as they say. How thrilling! The audience seems so close, I could almost touch them. I see their lips moving. They're singing along. Dawn Gardiner, you have done it! You have become a successful entertainer.

I do my grand finale and wait for the applause. I glance down at the second row. *Mother! Mother?* Is she smiling?

Who are these people taking my arms? I look up into the faces of complete strangers. Wait. No. I know you. Don't I?

"That was lovely, Donkey. How about we go and have tea?" Her face looks so kind. A lady with pale green eyes and grey curls.

"I could eat." I say, and she smiles at me, merriment in her twinkling eyes.

"I don't doubt it. Let's go find snacks."

"All right. I'm always hungry after a performance."

"And you did a fantastic job." Ethel says. *Oh! I recognize her!* And, once we're out in the hall. "Everybody owes you one for saving us from that Hell Choir."

I don't know what Ethel means, but she seems happy about it, so I don't say anything more. What kind of cookies are we having today? I hope they have chocolate chip.

Chapter Five

Gladys Peachy

Reverend Peachy forbade us to play cards. He said they were from the devil. While I had no doubt that there was a devil and that there were some activities that fell on his side of the fence, I never believed that playing cards did any harm. I knew that some people used them to try and tell the future, but when I was growing up with my older brothers, Ron and Joe, and my little sister, Glenna, we used them to play *Old Maid* and *Snap* and *Crazy Eights*.

When Paul and I first got married, before we had a place of our own, we lived with the Reverend John and Mrs. Adelaide Peachy for half a year. I used to hide my deck of cards in the same drawer where I kept my undergarments. I knew that no preacher man would dare to look in there. I wasn't willing to give them up. I guess they were my secret *vice*. I didn't smoke or drink or dress like a floozy. I just liked a good game of *gin rummy*.

Sometimes I felt guilty for my deliberate rebellion. Other times, I felt empowered. As a woman in those days, any small victory was a victory nonetheless. I don't know why I didn't leave them with my parents or my siblings until Paul and I could afford our own home. It seems silly to me now. I could have avoided an unnecessary conflict. I have never liked confrontations of any kind. It makes my stomach feel like an old ringer washer, churning and turning and stirring up dirt.

One afternoon, I was helping Adelaide peel potatoes for dinner, her honey-coloured hair (the same shade as Paul's) wound up in a bun and my curls wrapped in a kerchief. The floral apron she wore could have wrapped itself twice around her stick-thin frame. The reverend (I never dared to call him

John) was in his study preparing a new sermon to take with him on his next road trip. Paul was being interviewed for his first teaching position at Doris Campbell Elementary School. The younger Peachy children, 12-year-old David and 10-year-old Elizabeth (the Peachy family lost a boy to pneumonia in between Paul and David) were playing *Parcheesi*, one of the few pleasures their father allowed.

"I think it's lovely that you can make your own clothes, Gladdy." Adelaide spoke so softly, I could barely hear. I wasn't sure if that was her natural speaking voice or if she was just as terrified of the reverend as I was. "That dress is simple, but oh, it's lovely!"

"Thank you. My grandmother taught me." I picked a potato out of the bag. "She said that if a woman isn't pretty, she'd better be useful."

Adelaide set down her paring knife and slid her hand over mine. "You're a lovely girl. I don't know why anybody would ever say that you're not."

I sighed. "Grandma loved me. Of that I am sure. She just had her ways. She said things that she thought were funny, but…"

"Sometimes they weren't so funny. I understand. Believe me, Daughter, I know what it's like to wither because somebody's big fat shadow is blocking out your sunlight." She almost giggled.

My jaw dropped open. I almost laughed, but then I looked at Adelaide's face and she was dead serious. I saw that it was true too. She was white as a sheet, even in mid-summer. She wilted all right and long before her time, her flower ceased to be.

"Do you mean…?" I didn't know what to say.

Adelaide half-grinned. "They don't mean to be that way. Some trees are just so large and their branches so far-reaching, they don't even realize that they're stunting the growth of the smaller plants all around them. Sucking up all the water. Commanding all the attention. It's not even their fault, really. Can they help who they are?"

I never got to respond to that question. It was just as well. To this day, I don't have a clear answer.

A lion roared. At least, it seemed so. Reverend Peachy's voice was naturally loud and booming and, when his ire or his passion for the gospel or his indignation arose, it shook the house. Truth be told, I was never afraid he would become violent, but he had an authority that might have cowed a drill sergeant. I often wished I could see him square off with one, just to test my theory.

"Who brought these tools of the devil into my house?!"

My heart leapt into my throat at the knowledge of what it must be. Unless Paul or David or Elizabeth suddenly tried to sneak some dreaded Elvis Presley into the house, there was only one thing that could cause a vocal earthquake of this magnitude.

I gave Adelaide an apologetic look.

Reverend Peachy appeared in the kitchen doorway, David and Elizabeth in tow, and a mess of spades, clubs, hearts and diamonds in his broad, clean, preacher's hands. "Look at this, Mrs. Peachy. Look what I found our children playing with in the family room. Where did these come from?"

I gasped. Hiccoughed. Raised a hand to my mouth. "I... oh..." I felt ire that the children had rummaged through my private things. I dared not express that now. "They're mine."

Reverend Peachy looked shocked at first. His brow furrowed, lips tautened, rage palpable. "Daughter, perhaps you were unaware. The Peachy family does not keep cards in the house. These are used by fortune tellers, mediums, workers of iniquity!"

"Oh John, please. It's just a deck of cards." Adelaide shook her head.

"Addy. I won't be defied in my own home!" He held the offending items up in his trembling hand. "I won't have my children led into a life of debauchery!"

"By playing *Old Maid*?" Adelaide stood her ground, even though her tiny frame made her appear dwarfed in front of, as she had aptly stated, this big fat shadow.

"Our children will be led astray." He continued, revving up his preaching engine.

I suddenly felt as if we were in a revival tent... minus the raucous singing.

"They'll turn to witchcraft. Gambling! Alcohol!"

"We have good children. They know the difference between right and wrong."

"Obviously not! Look what they were doing!" He pitched the cards onto the table.

"John!"

"I... I'm sorry." I hung my head.

"Gladys, we welcome you into our family as a daughter, but we cannot allow you to bring evil into our midst. Go and gather up the remaining cards and dispose of them, please, before the damage is done and the children are tempted away from the path of righteousness." He turned to walk away, and then stopped to lob one more warning. "Perhaps some time in your prayer closet is warranted. Have no fear. The Lord forgives. You know what they say. Confession is good for the soul."

I looked at Adelaide. She gave me a knowing smile.

My admiration for her hidden strength blossomed in that moment. I thought she was just nice before, but that day, I saw something I both did and did not want. I wanted to have her grace under fire, her wisdom and her courage. I did not want to become almost a specter, who I was stifled and smothered, the mould of my being warped until I fit someone else's image of who I ought to be.

It was only a month later that Paul and I took a small apartment close to his new workplace. The Peachy home may have been bigger and prettier and easier to keep clean, but that little living space felt like Heaven because Paul and I had peace. We had our love for each other, our love for Jesus, our love for our fellow man. We also played *gin rummy* at least once a week. I used to laugh like the dickens every time I beat him. "There, Paul! That's what you get for growing up in a house with no playing cards!"

"Shhh! Don't tell my father. He'll faint." He would say, grinning.

Now, here I am, sitting in Activity Room #2, the games room, at Tranquil Meadows Seniors Villa. I'm sipping on a tasty cup of orange pekoe tea topped off with a splash of milk. Donkey wolfed down eight chocolate chip cookies before I grabbed the package and shoved it in the cupboard. Out of sight, out of mind.

We are all seated around a small, square table. Donkey is wearing a pretty white sweater, even though it isn't cold in here. She agreed to change out of the orange blouse, but not the purple pants, but white and purple aren't such a bad combination.

"Donkey, do you have any jacks?" Ethel smiles, watching her carefully look over each of the cards in her hand.

"Go and fish." Donkey giggles. "I think I'm going to win this time!"

I wish Donkey was having one of her good days. I'd rather play *gin rummy* or even *euchre*. Today, this is all our friend can handle, but that's all right. It's not like we're going anywhere special. Maybe she'll be up to a more adult card game tomorrow.

Ethel MacNarland

"I didn't know Donkey was such a talented performer." Agnes Holmes has a wide, exaggerated grin. "We could have planned something together. I would have done a dance number." She shuffles and taps with her feet.

"None of us knew." I shrug.

That is the truth. Donkey has been my friend for two years plus and she has never mentioned that she can sing. We've heard story after story about her kinda sorta famous son, but nothing about what she can do, what she must have been doing when she was young. Nobody just hops out of the gate being able to sing and step like that.

Agnes finally leaves our table, so we can start our card game. It's been steady all afternoon, ever since the Hell Choir left. The residents are raving about Donkey. I haven't heard a negative word. Well, no. That's not true. Jenny Logan, still dressed for tea with the queen, was put out that Donkey didn't wear, what she in her British vernacular termed, fancy dress. Jenny also mentioned that she should have been in charge of the clothing department and why hadn't anyone informed her that there would be a musical number by one of our very own.

Donkey is diving into the chocolate chip cookies and, by some miracle, we have managed to keep it off of her white sweater. I keep wincing and waiting for that one to bite the dust.

"Why didn't you tell us, Donkey?" I ask.

"Tell you what?"

"You're so talented. We didn't even know about it. Where did you learn to perform like that?"

The smile appears, then disappears, then appears, then disappears. "I don't know."

"I can't sing and dance like that. You wouldn't want me to even try. I would trip over my own feet, and my singing voice would make your tea get cold!"

Donkey laughs. "It would not."

I roll my eyes. "Yes, it would. I sing off key."

"Like the choir?"

"Yes. Like the choir."

"They were awful. Why do they come here?"

"Some people like to volunteer their time to entertain senior citizens."

"That wasn't entertaining. Not like I was when I went to the Jean Montgomery Institute of Music."

Lula's mouth drops open, even though she isn't finished chewing her cookie. "You went to the Montgomery Institute?"

Donkey nods, then looks away. "It was a long time ago."

"That school is top shelf." Lula picks up her teacup and mock toasts. "Well I'll be. Our Donkey was professionally trained. It wasn't Juilliard, but it was close to it."

"I couldn't go to Juilliard." Donkey frowns. "It was too far from home and my parents didn't want me to go. My mother thought I wouldn't be there to help with the chores. She never liked me. She preferred Eve instead."

Eve? Her sister? I knew that Donkey had one sister and a brother, Knight, although he was so much older than she was, she barely saw him during her growing up years.

Gladys pats Donkey's arm as if she were comforting a child. "I'm sure your mother loved you just as much as she loved your sister."

"She didn't. At least, she never told me so. Eve was always with her. She wore the best clothes. She went to all those fancy teas and socials. I was clumsy and ugly and I was left at home, until I got accepted to music school. Then, for a little while, my mother told her friends about me and displayed me for everyone to see. I felt awkward wearing Eve's clothes to those things. They never fit me right."

"She never got you your own clothes?" I ask.

Donkey shakes her head. "Eve got all the new stuff. I had to wear her hand-me-downs, but then, when I went to music school, I had to have costumes that were my own and Eve was jealous of me for a change."

The look of mischief on Donkey's face jars me. She seems like such a lamb these days, her mind tottering on the fence between here and Wonderland. It's easy to forget that she wasn't always that way. She has a history and the bits and scraps I've pieced together since I've known her make me confused. Did she have a happy childhood or a sad one? I suppose she's like most of us... a little bit of both.

"Well, I'm up for a game of cards, Ladies." Gladys, the sly fox, has managed to sneak the cookie package away from Donkey without her fussing over it. She has a deck of cards in her hand and a twinkle in her eye. She wants to play *rummy* or *euchre.*

"I like cards." Donkey smiles. "I know two card games."

"Oh! Tsk! You know more than two." Lula snorts.

"I can play *Old Maid* and *Go Fish*." Donkey rubs her hands together. "I'm going to beat you this time, Eve."

Gladys, Lula and I exchange knowing glances. It feels like going back to our grade school days.

Gladys grimaces.

Lula rolls her eyes.

I sigh.

"Are you sure you don't know how to play euchre?" Gladys asks.

Donkey's forehead wrinkles, emphasizing the deep creases that already frame her eyes. She grabs the deck of cards from the table. "Euchre? That's a grown up's game."

"Well we're..." Lula stops.

"What's the use?" I bite my lip to keep from giggling. "You go ahead and deal, Donkey. I'll be right back. Nature calls."

"You still pee the bed."

I stop dead in my tracks and turn back. "What did you say?"

"Mother loves you best, Eve, but that's only because you always blame me for peeing the bed. I know it's you, and soon, when we have our own beds and don't have to share anymore, she'll know your dirty little secret."

My heart goes out to her. *Did your sister pee on you? That's worse than me peeing on myself!* "You're right, Dear. I really ought to tell her the truth."

Donkey laughs. "You'll never do it." She starts dealing.

The rest of us smile, resigned to doing things Donkey's way, and I scurry off to the restroom before I have to change my pants.

Tallulah Pratt (Lula)

I'm so shocked. Donkey attended the Montgomery Institute. She never said a thing about it. Some of the most famous vocalists in the world attended that school. It was quite prestigious in its day, almost as much as Juilliard. Donkey must have been talented indeed to be accepted to a place like that. There's a lot more to that dotty little lady than meets the eye. I love her so!

I wanted to sing when I was a child. I could carry a tune. I just wasn't destined for stardom. Certainly not! My parents had no intention of allowing one of their daughters to traipse about the stage, dressed like a floozy! My parents had their ideas. They weren't uncommon sentiments in those days. Women were to be at home, faithfully tending to their families. They were to be kept in their place. I often dream of what could have happened if I had been born a little bit later, but I wasn't.

That's all right. I had Tom. He was a philandering jackass, but he was my philandering jackass. Without him, I wouldn't have had my beautiful children, Sarah, Shelley, Stephen, Susan and Sam. I thought naming them all 'S' names was cute. In hindsight, it was probably stupid. Still, I'm thankful for all of our children, even Susan, God rest her little soul. It wasn't scarlet fever that took her from us.

I can never be at peace near water. I still see her twinkling blue eyes, the mischievous grin. She had to test every boundary, defy me at every turn. That last turn took her past the buoy line where the children could swim safely. I am still haunted by the screaming of her sister, the adrenalin rush as I hurtled myself into the water to fetch her, but damn that current! Damn the dark hue of the river! I couldn't find her. Couldn't!

I dove down again and again. Sucked in another gulp of air. I groped, grasped, grappled with weeds, rocks, clam shells, sunken logs. Not once did I feel the telling sensation of skin against skin.

She was gone.

I came up empty-handed and empty-hearted. I nearly drowned myself trying to find her. Somehow my senses came to me and I realized that the other four would be in deep trouble if I went under too. Loosened from my apron strings too early, she drifted away... taking a piece of me into the depths with her. I still feel like something is missing from my soul.

I could have murdered Tom where he stood when he came home from the road (or was it Beulah Brantford's arms?). *Where were you? Why weren't you here? Maybe you could have saved her. You're a stronger swimmer!*

"It's no use fretting over things you can't change."

"You can say that again. Do you have any kings?" Gladys smiles at me over top of her hand of cards.

I didn't mean to think out loud, but since I'm doing it, let's go for broke. "Kings? I had one and he was a selfish old coot." My grin almost turns into a laugh.

Ethel giggles. "I had one of those too."

"Me three." Donkey nods.

"What about you, Gladdy?" I wink.

She gets a faraway look in those pale green eyes before she replies. "Yes. One selfish king and one incredible prince."

Ethel and Donkey keep laughing as if they know what she's talking about. I might know, but I'm not sure.

"If that means what I think it means, Gladys Peachy, then I

envy you your handsome prince. You were one lucky lady."

Gladys shrugs. "Why? You've got a handsome prince after you, Lula."

"Yeah." Ethel agrees. "Even if he is a little closer to his expiry date than some princes."

I huff, smoothing out my hair though there isn't a mirror in sight. "Oh! You girls! I am not going on a date with Emmett Muggeridge!"

"Why not? What's the harm?" Gladys eggs me on. "You don't have to marry him or anything. Just enjoy his company."

"That's how it starts." I dig in my heels. "It's all charm and smiles and then... boom! You're with someone that you think you know and then... and then..." My eyes mist over.

"Oh... dear... we didn't mean to upset you." Ethel pats my hand. "We forgot that this is the anniversary of losing Tom. Forgive us, Lula."

"That's right. We won't talk about it anymore today." Gladys looks for a tissue.

"I'm all right. I just... can we just... I would rather..."

"Play cards." Donkey pipes up. "I'm going to win this time!"

"That's how this started." I turn back to my hand. "Kings. Let me see. Go and fish, Gladys. I don't have a single one."

Dawn Kehoe (Donkey)

Chocolate chip cookies taste the best. Are these homemade? No. They can't be. I'm picking them out of a plastic package. Mmm... they're pretty good. I want another.

I must have knocked that performance out of the ball park.

Look! Ginger Rogers is talking to Lula and she says she wants to do a dance number with me. I'm not sure how that would work. Would she just tell Fred to kiss off and get himself a new partner? Who would lead? I know that sometimes women marry women these days. What is that about? I couldn't picture it. If I married a woman, I'd smack her silly the first day. As soon as she tried to put an apron on and take over my kitchen... whoa Nelly!

Slap!

That's a funny thought. Me slapping somebody. I've only ever done it to Eve and that was a long time ago. It was her own fault. I was supposed to go to a dance with Jerry Jones. Hubba hubba, he was a looker! 6 foot 2. Eyes of blue! It would have been perfect, but he had to go and lay eyes on Eve, all those waves of dark hair and ivory skin. Like all the boys in town, he went gaga and fell at her feet. So much for my dreams of actually dancing with a boy. It was back to the stage for me, but not before I had an all-out cat fight with Eve.

"You can have any boy you want! Why did you have to take Jerry? He was with me."

She looked smug. Triumphant. She finally had her revenge for losing out on the Montgomery Institute. "It's not my fault if he likes me better, Dawn. Maybe you should spend less time tap dancing and more time fixing your hair. You're a mess. It's a wonder any boy looks at you."

Slap!

My hand whipped out as if it had a mind of its own. You should have seen the shock on Eve's face when it connected with her high, jutting cheekbones. I thought she would hit me back. Instead, her brown eyes watered and she retreated, fleeing the family room, mounting the stairs, slamming the door to our bedroom, the latch clicking behind her to make sure I didn't follow.

"Oh! Cookies!" I grab one from the package. "I love these."

"Donkey. You've already had four." Lula protests.

"Leave her be." Ethel takes a cookie too. "Seriously, are you worried about spoiling her dinner? She eats like a horse."

"Neigh neigh." I laugh. "I do not. Horses eat hay, Ethel. I'm eating sweets."

"Oh Lordy." Lula grins. "What a silly old goose you are today!"

I grab another cookie. "Honk honk! I am not. Geese are grumpy and they've got those long, curved necks. I'm quite happy, thank you very much. Maybe I'm more like a duck."

"A quack?" Ethel taps her knee and starts laughing. "Oh! Yes. That's it."

I giggle too. "Yes. That's it. I'm a little quack."

I have three more cookies in front of me. Where did they come from? I thought there was a package. Maybe not. I do seem to be forgetful these days.

Chapter Six

Gladys Peachy

I am standing under a massive oak tree at the far end of Jack Robillard Memorial Park. It's twilight, that in-between corridor when the pretty pale blue of the daytime sky looks like someone spilled a bottle of indigo ink across it and the darker hue is bleeding into the lighter one, overtaking it in much the same way that my love for Paul Peachy is overtaking me.

I feel like Sleeping Beauty right now, awakening from a hundred years of sleep. I never knew there could be such life, such colour, such joy. They're just lips. They make smiles and frowns and they keep our teeth and tongue behind their gates when we aren't using them. Why then? As Paul's warm, full lips part over mine for the first time, why do I feel as if I am floating above the earth, tethered by the thinnest string? I tremble to the point where he breaks off our union.

"Are you cold, Gladdy? Do you want my sweater?"

I smile. "No. I'm fine. What about you?"

His eyes twinkle like Venus, who is sending down her beam over his shoulder. "I'm fine. Do you... are you... you don't mind?"

Mind? Has he gone crackers? "No. I don't mind. You could do it again if you like."

Paul laughs softly, leans in to kiss me again. So, this is euphoria? The last time I felt anything even close to this, I was on a ferris wheel at the Lanark County Fair. *Oh Paul. Can this moment freeze and just keep going on and on and on for eternity?*

He pulls away, a gentle hand brushing my cheek. I smile, look down, the expression fading.

"I'll be back in two weeks. My father has meetings scheduled ten miles away then. They'll be pitching the tent in Appleton."

I bite my lip. "It seems like forever."

"Don't worry." He pulls me into an embrace. "I can use the car. He lets me go all over the countryside putting up posters and handing out flyers. I'll pick you up and you can help."

"Okay." *What kind of a date is that? Oh, I don't care. I'd shovel dung if I had to... just to be beside him.*

He kisses me once more. "We'll have dinner after that. Just you and me... before we have to go to the meeting. You will come to the meeting with me, won't you? I'll make sure you get home afterwards."

I nod. *Home is wherever you are.* "I'll be counting the days."

"I'll be counting the hours."

"The minutes."

"The seconds."

We both giggle and embrace one more time before he takes my hand and leads me away from our secluded trysting spot. Walking toward my house side by side, I find myself treasuring this newfound place beside him and dreading the moment he leaves me.

Slap slap slap! Oh! Paul is hitting me over and over and... "Stop it!" I thrust my arms out to block the blows. I am being smacked in the ribs. "Ow!"

Where am I? Where is Paul? I awaken in the darkness. The little clock on the night stand reads 3:33. It's definitely a.m. The stars are peeking through the glass at me and... who is that?

"Who's there?" I cry out.

A stranger stands at my bedside. I can't see who it is. These blows are going to bruise me. I squint, trying to adjust my vision.

"No! I won't let you! Don't hurt him. He didn't do it. It was me."

Fear turns to annoyance as I recognize Donkey's voice, chiding me for something or other.

"Stop, Donkey! You're hurting me." She keeps swatting at me and I try to grab her arms, but it's not easy to do that without light.

"He's just a baby. You can't hurt a baby!" Donkey's voice pleads, her arms flailing.

Finally, I get a hold of one of them and pull. Donkey lurches forward, losing her balance and falling, not to the floor, but against my bed. I hold on as hard as I can to keep her from slipping down where she could be injured. It crosses my mind that I'm the one who is going to smart in the morning, but my instincts were always protective. I would have been a good mother. That's what Paul said.

"Donkey! There's no baby here." I don't know if she's sleepwalking or having one of her episodes. "Donkey! It's Gladys Peachy. I'm your friend, Gladys."

"Gladys?" Donkey repeats, her arms going limp. "He tried to hurt my Gabe. I couldn't let him do that."

"Who?"

"Lowell."

"Lowell?" I sigh with relief. At least she's saying her own husband's name and it's not Cary Grant.

"He was drinking. When isn't he? Gabe's only four. He doesn't know why he isn't allowed to make any noise."

I sit up, switch my bedside lamp on the dimmest setting and help Donkey slide her bottom up onto the mattress. Now I can see that her face is wet from tears. These are the real memories in her life. No wonder her mind wants to run away.

"Oh, Dear Heart." I pat her on the shoulder. "That's all over now."

"It is?" She takes in a few short, emotional breaths.

"You must have had a bad dream. Gabe is all grown up and he's safe. You're here with me and you're safe. And Lowell... well..."

It's like a light bulb goes on over Donkey's head. "The bastard is dead."

I am taken aback at her harsh language. But then, I think, how blessed I was to have a good man. No. Donkey wasn't being mean or harsh. In fact, from what I've heard when Donkey is lucid, Lowell Kehoe was indeed a bastard. Oh! I used vulgarity. I never do that. Well, maybe in this case, there's no other word that fits. I know that his mean streak came out when he drank. I never met him, but if he would harm his wife and baby, I know there's a dark place for him where he will never get out. I don't like to wish anyone to the eternal fire, but as I watch my friend, teary eyed and distraught in the middle of the night, mercy is not the first thing that comes up from the depths.

I give her a hug. No sooner does her body lean against mine than I hear a soft snore.

"No, Donkey. You need to go back to your own room."

She doesn't answer. She has gone back to a dead sleep. *Was she ever fully awake?* I sigh, lean back, and think about how doggone tired I'm going to be come morning.

Is that a sparrow already starting its dead of night song? "Play it again, Sam." If I have to lie awake here, cradling Donkey, I may as well be entertained.

Ethel MacNarland

Gladys has fallen asleep in the recliner beside me in the TV activity room. Thank goodness for that. She was one grumpy Gus at breakfast this morning. I hope she isn't coming down with something. I even saw her glare at Donkey. Now, I can't blame her. We all get short on patience now and again. Dear Donkey's brain goes on wild goose chases and she tries to take us with her. Anyone would get annoyed, but Gladys is a saint compared to Lula and I. She never says a harsh word. This morning, I thought she might bite Donkey's head clean off. To be fair, she held it in, but I could see it on her face as if someone had written it there in ink.

"She's snoring." Lula grins. "Poor sweet thing. She had to deal with Donkey in the middle of the night."

"What?" I am sitting on the white and blue paisley sofa beside Lula while Emmett tosses her wistful looks, wishing I would go and watch whatever movie is playing on TV.

"M'hm. Apparently, Donkey had a nightmare."

"She did? Gladdy never said a word at breakfast."

"No. She didn't want to upset Donkey." Lula glances across the room where Donkey is riveted to this morning's movie selection. "I joined her for a little stroll in the garden after we ate. I just had to know what put her in such foul humour today."

I click my tongue. "She sure wasn't herself. I can see why if she didn't get enough sleep."

Lula's stunning eyes narrow, her face taking on a pained look. "I hate to say this, but…"

"What?"

"Donkey forgets and she gets lost in her imagination and... I can live with that. I mean, she's been a good friend to me ever since the first day I arrived here. She had only been here a month when I came in and she made me feel welcome and I owe her for that."

I anticipate what she's going to say. I don't think I want to hear it.

Lula lowers her voice. "Donkey's problem is getting worse, Ethel. I think it is. Well, is it just me?"

I would like to say that it's just Lula's imagination. Oh, how I want to refute her statement and... why did she have to speak it out loud and make it real? Can't we go on pretending that everything is going to stay the same?

"It's true." I purse my lips. "Donkey's lucid times are getting farther apart. Sometimes the lucid Donkey and the fairyland Donkey seem to cross paths in mid-sentence. Oh... Lula..."

"Lordy, I don't want to know that. I don't want to face it."

"She's our friend."

"She deserves so much more than what's happening to her mind. It's sad."

"I'm so scared it will happen to me."

Lula gives me a look as if I've uncovered a secret. "You mean, it's not just me that fears that?"

I pat her hand. "In this place, everybody sees how bad it could get. We all live with the fear."

Lula smiles, tears misting over the blue of her eyes. "Are we overreacting? I mean, the woman is still relatively healthy. She eats enough for two. She can still care for herself, mostly."

I grin. "As long as we're there to wipe off the stains and make her change clothes."

Lula smirks. "And she's got a whooole harem of handsome husbands. I should envy that."

"But they're all dead. That's no good."

We both chuckle.

"The staff don't seem to notice." I shake my head. "Aren't they well paid to take note of these things?"

Lula swats a hand in front of her face. "They don't see because we cover for Donkey too well."

"So what do you suggest we do then? Spill the beans?"

"Don't you dare!" A third voice chimes in.

Lula and I turn to see that Gladys is awake and she is looking at us with obvious ire.

"Gladdy! You're awake." Lula chirps.

"Yes. I'm awake. And I'm telling you…" Her finger wags at us. "Don't you tell them anything about Donkey."

"But… what about…?" The ocean in Lula's eyes deepens. "…you can't keep this up forever. These middle of the night episodes have got to stop."

Gladys glares. "What's it to you, Lula? She's not sleepwalking to your room!"

"Maybe you should go back to sleep." I plead.

"I'm serious!" Gladys smacks the arm of the recliner.

"So am I." I reply. "You're over-tired and overwrought. Why don't you go to your room and have a little lie down? We can talk about this after you have a rest."

Gladys rubs her temples as if a headache were setting in. "I shouldn't. I won't sleep tonight if I do that."

"You won't sleep anyway if Donkey decides to keep you company." Lula folds her arms. "Maybe you should just get a double if you're going to have a roommate."

Gladys huffs. "Tsk. Lula! Oh…" She sighs. "You've got a point. And no, I don't know what we're going to do about this, but I don't want them to put Donkey someplace where… where she's confined and we can't see her anymore. She means too much to me. I can't bear the thought."

"Neither can we." I rub Gladdy's arm. "As long as part of her is still with us, we should band together and just… help her as best we can."

"Exactly. Imagine what it would do to her if she got stuck in that other building." Gladys lowers her voice. "You know, the one across the parking lot that nobody visits. Tranquil Meadows Plus… it stinks of pee… and other things too awful to mention."

Lula grimaces. "It's like being dead before you're dead. I never want to end up in there."

"And we don't want Donkey in there either. It's like getting sentenced to Alcatraz." I say. "I'm with you, Gladdy. We'll keep quiet."

We all join hands in a strange and secret pact.

"Lordy, I hope she doesn't tell any of the staff that she's married to Clark Gable. They're not playing *Gone with the Wind* today, are they?" Lula says.

I glance toward the TV. "Oh-oh. I think it's *The Man Who Shot Liberty Valance*."

"Great." Lula laughs. "It'll be Jimmy Stewart starring as

Ransom Stoddard."

"Not a bad choice." Gladys winks. "If I hadn't met my Paul, Jimmy Stewart would have been my second choice."

"Of course, John Wayne's in that movie too." I muse. "She could be his widow. That would still leave Jimmy Stewart free for you."

Gladys giggles. "Oh… we complain, but I suppose there's no harm so long as Donkey enjoys it."

"And as long as the staff don't find out. They might ship her off then." I shudder at the thought.

"They won't." Lula rolls her eyes. "As long as she dresses herself, goes to the bathroom, eats and isn't a danger, they won't bother. Still, we'd better keep an eye."

Just like that, we have become *The Donkey Defenders*. I know. It doesn't have as much panache as *The Avengers* or *The Untouchables*, but we are determined to help our friend. I just hope that doesn't mean Gladys has to lose any more sleep. I hope she's her old sweet self tomorrow.

Tallulah Pratt (Lula)

I can't get enough of the gardens here at Tranquil Meadows. They sure do spend a lot of time beautifying the grounds. I have always loved flowers and the tulips are in full bloom right now. There are purple and yellow ones along the cobblestone walkway, pink ones around the fountain with the sculpture of a young girl pouring out her water pot, and square boxes full of red bobbing blossoms set beside the lovely wrought iron benches.

Trees full of apple blossoms line the back end of the property and the cluster of lilac bushes beside them have buds, not quite ready to burst, but soon.

I don't know who thought of it, but I would like to thank the gardener who transplanted the wildflowers to that little patch just beyond the outdoor chess table. I mosey over there every day, especially in the springtime. Lilies of the valley smell like Heaven. Ladyslippers make me giddy like a schoolgirl.

Perhaps that's because my grandma used to take me for walks in the woods and we would find nature's secrets blooming amid the trees and brush. That is one of my favourite memories, strolling hand in hand with her, carrying a basket to pick flowers and wild berries and to collect interesting stones. I was happy with her. I was safe. I was allowed to be ten years old.

I was not yet a woman, Uncle Wally. Why did you do that to me? Didn't you know I looked up to you? Didn't you know I used to freeze sometimes when Tom tried to touch me? I was terrified! I couldn't stop myself from pushing him away and... that's why he had to find comfort in Beulah Brantford's arms. Wretched men! I can't trust them! I just can't!

"Lovely day, ain't it?" Emmett Muggeridge tips his fedora as he approaches the wildflower patch where I have been lost in an unpleasant reverie. His timing couldn't be worse!

"I love springtime." I say, hoping he can't tell that I was almost in tears. I should be grateful that he came along. Uncle Wally doesn't deserve even one more drop of water from me. Neither does Tom.

Emmett replies. "Lily of the Valley. It ain't as fancy or as famous as roses and orchids, but I have often wondered, is there a more beautiful flower in all of God's creation? Tiny. Delicate. To be handled with tenderness and care."

I am dumbfounded. What do men know about flowers? In my experience, they see them as something to be hastily picked up at the florist, offered up for anniversaries, birthdays and dates to get a woman into bed or to offer atonement for their sins. Emmett... well... he seems to actually appreciate them.

"I love the fragrance of them. Soft and sweet." I reply. I try not to, but Emmett fishes smiles out of me like a sportsman draws out trout from the water.

"Oh yes." He walks over to an empty bench and plunks his body down. "My mother used to wear a perfume with that scent. It would get all through her clothes, my father's clothes, my clothes. Sometimes I smelled like a woman." He throws his head back and laughs, showing off the full mouth of shiny teeth he still possesses. "I resented it at the time, but now... sometimes I come over here just to smell something that reminds me of her. Lord, she was a wonderful woman."

I don't like men. I don't trust men. For some reason, despite that, I find myself sitting down beside Emmett, eager to hear more about his life. There's an old adage. You know how a man will treat a wife by watching the way he treats his mother. Emmett seems to revere his mother as if she had been a saint or something. He couldn't be lying, could he? If he is, he's putting on the performance of his life because his face is enraptured as if she were here right now.

"My mother wore something floral." I think back. "It wasn't as pleasant smelling as lilies of the valley. Truth be told, it made me sneeze."

Emmett laughs some more. I didn't mean it to be funny, but he does have a pleasant laugh.

"What perfume do you wear, Lula?"

"That's... kind of a personal question, isn't it?"

"Is it? Because..." He leans forward and inhales with his nose. "I smell it every day. You share your fragrance with the whole world, so how can that be personal?"

I never thought of it that way before. "Oh. Well... in the interest of... of making sure I don't bother anybody's allergies, I will tell you that I wear something called 'Tahiti By Twilight'. My daughter Sarah bought it for me last Christmas."

"Sarah. She's the deaf one, ain't she?" Emmett pays attention!

"Yes. She had scarlet fever as a child and when she recovered, her hearing was gone. The poor dear."

"She's a lovely girl. And she seems to have done well for herself in spite of her challenges."

I smile wide. "She's smart as a whip. Speaking of flowers, she became a florist. Runs her own shop. She calls the shots. That's why I came to Ottawa after Tom passed away, to be closer to her. I am so proud of her. Nobody is going to take advantage of my Sarah! Not like..." I stop. The smile fades. "I mean... it's a relief to know that."

"I'm sure it is. Women have to be so careful in this world. I mean... men do too. It's just that..." Emmett's sigh is loud and long. "Around every corner, there seems to be a wolf waiting to devour the next woman to come along. Everybody is Little Red Riding Hood."

That surprises the socks off of me. Not literally. Emmett isn't getting any part of my clothing off! Is that clear? I just never expected him to be so... delightful... I mean... insightful. Aren't men primitive and only interested in sports and being between the sheets?

"Do you like to read?" Emmett asks.

"Yes. I love to read."

"Lately, I've been reading a lot of poetry. Some Longfellow. Wordsworth. One of those things I meant to get around to when I was younger, but you know how it is."

"Life gets in the way of our best intentions."

"So it does. I'm retired now, though. All that busyness. I thought it would never end."

We say nothing as a happy cardinal begins his flagrant and high pitched woo woo woo courtship song somewhere nearby.

"I remember wishing the kids would hurry up and get bigger, so they could look after themselves." I wring my hands. "All those messes to clean and the crying and read me a story and get me a glass of water and can I have a candy... and then, they were bigger. They were tying their own shoes and buttoning their own clothes and... they seemed to leave me behind like... a favourite sweater that they were still very fond of, but..."

"It doesn't fit them anymore." Emmett looks at me and, for a few seconds, it's like our souls know each other, have known each other, for a thousand lifetimes.

"Hello Lula, Dear. Emmett. I'm here for our morning constitutional, but I can come back another time if I'm... interrupting." Gladys grins.

I glare at her. "Gladdy. There you are. I've been waiting for you." I look at Emmett. "We were going to take a little walk. We have some things to talk about."

Emmett reluctantly takes the hint. "I see. Well, I wouldn't want to get in the way of important girl talk." He gets up and tips his hat to leave.

"Emmett?" He turns back to face me.

"Yes, Tallulah."

"Maybe you could bring one of those books next time?"

"I sure will."

His ear to ear smile imprints like a tattoo upon my heart. It shouldn't. I don't trust him. I sure enjoyed spending a little time with him in the garden. Maybe we can just be reading buddies.

I look at Gladys. I could smack that grin off of her face. She reads me so easily. She's my friend and she should be talking me out of this. Instead, she pats my arm and says, "It's about time."

That's the only nice word she has said all morning and I want to swat her for it.

Dawn Kehoe (Donkey)

My husband was the bravest of them all. He shot down that awful villain, Liberty Valance! Everyone was so surprised. I mean, who would have thought that such a slight and quiet man would be so quick on the draw in a gunfight? Ransom Stoddard, you're a hero!

Liberty Valance, on the other hand, was nothing but a mean old drunk who shot people and hurt little children for making too much noise. I hated him! I was afraid of him. It's not right when men like that make other people afraid to move or to speak or to even breathe!

Liberty Valance staggered in late one evening after yet another job that he had found, but was bound to lose. His shirt and tie were askew, his belt undone. His hair, normally dark and slicked back fell across his forehead in a way that signalled that we were in grave danger. I had seen that look before after many a whiskeyed afternoon.

I remember like it was yesterday. I heard his slurred words trumpeting up the drive. I peered out the kitchen window, my heart pounding as if someone were trying to escape out of my chest. I backed out through the archway as he came in, creeping up the stairs so quietly, as if I were a mouse trying to sneak a crumb to eat and not a resident in my own home. Up... up... up... and then he called my name.

"Dawnie. Where you at, Baby Doll? It's me!"

I am not your baby doll. That's what you call those floozies down at Marty's Bar! Hey, Baby Doll. Wanna dance with me?

I knew what he would do to me if I didn't answer, but it didn't matter. He would find a reason to do it even if I did. I had learned the hard way. There was no winning side to this fight.

I opened the door to Gabe's room where he was asleep already, as it was well after 9 o'clock and he was only seven. I woke him, put a hand to my lips --"Shhhhhh"--. I wrapped him in his blanket and did something that scared me almost as much as hearing that drunkard's voice bellowing down there. I led Gabe up that narrow stairway that took us to the attic, the one that Eve warned me was haunted. I don't know how I managed to get in there without being heard, but I did. Gabe's eyes were wide with fright. By now, he was used to the fact that that loud, booming voice meant the monster was here and he could go off like a bomb with the slightest provocation.

My plan, in hindsight, was foolish. I thought that we could stay perfectly quiet and still up in the attic and the villain would think we had left. He would tire of looking for us. He would pass out, fall asleep, and forget everything come morning.

"Dawnie! Dawnie! Where you at?"

I held my breath, clutched Gabe close to me, and prayed the rosary in my head, even though I didn't have the beads to turn over in my fingers. *Hail, Holy Queen, Mother of Mercy, our life, our sweetness and our hope! To thee do we cry, poor banished children of Eve...* And banished we were! Shoved out of the Garden of Eden and sitting, forlorn, in a huddled heap in a dark, foreboding attic. Isn't it odd that a person should fear a room within her own home? Isn't it even odder that a greater fear could drive her to that very place?

"Dawnie! You'd better answer, Baby Girl. Where have you gone? I'll find you. No matter where. You know I will!" I could hear Liberty Valance's anger rising, like the wind whipping up to usher in a thunderstorm.

"Mommy." Gabe's whisper panged my heart. What kind of mother can't protect her own baby?

I hugged him tighter, wishing I could conceal him inside my own body the way I did before he was born.

Smash!

Bang!

Ka-thunk!

I thought that must be our bedside lamp. It sounded like it was happening right beside me, but that was only because the master bedroom was right below.

Gabe trembled in my arms and I felt utterly wretched and disgusting. I was a complete failure. If my own mother were here, her look would be unbearable. I thought I might hyperventilate. I tried to slow down my breaths.

Curse words assaulted our ears. Banging. Pounding. Smashing glass. Other sounds that made me wonder what in the world that man was doing to our home. Would the house even be standing when he was done? Every noise cut through my courage like a blade.

And then, in a flash, nothing. Sudden silence. No shouts. No cussing. No destruction. A flicker of hope lit within me. *He is giving up? He'll go to sleep. He'll leave and go back to the bar.* I didn't care what he did, so long as we were safe.

Oh God!

Creak – creak – creak – creak – Creak – CREAK – dead air.

God?

I looked down into Gabe's face. I couldn't see it clearly. We were, after all, in the dark, but the tiny window at the top of the room let in a shaft of moonlight. It was enough for me to see that my son's face was wet with tears and the smell let me know that he had just soiled his pants.

Crunch!

Jiggle!

Twist!

I guess I didn't pray hard enough.

The door to the attic burst open and the stark light streaming from the hallway almost blinded me. I could barely even see the monster enter the room, had no idea what he was up to until I felt his arms grabbing my shoulders, lifting me forcibly from the ground, Gabe's terrified body sliding off of me and then scuttling behind a group of cardboard boxes. They would be a flimsy shield indeed, should the monster decide to pursue my son.

"No! Stop!" I may as well have been pleading with Satan.

"You're mine, Dawnie! Mine! I own you. Do you understand? You don't defy me!" One hand closed around my neck and now I was dangling like one of those bad guys in the wild west who just had the bottom drop out.

"Please…"

The word came out in a squeak. My windpipe was a broken straw. I breathed in a slight portion of air, but it wouldn't be enough. I began to see snippets of my life passing before me.

Eve, my parents, my elder brother Knight, before he went away, we all sat at the breakfast table on an ancient Christmas morning.

Me, singing and dancing on stage, Jean Montgomery smiling and fanning herself with a stray program leaflet.

My arm extending like a whip, the flat palm striking Eve in her starkly pretty face.

The painful and joyous birth of my Gabriel.

A loud, jarring explosion. A flash of bright light in the darkness. A strange, metallic smell, suddenly overpowering the odor of poop and must and whiskey.

Liberty Valance crumbled, both arms now clutching at his chest.

My body would not hold me up. I, too, fell, unable to speak, my lungs attempting to inhale with all their might. At first, my windpipe did not want to comply. It had been compressed so small and I thought my freedom might have come too late.

Heeeeeeeee... heeeeeeeeeeee... heeeeeeeeeeeeee... little bursts of air made it through and then made it back out of my body again. I leaned against a box, only so I wouldn't collapse completely to the floor.

What had happened? Why had the monster let me go? I was certain that my number was up.

Haaaaaaaawwwww... haaaaawwwww... More air, little by little, clearing my brain and relieving the pain, made it in and out of me.

I had the strength to look up now... barely.

The attic was still dark, but the door leading to it was open wide, letting in the light from the hallway. In my shadowed surroundings, I saw three things. The man who had just held my life in his cruel hands now lay in a heap of useless flesh and bones not three feet away from me. My son, Gabe, stood behind him with a blank stare and droopy, shitty pants. Beside him stood another man, tall and lean, with side-parted waves of hair.

"Who?" My first word was a raspy question. I thought I recognized the man, but...

"I heard shouting and screaming. I thought you might be in trouble." Ransom Stoddard stood there, backlit, radiating light like an angel from Heaven. He had been living next door to us for the last five years. This wasn't the first time he had come to our aid. I think he is the bravest man I've ever known and the absolute love of my life.

"Thank God you came." Bits of gravel seemed to come out of my mouth as I spoke.

"He almost killed you, Dawn."

My pot of tears boiled over and spilled down my face. I could let go now.

Ransom knelt beside me, sliding a comforting arm around my shoulders. "You don't have to worry now. You don't have to be afraid."

I knew that, but I was certain that this all-consuming fear would dog me for the rest of my life. Some ghosts remain.

"It'll be all right." Ransom let me lean into him for support as he helped me to my feet. "It was the only thing he could have done. I know that."

I saw, in the streams of light flooding in from the hall, that the man who shot Liberty Valance still held the gun. He would be my hero forever.

"It's a good thing this was only a 38 special. Not much of a kick. How old is Gabe?"

I looked at my son, his expression as blank as a new sheet of paper. I rushed to him, clutched him to my chest, not even caring that he stunk to high heaven. He didn't cling to me right away, but slowly put his arms up and around my waist. Only then did his tears break free.

"Mommy." He buried his face in my blouse.

Ransom Stoddard raised his hand, the one with the weapon in it. "Was this your gun, Dawn? Where did it come from?"

My gun? Didn't it belong to him?

"I've never seen it before." That wasn't exactly true. It looked familiar. I did have a handgun in the house. It was in a shoebox. I wanted it for protection, just in case... but I was so afraid of it, I shut it up in the attic someplace. Did the gun look like that? Maybe. I couldn't recall.

"Don't worry." Ransom's smile was handsome. "I'll explain everything to the police. It's best that way. I'm sure you would agree it would be better for the boy. You don't want them questioning him."

"Of course not!" I drew Gabe in tight. "He's just a little boy!"

Ransom Stoddard nodded. "I know just what to say. Leave it to me."

I will always be amazed at how brave Ransom was. What would have happened to me without him? To Gabe? Everything worked out for the best, even if I did have to take on that wretched job at *Smoky Joe's* to take care of us. A woman's got to do what a woman's got to do.

Oh! Look! The movie is over. What were we watching again? Something with Jimmy Stewart and John Wayne. They sure don't make actors like them anymore. Dinah Gillespie fell asleep part way through it. Look at her. Still snoring. If she wants to do that, why doesn't she go to her room and lie down? Why should we have to suffer through her snoring? I feel like reaching over and poking her... hard!

Look at Gladys, Ethel and Lula over there yakking it up. I wonder what they're talking about. Probably complaining about the food here. I'm sure I haven't eaten since yesterday. What kind of a place is this? Even jailbirds get bread and water, don't they?

Chapter Seven

Gladys Peachy

I am standing before a full-length mirror, the delicate lace of my mother's wedding gown surrounding me like a shroud. I never thought of myself as shapely before. In fact, wasn't it the sin of vanity to look at myself this way, contemplating how I went, in such a short time, from straight as an arrow to sloping and rising in perfect cadence, my figure smooth and rounded? Not too much of this or too little of that.

I smile at the way the curls frame my features. They used to be shorter than this, but I began growing them longer shortly after Paul asked me to marry him. Now they are the right length to weave flowers through the strands, and both my mother and younger sister, Glenna, worked on that for an hour this morning.

Today, I leave Gladys Early behind and become Gladys Peachy. Tingles of fear and excitement course through me at the same time. I marvel at how alike those two feelings can be. Are they a married couple too, like Paul and I are about to be?

I hear a light rapping at the door to my bedroom.

"Come in."

In strolls my tall and slender father, eyes misty, lips spread like a crescent moon across his face.

"Daddy? Do I look pretty?"

He shakes his balding head. "My Darling, I am stunned! I feel like I'm looking at your mother all over again and we are about to get married."

"Really?"

"You aren't my little girl now, are you, Gladdy?"

I reach out to throw my arms around him. He stops me. "You don't want to wrinkle your dress."

"I don't care." I put my hands on his tie and begin adjusting it. "I'm always going to be your little girl."

I relish the sensation of his strong hand against my cheek. "You're a lady now."

It sounds so regal when he says it. Truly, the right words from a father can give a girl wings to fly. "Maybe so, but I'm your little girl too. I have to be or I just won't go through with it."

He coaxes a stray hair away from my eyes. "Paul is a good man. To be honest with you, I wasn't sure at first. The life of a travelling preacher wasn't something I dreamed of for my daughter."

"Paul is going to be a teacher!"

He put a finger over my lips. "Yes, and still, you won't be living in the same town as me. One street over is too far for my liking and here you are, moving two hours away."

"It could have been worse." I flash a smile. "We could have been missionaries heading off to the African jungle. I'm so glad the Peachy family's house isn't all the way across the country. I'd be sad if I never got to see you."

My father's eyes meet mine and he searches my heart, or so it seems. Does he know that he walks and talks with me there, even when we're not in the same room?

"I know that a wedding is an exciting event for a young girl." He frowns for a fraction of a second. "A woman, I mean."

"Dresses. Flowers. Golden rings. It sure seems like a dream."

"Well…" He pauses. "Don't take this wrong, Gladdy, but… if that dream... if it ever becomes a nightmare..."

"Daddy!"

"Shhh..." The sudden fear I feel as he speaks is as foreign to me as wings on a fish. "Let me finish now. I hope everything turns out the way you want it to, but a lot of folks say that once you make your bed, you've got to lie in it. I disagree. You're my daughter. If you ever need to..." He points at the floor. "This is your room and this is your home and you will always be welcome here."

I rest my head against his chest, not even caring if I muss up my hair. "I wish I could have both of you forever. I don't want to leave you." Tears overwhelm me. "I don't want to leave him... how can I love two men so much?"

"Now now. We've got a telephone." His breath catches and I think we'll both be crying if we don't stop talking. "And I'm confident that Paul has got sound plans for the future and he thinks the world of you."

I look up and smile. "He treats me so kind."

"He'd better." My father's fingers wipe my tears. "I guess you'll have to fix up your face before we leave for the church. Your mother will have my hide."

I laugh. "All her hard work..."

"Be happy. That's what I want for you, and... don't forget to call... and come to visit... and I'm always your father..."

We stare at each other for a moment, as if we have to stamp the image of each other's faces into our minds... as if we might forget.

"I'll never forget you, Daddy." I say this to the air as I awaken at... what does my alarm clock say? It is almost four o'clock in the afternoon. Darn it! I knew I shouldn't have taken a nap.

Will I be able to sleep tonight?

My body doesn't want to get up. It feels heavy, like a sack of potatoes. With some effort, and more than a little whinging from my hips, knees and elbows, I manage to get up out of bed. Cobwebs line the walls of my brain, traces of sleepiness still clinging and I push through, willing this old body to the mirror. Don't I look a fright!

Splash splash splash...

I wash my face, straighten the curls that are now flat and will continue to be so until I can get under a shower head. I blow onto my hand, smelling to see if my breath will peel paint. I pour myself a small dose of mouthwash and gargle and spit, just in case.

My face stares back at me. I know it's me, but it still seems like a foreigner, but for the green eyes and curls. All these lines make me wonder if some farmer comes and ploughs furrows in my face while I sleep. Ethel would love that one. She has such a way with words.

Out in the corridor, the busy day has carried on without me. That is the way life will be soon. I will be gone and everything will continue, barely skipping a beat. It makes me feel small sometimes, but then, I realize that being on this planet at all is a miracle.

I pass one of the assistance desks. It's really a nurse's station, but they don't like to use medical words here. They deliberately avoid it, as if calling things by other names will make us all believe that we're at a spa resort instead of on the last train out of town. They're not fooling anyone.

Do they really believe that a person can live 70, 80, 90 years and be unaware when they get to the Last Chance Saloon? What a bunch of jackasses! *Oh Paul. That nap didn't do me a lick of good. I'm as cranky today as I was during the menopause years. I'm sorry I was so impatient during the hot flashes, flushes, hormone surges and strange cravings and urges.* What a pickle we women find ourselves in! Just when we think our monthlies are over, in marches something that makes those few days a month seem like a Sunday School picnic!

"Hello, Mrs. Peachy."

Evangeline Martin could light a candle with that smile. She's got the brightest, whitest teeth I've ever seen, but perhaps that's an illusion on account of her skin is as dark as a coffee bean. She is my favourite attendant here at Tranquil Meadows. She's a tall, heavy set woman with beautiful facial features, her cheekbones high, both lips full and fleshy.

"You can call me Gladys." I manage to smile, even though I still feel wretched and crabby.

"Oh yes. You told me that before. I can be forgetful some days."

"Join the club. It doesn't improve with age, you know."

Evangeline's laugh is hearty and her eyes narrow and sparkle. "You got that right, Gladys. I'm only 33, but my bones snap, crackle and pop like Rice Krispies."

"Mine too."

"They're getting ready in the dining room." She points down the hallway. "They've got roast beef tonight. It smells mighty good."

"I'd better go and get a seat then." I start off. "You never know when there might be a stampede."

Evangeline laughs again, but it's interrupted by a voice that grates on me like sandpaper. I feel guilty for it too. As a good Christian woman, I know I'm not supposed to judge people, but the first time I met one of Tranquil Meadows' administrators, Ms. Biddy Finneyfrock, a shiver went up my spine. That is not normal for me. In fact, my father would have told you that he felt I was the most naïve waif on the planet.

Biddy is a short form. Her real name is Bidelia. Bidelia Faye Finneyfrock. Her driver's licence fell out of her purse once and I saw the full name there beside an expressionless, washed out picture that looked just like she does every day, close-cropped bleached blonde hair, furrowed forehead and all. I didn't look on purpose, but still, she gave me the nastiest stare with her ice blue eyes, as if she were James Bond and I had discovered her secret identity.

I turn and begin walking toward the dining room, wishing to leave the women to their duties. I barely get five steps away when I hear something that piques my curiosity.

"Mrs. Martin." Biddy caws (Yes! Her voice does remind me of a crow.). "Is that Mrs. Kehoe's file sitting open on the desk?"

Mrs. Kehoe? Donkey? I almost turn around, but then Biddy would know that I'm eavesdropping.

Evangeline stammers. "I... I... oh... I guess it is. You see, I was preparing the paperwork like you asked me to and then a call came in and... and I answered that and then..."

"That information is privileged. We have discussed that before."

"Yes, Ms. Finneyfrock. You're right. I apologize."

Battleaxe! Why can't Bidelia Faye Finneyfrock stop terrorizing her own employees? I inch down the hallway, riveted to every word of this berating conversation.

"Please do not let it happen again. Imagine the fiasco if a resident or one of their family members were to see the confidential information contained in a file like this. For one thing, we could be sued, you included. This is for the good of everyone."

"Yes. I understand. We were short-staffed today. I know that's not an excuse..."

"No. It is not!"

I mimic Biddy's harpy-like beak moving. *Yakyakyak.* That woman drives me... well... she makes me want to sin! I am almost out of earshot now.

I hear Evangeline one last time before I turn to enter the dining room.

"I'm keeping an extra eye, just like you asked."

"Good." Biddy replies. "Remember what we talked about. And don't make it obvious! It must be business as usual. Understood?"

"Yes, of course. Business as usual."

"Keep me posted. Now, please put this file where it belongs."

What was that about? Questions well up within me. *Do they know she's starting to drift? Will they try to take her away?* I push those thoughts from my mind and sit at our usual table where I am the first to arrive. I pick up today's edition of *The Metro News* and begin thumbing through it, waiting for my friends and my food to join me.

Ethel MacNarland

I am writing words in my journal now that I wish I did not have to write.

Ignorance is bliss. Whoever coined that phrase must know how I feel at this moment. We have taken an oath to protect Donkey for as long as we can. None of us want her to end up in that God-forsaken place across the parking lot. They call it Tranquil Meadows Plus, an extended care facility for old folks who don't know their own names anymore. I call it the Grim Reaper Hotel. Folks check in... until they check out.

The thought of Donkey in that place is like a dagger through my heart, and yet, for all of our good intentions, we are losing her. I know that Gladdy and Lula mean well. When we're all together, I feel that spark of hope that says, "Maybe everything will be all right. Maybe Donkey is doing fine, in her own little way."

She slapped Dinah Gillespie across the face. That is not all right. In fact, it's downright horrific. Dinah is as much a wandering soul as our Donkey is. Half the time she thinks she's at *Best Western*. She tried to tip Evangeline Martin. Thought she was part of the hotel cleaning staff.

I wanted to watch Dr. Phil late this afternoon, so I went to the TV room. It was pretty quiet in there, thank goodness. People were likely hanging out in the games room, doing arts and crafts, strolling outside or napping. Even Gladys decided to lie down. She sure needed it.

I had barely made it through the door when I came upon a terrible scene. Donkey's face burned red with rage. I don't know what Dinah may have said to upset her, but there she was, berating the poor old gal without mercy.

"You can have any boy you want, Eve. Why did you have to take Jerry? He was supposed to go to the dance with me!"

Crack!

Donkey's hand whipped out lightning fast, connecting with Dinah's cheek.

"Donkey! Stop that!" I hurried over and grabbed her arm before she could do anything else.

Dinah stood there, a dumbfounded expression and a red welt forming on her thin, sunken in face.

"I'm sorry, Dinah." I turned back to Donkey. "Why did you do that to her?"

Donkey glared at me, her eyes rife with malice. "I know you're going to take her side, Mother! You always take her side!"

How do I deal with this? My thoughts kept racing like headless chickens scattering around my mind's barnyard. *How do I chide Donkey for doing something when she doesn't even know me?*

Donkey and Dinah stood there. I would like to say they were squaring off, but that would be a half truth. It was more like Dinah the Deer coming face to face with Donkey the Tiger. I had to do something.

I glanced this way and that way. The coast was clear. What a miracle that nobody wanted to watch television at that moment.

"Eve is cruel." Donkey pleaded with me. "You don't hear the awful things she says to me. Oh, what's the use? No matter what I say or do, you're going to give me that look..."

That took me aback. *Do I have 'a look'?* "What do you mean, Donk... er... I mean, Dawn, Dear?"

Donkey's eyes brimmed with tears. It was heart-wrenching.

"You're disappointed in me." Donkey frowned.

"I'm not."

"You're ashamed of me." Her lip quivered. "I try so hard. I really do, but I'm never going to be Eve." A heart's cry leapt from a place in her that I understood only too well. My own husband couldn't have expressed approval of me if his life depended on it.

"Dawn." I felt so awkward, and being in front of Dinah made it worse. "You're the kindest, sweetest, most talented person I know."

A small pause followed.

"You don't mean that." Donkey fiddled with the bottom of her sweater, avoiding eye contact.

I nodded and smiled. "I do."

I waited. I hoped my answer was enough.

"I'm getting hungry, Ethel. Is it time for dinner?"

"What?" I had to get a hold of myself. Of all the nerve! What bad timing! Why was I upset that she came back to reality?

The clock read 4:45 pm. Dinner would be served in three quarters of an hour.

"It's almost time." I gave a loud sigh.

"I hope it's something good tonight. Somebody told me we're having roast beef. I can't wait. They haven't fed me since…"

"You had ice cream at 3." I reminded her.

She hesitated. "Oh. So I did. It was… strawberry."

"That's right." How could I help but grin at her? As innocent as a lamb? A ferocious lamb with big teeth sometimes.

"Let's go to the dining room and find a table so we can all sit together." Donkey started for the door.

"Wait." The sound of my voice caused her to turn back.

I gestured toward Dinah, who had taken a seat and was now reading through a newspaper, which I noticed, was three days old.

"But I'm hungry, Ethel. Can't we go?"

"Don't you think you should apologize to Dinah first?" Now I really did feel like Donkey's mother.

"What for?" Donkey tilted her head to one side.

What should I say? I felt so torn.

The situation could have been much worse. It dissipated without any effort from me whatsoever. It was probably the only time in my life that I felt grateful for the wonders of dementia.

"Why does Dawn need to apologize?" Dinah piped up. "What has she ever done to me?"

Flummoxed. That word describes how I felt, how I still feel as I write this.

"Well I... I..." I pointed to Donkey. I pointed to Dinah. I was at a loss.

"I like Dawn." Dinah smiled. "We play checkers sometimes."

"I want to play again. Maybe after dinner?" Donkey said. "I think I'm going to win this time."

"All right." Dinah agreed. "Next time my cousin comes to visit, I'll introduce her to Dawn."

"That would be nice." I said.

"My great aunt on my mother's side is the mother of the queen of England, you know. I can't wait until she drops by again." Dinah raised the newspaper back up to her face.

"Really?" I had never heard such a load of crap in my life, but around here, you just roll with it.

"Yes." Dinah nodded.

I said nothing, which seemed quite appropriate since, apparently, the last ten minutes of my life never happened.

"See you later, Dawn." Dinah waved.

"Okay, Dinah." Donkey turned to walk toward the hallway that leads to the dining room. "Let's go, Ethel. I'm so hungry."

"All right. Lead the way."

There was nothing more to say. We left for the dining room, Donkey dreaming of food, and me, wondering how in the world am I going to bring this up to Gladdy and Lula. *Donkey. Please. Stay with us a little while longer.*

I don't want to lose my friend. In a way, haven't I lost her already?

Tallulah Pratt (Lula)

Tallulah Pratt! When will you ever learn?

I am 72 years old, so if I haven't learned by now... well... it's too late to teach an old dog new tricks, isn't it?

I always got roped into making and putting up decorations for the social clubs, the school dances, the wedding showers and whatever other shindig Clarence Falls could dream up. For a small town, there seemed to be something doing all the time and guess who got dragged in to help with the preparations?

Just because I have a talent for colour coordination and making ribbons and bows and such... well... did that mean I wanted to be saddled with the responsibility for making everyone ooh and ahh and make such a fuss over crepe paper and tissue roses? Certainly not!

I resented it.

I resent it now.

Yes. I absolutely resent the fact that I let Agnes Holmes and Evangeline Martin sweet talk me into sitting here making bows out of pink and purple ribbon. Can't they find some other poor soul to help with the spring social next week?

Apparently not. Agnes made it seem like the apocalypse was imminent if I didn't rush to the arts and crafts room right away with my fancy, top of the line scissors and pinking shears and glue gun and scrapbooking stamps.

So here I am. I've made the most adorable over-sized tulips for the walls. I used poster board.

See how busy I am helping, Jesus? You can hold off on the end of the world!

Oh, Lordy. For all of my complaining, I have to admit, it would all look as ugly as sin without my artistic eye for detail. I mean, think about it. They were going to have a theme with orange and brown as the main colours… in May! Are they out of their minds?! Thanks to me, the wonder decorator, we've got appropriate colours and spring flowers. Common sense has prevailed.

"We're about finished here, Tallulah." Agnes smiles. "I'm so glad you were here to lend us your expertise."

I could blush. "It was nothing special." I grin wide enough to catch a stray golf ball. "I must say, once we figured out what we wanted, the afternoon went rather quickly. Many hands make light work."

"What do you mean we?"

I am nonplussed to hear Jenny Logan's scathing tone. She is scowling, and the look doesn't go well with her perfectly coifed hair, polished nails, mint green, short-sleeved blouse and mid-length, forest green skirt. She's dressing to impress no one, the cranky cow!

I could slap that smug look off of Jenny's face, but Agnes runs interference.

"It was a fine group effort, Jenny. Look at all the progress we've made. I think your centerpieces for the tables are particularly lovely."

Agnes! You must be kissing up. Those centerpieces are drab drab drab. They need a little panache. Maybe a candle in the middle.

"A group effort?" Jenny snorts. "The group wanted to go with orange and brown.. until SHE came along."

"Now now. I'm glad we switched to a more... seasonally appropriate look." Agnes picks up one of my poster board tulips. "These pinks and purples are stunning."

I smile at Agnes.

Jenny sneers. "Hmph. Things were fine the way they were."

"Jenny. Please..." Agnes keeps her smile even while Jenny is raining on our parade.

"Perhaps we can do an orange and brown theme when autumn comes." I toss the old dog a bone.

"Sure." Jenny rolls her eyes. "By then, you'll be in the mood to change it again. You should get an award. Tallulah Pratt. Bossy woman of the year."

"Jenny!" Agnes' jaw drops.

Now, that dig was the last straw. I sharpen my tongue and launch. "And you should win an award for best dressed woman of the year!"

"Really?" Jenny smooths out her skirt.

"Yes. Jenny Logan. Best dressed woman of the year... 1930... if they ever decide to give out that award again."

Agnes' hand flies up to cover her mouth. "Oh. I... Ladies... we don't want to fight."

"Sure we do. This old cow has been a thorn in my side since the day I arrived here." I snarl. "She's always dressing as if the Queen was coming. Perhaps she should get Dinah Gillespie to arrange an introduction."

"I can wear what I like. It's nobody else's business." Jenny's voice is growing louder.

"Go ahead. Wear what you like." I'm on a roll now. "It's just a shame nobody else likes it."

"Bossy cow!"

"Jealous ninny!"

"Miserable harpy! You're nothing but a bitter and cruel old woman. Why, Emmett Muggeridge has tried to court you for half a year. Do you let him? No. Do you let him go and let some of the other ladies have a crack at him? No. All you care about is your own self! You string him along getting that sweet man's hopes up, and then you turn away and make him feel like a piece of dog doo on the bottom of your shoe. Isn't that right, Tallulah? Why don't you just come out and tell the truth?"

Everything just stops.

Jenny.

Agnes.

Time.

The beating of my heart.

I am in the bedroom now. Not at Tranquil Meadows. This is the room with the periwinkle bedsheets, the matching bedspread and curtains. Nothing is out of place or clashing, as far as the décor goes. Anyone would be proud to have images of this room featured in the pages of *Better Homes and Gardens.*

But, as beautiful as the room looks, here I lie with my husband of less than six months. His dark hair falls in an artfully sloppy slope across his forehead.

Tom is above me, blue eyes melding with mine, slight smile focused and wanting.

The precious deep night moments stitch a husband and wife together until they are one soul. I know this. I know it is my duty as his woman to satisfy his manly needs.

His ring chokes my finger.

His need chokes me.

I feel an old, insatiable fear rise up as his kisses turn from sweet to urgent. He explores a body that is both his and mine at the same time.

I swore an oath to love him.

I believe that I do.

Why does it happen this way? Why does the natural and holy lovemaking between Tom and I turn into this?

My mind flashes like a fork of lightning, revealing the secrets in the storm.

I see him.

I see Tom.

I love him.

I love Tom.

I see… Uncle Wally. *Oh God. Please. No.* He's dead. *Uncle Wally. Stop touching me. Stop touching me!*

"Stop touching me!"

The first time I uttered those damning words to Tom, he was as kind as anyone could be. He was gentle and rolled off of me, cajoling me with soft words that made me regret my rejection immediately.

Then came the second time. The third time. The fourth time. Every syllable that pushed his need from me shoved a blade into his heart and, eventually, my gentle husband's words took on an Arctic edge. I blamed him, but really, I created the warped man that he became.

A night came when I said, "Stop touching me" and he did not stop, would not stop, pinned my arms down and conquered what he had purchased with a little golden band.

I have never once enjoyed a sexual touch from a man.

How can I do a thing like that to a man as sweet as Emmett? I destroyed one man. I won't do it to another.

I open my mouth now to rebut Jenny Logan's hurtful accusation.

Jenny is no longer in front of me.

Agnes and Jenny are putting the craft supplies away. I am just sitting here, like a useless lump.

A useless lump. I think Tom called me that once.

"Lula?"

I look up to see Ethel and Donkey standing in the doorway.

"Oh. Hello, Girls." I paint on a smile.

"We're going to the dining room for dinner. Are you coming?" Donkey looks so excited. I wish I could be that happy over the prospect of food.

I glance at the clock.

"I guess it is that time." I nod. "All right. Let's go."

I am so grateful for my dear friends.

Dawn Kehoe (Donkey)

Eve is beautiful. I am ugly. My mother's eyes tell me that. She doesn't have to say the words.

I know it when I watch her help to French roll Eve's hair and powder her cheeks and smooth out the new dress she is going to wear to meet Mother's Literati Society and her Women's Community Auxiliary Club and the endless luncheons and high teas and garden parties.

I don't know why I want to go to those things so much. How exciting can it be? There are no games or sports and no one would be dancing or singing. Nita Fowler, one of my friends at school who also happens to be the mayor's niece, says that it's boring.

"Dawn, it's just a lot of people doing a lot of talking and you drink tea with your pinky sticking out *like so.*" (She stuck out her own pinky without holding a real cup.)

Sometimes when I find myself at home alone, I open the china cabinet, take out one of Mother's prized fine china tea cups and practice drinking tea at those fancy socials, my pinky rising to salute my mother ever so daintily. After a hundred tries, I have become a professional pinky pointer. I imagine myself attending one of those fancy do's, chatting about Jane Austen and quilting and the joys of sticking out little fingers to prove your high quality breeding.

Pride goeth before destruction and an haughty spirit before a fall. I read that someplace (was it Granny Gardiner's dusty Bible, the one Father inherited after she died?) Those words proved too true today and I am cursing myself at this very moment for being so foolish. Why didn't I do my tea rehearsals using one of the everyday cups in the cupboard? Why did it have to be our best china?

There are only five tea cups of that pattern in the cabinet. Apparently, the story goes, my mother broke the sixth cup herself when she suddenly was seized with labour pains that brought me into the world. The cup flew from her hand and smashed to pieces against the floor.

This incident is not as bad as the first time. I didn't send the cup crashing to the floor, but the hairline crack goes all the way down from the rim to the base. How am I supposed to explain? How foolish will it seem to them that I actually thought myself worthy to be with my mother and Eve, like Oliver Twist showing up to meet The Queen of England.

I am a blubbering fool. Heaves and sobs shake my body as if an earthquake is going on inside me. The utter wretchedness of it all seizes me and I surrender to it, salt water blurring my eyes as my fists clench and my teeth gnash and snarl.

"I am never good enough, Mother! Never good enough! Never never never never!"

"Donkey? Donkey, what has got you so upset? Stop your shouting! Give me the cup!"

I look up into the worried face of my friend, Gladys. Her grip on my arm is a little tight. Who knew she could be so strong?

"Gladys." I cock my head to one side. "What happened?"

She smiles. "I could ask you the same thing, Dear Heart."

I shrug. "Well, if you really must know, I put a crack in one of Mother's fine china cups." I giggle. "She doesn't know it though. I was smart. I pulled all the china cups out of the cabinet and I put that cup at the back where she won't notice it until she tries to use them and that won't be for a long time. By then, she'll never suspect that I did anything." A sudden worry grips me. "Was that a bad thing to do?"

Gladys pulls the teacup (not my mother's) out of my hand and smooths the hair back from my face. Not that it's long enough to get in my eyes anymore.

"That was a stroke of genius." Ethel says. "I would have done the exact same thing." She snorts. "If we had had fine china."

"You never had good china when you were a young girl?"

"No. I think my grandmother sold off a lot of her things during the depression years."

"Oh." I try to imagine that. "Were you… were you one of those families my mother warned me about all the time?"

Ethel's eyes widen. "What do you mean, Donkey?"

"You know, she always wagged her finger in my face and said, "Dawn Gardiner, don't you be mingling with those people from the wrong side of the tracks!"

Apparently, I said something funny because Gladys, Ethel and Lula all burst out laughing. Maybe instead of going to the Jean Montgomery school, I should have opted for clown college. I am quite the comedian.

Chapter Eight

Gladys Peachy

"No! No! Don't hurt him! Don't!"

A blast of thunder and a shout in the dark sets my heart suddenly hammering so hard that I feel as if it will tear through my chest cavity. My eyelids pop open, but all I can see are shadows. I can tell the shape of my dresser and desk.

"Stop it, Lowell! He's only a baby!"

Lightning's brilliance briefly illuminates the grounds outside my window and the scene within my room. Before the blue and yellow spots appear before my eyes, I see Donkey's tautened features, arms flailing, reaching out to invisible phantoms, the ghosts from her traumatic past.

Thank God I'm lucid this soon after being so violently awakened. If it hadn't been Donkey, it surely would have been the storm.

THWAP!

"Donkey!" I throw my hands in front of my face. Even though she can't see any better than I can, her blows connect with uncanny accuracy. "Ow! Donkey, no! Please, wake up!"

Ka-boom-a-room-room!

Thunder punctuates my weary plea. The noise is loud enough to wake the dead, but not Donkey, it seems. I marvel that she keeps swatting and wailing.

"Get away from him! Get away from my Gabe!"

"Donkey." I say more firmly. "It's Gladys. I'm your friend, Gladys."

Lightning hurts my eyes in the dark.

"Gladys. You can't be here."

"Why not?"

Thunk!

Her arm clips the side of my bed.

"Ow!"

Dead silence.

Ba-room-a-room-room.

"Donkey?"

No answer comes for a few seconds. A new flash of lightning reveals Donkey's eyes, open now, her expression puzzled.

"Where is Lowell?" A hint of a sob catches in her throat.

I bite my lip. "Lowell is dead, Dear Heart. He has been for a long, long time."

More thunder rolls.

"I'm in your bedroom, Gladys. How did I get here?"

"You were walking in your sleep." *And slapping me silly*, I want to say. "Perhaps… perhaps it was something you ate before bed."

"Oh, and Lowell? Lowell is gone? And my Gabe is…"

The lightning explodes overhead.

"Your Gabe is at home tonight. He's a wonderful singer." I smile. "And you're safe here."

A gust of wind sends stray branches scrawling across the pane.

"I'm safe." Donkey does not sound convinced.

I pat her hand. My eyes have adjusted to the lack of light enough that I can make out her frame. "You will never have to see Lowell again."

The lightning and thunder fall over each other and seem to come at the same time.

A haggard sigh follows and I reach to turn on my bedside lamp.

Click-clock-click. Nothing happens.

"Oh dear. The storm has knocked out the power."

"What do we do, Eve? I don't like the attic." She lowers her voice. "You were right. It's haunted."

Donkey has gone off on another imaginary journey.
I know there will be auxiliary lighting out in the corridor. I don't feel like opening my private door in the middle of the night… if it is the middle of the night. My clock is off with the rest of the electrical things in here. It could be near pre-dawn by now.

I glance outside as the lightning flickers again.

"Eve! It's too scary! Help me!" Donkey's voice trembles.

I have to do something before she gets in a frenzy again. I don't want the attendants coming in to find her like this.

"Dear Heart, why don't you come and snuggle in here?" I throw back a blanket and offer to share my bed, though it certainly was not made for two.

"But… but you forbid me to be in your bed. After you got your own bed, you didn't even want me on your side of the room, and I'm not to touch any of your things."

"It'll be all right. Just this once."

Donkey hesitates. She almost turns to go back into the hallway.

I open my mouth to speak, but then she changes her mind, turns back toward me and climbs into the bed.

"We hid." She says as I pull the blanket up to cover us. "We hid in the attic."

I want to tread carefully, to draw her back to reality, but I am also curious. "Who hid in the attic?"

"Me, Eve. Me and my Gabe. I was so stupid. I thought we would be safe there. You warned me never to go in that room. I should have listened to you."

No matter how tired I feel right now, can it compare to how tired Donkey must feel all the time on the inside? "You did what you thought was best. It's not your fault."

She snorts. "Why are you being so nice to me? What do you want?"

"Nothing, my Dear. I just wanted to comfort you, like a good sister should."

"Hmph. You've never done that before."

I don't know what to say to that. My siblings and I always treated each other kindly. Well, maybe we had the odd disagreement, but I could never complain that I was mistreated.

"Maybe I could start now." I reply. "I'd like to be a nice sister."

"Oh." Donkey is quiet for a moment. "All right then. Just don't steal my boyfriend again."

"I won't."

"Eve?"

"Yes."

"I almost died in the attic."

"I know. I'm sorry that happened to you, Dawn."

"Lowell came to see me last Sunday. It was Mother's Day."

This jars me. Donkey is blurring the past and the present and I don't know where to find the lines between them anymore.

"Last Sunday? But, Dear Heart, Lowell is gone."

She thrusts an arm in the air. "He gave me a bruise. He always was a brute. Why couldn't I see that? Why didn't I know that before I married him? Why didn't you warn me?"

Lowell was a brute. Of that I am sure. But he's been dead for years. I know that Donkey sometimes thinks she's married to a movie star, and maybe I would too if I hadn't had such a wonderful husband, but this? This isn't her usual modus operandi (I learned that term watching police shows).

"You're not answering me." Donkey sounds chagrined.

I sigh. "Well, um -- I -- I'm sorry." I don't know what else to say. "I wish you had never even met that horrible man."

"Thanks, Eve. I love you. I never thought you loved me back." She throws her arms around me as best she can lying on a bed that's too small for two. My bones ache a bit in her grip, something I may as well get used to because Donkey has just started to softly snore.

I wish I could fall asleep so easily. I wish I could fall asleep. I am troubled.

Let not your heart be troubled...

The familiar scripture verse ought to comfort me and restore my peace. It doesn't. Not now. *Lowell couldn't come to visit. She could be just mixing up her times. How far gone is she? How long before we can't protect her anymore?*

I slip an arm around her as she sleeps so serenely. I try not to make a sound, but tears are flowing, not down my cheeks, but sideways toward my pillow. My nose is starting to run. I try to keep the heaves light so as not to disturb my dear dear Donkey. *I am sorry sorry sorry that I wasn't there for you. God, in your kindness, help us to help her. Please. Help me!*

And in my mind comes a thought, an unpleasant one. I am not a suspicious person by nature. Why would I think that? Who gave Donkey that bruise? I see a face in my head. I shake the thought off. I am overtired and overwrought and I don't want to think about it anymore.

Help me sleep, God. Help me rest.

Ethel MacNarland

Stupid dream! Stupid stupid stupid! The first clue should have been the water park! I was climbing that set of stairs that leads to the top of one of those giant slides at Splashtopia. I went there last summer with Marianne and the girls. They shrieked with terrified delight all day going up the stairs and down the slides. I sipped lemonade and sat in one of the shallow kiddy pools within full view of them, but there was no way I was going to go on those slides myself.

So why did I? Why did I climb to the top of those steps in my dream and torpedo down that slide, arms raised, voice yelling, having the time of my life until I woke up and realized I was peeing all over myself?

I thought of jumping out of bed and fleeing toward the bathroom, blurry as it is without my glasses on, but I sighed and realized how foolish that idea was. It was too late. Trying to get to the bathroom in mid-pee-flood would only move the mess to both the bed and the floor and it was going to be hard enough to hide the evidence of what I had just done on the sheets. I couldn't hope to bend down to the floor to clean that too.

As if one leak wasn't enough, I felt so overwrought and silly and childish... well, didn't I add insult to injury and start sobbing and blubbering like a fool! I couldn't help myself. It just pushed its way up like an oil gusher and before I knew it, my face was soaked, the tears dripping down until they left this wrinkly old face and landed on the shoulders of my already soaked nightie.

That is how I ended up a sneaky old criminal. Well, maybe criminal is a strong word, but I do feel like one and I don't know how they do it, those burglars who sneak into people's houses and banks and jewelry stores. All I feel is panic.

So I am showered and dressed now (I won't go out in the corridor smelling like that!). I am wearing a pale yellow blouse with a faux lace collar today. I have sprayed enough air freshener in here to kill a cow. I crack open the door to my room, so thankful that I woke up early enough. The full hustle and bustle of the day has not yet begun.

I can hear some cling clang in the distance. The kitchen staff must be prepping to feed us. The squeak-squeaky-squeak of the wheels of some cart and the faint strains of *That's Amore* let me know that Guy the Whistling Janitor must be on duty already, but the night stillness, that dead quiet that seems serene and creepy at the same time in a facility like this, it is only starting to give way to the sounds of early morning clatter and shift changes.

Knees almost knocking with anxiousness, I inch one foot into the corridor with my guilty bundle of smelly sheets. Along the wall I creep, heart pounding, ears straining to hear footfalls, approaching voices, karma coming to make me pay for the bad deed of peeing the bed.

Just a little ways down the hall lies an alcove, a spot where the hallway widens and the cleaning staff always leave a white bin there with a plastic lid that has 'linen for laundering' scrawled across the top in permanent marker. This could be my salvation if I can just get there without being discovered.

One step, two steps, three steps… *oh please don't find me here, Evangeline Martin… or worse… Biddy Finneyfrock!* It's a bit early for them to be in, but you never know.

I am getting closer and freedom is barely ten feet away. Oh, the exhilaration; the panic giving way to utter joy as I raise the lid on that bin and slam dunk the evidence into it. Ha! *All the linens look the same! I'm home free!* I close the top and I am about to make my way back to the sanctuary of my room.

Not so fast, Ethel MacNarland!

If the staff come into my room to clean and find my bedding already stripped, they'll figure me out. I'll be a spokeswoman for *Depends* faster than you can say, *Tinkle tinkle little star.*

I stare at the closed door beside the dirty laundry bin. It's got supplies like bedding and towels and tissues and all kinds of things that we are allowed to ask for, but not just go and take by ourselves. We pay them up the wazoo to stay in this place, but we've got to ask for extra supplies like school kids.

I look both ways to see that nobody has wandered into view. The coast is still clear. So Ethel, late-starting career criminal, quietly turns the doorknob and slips into the supply room. If only it were the vault at the bank. I might actually find something in here to steal that is worth this guilty feeling.

All right, I need to focus. The walls are lined with metal racks, each with four or five shelves. I scan past ugly blue-striped pajamas, towels, tissue boxes, lotion bottles and shampoo, and then finally spot my quarry. Shelves of stark white sheets and flannel blankets with one navy stripe across them; they're not beautiful, but they're clean and dry. I grab a fresh set and now I can make up my bed and they will never know what I've done, if I can just make it back to my room undetected.

I can't stand this scared sensation anymore. I've got to get back back back right now now NOW!

In a tizzy, I pull the supply room door open wide, ready to make a mad, speedy escape. I step back into the hallway, just a short dash away from freedom. *The clean bedding police will never catch me!*

"It's Ethel!"

What?! That is the worst possible thing I could hear at this moment. What is Gladys doing here?

"Has Ethel taken on a new job as part of the housekeeping staff?"

I would know Lula's slightly pompous tone of voice anywhere. I turn to see Gladdy, Lula and Donkey standing there, inquiring minds wanting to know why I am committing grand theft linens. I do not get embarrassed easily. I never have. I feel the blood rushing to my cheeks just now and I don't like the way it makes me feel... small.

"For your information..." I pause and lower my voice. "...I need... I needed..."

"A part time job in housekeeping." Donkey's smile is serene.

I huff. "I've got to get back to my room before..." I look both ways down the corridor. "...before I'm discovered."

"Ethel MacNarland..." Lula's blue eyes narrow. "Why on earth are you suddenly doing the job of the housekeeping staff? Something is mighty fishy here."

I bite back a tear and the urge to punch and kick and bite my way past the girls to the safety of my room. I can't make up anything to justify myself. I want to. Nothing comes to mind.

Gladys Peachy ought to get an award for being both sensitive and wise. "Ahhh… you… um… had a little trouble in the night, Dear Heart?"

My eyes go wide.

"The kind of trouble that you don't want the staff to see?" Gladdy's voice is soft and kind.

I nod.

Lula swats my arm. "Why didn't you just say so? Come on. We'll help you and then we can all go and find a good table in the dining room."

"I'm hungry. I hope they give us bacon." Donkey's eyes glisten like a child waiting in line to see Santa Claus.

What? They're not going to mock the septuagenarian bed wetter? These girls are such good friends. Why didn't I know them back in my younger days? I feel this fullness inside me, and also an emptiness… all those years that we could have known each other.

"Come on, Ethel. Let's get you back to your…" Gladys stops mid-sentence. "Oh dear."

"Oh dear?" I don't like the sound of that.

"It's Biddy Finneyfrock!" The sound of her name on Donkey's lips makes my blood run cold.

"What's she doing here so early? My boat is sunk." I fret, glancing around quickly to see if I can find a place to hide the 'stolen' goods.

"Hmph!" Lula puts a hand on my shoulder. "That tyrant of a woman is not going to get the better of me."

"Of you?"

"Of us." Lula's grin is, dare I say it, smug; her intense blue eyes focused and ready to fire.

We are tucked into the little alcove where the supply room door is located. Lula steps out of there and takes a few steps, intercepting Biddy's approach.

"Ms. Finneyfrock. What a fortuitous coincidence! I was just mentioning that I wanted to see you today and, Lordy, there you are!" Lula's lie sounds prissy and polite and it makes me want to laugh.

"Good morning. Mrs. Pratt." Biddy's voice also sounds polite, but unlike Lula's, there is no warmth in her tone.

"Good morning." Lula keeps her engaged.

Gladdy keeps peering over my shoulder to see what's happening. "Not yet." She whispers. "She's still coming this way. Don't turn around or she'll see the linens."

I nod. "Don't worry. I'm too scared to do anything."

"What can I do for you?" Biddy asks.

"Where did you get that broach you're wearing? It's stunning. Really brings out the roses in your complexion."

Lula, you have got to be kidding! Ms. Finneyfrock's skin is almost ghostly; pale face, ice blue eyes and spiky bleached blond hair that reminds me of a newly mown lawn.

"My broach?" Biddy's pitch never changes. "You wanted to see me to discuss jewelry?"

"No. I should say not." Lula's feathers are ruffling. "Although I have to say, the um… the pearls in the center are just gorgeous."

"Mrs. Pratt, I really don't have time to…"

"I wanted to discuss… to discuss…" Lula stops. "…the spring

social is coming up!" Inspiration strikes. "Yes, that's right. The decorations are prepared, but there needs to be some adjustment to the menu."

"It is barely 7:30 in the morning." Impatience rises in Biddy's voice. "If you wish to discuss such matters with my office, I would be happy to make an appointment to see you, but I really don't have time…"

Lula's attempt to run interference is failing. I know that I am about to be caught and my untamed pee secret will be out. I brace myself for the inevitable.

"We want bacon!"

My heart leaps into my throat.

Gladdy's mouth forms a capital 'O'.

"Why don't you give us bacon?"

Gladys mouths the word 'Donkey' and grimaces.

Is our friend about to betray her fluttery wandering mind to the most distasteful seniors' home administrator since Hitler?

"Donk… er… Dawn. We were just discussing…"

"I heard what you said, Lula." Donkey retorts. "What I want to know is… why does the kitchen here refuse to ever serve us bacon? I like bacon. Lula likes bacon. Don't you, Lula?"

Gladdy has a mischievous smile on her face now. What is up with that? It's not that amusing. I'm still trapped here like a terrified pissing bandit.

"Well, yes. Yes, I do like bacon." Lula agrees. "Perhaps we should discuss the inclusion of…"

"Come on!" Gladdy whisper shouts to me.

"What?"

She grabs my arm and starts walking me out of the alcove and down the corridor.

"Gladdy! She'll see!" I protest, but yet, I go with her.

"We only want to serve healthy food." Biddy's lame explanation of the merits of a bacon-less life starts fading in the background as we pick up the pace and walk-run away from the scene.

"Thank the heavens above!" I say as I turn the knob and enter my own room. "Oh, Gladdy! My heart! It's beating like a jackhammer…"

Gladys slides into the desk chair and I fall onto the dry end of the bed, laughter bursting out of both of us like a newfound gusher from an oil well.

Tallulah Pratt (Lula)

It happened again. There I was, walking down the corridor from my room toward the dining hall. I know that they don't serve breakfast until 8 o'clock, but my plan to take a stroll through the garden just after sunrise was put on hold by the sudden arrival of spring rain showers. So much for early communing with nature.

So I decided to go to the dining room and save a seat for the girls. The staff will let me have a cup of tea while I read the morning papers and find out which dummies are up for re-election this year. Not that I care. Not anymore. At my age, you realize that politics is the same cheesy pop music playing over and over again on the radio. The tune changes a little. They phrase the lyrics a different way, but it's the same old song and dance.

Well, as I was saying, I was on my way to the dining room at an ungodly hour when I saw them. The door to Gladdy's room opened and out she came, Donkey following close behind her. She tried to give me some cockamamie story about Donkey coming to fetch her for breakfast, but you have to get up pretty early in the morning to fool this old bird, Gladys Peachy. All right. I know that it is pretty early in the morning, but not early enough.

Donkey still had her nightie on and her hair was utterly mad. She looked like Albert Einstein, for goodness sake! So I know she invaded Gladdy's room in the night.

I will discuss that with Gladdy later. It wouldn't have been appropriate in front of our dotty friend, so I did the sensible thing and went with them to help Donkey pick out something to wear that doesn't clash or have yesterday's chocolate pudding on it. I must say she looks radiant today. I convinced her to go with a robin egg blue, short sleeved blouse with geometric shapes all over it and navy pants. She looks sharp and the busy pattern will help to hide whatever she decides to spill on herself. Tallulah Pratt, you brilliant vixen, you!

I did my best to tame her wild hair. It looks all right, though she needs a cut at the salon. I know that she doesn't really care if she looks good these days. Mercy! All her husbands are dead and she doesn't seem interested in suitors anymore. That's just like me. I do not want to be pursued by men! I have had enough of their philandering ways.

That is why I don't understand my own body. Why does my stomach seem to be housing a flock of frantic butterflies?

I mean, the morning was eventful enough. After the incident with Donkey, I ended up having to rescue Ethel, the poor thing. Her bladder runs amok. She almost got caught sneaking new linens from the supply room. I had to run interference with none other than Biddy Finneyfrock, the terror of Tranquil Meadows!

I'm proud of myself. I handled it with finesse. I complimented her on that godawful broach she was wearing. Where did she get that thing? A blind jeweler? I can't believe someone actually made something that looks so gaudy.

And now, all of the early morning excitement is done. The rain stopped just after breakfast. The sun has peeked out from behind the scattering clouds and I am sitting on a dried out bench in the garden, breathing in the scent of the newborn lilac blossoms and lily of the valley. Bees are buzzing here and there. A robin is cheery-upping for all he's worth nearby, and I am feeling so strange.

It's foolish! What is wrong with me? I'm wringing my hands until the knuckles turn pale. My insides feel squishy and jiggly like a bowl full of Jell-O. Am I coming down with something? It feels familiar, but it couldn't be that silly schoolgirl feeling... that... oh! There he is!

"Good morning, Lula. My, but that is a pretty colour on you." Emmett Muggeridge doffs his fedora and smiles, hazel eyes soft and glassy.

I never noticed before, but his pupils have a mysterious dark ring around them, framing the bluish green pools in and making me wish I could dangle my feet in their translucent waters.

"Oh." I feel my face flush. "This old thing." I pulled this cream and teal blouse out of the closet this morning, wondering why I bought it months ago, but never thought to put it on. The top half is adorned with an artfully arranged row of peacock feathers. "It's nothing special." And yet, I still preened in front of the mirror for 20 minutes before wandering out here.

"May I?" He indicates the bench I'm sitting on.

"Well... all right."

Emmett sits beside me, which makes a shiver slither up my spine. Is it a good feeling? Uncle Wally used to make me shudder too. A sudden urge to run seizes me.

"I brought a book." Emmett pulls a hardcover volume from under one arm. "You asked me to, remember?"

Uncle Wally's image shimmers and vanishes from my mind. I look at the title. *"Poetry for Old Souls.* I've never read that one." I reach out and touch the smooth cover, run a finger across the inkwell and quill that grace its surface.

Emmett shrugs. "I found it in the lending library here. It used to belong to a Katherine Knowles."

"And how do you know that?" *Are you just like Tom? Was Katherine Knowles one of your conquests, Emmett?*

"Easy." Emmett flips the book jacket open. "Looky here. It was a gift." He reads aloud. "To Miss Katherine Knowles. Christmas 1985."

My suspicious thoughts were for nothing. "Lordy, someone gave her poetry. It must have been…"

"A suitor?"

I fiddle with the top button of my blouse. "Yes. Who else would give that kind of gift?"

"Hmm…" Emmett stares at the inscription again. "And did she return his interest?" His head snaps up, eyes boring into mine. "Or did she spurn his advances at every turn?"

I bite my bottom lip trying not to giggle like a stupid floozy. "I suppose they had a whirlwind courtship and then…"

"And then?"

"He left her for another woman." My eyes tear away from his as a memory flashes before me; my furious fingers pouring prewash treatment on one of Tom's white dress shirts, trying like the dickens to get that ugly homewrecker's lipstick stain out.

Emmett's tone never changes. "What makes you think that? Maybe they lived happily ever after."

My voice comes out like I just swallowed a mouthful of gravel. "If they were happy, why is this book here in the lending library? Why didn't she keep it and treasure it forever and ever? That's what I would do if a suitor… I mean… if someone I truly loved gave me a beautiful gift like that."

"Would you really?"

I look up into his kind face again. "I kept the first gift Tom ever gave me. It was the ugliest little piece of tin ring that you ever did see."

Emmett laughs. "You met him when you both were young?"

"Yes. Barely out of our teens. He was only beginning his new job then, so I had to settle for something that made me itch like crazy. Still, I refused to get rid of it, even after we were married and I had real gold on my finger."

Emmett looks skyward. "Lorna hand embroidered me a handkerchief."

"A handkerchief? That's not as intimate as a ring, but…"

He shakes his head. "But…" He reaches a hand into the front pocket of his trousers and begins pulling something out.

I gasp. "You kept it… after all these years."

He opens it up, the white fabric wrinkled and slightly yellowed, but I must say, the stitches still strike me as exquisitely crafted; red rose petals distinct and perfect.

"I carry it with me everywhere." He confesses. "It makes me feel like she's still with me in some small way."

"She must have been a wonderful woman."

He nods. "I was truly blessed." His hand slides gently over mine. "And I swear to you, Tallulah, I don't know what kind of fool man betrays the woman he loves, but I kept my vows and I gave Lorna all of my heart in the good times and the bad. That is what a woman deserves."

What do I say? Can I say anything with my breath catching in my throat this way? Emmett Muggeridge! How dare you say the most beautiful thing I have ever heard in my life! Can I resist your heartfelt confession? Dare I believe it?

"I… oh… uh…" I search for the words that will make me feel like I'm on solid ground. Everything seems to shift beneath me. "We… could we read some of the book together?"

Emmett just stares at me.

Please. Don't push me into something I'm afraid to give.

"Of course." He picks up the book and flips through some of the pages. "That's what I brought it for."

I manage a smile. I always dreamed of meeting a man who liked poetry. The best I ever got from Tom was *'Roses are red, violets are blue, marry me, darling and I will be true.'* What a load of codswallop that was!

"Hmm…" Emmett leafs through and stops almost mid-way through the book. "Here's an interesting one." He clears his throat. "Late Summer Wine by H.M. Brown."

"I've never heard of that poet before."

"Nor I." He smiles. "Let's give old Mr. Brown a try."

"All right." I lean in closer.

"The nightingale's song as the evening wears on

Falls softly like silk on my ear
The deepening hue of the rich twilight blue
Makes the first evening twinkle appear

O love, take my hand, maybe not as you planned
Just the same, let our worn hearts entwine
I have tasted young love, but by Heaven above
Nothing's sweeter than late summer wine"

I don't know if the poem is good or a trite piece of trash, but it doesn't matter because Emmett's velvety baritone makes the words flow as soft as butter on toast and the syllables stream over my heart with sentiment and sweetness and I find myself almost caught away. Almost. I want to. I want to let myself fall into the current of romance, but how can I?

"Oh, Emmett." I whisper.

"Tallulah?" His eyes glisten. "Would you let me ask you a question?"

"Yes."

His grin may be impish or just hopeful. He takes off his hat and I feel the hair bristle on the back of my neck as he speaks. "Please, will you let me escort you to the spring social?"

"Oh, Emmett!" The whisper turns sharply to scolding. Leaping to my feet, I feel a tirade coming on. "You are impossible!"

"Yep."

"Incorrigible!"

"Absolutely."

"And I... I don't think... I mean... I can't believe..."

Mid-rant, I see a figure approaching, obviously fixated on our little tryst. I pause for a few seconds, ire rising at the memory of how she berated me and cut me to the bone. Well, Emmett Muggeridge! I may not always fall for your sweet talk, but I never miss an opportunity for revenge.

"Emmett." I whirl around to face him, anger turning to a soft coo.

His bewildered expression almost makes me laugh.

"Are you mad at me?" He asks, backing away as I advance upon him, one brazen hand reaching out to touch his cheek.

"No. I... I think I was just surprised, that's all."

His smile returns, but more timorous than before. "Surprised? Well, that's all right then."

I give him my best red-headed minx stare. Maybe, at my age, it's not sultry, but he responds the way that men do anyway. He's a deer caught in the headlights. "I would be delighted to attend the spring social with you." I shrug. "Though I don't have a thing to wear."

His fear turns to gleeful schoolboy delight. "Yahoo! Oh, Tallulah! You just made me a happy man!"

"Don't be happy too soon." I shake my head. *Am I crazy? What have I just done?* "I'm a handful, Mr. Muggeridge. You may have just caught a tiger by the tail."

He sticks his hat back on his handsome head. "I'll take my chances."

"I'm sorry to cut our book reading short, but I've got to go and see what Gladdy and the girls are up to. It'll be lunch time soon."

Emmett nods. "So it will. The morning has just flown by. You go on ahead and give my regards to your lady friends. I'll be seeing you around."

I walk down the pathway toward the entrance. Did I say walk? I am not walking. I am strutting! Every gloating footstep makes me feel as happy as a clam, Jenny Logan's scowl filling me with absolute glee.

"Good morning, Jenny." I quip. "I see you're dressed for high tea... in 1944."

A gloating laugh escapes me. I am very nearly floating on air. I look back toward Emmett and say, deliberately loudly... "Goodbye, Emmett. I can't wait to dance at the spring social with you!'

Jenny looks positively crestfallen. Isn't that a scream? I am naughty... sinful, even, but I haven't felt this good in years.

Dawn Kehoe (Donkey)

Lowell came to see me. He gave me a nasty bruise! See? It's right there on my hand.

Gladdy told me that Lowell is gone and he's never coming back, but I know better. He's not gone! He'll never be gone! Why was I so stupid? Why did I think I could ever escape?

I think I'm safe for now. He's like one of those vampires and he won't come out in the daylight... or maybe he's afraid that my best friend, Gladys Peachy, will catch him and send him back to wherever the dead go... the bad dead, I mean. I know where good people go. I know about Heaven. Jesus loves me. Jesus would never hurt me.

I could just cry... I could just... hey... where am I? What am I doing here? That's Gladdy and Lula... and Ethel is carrying fresh linens. What is she doing that for? She sounds upset.

She's talking to Lula. "For your information, I need... I needed..."

"A part time job in housekeeping!" I reply. I don't think that was the right answer. The girls carry on as if I'm not included in the conversation. They do that sometimes. It's okay. I'm used to it. That's what Eve and my mother used to do too.

My mind wanders down the hall toward the dining room. I

wonder what we're having for breakfast. "I'm hungry. I hope they give us bacon." I didn't know I said that out loud, but I must have. Lula just swatted my arm.

I can't wait to eat. Where are we going today? The restaurants around here sure aren't five star.

Well, would you look at that? Here comes the head chef now. Where's his white puffy hat? Whatever possessed him to take a lawn mower to his blond hair? It's all spiky and short. Unflattering, if you ask me.

Lula is chatting it up with him. What is she saying? She needs to discuss the menu? Yes! Lula, you are a genius! That's exactly what we should do. If we want five star meals, we should go right to the source.

I chime in. "We want bacon."

Lula is giving me a strange look. What's the matter with her? What kind of a restaurant doesn't serve bacon? For Pete's sake, we're not Jewish!

"Why don't you give us bacon?" I glare right into the face of that chef. I want him to know I mean business!

Lula pats my arm... patronizing me! "Donk... er... Dawn. We were just discussing..."

"I heard what you said, Lula." *Does she think I'm deaf?* "What I want to know is... why does the kitchen here refuse to ever serve us bacon? I like bacon. Lula likes bacon. Don't you, Lula?"

Hmm... the chef looks kind of mad. I don't understand why. It's his job to make the customers happy. If throwing a little bacon on the fire will do the trick... well, I should have it so easy. It was never that simple for me to make my mother happy... or Eve... or my little Gabe. I've spent my whole life trying and failing to make other people happy. That makes me feel... it makes me feel...

??????????????????

Hey! How did I get here? And would you look at that? We're having macaroni and cheese. See what I mean? This restaurant is definitely not five star. Oh well. I'm hungry. Where's my fork? Somebody put this thing on me... what is this...

"I don't want to wear a bib! That's for babies!" I scowl.

"Now now, Donkey. It's to keep your clothes clean. See? I'm wearing one too." Lula smiles at me.

"And me too." Gladdy points to her own bib.

"Me three." Ethel nods.

So, what then? Are we all children? It would seem so. Mac and cheese is a kid's food.

"All right." I give in, but not gladly. "Just answer me one question."

"Anything, Dear Heart." Gladdy pours a splash of milk in my tea cup.

I look around. Everybody is eating mac and cheese. I find that confusing.

"Why are we having macaroni and cheese for breakfast? That is the craziest thing I've ever heard!" I take my fork and swirl it around the plate.

I look up because nobody is saying anything. They're looking at each other as if they have some secret.

"Donkey, we had breakfast hours ago." Lula frowns, but then smiles again, but it's not a real smile. It's like a clown's painted on expression. "Don't you remember? We had oatmeal and toast and a boiled egg."

I think... hard. I seem to recall something about... well, I remember a piece of toast falling on the floor, but that can't be real. Why would anyone do that?

"Are you lying to me? Are you playing a joke?" I glare at Lula.

She shakes her head. "No no, I'm serious." Her earnest blue eyes won't move off of me. If she doesn't start eating soon, her food will get cold. "Trust me. It's lunchtime and we're going to have a movie this afternoon. They're setting up a big screen for us and everything."

"Yaaay!" I yell at the top of my lungs.

"Oh! Donkey! Shhhh…" Gladdy grabs my hand. "Let's use our indoor voice, shall we?"

"When are we going to the movies?" I ask.

"Soon." Gladdy indicates my plate. "Why don't we eat our lunch and then we can go, hm?"

I pick up a forkful of macaroni and stuff it in my mouth. "Okay. I hope they have popcorn."

"They will." Lula says. "They have one of those big theatre-style popcorn machines. Oh, I love the taste of hot butter poured over a big bag of corn."

I grin. "I'll try not to pour it over Eve's head again."

Ethel bursts out laughing. "Donkey! You didn't!"

"I told her it was an accident." I remember that like it was yesterday. "But, it wasn't. That's what she gets for stealing my boyfriend!"

All the girls are laughing now. What's so funny? I'm not sure, but this mac and cheese isn't half bad. Are they sure this is lunch and not breakfast?

Chapter Nine

Gladys Peachy

I remember the first time I stepped into a dress shop, swishing and swashing the hangers across the racks to find the perfect new outfit to wear for an evening out with Paul. I had been working half the summer stacking books at the local library, a position which, I have to confess, only came about because my father, bless his soul, knew the librarian.

It was the early days of our courtship. I wanted Paul to only have eyes for me. I wanted him to take one look at Miss Gladys Early and never want to look at anyone else. That is why I dawdled for over three hours trying to find the right colour, the right fabric, the right price for my budget.

I know how it is when a woman is trying to capture (and keep!) a man's fancy, but then again, I was a silly teenager back then. What did I know about the ways of romance?

This is a totally different circumstance. By age 72, finding something to wear should be a little less fussy. That is particularly true when you claim to have no more interest in love or men or courtships.

Still, I suppose I should be more patient. I shouldn't be sitting here tapping my foot on the carpet as if the sole of my shoe were a machine gun.

Tappity tappity tappity tap…

"Lula, are you still alive in there, Dear Heart?" At our age, you never know, do you?

A voice echoes from the other side of the dressing room curtain. "Gladys Peachy! Of all the cheek! I most certainly am alive!"

SWOOSH!

The curtain pulls back and Lula is standing there in a bright yellow suit jacket and skirt, one hand on a hip and the other looking as if she has to lean like that to hold up the wall.

"What do you think? Too business-like? It's a dance, not a job interview." Lula's blue eyes twinkle under the lighting.

I don't want to tell her the truth. It would be mean. "Well…"

"Oh come on, Girl. That's why I brought you with me when I decided to take the Tranquil Meadows weekly field trip to the Carlingwood Mall." She bends both arms upward and does a little pirouette. "You're going to save me from buying something ugly or flashy or out of season or…"

"You look like a banana." I cover my mouth with my hand. "I'm so sorry. I shouldn't…"

Lula rolls her eyes. "Please. Don't hold back how you feel on my account."

"I apologize, Lula Dear. I just…"

"Well, at least you're not just blowing sunshine up my behind." She shrugs. "Really? A banana?"

I nod. "Yes, and the last one made you look like a giant eggplant. I like solid colour. Just… the style wasn't right. It didn't flatter you. I don't know… it seems like we've been here for hours. I'm getting hungry." I feel a little fatigued too, but I don't want to make her feel bad.

Lula grins. "You're beginning to sound like Donkey."

I laugh. "Yes, I guess I am. It feels strange not having her here with us."

"Yes, well, Ethel promised to keep an eye. Imagine if we had brought her along. She'd be picking out a dancing dress for a date with Bing Crosby." She heads back into the dressing room. "Hold on. I've got one more to try and then we can go for lunch at that Chinese place in the food court."

"Wok 'n' Roll? I love that spot. They make the most delicious chicken almond guy ding." My mouth starts to water just thinking about it.

Lula keeps talking from behind the curtain. "It's the general tao chicken that I can't get enough of. A little bit of kick to be sure, but it's got more flavour than that tasteless mac and cheese they gave us two days ago in the dining hall. All that money we pay them and that's the best they can whip up?"

I can hear the strain in Lula's voice as she struggles to get out of one dress and into another.

"Can I ask you something?"

"Of course you can, Gladdy. You're my dearest friend in the world."

I hold back a giggle. "I'm glad you agreed to let Emmett escort you to the spring social, but…" I hesitate. "… well… aren't you going to an awful lot of trouble for a man that you aren't interested in dating?"

SWOOP!

Trouble was not the word I should have used. Tallulah Pratt, 72 and still formidable to look at as a woman (at least, I think so), is standing there like a tiger ready to stake a claim and stalk her prey. I suddenly wonder if Emmett Muggeridge knows that touching fire can get a man burned.

"What do you think?" Lula asks, mischief written all over her face. "This is the one. Tell me, it's the one!"

My jaw drops. "Oh, Lula. You look… that is… that is enough to put a young woman to shame."

Emerald green was made for redheads. The fact that the dress is not a solid emerald hue, but a blue-green brocade with raised golden leaves, ruched sleeves and a slightly flared skirt flatters Lula's porcelain skin (even the smattering of light freckles on her arms) and the carrots in her hair and the intense blue gemstones of her eyes. Lula's high-pitched laugh sounds like a teenager getting ready for the prom. "I've got the perfect jewelry to go with it. Eat your heart out, Jenny Logan!"

I don't know what provoked that crack about Jenny, but just look at Lula. I see a happiness in her face... a youthfulness that has always been missing. I know that we are not in our prime anymore, but keeping that childlike wonder is vital (at least I think it is) to living longer. She's a woman who has known much turmoil in her life. Maybe not quite as dramatic as Donkey, but my dear Lula has been hurt by the storms of her younger years just the same.

I set a hand on her arm and say the words that I feel are the God's honest truth: "Dear Heart, poor old Emmett isn't going to know what hit him."

Ethel MacNarland

Donkey is married to Frank Sinatra. Not in real life, of course, but *From Here to Eternity* was playing on the classic movie channel after breakfast and now, the poor gal is in pitiful mourning, widowed to Old Blue Eyes.

I am sitting on the white sofa with the blue paisley pattern on it while Donkey is reading something or other in one of the recliners. It's almost time for us to head to the dining hall for lunch, but not yet. She is so relaxed over there. I don't want to disturb her until I have to.

Gladdy and Lula went on the Magic Bus with the staff of

Tranquil Meadows for their weekly trip to the mall to shop for a dress for the spring social. I could have gone, but I tried shopping with Lula once and the corns on my toes ached for days after. So I took a rain check and told them I would be on Donkey duty until they get back.

It's a good thing I did now that she has decided to be the widowed Mrs. Sinatra. *You were Dawn Gardiner... not Ava Gardiner, Donkey!* I could never have seen myself married to that old crooner, handsome as he was. He was too high maintenance. What am I saying? My own husband kept me on my toes. *Where's the newspaper? Is that what we're having for supper? I found a wrinkle in my shirt, Ethel. Didn't anybody ever teach you how to use an iron?*

I came close to ironing Laird's shirt with him still in it! Ha! That would have been hilarious. Well, all right, I didn't wish the man to burn. A little appreciation would have been nice though.

"Good morning, Ethel. Isn't it a lovely day?"

I start. I was so lost in my own thoughts that I didn't even see Pete Marsden sit down beside me.

"I'm sorry." He grins. "I didn't mean to give you a fright."

I swipe a hand in front of my face. "Oh...pshaw! You didn't scare me. I was just.."

"Reminiscing?"

"Not exactly." I try not to laugh.

"Where are your partners in crime this morning?" Pete is playing with his watch, nervously winding it even though I know that it's got a battery and the little knob is just for show.

"My what?" I give him a puzzled look. "Oh, I get it. Donk... I mean, Dawn is reading over there and Gladdy and Lula went on the mini-bus to the mall today."

"Ah, and you didn't go with them?" The sun is slowly moving higher in the sky, but it's still low enough to cast a beam through the windows and make the bald scalp underneath Pete's thin comb-over glisten.

"I wasn't up for a long walk on those concrete floors. Shopping with Lula is exhausting."

Pete chuckles. "I would imagine that woman is hell on wheels."

"She's what?!"

"I just mean…" He catches himself quickly. "I mean that… a… a woman like Lula is used to… in my experience, she would be used to the fine things and…" He casts a pleading glance my way. "…and the cheap five and dime things just won't do."

I soften. "You're right. Lula is a great friend, but she does like to have everything just so."

He shrugs. "There's nothing wrong with that. I just can't see that it would make a shopping trip very relaxing."

A loud laugh bursts out of me before I can stop it. "Relaxing? Oh Heavens, no! By now, Gladdy must be beyond tired. I almost feel guilty for letting her go without me, but why should we both have aching feet this afternoon?"

Pete puts his watch back on his wrist. "Actually, I'm glad you didn't go…"

"You are?"

"Yes, Ethel. I know we were interrupted last time I brought this up, but…"

I know what's coming. A feeling of dread comes over me. I don't think I want to date anyone, as sweet as Pete is.

He looks like he might blow up if he doesn't get his question out. "Have you had time to think about my request to escort you to the spring social? It would be nice to have a dance partner and have a bit of fun."

I can't argue with that logic. It would be nice, so long as it was just an innocent evening of dancing and nothing more. Could we do that? I'm in my seventies. You would think I would have this all figured out by now. Hey Kids! Guess what?! You never do figure it all out!

I hesitate, unsure of what answer to give. "Well, I was thinking…"

"Heyyy! There you are, Amore!"

In he strides, larger than life, still sporting a full head of black (and a little white) hair, beating his chest with his hands to show me his virility (or maybe to look like a gorilla, I don't know which). Nino Fabrini, five foot five, still fit, voice volume on loud and-a accent-a very Italian, stands in front of me and strides right over any attempt at courtship by Pete Marsden.

"Bella bella, my darling Ethel, allow-a me take-a you out to the dance. I waltz like-a Fred Astaire. I sing…" And here, he demonstrates a voice that might give Al Martino a run for his money. "Alle porte del sol, ai confini del mar…"

I open my mouth to speak, but his presentation isn't finished.

"I make-a you happy woman, treat-a you like a queen. What you say to Nino, hey? You say yes?"

All I want all of a sudden is lunch. I don't care what they serve, but I want to bolt to the dining hall and pretend that I'm not sitting here, Pete looking like a sad hound dog on one side and Nino looking like an over-confident rooster on the other. I envy Lula. All she has to contend with is Emmett.

The air seems thick just now with both men waiting for an answer from me. What would they say if they knew I was thinking of saying, *"See ya later. I'm off to join the circus!"*

The last thing you think will happen to you in the twilight years of life is a tawdry love triangle. I mean, it never happened to me when I was a young, doe-eyed maid. I don't think a lot of men were looking my way. If they were, I didn't know about it. Laird happened along and I took the first train to matrimony. In hindsight, would I do that again? I'd like to gush and say, *"Yes, of course!"* I'm grateful for my children, aren't I? If there were a way to have them while skipping the part where I married Laird...

"Well, Ethel. What'll it be?" Pete asks ruefully. "Me or the spaghetti man?"

Nino's dark eyes grow wider. "Hey-a Pete! No say-a nasty things about me." He turns his attention back to me. "Look-a here, Amore. Bigga hair, bigga smile..."

"Bigga mouth." Pete adds, sulking.

"You watch it!" Nino's fist is up now. "You a wise guy, hey? You wanna piece o' me?"

Pete stands up, raising his fists in defiance. "I don't mind if I do. Come on, Fabrini! Let's have at it!"

"Let's not!" I try to interject.

"Who wanna go out-a with baldy, hey?" Nino taunts.

"Who wants to go out with a guy with black eyes?" Pete retorts.

I attempt to get between the rival rams before their horns collide. "Gentlemen! Nobody is getting a piece of anybody today." I realize that sounds a little bawdy in today's lingo, and that's a little bit funny to me, but I don't think it would be good to laugh at this moment.

"Ethel, you a lady. You stay outta this." Nino is breathing so hard, his nostrils flare like an angry bull.

"Stop it!" My words are useless. It seems as though I'm going to have to watch these foolish old farts go at each other for a date that I don't want.

"Mr. Fabrini, calm down." Evangeline Martin's voice breaks through the insanity.

I see her standing beside me now with one of the maintenance men. I think his name is Phil… or Paul… or Pat. I can't remember.

Upon seeing Evangeline, Pete's stance relaxes immediately. Nino Fabrini still looks piqued, but momentarily, he backs off and drops his arms to his sides. "You lucky." He gesticulates with his fingers under his chin. "Maybe we meet another time."

I think Pete is going to react and let his temper flare again, but for now, the storm has passed.

"I'm sorry, Ethel." He shakes his head. "It's not fair. I was giving you my best pitch and he comes along and butts into our business!"

Nino opens his mouth to protest. "All's fair in-a love and war."

"That may very well be…" I fumble for the right thing to say. "I'm sorry, Evangeline. Things got a little out of hand, but it's all right now."

"Are you sure?" Evangeline is usually smiley, but right now, her lips are pursed and she does not look impressed. "If these men are harassing you, I'd be happy to put a stop to it."

I sigh. "Thank you. I think it's under control now. Thank you for your flattering offer, Pete and Nino. It's all a bit overwhelming. We still have a few days until the social and I need to think it over."

Pete nods. "All right. We'll wait for your answer."

"You pick-a me, I make-a you feel like a real lady." Nino pats his own chest.

I nod. "Give me a little time and I'll let you know. In the meantime, I think I will go with Dawn to the dining room and see what they're serving for lunch."

"The spaghetti!" Pete exaggerates the syllables, which incurs a wrathful glare from Nino, but since I'm not deciding anything right now, he retreats out of the TV room and, for the time being, all is well that ends well.

Tallulah Pratt (Lula)

Gladys Peachy, you are a lightweight! Well, you're the best friend a girl ever had, but when it comes to shopping, you can't keep up. Just look at her! She's practically dragging herself across the floor to the mall entrance so we can get back in the little mini bus and head home.

I must say, we had ourselves a wonderful time. I found the perfect dress for the spring social. I even got a new pair of shoes to match! They're not as high in the heel as the ones I wore years ago, but that's because I'm a little older (not old!) and wiser. High heels are a form of torture that we women allow, and for what? To catch the roving eye of a man? They're awkward and they make my feet ache. I won't wear them anymore. That's why I got a sensible, low-heeled and pretty pair that will make me feel like the belle of the ball.

"All abooooard!" Benny, the driver, calls in his happy-go-lucky, singsong voice. I don't know if he's driving a bunch of seniors around in this overgrown van or a group of kindergarten children. To be fair, as I look around us, some of the passengers are a bit like children... there's Dinah Gillespie. I notice a shopping bag in her hand. What did she buy? I bet if I asked her, she couldn't tell me. It could be stockings or a box of truffles or something ridiculous like a screwdriver. She's as far gone as Donkey, if not more so.

Jenny Logan looks as miserable as ever. I'm glad she's sitting near the back. I won't have to look at her once I sit down. I can't imagine shopping being pleasant in those shoes! Who does she think she's impressing? Certainly not me!

Gladdy takes the window seat while I take the aisle seat beside her.

Emmett smiles at me from across the way. My insides feel like there's a balloon in there and it inflates when I look at him. What is wrong with me? What has possessed me to go to the dance with him? I can't very well back out now. When would I have another opportunity to wear my gorgeous new dress?

"Did you have a good time shopping?" Emmett asks, a wry smile on his handsome face.

"It's always nice to get out for a while." Gladdy answers, filling in the awkward silence. "But, boy, am I pooped! I may need a nap to recover."

Emmett nods. "I can imagine. You ladies must have been mighty busy."

Gladdy lets out a little laugh. "You can say that again."

I finally find my voice. "Well, there were sales on." I'm lying, of course. I don't want to boost that man's ego by letting him know I was searching hither and yon for a suitable outfit for the spring social. "I never could resist a sale."

He smirks. "That word does seem to draw women in like a piece of steel to a magnet."

Emmett reaches across the aisle to grab my hand. What a bold man! I slap his fingers and draw mine away. "Mr. Muggeridge!

You are being rather forward!"

His laugh is hearty and annoying and strangely captivating. I instantly rue slapping him. I could be enjoying the warmth of that large hand right now, but what would people think of me? Do you know what? For all of Tom's philandering, I never once strayed away from him. I never even considered cheating on him, not even that one time when Tom's good friend, Lou, offered himself to me. I was ashamed. It felt as if I was dirty and tawdry. Why did I feel that way? I didn't do anything wrong!

"I wonder what the girls are up to." I turn to talk to Gladdy.

To my surprise, she has fallen asleep with her head against the glass. I don't know what she did that for. It will only take half an hour to get back to Tranquil Meadows. Maybe Donkey kept her up all night again.

It doesn't matter now. I lean back in my own seat and close my eyes and relax and as I drift off, a little dream passes before my eyes. There I am in my wedding gown dancing around and around while the music plays. *I'll be loving you always. With a love that's true always.*

I am a vision in lace laden with tiny pearls.

Enraptured in my fleeting happiness, I look up, expecting to see the familiar face, the eyes of the man I married, Thomas Pratt. I see the face of Emmett Muggeridge.

I start!

Pop! My eyes open.

I gasp!

"Lula, is everything all right?" Emmett asks.

Have you been watching me sleep? Did I drool? "I..." I look across the aisle at him. "Well, I guess I'm a little tired. I fell asleep."

"A little dream?" He prods.

I smile, trying to look natural. "Yes. That must be it."

"You don't remember?"

"That's right." I fib. "It's all fading. You know how dreams are."

"I do." He is wearing an impish grin.

I look down and realize… well, of all the cheek! How long has his hand been holding mine? I feel a sudden urge to pull away, but then I don't. Lordy, his hand is warm and strong, and right now, I just don't want him to let go.

Dawn Kehoe (Donkey)

"Eve! You're a shameless hussy!" I could slap that smile off of her face right now!

I raise my hand to do it, but she grabs my wrist.

"No, Donkey. No hitting."

Why not? She deserves it. "You took my boyfriend, Eve." She doesn't even look sorry.

"Donkey. It's me, Ethel. Snap out of it!"

"I watched you just now." I accuse her. "I saw those boys fighting over you. See? You can have any boy you want. Jerry was mine!"

Eve huffs, loosens her grip on my arm.

I don't have the energy to fight anymore.

She puts an arm around me. "Let's talk about it over lunch, all right? What do you think of that idea?"

"Lunch?" My stomach growls. "I could eat."

"Good." She leads me out of the living room into the hallway.

I don't remember our house having such a big hall. Wait a second. This isn't our house.

This isn't…

That isn't..

Who is that…

Where…

My name is Dawn Gardiner. No. I'm Dawn Key… I'm Donkey!

"I think we're having barbecued chicken." Ethel smiles as we head toward the dining hall.

"It smells good." I reply. "Ethel, where did Gladdy and Lula go? Did they move away and not tell us?"

Ethel laughs. I don't find it funny, but she seems to think everything is a big joke.

"Gladdy and Lula went to the mall today. They'll be back this afternoon."

I feel frightened, as if everybody knows something that I don't. "Are you sure they didn't just go away?" My eyes fill with tears.

Ethel takes my hand and shows me to our usual table. "I'm sure. They'll be back around 3 o'clock." She promises, looking right into my face. "Lula wanted to find a new dancing dress for the spring social."

"Who's she going to dance with?"

Ethel ties a bib around my neck. I want to stop her, but my arms feel heavy and tired.

"Emmett's going to escort her. Isn't that nice?"

"Emmett is a nice man." I know that's true. "I'm not going to dance with anybody. It's too soon after losing my sweet Maggio."

"Maggio?" Ethel gives me a funny look. Then, she nods. "Ah… gotcha. Sinatra. Old Blue Eyes."

I frown at Ethel. "How did you know he had amazing blue eyes?"

Chapter Ten

Gladys Peachy

I don't have a date for the spring social tonight. It's just as well. I have only given my heart to two men in my life; my father and Paul Peachy. I don't feel lonely. I feel blessed. Of course, I miss both Paul and my father sometimes, but there is no emptiness within; just gratitude and a fullness that makes me feel peaceful and satisfied.

I wish I could say the same for my dearest friends, but when I look into the eyes of Ethel, Lula and Donkey, I see pain, unfulfilled dreams, regret and sorrow. Is it arrogant of me to think that? I don't mean that I'm better than they are. I just wish their lives had been this complete. The only thing ever denied me was the joy of motherhood, but I don't want to think about that right now, so I push the memory away.

I have work to do.

I put on a clean, pastel purple dress. It's the same one I wore to church this past Easter Sunday. It has a belt with a silver buckle and it looks like a two-piece outfit, but it's not. I've got a set of white pearl earrings and a necklace to go with it. I suppose I won't look the picture of glamour, but I will not be whirling and twirling on the dance floor in the auditorium.

I volunteered to help with the hospitality; that is, I am going to lay out the punch and the sandwiches and the napkins and whatnot, and I will be smiling and greeting people at the door.

There's a table set up with a ballot box on top of it. Everyone who comes to the dance will receive a raffle ticket. I have the door prizes in a bin beneath the table. No one will see it because the white linen table cloth goes all the way to the floor.

Agnes Holmes drafted me to help once she realized that I don't have an official date. Lula thought I should be insulted by that. I'm just glad to be useful.

Oops! I'd better hurry up! I promised Agnes I'd be there by 6:30. Where are my shoes? There they are on the bed. All right, let's get moving.

I'm off like a herd of turtles. The auditorium is way around on the other side of the building. I follow the corridor past all of the ladies' rooms and have nearly passed half of them when Donkey's door opens suddenly, her frantic form scurrying out, eyes and mouth wide, as if some terrible monster were chasing her.

"He's here! He's here!" Donkey's voice is too loud.

"Donkey? What is it, Dear Heart?" I try to calm her, placate her. I check my watch and wince, hoping I don't keep Agnes waiting too long. "Did you fall asleep? Did you have a nightmare?"

"He hurt me! He's a bad man!" Donkey lets me put my arms around her. Her fingers dig into my dress and I wonder if I will have to go and change into a clean one.

"Who's a bad man?" I ask.

"He is!" She is staring at someone who isn't there.

"My dear, dear Donkey…" I reason. "…there's no one here except you and me."

"No, Gladdy. You're wrong."

Thank goodness she recognizes me.

"He's here." She repeats, raising a finger to point down the empty corridor. "I just saw him. He hurts me all the time."

I know that Lowell hurt her. He did more than that. He almost

133

took her life. It makes me sad to think of it. I need to bring Donkey back to the present.

"Why don't you come with me?" I say, noting that she's not exactly dressed up, but she looks clean. Her pretty pink blouse actually looks nice with those grey pants. "You can help me set up for the dance."

Donkey looks up into my face, eyes pleading. "Will he be there?"

I shake my head. "No. I promise he won't be there. I won't let him come."

That seems to do the trick. Her smile returns and she relaxes. Like it or not, Agnes, Donkey is now on the Hospitality Committee.

Ethel MacNarland

I hate it hate it hate it! It makes me feel more like a baby than the bibs Donkey is always complaining about. I don't want to wear that! I won't!

I sit down on my bed, bottom lip jutting forward in the biggest pout since I lost at marbles in the schoolyard in Grade 3. I used to love the feel of the smooth glass between my fingers; alleys, beauties, it didn't matter. Marbles were treasure to a kid back then and I had a tin (real tin!) can full of them.

A frustrated sigh escapes from deep within me. It feels like I'm losing yet another battle.

I glare, hate brimming in my lower lids in the form of angry tears that don't quite spill over onto my cheeks. "Miserable adult diapers."

I look at the label on the plastic package... Depends. The word diaper isn't printed anywhere, but they're not fooling anybody.

I suppose this is better than using cloth and two safety pins. I burst out laughing at that thought, bitter as it is.

"Well, let's see. It says they're like real underwear, except with odor control and absorbency." I'm not convinced, but I pull out a pair and take the towel off of my freshly showered body.

Sliding one leg in, and then the other, I pull them up over my lumpy, bumpy, kind of wrinkly frame. I have never been a fat woman. I wouldn't say I was skinny either. I'm an in-betweener. I grin and shrug. "Hmph. The magazines only want stick women these days. They want women to look straight and bony, like a gangly pre-teen boy."

I don't want to pursue that subject right now. I was never destined for a magazine cover, except maybe *'Disgruntled Housewives Weekly'*. That makes me laugh again. I'm in fine form today, despite being sentenced to adult diaper jail. I can't even blame Biddy Finneyfrock for that. I realized after the bed peeing incident that my bladder is running the show.

The last thing I need at the spring social is to spring a leak! So, I broke down, went to one of the little shops that are set up in the lobby and bought these stupid things. If I have to surrender to this overactive pee factory of a body, I'm doing it my way and on my terms.

What a surprise! The panties slide up and on rather easily. I pull on the elastic at the top and let it snap back. Snug. Not too snug. They might even be a little bit comfortable. The night is young and the jury is still out on that.

I catch a glimpse of the time. I'd better hoof it! It will be time to go soon.

I pull a pair of stockings on, grunting and groaning as if I were running the gauntlet. Ha! Phew! I need to catch my breath. At least we gals don't have to squeeze into girdles anymore. That was a throwback to the days of medieval torture.

Lula went shopping for a new dress, but I have a pretty one that I hardly ever wear. It's light and airy with blended pastel swirls on top and a pleated, loose skirt at the bottom. I can swish and sway and feel girly with a skirt like that. It's pink!

As I pin my favourite silver broach on, the one with the mini white roses and pearls, I smile at my reflection. I don't look half bad for an old bird.

Now, where is that little tube of lipstick that I never use? I open the top drawer to my side table and push aside a deck of cards, my diary, pens and some batteries. There it is! *Ruby Smoke...* that's the only shade of lipstick I own.

Rap rap rap!

Someone is at the door. I check the bedside clock and sigh. He's right on time. Well, that can't be difficult when you didn't have to race across town through traffic.

I check myself one more time in the mirror, hastily drawing across my lips, smacking them together and then grabbing a tissue to absorb the excess. I shrug and salute myself. This will have to do.

I slide both feet into the fairly comfy white flats I always wear for dress up occasions and sashay across the floor toward my door. The voice on the other side of it sounds pretty chipper, singing: "Luck, be a lady…"

I pull on the door handle, grateful that I'm not hearing *To the Door of the Sun*.

"You look like a million bucks, Ethel." I smile back at Pete Marsden, his grey suit and silky, striped pink tie adding a debonair air to him, despite the silver comb-over. Together, we will look like a pair of dotty septuagenarians, but it's all right. We're all in silly mode this evening.

"Thanks, Pete. You don't look so bad yourself." I smile and grab the smaller purse that I use for special occasions.

"Are you up for some dancing and snacking and crazy smooching in the moonlight?" Pete offers me an arm and I take it. We start to stroll toward the auditorium as if we really are teenagers going to the spring prom.

"Dancing and snacking are on the menu." I reply. "I don't know who you're going to do the crazy smooching with."

"Either way, I'm sure glad you accepted my invitation and ditched Nino Fabrini."

"Me too." I let that slip out without even meaning to. "Well, you did ask me first."

A lot of couples and singles are heading the same way we are. This is going to be quite the event, and I was going to sit around, mope in my room and not pick anyone to escort me. That would have been downright stupid.

I feel a happiness welling up in me. I'm going to enjoy a dance. Me! Ethel MacNarland! In my seventies! Best of all, I have almost forgotten that I'm wearing those cursed Depends!

Tallulah Pratt (Lula)

Tallulah Pratt! You are the picture of glamour!

I may be biased, but look at that foxy femme fatale staring back at me from the mirror! I liked this dress when I tried it on at the mall, but I love it now. I went to the little in-house salon that they have in the lobby here. My hair is freshly done. I'm wearing evening make up! I'm ready to knock 'em dead and make Jenny Logan positively green with envy.

I am wearing a pair of gold button earrings with an emerald at the bottom. My beautiful daughter Sarah gave them to me for my birthday last year. I am having trouble with the clasp on the matching necklace. I am trying to see it in the mirror; to look and see where to attach the two ends, but damn my silly vanity! I really do need to see that eye doctor.

After a dozen tries, some huffing and almost a swear word, the clasp finally hits its mark and I turn the chain around so that the attached ends are now at the back of my neck and the pendant is dangling above the neckline of my dress.

I know that they have irritating signs all over this building saying "No scents is good sense", but I like to smell good and I pay through the nose to live here. So I take the fancy, multi-faceted bottle from its glass tray on my dresser, lift my head up and push the button to release a spray of *Tahiti by Twilight*.

There! Now all I have to do is slip on my shoes, grab the adorable little gold clutch that I have owned for at least 20 years and voila! This chick is ready to fly the coop.

I glance at the big numbers on my bedside digital clock. It's time! I feel an urge to rush out into the corridor to find him, but that would be foolish. He is going to come here. He will offer me his arm like a gentleman should and I will walk beside him through the doors of the auditorium. I am a woman of dignity.

I sit on the side of my bed and wait. Minutes pass... or it may be seconds.

Where is he? He had better not be late! Worse than that... a terrible thought occurs to me. *What if he changed his mind?* I can see Jenny Logan's smug, condescending smile as she dances around and around the floor with Emmett Muggeridge! That feels like a slap in the face... like Tom Pratt and his mistress on the side all over again. I am always the last to know these things. I am always the fool!

Tears well up in my eyes. Thank Heavens for waterproof

mascara! I grab a tissue from the bedside table and dab at the water before it can roll down my cheeks and mess up the face I spent 20 minutes putting on.

Suddenly, I notice something on the floor by the door. I walk over to pick it up. It's a piece of paper... stationery, to be precise, face down on the floor. How odd! I do have stationery, but it's not light blue. It's white with a spray of gardenias at the top. Where did this come from?

Turning it over, I see handwriting with rather exquisite penmanship.

"Oh!" I gasp, backing up and sitting, almost involuntarily, back down on the side of the bed.

It's a poem. I read the words through a teary blur.

"Never Too Late

No matter the day
No matter the hour
It's never too late for love

It comes across gently
Yet holds such great power
It's never too late for love

Though the snow touch the mountains
And the boughs slightly bend
Put your hand in mine
And it's springtime again

It's never too late
No, never too late for love"

The bottom of the poem is signed... "Emmett Muggeridge". My hand goes to my mouth. *Emmett wrote this.* I sigh, anxious and elated. *Emmett wrote this... for me!*

Where is he? Where is Emmett? Just a moment ago, I doubted his sincerity, accused him of imagined infidelity. Now... my heart is so full… I am overcome with conflicting emotion. A furious desire pushes me. I am compelled to see him, to touch him, to be with him!

With more passion than is wise for a 72-year-old woman, I launch myself toward the door of my bedroom.

"Emmett?" I grab the doorknob and pull it open. "Emmett? Where…?"

I am stopped mid-sentence. A perfect red rose stands in mid-air, offered to me at the end of a large, warm hand that is attached to an arm that goes all the way up to a shoulder, a neck and a smiling handsome face. *Emmett! You are disarming me and I am happy, and so very afraid.*

That overly-confident vixen that stared back at me in the mirror is cowed right now, and also pleased. He has switched to a different fedora to match the navy, pin-striped suit he is wearing. The tie is a rich, smoky blue, but there are balloons shaped like hearts, a big one at the bottom, tapering off into smaller ones towards the top. I put my hand over my mouth to stifle a giggle.

"My granddaughter picked it out." He smiles as I accept the rose from his hand. "When I told her I had a date for the dance, she made me promise to wear it."

"Thank you for the flower." I reply, still grinning about the tie. "And… and for the poem."

He lifts his eyebrows. "You don't find the poetry too kitschy?"

"No." I shake my head. "Not at all. It reminds me of something Cole Porter would write." *It's De-lovely*, I almost add, but how silly would that sound?! I open the door of one of my upright cupboards and grab the little pressed glass vase that I use whenever Sarah visits and inevitably brings me flowers from her shop. "Let me put this in water and then…"

"We can head off to the big do."

"Yes. The big do." I repeat, my smile warming me all the way to my toes.

Dawn Kehoe "Donkey"

I smell the whiskey on his breath.

I see the red lines around the darkness of his eyes.

His body weaves a little when he walks and he takes a misstep, steadies himself, smiles. It's not a happy smile. It's crooked. It doesn't bring me comfort. It makes me feel like I might wet myself, like my knees might buckle and send me crashing to the floor… through the floor… down to the pits of hell. Even that would be an escape.

But there is no escape. Not for me. Not for foolish Dawn Gardiner who believed Lowell Kehoe when he said he loved me; when he promised we would have a wonderful life together with a white picket fence and a house and a garden. I thought I would buy china teacups and invite ladies to my beautiful home for high tea and cakes. I would invite them. Then I would never have to feel the blade of unworthiness that sliced through me every time my mother chose Eve and left me out.

All I did was trade one devil for another, and the second one was worse… and bigger, but I didn't see it. How stupid could I be?

"Give it to me." Lowell snarls, closing in on me like a wolf cornering prey.

"I can't. I don't have it." I back up one step… two… three… until the wall is behind me and he is in front and there is nowhere to go.

"You do!"

His strong hand grabs my wrist… hard. It hurts! *Don't break the bones!*

"I don't want to." I resist even now, in my foolishness. "You can't make me!"

He puts the pen in my hand. He drags me, unwilling, over to the desk. I look up and see a photograph of me with my grandsons. I have grandsons?

"Sign here." His hand squeezes harder and I wince with the pain. "Stop fighting me. It's only a hundred dollars."

I look down at the desk. I see a cheque there. It says one hundred dollars. The chequebook is mine, but that is not my handwriting.

"Sign it!" Lowell's anger is rising again. He forces me to sit on the chair. He slams his fist down on the desk.

"Oh!" I jump, my heart pounding with the fright of it. I feel tears welling up in my eyes. I don't want him to see them.

He made me... he... Lowell... it was Lowell... was it Lowell... was it...

????????

"Why don't you come with me? You can help me set up for the dance." Gladys Peachy's voice surprises me. What is she doing in my room? What dance? Wait a second. This isn't my room. I'm... I'm... Donkey. I'm a donkey. No. Ha! That's silly. I am not a donkey. I'm Donkey and this is my very best friend, Gladys Peachy.

She wants me to help her set up for the dance.

A fearful thought comes to me and I look up into Gladys' kind eyes. "Will he be there?"

Gladys shakes her head. "No. I promise he won't be there. I won't let him come."

I smile. Gladys always tells the truth.

We start walking down the hallway. I hope they serve snacks at the dance. I haven't eaten since… yesterday. No. I ate today. I think I did. I remember pudding… two helpings. I'm hungry again.

"There will be sandwiches and cookies." Gladys says, a little grin on her face.

I giggle. "In china tea cups?"

She gives me a funny look. "I think they'll be plastic, Dear Heart, but the fruit punch will be lovely."

Fruit punch in plastic cups. It's not quite high tea, but I can live with that.

Chapter Eleven

Gladys Peachy

I remember my father waltzing around our kitchen floor with my mother, her face enraptured as their eyes met. What a beautiful example they set, showing their children that love was not a fleeting thing. Nurtured properly, love lasts a lifetime.

I remember the first time Paul tried to dance with me in our own apartment. He was the picture of peaceful confidence most of the time, but all of a sudden, his handsome cheeks flushed and a nervous giggle burst out of his mouth. I wanted Fred Astaire and I was getting Jerry Lewis.

"I'm sorry, Gladdy." His words stumbled over themselves much like his two left feet. "Well, you know how my father is. We were never allowed to dance."

I rolled my eyes. "Let me guess. Dancing is…"

We finished the thought in unison. "…of the devil!"

Then we both laughed and I let Paul off the hook, choosing to throw my arms around him, lean my head against his chest and hug him instead of making him dance with me anymore.

"Oh, Paul." I told him, and I meant it with all of my being. "I don't care if we dance as long as your arms are around me every single day for the rest of my life."

And do you know what? Right up until the day he died, they were.

So it doesn't bother me to watch people dancing now. I wouldn't want to be held by anyone other than my Paul. I am enjoying greeting people, running the door prize draw, rushing here and there to make sure that the party goes off without a hitch.

Lula and Emmett just walked in the door. My, but she is strutting like she is the queen of the prom. She has Emmett's arm and I wouldn't want to be the one who tried to pry him away from her grasp. She has gone from resisting his courtship to staking a claim as if she had found gold.

Ethel has been escorted to the social tonight by Pete Marsden. Pete looks so happy about it. Meanwhile, Nino Fabrini is scowling and glaring at them from his chair, a glass of punch in his hand. I know that he asked Ethel for a date tonight too. Imagine that! Two men fighting over her! I don't have a lineup of suitors after me. What a relief that is!

I know that some women like that sort of thing. I know that Ethel doesn't like it. She fussed for two days trying to make a decision. She told me she was going to skip the spring social and move to a convent. Haha! She's such a cutup! I'm glad she changed her mind. Look at them dancing to "Smoke Gets in your Eyes". Pete seems quite taken with Ethel. I don't know if she feels the same, but they look like they're enjoying themselves.

Looking over the crowd, I feel a wave of sentiment washing over me. When we are young, we just don't know the secret. We don't have a clue that those people with the white hair, the wrinkled skin, the slower steps… they may look older, but deep inside, they are still the same; longing for connection and wishing for love. I see it every day. People here are missing loved ones who have gone, wishing loved ones would come to call and even searching out companionship, like dear Emmett seeking out Lula.

I sigh, satisfied that everyone seems to be gabbing it up, dancing or snacking and having a good time.

Amid the hum of conversation, I hear a sound that doesn't belong here, not on such an evening of fun and celebration. Are my ears deceiving me? Do I hear... I still have sharp hearing despite my age. I'm sure that I'm hearing the sound, quiet as it is, of crying.

Donkey! That is my first thought. Where is she? Is she all right?

I scan the room and don't see her at first. I spot her at last. What is she doing? She is giving Dinah Gillespie a glass of punch. I almost laugh. She is handing her the cup as if it were high tea time, pinky sticking out straight as an arrow, but if Donkey isn't the one crying, then who is it? I start to wonder if I'm imagining it.

I see nothing out of the ordinary until... no wonder I could hear it. The noise is coming from behind me. Jenny Logan, dressed in a stunning cream, lace-trimmed dress is sobbing, hot tears splashing down her face, a tissue raised to stop the flow of salt water from messing up her clothes. Heavens, but she is the picture of misery! My heart feels pity for her.

"Jenny? Dear heart, what's got you so upset?" I rub her arm. "Can I get you anything?"

She shakes her head. "Not unless you can... oh..." Her tears turn slightly to ire. "That Tallulah Pratt! How could she? How could she say yes to Emmett?"

I recall now that Lula and Jenny did get into a tussle over Emmett. They seem to be like oil and water.

"Well..." I don't know how to answer that. "He has been asking her for a while now. I suppose she thought it was the nice thing to do."

She blows her nose into a tissue. "I was hoping he would ask me. I mean, she's been spurning his advances for months."

I couldn't argue with that.

"But, she said yes and now..." Jenny bites her bottom lip. "I have nobody to dance with... nobody to enjoy the social with... I feel like a fool even being here."

"Oh now, of course you're not a fool!" It suddenly feels like I'm a teenager again, comforting one of my school friends who didn't get asked to go to the prom. "You know, there are all kinds of people here who didn't bring a date."

"That empty-headed Dinah Gillespie. She doesn't even know where she is! She thinks the queen is here somewhere."

I glance over and notice that Dinah and Donkey still appear to be getting along. Thank the Lord for small miracles.

"I don't know about that." I concede. "But there are a lot of people to talk to here. Perhaps if you mingle a little..."

"I don't want to mingle." She sobs. "I'm not good at mingling!"

Help, Father God! Help me to help Jenny. I hate seeing anyone sad, especially at an event that is supposed to be a few hours of fun.

Scanning the crowd, my eyes land on just the thing!

"Jenny, I'll be right back. I need to... uh... help with something. You stay here."

She just nods hopelessly and I scoot across the floor, past waltzing couples and chatting friends eating snacks and drinking punch. I hope I'm right. I hope I don't make things worse. Well, it's worth a try. Nothing ventured, nothing gained.

"Hello." I say, offering the sweetest smile I can.

"Bella?" The permanent scowl on Nino Fabrini's face instantly turns to a grin. "You like-a to dance with Nino? I make-a you feel like a girl of 16!"

He is grabbing my hand to lead me to the dance floor. "No. Thank you, Nino. I can't. I'm on duty tonight... at... at the buffet table and the door."

"Nonsense!" He shows off a mouthful of teeth when he smiles. "You can have-a nice-a time, hey?"

He is pulling me and I am almost helpless to stop it. "No no, really, Nino. I wanted to ask you for... for a favour. I need a man."

His grin is a mile wide now and that did not come out right at all.

"You need a man and you come-a to me? That is so beautiful... so-a romantic, no?" He pulls me in close, pressing his cheek to mine.

I pull away. "No, you don't understand. Please... it's not for me. There is a woman here and she's crying and she needs..."

Nino stops dead. His face takes on a pitiful expression. "You mean-a somewhere a woman cry, Bella?"

"Yes. I was hoping you might... well..." I feel awkward. Lula would be so much better at this, but I go for broke. "You're a... a real man and that's what she needs. A hero to sweep her off of her feet and dance with her and make her feel..."

"There is-a no time to waste, Bella. Where is this lady in distress?" He presses his fingers together and raises them in the air. "I come in-a like a knight in armour. Me... Nino Fabrini! Take-a me to her."

So I do. I take-a him across the floor to where Jenny is still crying and feeling sorry for herself, her head down, spirits lower than her shoes.

Nino's eyes soften. For all of his pompous strutting, he seems genuinely concerned. He reaches out a hand toward Jenny, who still isn't paying attention.

"Oh... Amore..." He begins and I back away just a little, enough to give them room to connect, but still close enough to be nosy and see what's going to happen.

Jenny looks up, sadness and bewilderment on her face.

"Nino?"

"Yes, Amore. It is Nino." He smiles. "Why you sit-a here all alone? Why you look-a so sad?"

She shakes her head.

He takes the tissue from her hand and tosses it away.

"No more-a sad." He says. "Bella, you come-a with Nino, hey? You come-a dance with me and I make-a you happy happy girl."

Jenny looks stunned and says nothing.

"Come now." He takes her hand. "You look-a so beautiful... dressed like a queen."

With that, I watch as Jenny rises from the chair where she had been sitting and sulking and she lets Nino lead her out to the dance floor.

I look up and whisper a 'thank you' to Heaven. Now, Jenny isn't crying anymore and Nino isn't scowling at Ethel and Pete. I just killed two birds with one stone.

Ethel MacNarland

Who knew that Pete Marsden was so light on his feet? He definitely knows how to lead a lady around the dance floor.

I don't know why I'm surprised by that. All of the residents here are more than a bunch of old relics waiting for our time to expire. We have had lives; experienced the joys and sorrows of youth.

Who knows what amazing stories lurk behind all of the faces that I see and interact with every day? I bet I could interview every person here and have ten years' worth of books to write.

I always dreamed of being a famous author... like Margaret Mitchell or Harper Lee. I wouldn't mind being a not so famous author either, churning out dime store novels or those Harlequin romances. At least someone out there would be reading my words. That would be such a thrill.

Pete is smiling at me. That grin hasn't left his face all evening.

"Do you remember doing the jive, Ethel?" He asks, hinting that he just might try it.

"Oh goodness, Pete! That was a long time ago. I don't know if I remember how." My heartbeat speeds up a little just at the thought.

He laughs. "We don't have to be fast and fancy." A mischievous twinkle is in his eye. "Let's have some fun."

As if on cue, Bill Haley's *Rock Around the Clock* comes on and that song was made for jiving. Pete takes my hands in his and starts to do the moves that I am sure I have forgotten. He pulls me forward. He pushes me back. I feel the rhythm go through me like an invisible firework bud, traveling up and up and exploding, sending excitement coursing through my entire being.

"Oh!" I giggle like a child as he whirls me around. "I guess I do remember after all."

"Sure!" He says. "It's just like riding a bicycle."

"I have never ridden a bicycle." I confess.

His eyes widen. "Are you kidding me?"

"Nope. My parents never got me one."

"Well, isn't that something! I rode my bicycle every spare moment I had. My first wheels."

Around and around we go, the song propelling us on. I have to admit that I haven't had this much fun in a long time. I don't feel tense around Pete. Not like I used to around my own husband, Laird.

The song is nearly over, which is a good thing because we are getting winded now, even though our version of the jive is less rambunctious than it would have been had we met during our younger years.

One more whirl around and it will be done, but then I see Pete's exhilarated smile change. The corners of his mouth turn downward and his eyes squint; pain written all over his face. He lets go of me, one hand reaching around to his lower back.

"Pete! Pete, are you all right?" I take his free arm. "Let me help you to a chair."

"Ohhhhh… oh, my back." He winces.

I'm not alone now. A couple of staff members have hurried to our rescue and several residents are also standing around us. Gladys offers me (and Pete) a consoling look and Donkey… well, I'm not certain if she realizes what is happening or where she is. Who knows with her? She is standing nearby though as is Agnes Holmes.

"Oh dear, Pete." Agnes shakes her head. "Your sciatica again?"

As the attendants help Pete into a seat, I see the colour gradually returning to his face, his contorted features becoming more relaxed.

"I'm okay. I'm okay." He raises a hand to reassure his rescuers and me. "It's just… yes… a little trouble with my sciatica.

Maybe... maybe..."

I sit beside him, feeling guilty for helping to cause his pain. "Maybe we should stick to the waltz from now on?"

The grin returns to his face. "If you insist." He adjusts to a more comfortable position. "But, boy, that was fun, wasn't it?"

I can't help but smile back at him. "It was fantastic."

Tallulah Pratt (Lula)

Emmett Muggeridge! What in the world are you doing to me? I'm wearing a ridiculous smile as we whirl and twirl to the music under that kitschy-looking disco ball that is casting spinning shadows and light onto the floor. I'm thinking insane thoughts like *Hold me, Emmett. Hold me forever and ever and never let me go.* I am saying sappy things, like "Oh Emmett. I feel so happy, like my heart has wings attached and I could fly right up to the heavens."

He isn't helping matters. Emmett looks so handsome. His hazel eyes connect with mine as we dance and I am swept up in their pools of mysterious joy. His smile sends butterflies fluttering about in my stomach. I am a right mess! I am a helpless insect caught in the Venus fly trap!

I am 72 years old. Well, that is much too old to fall in love like a silly school girl, isn't it? Maturity means leaving all of that fairy tale nonsense behind. It would be perfectly fine to have a gentleman friend to walk with and play cards with and maybe even have a meal with, but this crazy, out of control feeling... I don't know if I like it. I don't like feeling as if my insides will fall out any second. I don't like being self-conscious about a hair being out of place or a piece of spinach getting caught between my teeth without my knowing. Those awkward scenes are for teenagers and it has been more than 50 years since anyone could call me that.

I excuse myself and head to the ladies room to try and get myself together. All the dancing and cooing and wooing have almost left me out of breath and a little break is just what I need to screw my head back on straight.

Wouldn't it be just my luck to walk out of the stall to wash my hands just as Gladdy comes out of the stall at the end? I wanted to be alone so I could talk myself out of this crazy predicament.

"You look stunning tonight, Dear Heart." Gladdy smiles as she rubs her hands under the water.

I know that, but it's nice to hear her say it. "Well, thank you. It does feel nice to wear something other than casual clothes for a change, but I wouldn't want to pull a Jenny Logan and do this every day."

She turns off the tap and reaches for a paper towel. "No, not every day."

"By the way, I saw what you did for that foolish old cow."

Gladdy gives me a puzzled look.

"Jenny Logan. You sent Nino Fabrini her way. I don't know if that was a blessing or a curse." I giggle.

Gladdy chuckles. "It seemed logical. Jenny was upset because she didn't have a date and Nino was going to spend his whole night scowling at Ethel and Pete. I ran interference... awkwardly, I might add. I don't have a lot of experience at playing Cupid."

I open my purse and rummage through it to find my tube of lipstick. "Yes, well, Cupid is trying to work overtime right now. Of all the cheek!"

Gladdy's wry smile irks me just now.

"You and Emmett seem to be having a good time." She pries with all the innocence of a predatory animal.

"We are having a good time." I smooth a fresh coat of *Autumn's Kiss* across my lips. "Maybe too good."

"What do you mean?"

"I mean… when is all this going to blow up in my face? What am I doing, cooing and crowing like a lovesick 16 year old? It's not right. It's foolhardy!"

"Tsk." Gladys chirps. "You're overreacting."

I give a loud, forceful exhale. "I just can't do it, Gladdy."

"Do what? Enjoy yourself?"

"No!" Bitter memories pass before my mind's eye, quick as a flash. "I know how these things end! I know what happens and I am setting myself up for a big fall."

Gladdy shakes her head. "Oh, I don't believe that!"

"I do! Sure, we're having a wonderful time tonight. We might even have a string of lovely days and nights. It will seem like a dream, but dreams end when you wake up and I think it's time I woke up and realized that it's time to get off this carousel before I give my heart away and then find out he traded me in on some other floozy. If it looks too good to be true, it is! It might be too late for me already. I look into his eyes and my heart does flip flops. It's just… too much!"

Gladys Peachy is the sweetest, kindest woman I know, but right now, as I look at her reflection in the wide mirror of the ladies' room, she does not look either sweet or kind. If I didn't know any better, I would say she looks cross!

"Tallulah Pratt!" Her words come out stern and her hands are firmly planted on her hips. "You listen to me! I am truly sorry that Tom cheated on you and I'm sorry that it hurt you, but Emmett Muggeridge is a fine, upstanding man. Why, you yourself have been telling me just how amazing he is for days now. We shopped until my feet felt like falling off just so you could get the right outfit for the dance tonight."

A pang of guilt shoots through me. "I know, Gladdy dear. I'm so sorry about that…"

"I'm not finished!" Her abruptness takes me aback. "Does Emmett have an alter ego? Is he Jesus?"

I almost laugh. "What? Are you losing your marbles? No, he's not Jesus."

"Well, then…" Gladdy raises an eyebrow. "Maybe it's time that he stopped paying for other people's sins."

My mouth drops open.

"That's right." She nods in agreement with herself. "Emmett Muggeridge is not Tom Pratt and he does not deserve to be punished as if he was."

Time seems to stop. Am I still breathing? It's as though someone has clicked on a painfully bright light.

Gladdy was just rude, abrupt, curt and absolutely right.

I thank her, take a deep breath and go back into the auditorium.

"Would you care for a glass of punch?" Emmett asks upon my return.

My smile is electrified with ten thousand volts right now. Something inside has broken free, like a mustang from the corral. Chalk it up to Gladys Peachy and her wisdom or the magic of music and a cheesy disco ball, but I am ready to throw caution to the wind, that same caution that almost caused me to throw in the towel just a few minutes ago.

"Emmett." Sliding my arm around his, I lean my head against his shoulder. "Do you feel like… taking a walk?"

He sets the glass of punch on one of the tables. "An evening stroll in the garden?"

I giggle. "That sounds lovely."

The sun's eye is almost below the horizon as we wind our way along one of the paths, two silhouettes among the flowers, the evening star gleaming above as the daytime blue begins to give way to deeper shades of indigo.

"I hope you're having a good time." Emmett says.

"I'll say I am."

"Good." He points to the evening star. "Are you making a wish?"

"At my age? Isn't that a bit silly?"

Emmett stops walking and turns to face me. "It's never too late to dream. I believe that's part of what keeps us from going all dotty."

I gasp. "Is that what it is? I don't understand it… why Donkey doesn't know where she is half the time, but I'm fine."

He shrugs. "I don't know if that's what the scientists say or not, but it's a theory I have. So I am going to keep on dreaming and wishing and being hopeful for as long as I can."

Looking up at his face, those sparkling eyes, it would be easy for a girl to dream and wish and hope. "You make it sound easy." I feel a pang of regret for all the years of optimism I have missed. Can I truly feel good about the future? Can I stop expecting the bottom to drop out all the time? I don't know, but Gladys has made me think that it's worth a try.

"It is easy." Emmett laughs. Then, perhaps seeing the

seriousness on my face, he says. "Well, it could be easy."

"How?"

He looks mischievous. "Two heads are better than one."

"Oh, Emmett!" How forward!

"I'm serious, Tallulah. You like poetry? Try this on for size." He clears his throat.

"What do you say, my blue-eyed girl?
Do you want go to steady? Let's give it a whirl.
Life is an adventure and it would be bliss
To see you every day and to give you this…"

Emmett!

I was about to say his name.

Just like that… I mean… no warning or anything… just like that!

Emmett's lips brush against mine as soft as a feather and as warm as a summer day.

I am Tallulah Pratt. I am 72 years old, and I have just been kissed!

Dawn Kehoe (Donkey)

People are dancing. I don't think my mother will approve. I hope she doesn't come home while this party is going on. Oh, Eve! I don't know what possessed you to think we could pull this off! Mother will have our heads. No, wait. It's more like… Mother will have my head. It doesn't matter that this was your bright idea. I know I'll get the blame.

Where did you get that cute shiny ball?

Oh my! You brought out Mother's china tea cups?! Are you

insane?

I suppose they are pretty. Maybe I'll have some of that fruity herbal tea over there. If you're going to neglect your guests, I guess I'll have to act as the hospitable host and pass out the tea.

I hate to break it to you, but the tea got cold. I would make more, but this is your show. So I'll just let all your friends think you're a bad hostess. Haha! That ought to teach you for stealing my date. Jerry Jones is going to know how awful you are!

Hey… hey, don't I know her?

How did Gladys Peachy get here?

How do you know her?

She's my friend, Eve. Mine! Do you understand?

I can't believe it! It's not enough to take my boyfriends. You have to steal my best friend too?

??????????????????????

"I hate you I hate you I hate you! I hate…" What… who…?

"Come on, Dear Heart." Gladys is right here beside me. Wasn't she just over there?

"I think you're a bit tired, Donkey." Ethel is on the other side.

They've got my arms and we're going… where are we going?

"Are we going to the dance?" I ask.

Gladys and Ethel are smiling, that funny look that people get when it's a private joke.

"It's late." Gladys has my purse as well as hers on her other arm. "We're all ready to head to bed." She yawns. "I'm exhausted. It's been a long day."

"You can say that again." Ethel agrees.

I notice that Ethel is wearing a pretty dress. It has pastel colours on the top and... I wrinkle my nose. "What's that on your dress, Ethel?" It looks wet and kind of purplish. "Did you spill something?"

Gladys bursts out laughing. What's so funny?

"Sort of." Ethel replies.

I look down and notice that there are droplets of that purple stuff on one of her shoes too.

"I had a lot of fun tonight." Gladys says.

"Me too." Ethel chuckles. "Now Pete's flat on his back with a fussy sciatic nerve and..." She looks down at herself. "I've got a date with the dry cleaners in the morning."

I don't know why that's amusing. I'd be upset if my pretty dress got stained like that.

"Here we are, Donkey." Gladys smiles as we reach the door to my room. "Sweet dreams. Shall we meet for breakfast in the morning? Same time same place?"

"Yeah. Breakfast sounds good. I'm hungry."

They exchange funny looks.

"You ate like a trooper at the dance." Ethel says.

"I did?"

I don't recall, but Ethel would never lie to me.

"Goodnight, Dear Heart." Gladys says as both girls release my arms.

I reach for the door knob, but Gladys laughs again and I turn to look at what's so hilarious.

"Do you want me to... get rid of that?" She asks.

"Get rid of what?" I look down and see that... whoa now... where did that come from? I am holding a crumpled plastic cup. What's that doing there? It's got leftover drops of purple liquid clinging to the bottom and the sides.

"The evidence." Ethel's shoulders are bobbing up and down as she starts laughing again.

I don't understand what she means, but I do what Gladys asks and hand her the cup. I decide to turn in and go to bed. Maybe tomorrow will make a little more sense.

Chapter Twelve

Gladys Peachy

May has given way to June which has almost given way to July, the temperatures inching their way up and the humidity following right along with it.

I am torn between two opinions. The air conditioning in here makes me shiver and need a cardigan, but without it, I'd be soaked in perspiration. So which do I prefer? Shivering or sweating?

I am sitting on the white and blue paisley sofa beside Ethel. Lula is out strolling in the garden with Emmett, like she has been doing every morning since the spring social. Across the way, watching this morning's classic movie selection are Donkey and Dinah Gillespie. I squint, trying to see the screen.

"What's playing this morning?" I ask no one in particular.

Ethel grins and replies. "Paint Your Wagon."

We look at each other, trying not to laugh, but neither of us can help it.

"So…" I whisper. "She's going to be Clint Eastwood's widow today?"

Ethel slaps her knee and guffaws, before whispering back. "But Old Clint's still alive."

"That won't matter to Donkey. She'll be mourning the loss of her one true love. He's a cowboy in *Paint Your Wagon*…"

Ethel sings her variation of the song: "And he calls the wind Mar-i-ah"

Now we are laughing so hard, my side is starting to hurt. I'm a little winded, just from laughing. I guess it doesn't take much at this age.

Ethel is reading this morning's copy of *The Citizen* daily newspaper. I am working on a crossword puzzle and looking for a five-letter word, 6 across, and the clue is 'the end of life'. Oh, that's an easy one. I pencil in the word 'death'.

"Well, would you look at that?" Ethel shakes her head. "Such a fuss they're making for tomorrow."

"I don't blame them." I reply. "It's not every day that the Queen comes to visit. She'll be on Parliament Hill tomorrow for Canada Day."

Ethel shrugs. "That's amazing to me. She's got a few years on us and she's still traipsing around the globe like that. I get tired walking to the dining hall."

That makes me want to laugh. "Me too. I'm getting winded right here just from laughing so hard. I don't believe I could handle doing one of those walkabouts with crowds of people fawning over me and gawking. I'd be so uncomfortable."

"Not to mention it's summer now. It's way too hot! She's going to pull a Jenny Logan and wear a dress with matching hat and shoes. I'd fall over from the heat."

I feel a little lightheaded just thinking about that. "I remember waiting in the crowd to see her when she was here for her Golden Jubilee."

Ethel's jaw flies open. "You stood outside waiting for The Queen?"

"I did. She was in a horse drawn carriage and looked so lovely in a bright green dress and hat. I waved and waved until my arm hurt and she waved at us, you know, in that elegant way that she does."

"Hmph. You could have saved yourself some trouble. Just be like Dinah Gillespie. She believes that she's having tea with The Queen at least twice a week."

I double over laughing again. I feel a little guilty for it. I mean, isn't it a little rude to talk about poor Dinah like that? Oh, but it's the truth! She has it in her mind that she's related to royalty and Donkey is probably widowed to royalty. All in all, this is a regular fairy tale kingdom. There you go, Ethel. For a change, it's me coming up with a funny line.

Ethel MacNarland

I'm glad that I'm sitting with Gladdy on the white and blue paisley sofa this morning. There's Pete Marsden across the room making eyes at me again. I'm glad that his sciatica has eased off. I felt bad for dancing with him last month and causing it to flare up in the first place, but now that he's all better, he can just cut that out.

I didn't mind going to the dance with him. We had a lot of fun, but now he has other notions. He's always going on about what he calls 'pitching woo'. Well, I'm going to take a hold of him and pitch that woo right out of his mind! He's as persistent as that lone mosquito that buzzes around your head when you turn out the lights.

On the bright side, at least I don't have Nino Fabrini to worry about anymore. He has set his sights on Jenny Logan. Oh, Gladdy! What a stroke of genius that was! Nino is off my case and Jenny isn't pining over losing Emmett, and boy, has she lost him. He and Lula are spending an awful lot of time together. I'm happy for them. Emmett is a sweet man, but I don't think I want that kind of thing in my life.

It's nothing personal, though it's hard to tell that to Pete. Every time I try to explain it to him, he gets this wounded little puppy expression and I feel like a heel. I kind of envy Donkey. All her husbands are dead. Ha!

Tomorrow is Canada Day and apparently, they are going to be having a tea party outside in the garden. They're going to set up tables and serve us tea (hopefully iced tea, it's supposed to be hot!) and fresh strawberries and cream. That sounds wonderful.

After that, Marianne and the girls are supposed to come by and take me for an outing. One of the nearby parks is going to have a magic show, rides for the kids, a country music band and fireworks after dark. I got my temporary get out of jail free card from Biddy Finneyfrock's admin staff. So I won't be back until 11 o'clock.

"Seriously!" I huff. "Pete won't stop making goo-goo eyes! What does he think we are? Teenagers?"

Gladdy laughs. "He thinks you two are in a romantic movie."

I shake my head. "It's a romantic comedy... or maybe even a tragedy."

More laughter, and now Gladys is coughing a little.

"Are you all right, Gladdy?"

She puts up a hand, but the cough is still going and she can't talk.

"Gladdy?"

I reach over to pat her on the back, alarm flooding through me as her face is getting red and she is out of breath.

"Gladdy! I'll get help."

I don't have to. Pete, seeing our predicament, has shot out of the room as fast as an old fart can go, returning presently with

Evangeline Martin in tow.

"What happened?" Evangeline asks, her dark eyes jarring in their intensity.

"We were just laughing and talking and then..." Fear brings tears to the brink of my lower eyelids.

"Here. Will this help?" Pete has a cup of water in his hand. I'm supposed to be annoyed with him, but right now, he's earning brownie points.

Evangeline takes the water and proffers it to Gladys, who is still coughing, but it seems to be subsiding a little.

I am not a praying woman like Gladys is, but at this moment, what the hell? *God, she's one of yours and yes, she's an absolute angel, but could you let us enjoy her down here for a little while longer?*

Gladdy's shaking hands take the cup as Evangeline holds her by an arm, keeping her steady, protecting her from falling. She opens her mouth, but still can't talk. She manages a little smile and then takes one sip, and then another.

"Nice, slow breaths." Evangeline returns the smile. "In..." She inhales through her nose. "...and out." She exhales through her mouth. "That's it."

"I'm..." A gargling word comes out of Gladys' mouth. "I'm... all right..."

"Oh, Gladdy. You just scared me so bad. If my hair wasn't already white; it would turn that way." I pat her hand.

Evangeline sits beside Gladys on the opposite end of the sofa that I am sitting on. "How are you feeling, Mrs. Peachy? We can take you to the clinic if you like."

There is a clinic built in to this facility. Technically, it's not a nursing home per se, but if Gladys needs medical attention, they will whisk her off to see a doctor without ever having to leave the grounds, unless it's serious enough to require a hospital stay. That would be done off site. Those requiring more constant and intensive supervision, medically speaking, can be transferred to Tranquil Meadows Plus, the building across the way which, minus the barbed wire, puts me in mind of a concentration camp.

"It's just… a tickle in my throat. I get it now and again." Gladys says, her voice still raspy, but stronger. "I'm sorry that I alarmed everyone." She grins warmly. "And you are supposed to call me Gladys."

Evangeline now has a full-toothed smile, the bright white of her teeth shining like a light against the rich darkness of her skin. Gladys, Lula and I have come to a consensus. Evangeline Martin is beautiful. She puts that skinny blond Finneyfrock dame to shame.

Gladys puts a hand on my arm. "I'm so sorry I frightened you, Dear Heart."

She certainly did. We are all in our senior years here. I have no delusions of immortality, but I don't want this ride to end yet, not for any one of us. Is that too much to ask?

Tallulah Pratt (Lula)

The air hangs heavy and the heat is rising, even at this time of the morning. Summer has surely arrived with a vengeance.

What do I care? I am barely noticing the weather. I have noticed that the gardens here have some yellow and pink rosebushes blooming that are spectacular to behold. The fragrance surrounds us like nature's own perfume bottle. How grateful I am not to be allergic to a thing in this world as I breathe it in!

"What's the matter, Tallulah? Can't make up your mind?" Emmett coos and prods with one of the million questions he asks me every day.

"Well, I guess that's true." I smile and savour the incredible feeling of my hand nesting like a happy little bird inside his. "I do like Wordsworth and his host of golden daffodils on the hill."

Emmett's soft laugh thrills me. Weeks ago, I would have thought that idea crazy, but I am afraid I have consumed the Kool Aid, so to speak. I am immersing myself in the intoxicating waters of infatuation… or stupidity, whichever it turns out to be.

"I like him too." Emmett swats an intruding bee away with a wave of his hand. "But my favourite has got to be… hmm…"

"Hmm? What do you mean hmm?"

He shrugs. "It's hard to pick just one. Today, I might be in the mood for Shakespeare's sonnets. Shall I compare thee to a summer's day…"

I smile and lean my head against his arm. "You are a charmer, Mr. Muggeridge."

"But then again, tomorrow I might fancy Elizabeth Barrett Browning, you know, how do I love thee, let me count the ways…"

I am positively blushing now. Me! Tallulah Pratt! When do I ever blush?

"Then, on another day, I might be satisfied with something more mundane, yet just as sentimental…" And here, Emmett attempts to sing. "…and then I go and spoil it all by saying something stupid like I love you."

I don't know why, but his awkward warbling almost brings a tear to my eye. Lordy, what is happening to me?

"Frank Sinatra?"

"Not quite." He laughs.

"It was a good effort just the same."

"And I meant every word."

All at once, I realize what a fool I am! I am letting him get away with such blatant sentiment and doing nothing to stop it. *Oh, Emmett! This is dangerous for me! It might not be such a good idea for you either. Can't we keep it safe? Leave four letter L words right out of it?*

Lo and behold, it is as if that man reads my thoughts. As if on cue, he stops walking, turns to face me and puts one hand under my chin to raise my suddenly drooping head.

"Lula, are you fretting again?" I know he knows the answer.

"It frightens me, Emmett. I am not a walk in the park, you know! I mean, I know that we are walking in a park, or the 'gardens' as Biddy Finneyfrock calls them, but you don't realize… you don't know what kind of a woman I am." *Cold as an iceberg and just as deadly, Tom said.*

He chuckles softly, those captivating hazel eyes hovering over me like some divine, benevolent orb.

"I think I know you well enough."

I shake my head. "You don't. Heaven help you, you don't! I don't deserve poetry and romance and joy."

This fear embarrasses me. It is the stuff of childhood, of cowering under blankets for fear of the thunder and lightning, of monsters lurking in dark, cobwebbed closets, of Uncle Wally promising me ice cream and instead, giving me a feeling of being the dirtiest, slimiest creature that ever walked the earth.

"How can it be?" Emmett shakes his head, holds tightly to my hand so I don't run off. "You are a tempest. You know what you want right down to the colour of table napkins."

I feel as though my breath is caught in my throat, trapped in that cavernous tunnel with no escape.

"And yet…" He inhales deeply, his smile never wavering. "One mention of the word love… one attempt to lead you into the tangible, invisible energy that makes life on this monotonous sphere worth the living, and… well…"

"I am not afraid of love." I confess. "It's not the sweet courting. I could do that till the cows come home and never grow tired of it."

He lifts my hand up to his lips and kisses it.

I continue. "I enjoy your company and your affection and the way you recite poetry and the eloquent way you have of turning a phrase. I love all of that." My heart seems to be pounding at the bars of my ribcage now, seeking flight, resenting the life sentence that we are all born with. "I just… I…" How can I speak of things I don't understand myself? I certainly do not want to spoil the mood by bringing up old dead ghosts. What good would that do?

"Come with me." Emmett leads me to a bench that sits by a chattering fountain. "Sit right here. There's no rush. No pressure. No place we have to be for a while."

Skittish as a wounded bird, I follow him, craving his presence and yet filled with a foreboding that, in the end, all I will do is wound him, a heart that is worthy of walking in perpetual sunlight. Emmett is such a sweet soul. What has he gotten himself into?

We sit facing each other without any words at all for a

moment; the noise of the water mirroring that of my troubled mind. I hurt Tom in the end. I drove him into the arms of that insufferable woman. Emmett thinks I'm a good person. I'm nothing but a fraud!

"Do you want to talk about it?" Emmett breaks the silence and I start, head snapping up to find his eyes staring at me with such kindness... a kindness of which I am utterly unworthy.

"Not particularly. I don't know what to say except... well... you should have someone... better. I am not... not..."

"Looky here." Emmett's tone, cooing and romantic before, turns not harsher, but intense, steeled with purpose. "I know my own mind. I know what I want. You make me happy, Tallulah. My heart sings like a canary when I see your face. I want you to know that."

"But if you knew..."

"I don't care about the past." Emmett looks away for a second. "God, you... do you think I don't have any regrets in my past? Do you think I've led the perfect life?"

That jolts me. I have been so wrapped up in my own shameful secrets. "But, what if I'm not... what if I don't..."

"Enough." He takes both my hands in his now, leans in and parts my lips with his, and I am warm all over. It feels like I am flying above the earth and the sky and the moon and the stars. He continues with his words then, our hands still together, our faces inches apart. "Whatever happened to you, let me help make it better."

"Emmett..."

"Whatever bad memories you have, let's make some good ones to take their place."

His words send shivers through my body.

"Whatever sins you think you've committed, forgive yourself and let's move on. A lifetime is too long to carry such burdens."

"It's hard." Tears fill my eyes.

"Only when you try to do everything alone." He bites his bottom lip and grins. "You don't have to do that. I'm willing to walk through any storms with you and I won't complain either. I'll be so grateful just to have you. Don't you want to be with me?"

That makes it so simple. That one little question cuts through all the static. *Don't I want to be with you?* I already know the answer.

"Yes." I nod like a kid who just got asked if she wants a candy. "Yes. I want that very much." That realization makes me feel both confused and peaceful.

A soft laugh comes out of his mouth before he lifts my hands to his face and kisses them over and over again. "Then, be with me. The past is dead and gone and it's only you and me now. And I just can't help myself. Tallulah, I am lock, stock and barrel in love with you…"

I love you too, Emmett! I love you madly!

And I do. And I don't want to. And I think this is utter madness. And I ought to tell him the truth; tell him that he is slaying my inner dragons and completely winning over my heart. I know he wants to hear the words… the truth…

I open my mouth to say it.

The words will not come.

Dawn Kehoe (Donkey)

"The Queen is coming to visit." I heard that someplace. I can't remember where.

Dinah Gillespie's face lights up with a dopey smile. That poor gal got the short end of the stick in the looks department. It's not her fault and I won't say anything, but she looks like the wrong end of a donkey.

Donkey! That's me, isn't it?

"I'm having tea with her." Dinah says. "At Buckingham Palace tomorrow."

She is? Why wasn't I invited? I bet Eve is going, and she should go. For all my complaining, Eve knows how to dress the part and walk the part and talk the part. She's perfect! So it's not surprising to find out that she gets to have tea with The Queen, but why in the world is Dinah invited? Is she part of the serving staff?

"I hope I get to see the Corgis." Dinah's beady eyes are aglow. "Sweet little dogs, although if I were a queen, I would want miniature poodles... apricot..." A girlish giggle comes out of her mouth. "...or maybe a pretty calico cat."

"What about a parakeet?" I ask, remembering that chirpy little blue one that my mother had when I was a child. It used to sit on her finger and eat a cracker. I wanted it to sit on my finger too, but I wasn't permitted to touch it.

"There are royal swans in the water." Dinah says. "They're swimming in the canal right now, a gift from The Queen."

I wrinkle my nose. "What? They're still alive after all these years?"

"No no." Dinah laughs. "These ones are their great great great grandchildren... or something like that."

"Oh. Swans are nice."

Dinah nods her goofy head. "Quite, but they're not as nice as a calico cat."

I feel dizzy, like I'm traveling in circles.

Clint Eastwood is on TV this morning, but I can't hear the movie very well. Somebody is coughing way too loud. How rude is that?

I'm hungry. When is lunch?

Where am I? I don't know this place. Where is my son? Gabe? He's just a little boy. He's... no, wait... he's a man. He has children... I have grandchildren! Tyler is such a sweet boy. He sings in the Glee Club at his school.

Connor is older. He's 15 now... no, I think he is 16 or 17.

Lowell is gone...

He was here just the other day...

But he couldn't be...

I want lunch...

I hope they give us bacon.

Chapter Thirteen

Gladys Peachy

Fresh strawberries make me think of Heaven. I imagine everything tastes this sweet there. These berries were picked fresh. I can tell. They're pulpy, yet soft. They almost melt in my mouth and a dribble of juice runs down my chin. I find myself grabbing a napkin in a hurry. I don't want to stain my light green summer dress.

"Maybe you should wear a bib, Gladys." Donkey grins impishly as she says that. "Join the big baby club."

I suppose I deserve that, even if my vain attempts at getting Donkey to put a bib on are only for her good. Besides, I'm just grateful that she seems to be 'all there' today.

"Maybe you're right, Dear Heart." I reach for my cup of tea. "I am a little clumsy today."

"It's hard to eat fresh strawberries without a little dribble." Lula sets her spoon down. "It almost makes me feel like a child eating a sticky piece of candy."

"It's nice to have you with us today, Lula." I wink at her.

"Yeah." Donkey chimes in. "Ethel left early and went somewhere with her family. She won't be back until after dark."

"Well, Lordy…" Lula looks incredulous. "Of course I'm with you. Aren't I with you every day?"

Holding back a sudden urge to laugh, I approach the topic delicately. "Lately, we've been more of a threesome than a quartet."

Lula's blue eyes narrow and I wonder if she is getting annoyed with me.

"That's right." Donkey doesn't restrain herself. She giggles like a big kid. "You spend a lot of time on the arm of a certain man in a fedora."

Lula mouths the letter O. "Oh! Tsk! I do not spend that much time with Emmett!" She adjusts the brim of her lovely pale blue sunhat, the one that matches the sundress she's wearing and makes her look positively radiant.

Donkey is relentless. "You spend so much time with him, I'm starting to forget what you look like."

Can it be? The unflappable Lula is turning red in the cheeks, and it's not from a sunburn.

"Really! You girls!" Lula frets.

"It's all right, Dear Heart." I set a hand on her arm. "We're happy that you're enjoying his company. I'm surprised you're not spending time with him today."

Lula huffs. "I can't."

Donkey and I exchange funny looks.

"He's off on an outing with his children." Lula puts a splash of milk in her new cup of tea. "They're taking him on some kind of picnic. Apparently, they used to do that as a family… Emmett and his wife…" Lula scowls. "…and they want to keep the tradition alive."

A memory flashes before me; Paul carrying my freshly-packed picnic basket from the car to that beautiful sandy beach in Fitzroy. We would eat our picnic, walk barefoot up to our ankles in the river and then watch the sun sink below the waterline, the shrill cry of the gulls greeting our ears as they rose and dipped on the playful current of the breeze.

"That sounds like a lovely tradition." I feel an ache for Paul and those happy days, and just like always, I know it will pass.

"I'm sure it is. Emmett invited me to go along with them."

"Why didn't you take him up on it?" I shake my head.

"I don't know." Lula sounds irritated, probably more with herself than anyone else. "Maybe I was a little..."

"A little what?" Donkey leans in to hear better. I notice she has some cream on her nose. It's not on her clothes though, which is a miracle.

"A little nervous." Lula replies. "I mean, I don't know if I'm ready to go on a family outing." She makes quotation marks in the air with her fingers when she says the phrase family outing.

"Why not? A day in the park would be fun." I spoon another strawberry into my mouth.

"Why not?" Lula's blue eyes narrow. "Lordy, I can't believe you're asking me that. If I go out with Emmett and his kids, that will be like saying we're an item."

"You **are** an item." Donkey's tea just splashed over the rim and onto her pretty short-sleeved blouse.

"It will mean that we're getting serious!" Lula grabs a napkin to help Donkey wipe up the little mess she just made.

"Admit it." I coax. "You have strong feelings for Emmett, don't you? He certainly has feelings for you, so it is getting a little serious."

Lula tears open a sugar packet and pours the contents into her teacup. "Not that serious! I'm not ready to meet his children and parade our courtship in front of them so they can ask a million questions and maybe..." She pauses. "...maybe they'll get angry at me as if I was trying to take the place of their dead mother..." The spoon clinks against the porcelain as she stirs.

"...WHICH I AM NOT! Just so we're clear."

"I like these napkins. They're white with little berries on them." Donkey opens up one of the paper serviettes that they put out with the food.

"So, are you telling us..." I consider my words carefully. "...you aren't that fond of Emmett? This is just a little dalliance or a friendship. What are you telling us, exactly?"

Lula raises the teacup to her mouth. "I enjoy Emmett's company, but I'm saying that it's not serious enough to go on a family outing. In fact, when Emmett gets back, I mean to tell him that we should cool things off for a while. We should slow down."

"I see." I try not to grin, but I can't help myself. "So you don't mind then."

"Mind what?"

Lying is sinful. I know that, but this one seems to be for a good cause. "Well, maybe I shouldn't say anything."

"Gladdy, you've come this far. Spit it out." Lula is glaring now.

I can't look her in the eye. It's a little fib. It's not sinister or anything, but I am not a natural born liar. "You see, Jenny Logan is hoping to have a nice, friendly cup of tea with Emmett. She and Nino are on the outs. She's planning it really soon and I suppose it's a good thing that you're not too serious about him and you really don't mind if..."

"Why, that conniving witch!" Lula's eyes go wide.

"Now now, Dear Heart..."

"I'll rip the hair right out of her head! How dare she! Why are she and Nino at odds? How could she think she has a chance with my Emmett?"

Lula is heated enough right now to cause the table next to ours to turn and look our way.

"It's all right." I say to them. "Religion and politics... very contentious topics."

"I can't believe it! What a shameless... oh!" Lula's temper is flared to the point that if she were a peacock, her tail feathers would be fanned out to make her larger than life.

"I get up and pat Lula's shoulders. "Now now, calm down. You'll catch heat stroke if you get yourself all worked up."

"But how could she..."

"Hush now. It was only something I overheard. I'm sure it was nothing." I'm quite sure actually, as I only said that to get Lula's reaction. "There's nothing to worry about. Emmett won't have tea with Jenny. He only has eyes for you. Isn't that right?"

"And anyway..." Donkey chimes in. "The two of you aren't that serious."

"Oh! Tsk!" Lula swats Donkey in the arm.

Donkey starts to laugh.

Lula scowls at her, but then quickly softens. "Who am I kidding?" She sighs. "I'm falling for him, Girls. What on earth am I going to do?"

Ethel MacNarland

"Look out, Gramma!" My granddaughter Erin cries out.

I turn just in time to see a Frisbee passing by, much too close to my head for comfort.

"Laird MacNarland! You be careful with that!" Sylvia, my son Tim's wife, scolds her son as she helps my daughter Marianne set out potato salad, sandwiches, cole slaw, pickles, and a cheese and cracker tray.

"Sorry Mom." Laird hangs his head in contrition.

"Don't apologize to me. You almost hit your grandmother!" Sylvia unwraps plastic forks and sets them on the picnic tables (they pulled two of those together to form one long one) that has been covered with a couple of plastic, white tablecloths peppered with pictures of red maple leaves.

"I'm sorry, Gramma." Laird half grins. "I'll be careful."

He has a twinkle in his eye. They're the same shade of grey as his grandfather's were, but they lack the steeliness that he had. I grin back at him, grateful that he seems to be turning into a kinder, gentler Laird MacNarland.

The heat is rising and the humidity along with it today. The waves of the Ottawa River lap hungrily at the shoreline, a fresh breeze from the water giving us intermittent relief from the hot summer sun. I find a shady tree nearby where someone has set a row of lawn chairs. I pick one and sit down, fascinated by the cluster of boats, hoisted white sails leaving the marina for deeper waters.

I watch Laird and Erin and their Frisbee game while Lacy and Savannah are busy trying their hand at badminton, a game I much prefer to Frisbee. For one thing, nobody ever got knocked out getting hit in the noggin by a stray badminton birdie. Haha! That's a funny thought. Stifling a giggle, I watch the girls trying, mostly in vain, to hit the target with their rackets. They're awful! It's okay. I don't think they're trying out for the Olympics anytime soon.

"Would you like me to make you up a plate?" Marianne smiles at me. She looks lovely today with her blond hair braided down her back, wearing sporty navy shorts and a white tank top. It makes me happy to see her wearing what she likes. Laird seemed to get pleasure in life from doing two things; picking on me and then, if that bored him, picking relentlessly on Marianne. *You're not going out of this house wearing that! Look at you, eating cake. You'll be a fat sow like your mother. I will not have you dating that boy. His family is trash.* Meanwhile, that's probably what the boy's family was saying about us.

Laird tried picking on Meg too, but she wasn't as delicate as Marianne. She would never fall for it. She could match mean barbs with Laird as quick as you please and, crazy as it sounds, he never scolded her for it. He would smile. He thrived on lobbing verbal grenades and promoting family warfare. Meg mastered the art of intercepting his hurtful missiles and shooting them right back at him.

"I can do it." I say, starting to get up from the chair. "You don't have to go to any trouble."

Marianne sets a hand on my shoulder and gently eases me back down. "It's no trouble, Mom. I'll get it for you. Just tell me what you'd like."

Arguing with her would be pointless. She is bound and determined that old age makes one helpless. "All right, Dear." I almost say 'dear heart' and smile at the thought. Gladys Peachy must be thinking of me. "Did you make devilled eggs? You know how I love those."

She nods. "Of course, and Sylvia made ham and cheese sandwiches."

"I'll have that and some salad too. I'm peckish today."

"Okay. Be right back." And off she goes to do for me what years ago I did for her. She's a good daughter. Perhaps she is a bit overprotective of me, but then again, she spent a long time watching my spirit take a royal beating by that ogre of a father of hers. Ha! Picturing Laird as that big green ogre in the Shrek movie that the grandchildren like so much makes me laugh!

Then, I get a strange thought. *Does that make me that dumb as a post donkey friend of his... or his ogre wife?*

"Kids! Time to eat!" Sylvia's voice booms out across the field.

It's kind of funny too. Sylvia can't weigh more than 105 pounds soaking wet, but her voice comes out with a gravitas that makes me think she could cow a troop of marines. It's not a mean voice, just loud and meaning business.

"Are you enjoying yourself, Mom?" Tim leans against the tree and takes a drag from his cigarette, gazing with longing eyes at the water. "It's a beautiful day."

"Yes, Son." I nod. "I'm always happy when we get together as a family." I notice a little grey starting at the edges of his dirty blond hair.

"It's good." He smiles and turns to look at me. "I wish Megs was here with us, but she's off looking at dead artists' paintings."

"Me too. I miss her."

"And Dad."

I almost cough, but manage to hold it in. "Yes, I guess the circle isn't complete without everyone in it."

He chuckles. "Oh Mom. You're terrible at poker faces."

"Pardon me?"

"I know you don't miss Dad."

His candor takes me aback. "Well, I... I... I'm sure I..."

He swats a hand in front of his face. "Don't worry. I don't expect you to. He was fine with me, but I know he was hard on you."

Is that it then? Does my son feel sorry for his foolish old mother? It stings. It pricks me to the core.

Choking back the urge to cry or shout or something, I say. "Young Laird is the spitting image of your father." He really is, though the hair is a bit longer, the blond curls more pronounced.

Tim nods. "I notice it too, though he's…" He pauses. "…he's got the look but not the…"

I almost say hate, but that's a harsh word for a son to hear about his daddy. So instead, I use the word. "…hardness?"

"Yeah." Tim throws his cigarette on the ground and grinds it into the dirt with his shoe. "I was afraid I'd be just like him."

"Oh, Tim. You're nothing like that."

He sighs. "Oh, but I could have been. God help me, Mom. I could have followed in his footsteps and made life miserable for Sylvia and the kids."

"You're a good father. Look at your children. They're happy and free-spirited."

He chuckles. "A bit scatter-brained like their father. Thank God for my organized wife."

"They're not frightened of you." I bite my lip, not wanting to bring up dead memories.

Tim's eyes look less dreamy now, a little bit sad. "I wasn't afraid of Dad. He didn't pick on me, just you and Marianne."

"Well, he was a little outspoken."

"He was a horse's ass, Mom!"

"Timothy!" I hear Laird Sr.'s harshness just now in the edge of Tim's tone, though his ire is not directed at me.

"He was! Yes, I loved him. I named my son after him, didn't I?" He plops himself down in a chair beside me. "I just…" He shakes his head. "I've been going to counseling."

That surprises me. "Counseling? What for?"

He hangs his head. "Anger issues. Childhood issues. Sylvia encouraged it."

"But, why?"

"To save my marriage, Mom."

"To save your…" I had no idea their marriage was in trouble.

"She's right. Don't be angry with Sylvia." Tim takes my hand. "I just close off sometimes. I won't let her in. My counselor says I've been bottling my feelings for years."

I put my other hand over his. "Oh, Tim…"

"Listen, Mom. I just want to tell you… I'm sorry."

My breath catches in my throat. "Whatever for?"

"I didn't stand up for you." His eyes are misty now. Are those tears? "I didn't stop Dad from berating you and Marianne. I didn't say or do anything. I was…" He stops. "…a coward."

I gasp. "You were not a coward!"

"I was silent."

"You were a child. What were you supposed to do?" My heart beats faster. The thought of my Tim thinking this way for all of these years feels like a knife piercing through the heart. "You have always been a good son. Your father's bad behaviour had nothing to do with you and I… I never expected you to do anything to stop him."

"But, I could have."

"You couldn't." I pat his hand. "The best thing you ever did for me is to grow up and become a good man, and you are… and I couldn't be prouder if I tried."

A silence passes between us. All I hear are the delighted squeals and laughter of my grandchildren, the barking of a nearby dog, murmurs and snippets of conversation and the low whine of someone's radio playing something noisy and irritating. The blue sky hovers over us like a canopy of grace. Oh! That's a nice phrase, isn't it? Canopy of grace! I should write that down.

"I love you, Mom." Tim finally manages to say.

"I love you too, Son. I always have and I always will."

He raises my hand up to his mouth to kiss it. "I think everything will work out for us all in the end."

I smile. "That would be wonderful, wouldn't it?"

"I hope Sylvia is happy with me... with my progress. I hope she... I can't imagine life without her... without seeing the kids every day."

How my heart lurches in my chest at the thought of my son in pain! I am not sentimental by nature, but I'm not cold and hard either. This is my Tim, my beautiful boy, the one with the rosy-cheeked grin. "Listen to me. If Sylvia didn't want your marriage to work, she wouldn't have asked you to go to the counsellor. She obviously wants to work these things out."

He nods. "Yeah. Thanks. I guess she does." He reaches for that wretched cigarette package again. "You know, I've started writing."

I cock my head to one side. "Writing? I didn't know you had an interest in that."

He holds the unlit cigarette in one hand and pops the package back in his shirt pocket. "Yeah. I just never... I like mysteries. Crime thrillers. I think I might try my hand at it... when I'm not teaching at the college."

"Well, that's wonderful!" I chuckle. "I always dreamed of being an author."

"You did?"

"Sure I did. I just never…"

Tim's brow wrinkles, giving him a pensive look. "I remember! You were always journaling. I never thought…"

"Yes, I was always journaling and your father thought I was so foolish. He would tell me to…"

"You should do it!" The cigarette falls to the ground. He turns in the chair, reaches for my hand again, lifts it up as if we just won an Olympic event. "Mom! Why don't you do it? Why don't you pursue your dream?"

I burst out laughing. "At my age? In case you've forgotten, I am 72 years old."

He gets up and a huge smile crosses his face. He claps his hands together. "It doesn't matter! Don't you see? Grandma Moses was in her seventies when she started her career as an artist. What does age have to do with it?" He kneels down in front of me, grabs the arms of my chair. He is as animated as a hyperactive schoolboy. "Dad's not here to tell you not to. Nobody is going to stop you. Why don't you try it? I have a friend who owns a publishing house. Write something and I know I can get somebody to read it."

Butterflies flit about in my stomach just now, and it seems like a flock of birds are tweeting around my head. "Well, I… I could try." A flicker of hope begins to burn within me. "I'll tell you what." I pinch his cheek, though it's not so rosy and chubby anymore. "That counsellor is certainly earning his money."

Tallulah Pratt (Lula)

Gladdy, Donkey and I are trying for a Guinness World Record

for how many strawberries can be eaten in one sitting. Who could blame us? It's almost the end of the peak season for them. Canada's climate is cold and the growing season is short. This time next week, we'll be switching over from fresh strawberries to raspberries and then, eventually, blueberries.

We had wild blueberry bushes on the hill out back of our cottage. Summers were made even sweeter when the kids catapulted up the hill yelling and laughing, baskets in hand, and returned with them filled to the brim, their faces and hands stained with the juice.

I made wild blueberry tarts, pies, muffins and cobbler. The children would devour the treats with such delight. I even held Tom's attention when we were at the cottage. His work holidays left him no opportunity to escape to Beulah Brantford's embrace. Later on, after I discovered his infidelity, that fact gave me great satisfaction. In the end, Tom chose his marriage, his children, his summer cottage, and his picture postcard life over that foolish wannabe homewrecker!

Now, here I sit, eating strawberries and drinking tea with my dear friends. I have a new man courting me and I'm still not sure how to handle that. Should I let things get serious between Emmett and me? A little voice in the back of my mind is screaming, *"No! All men are the same!"* But how can that be true? Emmett is a decent man. I suppose, before he fled to Beulah's arms, Tom was a good man too.

That is why I'm confused. It has to be my fault. There has to be something wrong with me; something that turns a good man bad.

"Lula?" Gladys is calling my name.

"Yes, Gladdy."

"Did you hear what I said?" Gladdy's grin is full of mischief.

Donkey laughs. "You were daydreaming about Emmett."

"Oh! Tsk! I was not!" I can't help but smile at Donkey. She is remarkably lucid today.

Donkey begins to sing. "Lula and Emmett up in a tree. K-I-S-S-I-N-G!"

I give Donkey a swat, not because I'm actually upset with her, but she loves getting a rise out of me. Sometimes, she succeeds, but right now, I am just enjoying this day when she seems to be with us and not living in some other universe with a gaggle of dead husbands and fog all around her.

"Good afternoon, Ladies. How are you enjoying the strawberry social?" Evangeline Martin's full-toothed smile seems strained. Has Biddy Finneyfrock been at her again?

"Strawberries are my favourite!" Donkey raves. "My second favourite is bacon!"

"They are delicious." Gladdy agrees. "Please thank the staff for going to all this trouble."

Evangeline nods. "I certainly will, Mrs. Pea... I mean... Gladys."

"Ah, you remembered." Gladys beams with happiness.

"I did." Evangeline's smile flees away. "I need to ask... have any of you seen Mrs. Gillespie this afternoon?"

"Dinah?" I try to remember. Heaven help me, sometimes recalling what I did an hour ago is a chore at this age. "Now that you mention it, no. I haven't seen her at all."

Gladdy shakes her head. "I haven't seen her either, but there are some people away with their families for the holiday today. I know Ethel is with her children and so is Emmett. Could she have gone on an outing?"

Biting her ample lower lip, Evangeline looks worried. "A few people are away…" She looks over the crowd. "…but we always know about that. It's a rule here, as you know, to let the admin staff know when you're going out, just so we don't get alarmed if you're gone."

A fearful thought shoots through me like a bullet. Dinah Gillespie is not a close friend, but she is a bit like Donkey, dotty and forgetful and living in another world. I don't wish any harm to come to her, or to anyone else, even that insufferable Jenny Logan.

"Could she have gone to her room for a nap?" I inquire. "Perhaps she just didn't want to take part in the social today."

"We've checked everywhere in the building." Evangeline says, then puts a hand to her mouth as if she has told a secret that we're not supposed to know. "I… if you haven't seen her… well, just don't worry about it. Enjoy your tea, Ladies."

With that, she rushes over to the newly arrived Biddy Finneyfrock, worry written on her face.

"Oh dear!" Gladdy wipes her face with a napkin. "Poor Dinah. I hope she's all right."

"Me too." I shudder. "I hope she didn't just wander off the grounds."

"I'm sure they'll find her. If she's on foot, she couldn't get that far." Gladdy downs the last dregs of tea from her cup. "I'll say a little prayer."

"Gladys Peachy, you are sweet beyond words." I say. "I agree with your prayer. May Dinah be found safe and sound."

"I don't know why you're all fussing over her." Donkey pipes up. "The Queen is visiting. I heard that somewhere."

My heart sinks. It seems that Donkey's lucidity is slipping away. It was nice while it lasted.

"Dinah told me that she's going to visit The Queen today at Buckingham Palace." Donkey pops another piece of strawberry into her mouth.

I chuckle. "Donkey dear, you know we live in Ottawa. There's a big ocean between us and Buckingham Palace."

Donkey shrugs. "That's just what she told me. It's not my problem how she crosses the ocean."

Gladdy's brow lowers and she gets a strange look on her face. "No, but Dinah wouldn't have to cross an ocean, would she?"

What? Is Gladdy losing her marbles too? "What do you mean? Buckingham Palace is in London."

"I know that, but it's been all over the papers. The Queen is here. She's visiting Parliament Hill today." Gladdy's head snaps to attention, her mouth gaping wide enough to catch flies. "Oh Lula. I'm having an awful thought. Where is Evangeline? We need to talk to her right away."

I scan the grounds and see Evangeline, still yakking it up with Drill Sergeant Finneyfrock across the way. I point. "Gladdy, are you sure you want to talk to her right now? Biddy is there. It's a wonder the sun still shines when that woman comes around."

Up from the chair Gladys rises and begins walking, as fast as a 75 year old with a bum knee can.

What can I do but follow? I ask Donkey to come, but she's too involved with her favourite pastime, eating everything in sight. So I hoof it across the lawn behind Gladdy and catch up a few seconds later.

"Evangeline? Evangeline!" Gladys calls out.

Evangeline turns at the sound of her name. "Yes, Gladys."

I see the scowl on Biddy's face and I know what's coming. "Mrs.

Martin! We do not call the guests by their first names here! How many times have we been over this?"

A cowed Evangeline bows her head, turning it back toward her supervisor. "Yes, Ms. Finneyfrock. I apologize."

Gladys, in a sudden burst of... well, what do I call it? It could be outrage, but her tone stays as even and compassionate as ever. In a moment of valour (after all, we are talking about Biddy Finneyfrock), Gladys speaks: "Why, Ms. Finneyfrock, I asked her to call me Gladys, if you don't mind."

Biddy's head turns, as if she has just noticed vermin walking into her line of vision. "Mrs. Peachy, that is very friendly of you, but we want to maintain an air of professionalism at all times here at Tranquil Meadows."

Biddy thought that would be the end of it, but her answer did not satisfy Gladys, who spoke again. "I pay a lot of money to stay here. Is it too much for me to have the staff greet me in the way I prefer? I like Evangeline. She's one of the best people you have working here and if I want her to call me Gladys... well... that is between her and me."

I grin. I would never call Gladys mousy, but she has never struck me as a lionheart either. Perhaps she is a lion beneath that sweet, churchy exterior. I love her even more. No, not just that. I like her.

Biddy's ice blue eyes lock on Gladys and, for a second, I think she's going to launch into a verbal attack similar to the ones she lobs at her staff. Gladys is right though. She is the one who pays to be here. She is one of the reasons that this place even exists and Biddy understands who pays her salary, when she gets reminded from time to time.

"Very well, Mrs. Peachy. You're right. I want... we want our residents to be happy here." Biddy's attempt at a friendly smile comes off as warm as a dead fish, but she gets an E for effort. "If you'll excuse us, we have a very important matter to attend to." Biddy motions Evangeline inside the building.

"Wait!" Gladys cries out. "That's what I need to talk to you about."

Biddy and Evangeline stop dead in their tracks, turning to face us again.

"Have you seen Dinah Gillespie, Glad... er... I mean Mrs. Peach... I mean... have you seen her?" Biddy asks in a momentary state of disarray that would be comical were the subject matter not so serious.

Gladys frowns. "No, but Donk... Dawn says that Dinah was adamant yesterday about going to visit The Queen."

Biddy's brow furrows.

Evangeline's jaw drops open. "You don't think she..."

"I don't understand." Biddy replies. "She's going to fly away and visit The Queen?"

"No, you nin..." I stop myself from saying, you ninny. "You need to understand. The Queen is here today. She's visiting Parliament Hill."

Biddy and Evangeline look at each other, a pregnant pause in the air between them.

"She could have taken a taxi." Gladys says.

I have a terrible thought just now. "Which transit bus would she have to take to get to the Parliament Buildings?"

As if a magic fairy waved a wand to unfreeze them, Biddy and Evangeline suddenly run toward the building as fast as they can, leaving Gladys and I to shrug and stare at each other.

"Lordy." I say. "How on earth will they find her in that crowd?"

Dawn Kehoe (Donkey)

Hmph! You would think the whole place was on fire! Staff members are rushing here and there. The residents of Tranquil Meadows are jabbering with each other. The noise reminds me of a hive full of bees.

Hey! Who cares? There are strawberries left and I'm scooping them into my bowl. To the victor goes the spoils!

Look at Gladys and Lula over there, chatting it up with the staff. Are they trying to score points or something? It won't work. I told that old battle-axe Finneyfrock weeks ago that I want bacon for breakfast. Do you think she'll give us any? Not on your life! It's porridge and toast and eggs and Bran Flakes. Guess who doesn't need bran to go to the toilet? Dawn Kehoe, that's who!

The ladies are coming back over here. Too late! I have commandeered the last of the berries!

"I feel just awful." Gladdy says as she sits in her seat.

Lula sits down too. "If Dinah Gillespie snuck out to see the Queen, Lordy, I don't know how they're going to track her down. There will be thousands upon thousands downtown for Canada Day and to catch a glimpse of the royal visit."

"And it's so hot." Gladdy shakes her head. "It's dangerous for her to be out there all alone…"

"With only half of her marbles." Lula adds.

Gladdy and Lula exchange funny looks, and then they stare at me, misty eyed, like they were watching a newborn baby or a cute litter of kittens.

"I'm so thankful we don't have to worry about Donkey doing

that." Gladdy pats my hand. "Do we, Dear Heart?"

"Do we what?" I ask, mouth full of berries and cream.

For some strange reason, Gladdy giggles. "You would never just run off and not tell us, would you?"

"I would if I smelled bacon." I grin.

"Oh, tsk!" Lula huffs. "Donkey, you are such a card!"

I don't have a clue what Lula is on about. Maybe my friends are getting a little light in the head. That happens sometimes as people age.

Chapter Fourteen

Gladys Peachy

Dear God,

It's me, Gladys. Thank you for another lovely day. I am thankful to be alive and to be safe and sound in a place where I have everything I need. What a blessed life I have! You have treated me with such kindness for all these years.

My heart is troubled this morning. I know that you say to cast all my cares on you, so that is what I'm here to do. I feel like crying rivers of tears and I couldn't tell you why.

They searched all afternoon yesterday for Dinah Gillespie, and well into the evening too. I saw people rushing about. I heard phones ringing non-stop in the hallways. I saw police officers at the attendants' desk. Dinah's family... I believe it was her daughter and son-in-law arrived and lit into Evangeline with a fury. Staff spoke to each other in hushed tones, stress written all over their faces.

The gossip spread among the residents here like a fire through dry brush.

They found her body by the side of the road.

She ended up on a bus bound for Montreal.

She broke free from the crowd downtown and made a beeline for The Queen and now she has been arrested.

I understand now why tabloid headlines sell papers. None of these rumours are based on facts; just the idle speculations of wondering (and sometimes wandering) minds.

I didn't care for the mean-spirited content of some of the fictions being told about Dinah. I pray that isn't what they say about me behind my back. Are people really that savage? Maybe I always knew that, but I don't want to know. I'm 75 now. Can I go on believing in goodness and kindness and what's right prevailing over what's wrong? They used to say nasty things about Jesus too, didn't they? They called him a drunkard, an illegitimate son, a devil! Nothing has changed.

Anyway, this is just another prayer, as if you can't remember that I asked you before, please bring Dinah back to us. I pray that she hasn't met a terrible fate. I feel sad for her and could you please watch over Donkey too? The thought of her lost in the unknown out there frightens me.

I know you say not to be afraid. I don't think you were scolding us when you said that. I think you are well aware of human nature and you know that fear preys on us like a ravenous wolf, wanting to devour every spark of light we've got. I choose to trust you and I thank you for watching over us all and…

Rap rap rap!

I jump at the sound of a knock at the door.

"Who is it?" I call out, rising from my knees and checking myself over to make sure my clothing is on straight.

"It's Lula. Can I come in?"

I rush across the floor and open the door. "Any word?"

She breezes in, pale blue blouse emphasizing her amazing eyes. "They found her."

My heartbeat goes from kathump kathump to kathumpkathumpkathump.

"Oh, Gladdy!" Lula grabs my arm and helps me over to the bed.

"I'm sorry." The tears surprise and overwhelm me. "I don't know what's wrong with me."

Lula sits on the bed beside me, hand rubbing my back with the gentleness of a mother. "I do. It's a traumatic thing for everyone. You've got such sensitivity in you."

I shake my head. "I think I'm terrible."

"What?! That's ridiculous!"

"No, it's true."

The blue water deepens in Lula's eyes. "Stop that, Gladys Peachy! You are a wonderful woman. Everybody seems to know that but you."

Sniffling and blubbering like a foolish child, I reply: "The thing is, I would never have thought this about myself. I mean, I'm sorry that Dinah went missing. I truly am."

"We all are."

I match Lula's gaze now. "But a wicked part of me is thankful that it's her and not... and not Donkey!" I begin to wail. "Do you see what a terrible thought I had?"

Lula wraps her arms around me and pulls me tight to her chest, and I know she's fussy about not getting her clothes stained, but I am crying like the dickens and salt water is leaking all over her.

"Come on now." She kisses the top of my head. "You are beating yourself up for something that would cross anyone's mind. We all have certain people who are higher up on our list than others. It's what makes family and friendship so darned special, isn't it?"

"Yes, but Dinah..."

"Nobody is wishing anything to happen to Dinah, least of all you." She squeezes a little harder.

"But it was a terrible thought." In my mind, I see the angry eyes of Reverend John Peachy scolding me without a word, knowing that I am guilty as charged.

Lula sighs. She pulls out of the embrace, puts a hand on both of my arms and sticks her face right in front of mine. "Now, you listen here! I've been to church plenty. I believe in God and Heaven and all of those things."

"You do?"

"I surely do. I went to Mrs. Farrell's Sunday School class and learned Bible verses off by heart and I'm pretty sure that you're feeling guilty because we're supposed to love our neighbour and you had some thoughts that…"

"They were sinful." I frown and the tears threaten to spill over onto my cheeks again.

"But, Gladdy, don't you know? Bad thoughts land on everybody. We just have to decide what to do with them."

Lula is waxing wise right now and I didn't know she had it in her.

"You can't stop the birds from flying over your head." Lula grins. "But you can sure enough stop them from building a big old nest in your hair. So when the bad thoughts come, you shoo them away!"

Eureka! A light bulb seems to switch on over my head.

"You're right." I smile back at her. "I guess I just didn't like knowing I could think such a thing."

"Welcome to the human club." She pokes me in the arm. "Shall we go collect the girls for breakfast?"

I wipe my weepy eyes and blow my nose into a tissue. "Okay. I'm ready." We head for the door, but I stop mid-way. "Wait! You didn't tell me. Dinah… what happened, exactly?"

Ethel MacNarland

Dear Diary,

I have taken my son's advice and decided that it's not too late to pursue my dream of being a professional author. I'll let you know how that works out. I think I might faint if I ever actually get paid for writing words.

On a sad note, when I got back from the fireworks last night, Tranquil Meadows was as somber as the morgue. What a disconcerting thought that one of our residents, Dinah Gillespie, has gone AWOL and nobody can find her.

Gladdy and Lula were still up when I rolled in around 11 o'clock. They filled me in. I would like to say that such terrible news made me lose sleep, but after an entire day outdoors, I was out like a light almost before my head hit the pillow. I had strange dreams too. My husband Laird laughed at me, chided me, telling me what a foolish woman I was, actually thinking that someone would want to read my writing.

If I had known it was a dream at the time, maybe I would have told him to stuff a sock in it. I just took it. Didn't I always? Well, I can say it now and he's not here to argue about it. "Laird MacNarland! Stuff a sock in it! I don't have to listen to your rude commentary anymore!"

Wow! That felt good!

Rap rap rap!

Now who can that be at this hour? I haven't even had breakfast yet.

Upon opening the door, I see Gladdy and Lula standing there, Lula dressed in a lovely pale blue blouse that makes her eye colour pop, and Gladdy wearing a collared pastel pink tee shirt with one button. It kind of looks like a golf shirt, but the collar is a little too frilly for it.

"Rise and shine." Lula grins. "Are you ready for breakfast?"

In answer to her question, my stomach growls. "I guess I am."

"We can pick up Donkey on the way." Gladdy says. "I'm surprised I haven't seen her yet this morning. She's usually the first one up, urging me to get to the dining hall fast before she starves to death."

I slide my feet into a pair of white loafers and check my appearance in the mirror.

"You look fine." Lula says.

It must be true. Tallulah Pratt would never just humour me if my face was dirty or my hair askew.

"Can you believe it?" Lula converses as we walk toward the dining hall. "They found our dear Dinah like a poor fallen bird on Wellington Street last night. I don't know where she was or what she was doing. I guess she really was trying to visit The Queen, but…"

"I hope she's all right." I say, noticing that Gladdy's face looks as if she's on her way to a funeral.

"I'm not sure how she is." Lula continues. "I only know they found her downtown because I overheard a couple of the night shift attendants talking about it in the hall by the lending library."

Gladdy shakes her head. "That poor woman, lying there like that for God knows how long. All those strangers around her. The thought of it makes me…"

"Come on now." I grab Gladdy by the arm. "Don't dwell on it. It will torment your mind."

"I'm just so sorry. I'm worried that it could happen to Donkey." Gladdy sounds like a scared child.

I come to a dead halt. "We are NOT going to let that happen to Donkey. Got it?"

"Yes." Both ladies chirp in unison.

"Good." I start walking again. "One thing I don't understand."

"What's that?" Lula asks.

"Lula, what were you doing eavesdropping by the lending library? That's nowhere near where the ladies' quarters are." I feel a grin coming on, and the mischief I am stirring up makes me feel like I could giggle; a welcome change from the Dinah-shaped cloud hovering over our heads right now.

Lula's cheeks go redder than her hair. "Oh! Well, I... I... what do you care, Ethel? I just overheard it, that's all."

"During the night shift? You were up awfully late..."

"What if I was?"

I go for broke. "...or awfully early."

"Stop that!" Lula looks like a cat that has been caught swallowing a canary.

"Did you see Emmett when he got back from the fireworks last night?" I pull a Groucho Marx and raise my eyebrows up and down and up and down.

Gladys finally clues in to what I'm talking about. "Oh! The men's quarters are on the other side. You would have to pass the library!"

"Gladdy!" Lula's jaw drops. "Not you too!"

"Oh, come on! We're not teenagers." I urge. "Just tell me, did you stay with Emmett?"

After a pause, Lula speaks. "It's not what you think. I'm not some shameless floozy!"

I bite my lip to stifle laughter.

Gladdy's face looks shocked. "Dear Heart, we would never think that about you."

"Well, the truth is…" And here, a slight grin appears on her face. "…I missed him. I really did. It seems so foolish."

"It does not. It's lovely." Gladdy smiles.

"So I just thought I would greet him and say goodnight." Lula's cheeks grow a little crimson again. "I waited in the lobby for him to come home, and then of course, I had to tell him about Dinah and he had to tell me about being with his children and what a time he had and so… and so we grabbed some tea and a little snack and went to his room, but just to talk! It was just to talk. You have to believe me!"

I can't help myself now. I start to laugh.

"Oh, Ethel. I swear it was only to…"

"We believe you." Gladdy says. "So you were talking up a storm…"

Lula nods. "We were talking and talking and, Lordy, then we talked some more. It's a wonder our jaws can still move, and it was so comfortable." She gets a wistful look in her eye. "It felt like I had just slipped into an outfit that fit me to such perfection, why, I couldn't picture myself ever taking it off."

Lula, you lucky lady. I wish that I had known that with my husband.

"Plus, I was a little upset about Dinah being missing…" Lula shrugs. "So Emmett wanted to give me comfort and he held me for a while. He just held me."

"My Paul used to do that." Gladdy says.

"Anyway…" Lula lets out a chuckle now that the cat is out of the bag. "I fell asleep. It's that simple and it's not tawdry at all. I fell asleep in the arms of a man and I can't remember the last time that happened in my life. I hope you ladies don't think less of me. I'm not… I'm not…"

"You need to stop worrying about what we think." I reply. "You enjoyed some special time with what seems to me to be a good, kind man who is happy to be with you."

"I know." Lula shakes her head. "At 72, who would believe it? Certainly not the writers of those sappy romance novels. Haha… imagine that!"

I bite my bottom lip. "We'll put you and Emmett on the cover of one."

Lula has a loud giggle now. "Don't be ridiculous!"

Gladdy joins in the fun. "And we'll call it *Hot Man in a Fedora*!"

We have to stop walking because we're all in a full on laughing fit.

"Oh, I love you girls." Lula manages to get out, bent over and slapping her knee. "We'll have to change the names."

I chime in. "Okay, we'll call him Studley McDreamy."

Gladdy is grabbing her ribs. "Stop it… I can't stand it…"

A door cracks open at the raucous noise and Donkey's head peers out into the hallway, curiosity written all over her sweet, wrinkled face.

"Are you girls having a party without me?" She asks.

I notice that she is fully dressed in a lime green blouse and mustard-hued stretchy pants, a definite infraction if the fashion police were here. I grin about it freely. How will she know the difference with us laughing so hard over Lula and Emmett's septuagenarian romance?

Tallulah Pratt (Lula)

His words danced over my heart as soft and sweet as a baby's sigh. I leaned on his chest and heard the lullaby rhythm of his heartbeat beneath my ear. This morning, I feel like a stray jigsaw puzzle piece that is finally connecting to the one piece that fits, that has always fit me, but isn't that a betrayal to Tom? Yet one more reason why he cheated on me?

A reply seems to come to me out of thin air. *Jigsaw puzzle pieces sometimes connect to more than one other piece, don't they?* I suppose so, and Tom is gone. I did not jump into the arms of another man while still attached to the one I married. So I'm one up on you, Tom Pratt!

I never dreamed I could feel like this. I was never a 'cuddler'. There was always too much to do; cleaning and shopping and putting everything into its rightful place and making sure it all matched perfectly. It wasn't very feng shui, but it was Tallulah shui! Wouldn't Ethel love that line?

My dear Emmett, you were gone for a few hours and it felt like a part of me was missing. I ought to swat you silly for that! I don't know if I like that feeling of emptiness when you're gone. It's too much like depending.

"What's on your mind, Lula?" Ethel's smile is downright mischievous.

I should never have told the girls I spent the night beside Emmett. I won't tell them that already, I am longing to lie beside him again.

"I'm hungry. That's all." I lie. Well, maybe not so much. My stomach is growling.

"Of course you are." Ethel replies.

"Me too." Donkey says as we make our way toward the dining hall for the first meal of the day.

"I'm surprised you didn't just wait around and let Emmett walk you to breakfast." Gladdy says, and I know she is being just as incorrigible as Ethel, but her face looks as guileless as a toddler, so I can't even scold her for it!

Pursing my lips tightly together, I put on my best austere voice. "I will have you know, you naughty little vixens, that as soon as I awoke in the middle of the night and realized what I had done, I snuck back to my own room. Imagine! The staff could have seen me or… somebody could have!"

Ethel is cracking up again. "Are you 16 years old? Did you miss your Daddy's curfew?"

I huff. Why can't Ethel see how serious this is? "No, but what would people think? They might assume I was… that we were…"

"Should I call the police and have you arrested for the high crime of sleeping?" Gladdy asks.

"Gladdy, you should be on my side here." I glare at her.

"What do you mean, Dear Heart?"

"Don't you dear heart me! You're a God-fearing woman, aren't you? Don't you see how improper it would look for people to see me coming out of Emmett's room in the middle of the night like some flirty little tart?"

Gladdy smiles sweetly. "I am a God-fearing woman, as you put it, and I think it would be wrong of me to make a snap judgment about you even if I did see you coming out of Emmett's room."

"Why did you come out of Emmett's room?" Donkey finally catches up with our conversation.

"That has not been my experience with nosy church women." I confess, remembering things I would rather forget. "Even if you aren't doing anything wrong, sometimes they'll just make something up or accuse you or… well… it's hard to please some of them."

Gladdy nods in agreement. "I have run into those types in my travels." Her eyes narrow. "I learned to give them plenty of room. Smile and nod and get out of there. I made a deliberate choice to hang around the ones who cared about building people up rather than tearing them apart."

"Oh!" I laugh at her bluntness. "I wish I had known you back then."

"In the long run…" Gladdy says. "…I wouldn't worry too much about those types of people. The ones trying their best to find skeletons in your closet usually have a big pile of bones rattling in their own."

"Bravo, Gladdy!" Ethel claps her hands. "Can I use that line?"

"Huh?" Gladdy looks confused.

"That line, it's a gem. Can I use it?" Ethel is beaming now. "I've been dying to tell you. I was talking to Tim yesterday and he's writing a book."

I smile. "Ethel! That's lovely! Good for him!"

An emphatic nod follows, and then Ethel adds. "And he knows that it has always been my dream to be a writer and he told me I should go ahead, even at my age, and follow my dream. So I'm going to write a book!"

We all stop walking for a moment. It seems that the conversation drops too as we wait. For what, I could not say.

"Well, what do you think, Girls? Do you think I'm crazy?" Ethel's smile changes to a frown. "Oh God! You do! You think I'm nuts to do this. I mean, I'm 72! That's a heck of a time to start a new career."

I grab her arm. "No, Ethel. We're surprised, that's all."

"It's inspiring." Gladys interjects. "I'm excited for you and I can't wait to read what you write."

Ethel giggles. "It's going to be fun and a lot of work."

"But it will be worth it." I assure her and we start to walk again.

We might have kept going right off the edge of the earth, bantering back and forth about Ethel's new adventure, but we are interrupted now by the sound of a clearing throat.

"It seems to me..." Donkey says. "...that you ladies have forgotten all about our breakfast."

I look up. "Oh! So we have. We walked right past the dining room."

We stop, about face and turn around.

Dawn Kehoe (Donkey)

Dinah Gillespie went to visit The Queen and she got lost at Buckingham Palace. They found her on the grounds. She up and fainted!

I'm hungry. I hope they give us bacon today. I told the chefs here to get some, but they don't listen to me...

My husband died... I think he did. He was a great white shark... I mean... haha... of course he wasn't... he was EATEN. Yes, that's it! He was eaten by a great white shark. That's what I get for marrying an arrogant fisherman. I mean, he should have listened when the chief of police told him to get a bigger boat…

I dreamed of that shark… I dreamed it was shut up in my spooky old attic…

What are the girls going on about now?

"Why did you come out of Emmett's room?" I ask. That's what Gladys just said, but it makes no sense to me.

I'll never know because they are ignoring me again and they've changed the subject.

Ethel is writing a book. It will be a New York Times bestseller, I think.

"It seems to me…" I tell them. "…that you ladies have forgotten all about our breakfast." They were too busy jabbering about Ethel's new book to notice that we're here. "Come on, Girls! Let's get in there before all the food is gone!" I feel suddenly anxious.

They laugh at me. What's so funny about going hungry?

"Dear Heart, I promise you they won't run out of food." Gladys pats my back and we head inside.

Well, if she says so, I guess it's all right. Gladys Peachy never lies. I think she used to be a nun or a missionary or something holy like that. Sometimes she reads a Bible. I have one of those. I did try to read it. I don't remember all the words, but there were some nice stories in there. Was it written by Shakespeare? The way the words are, it's kind of the same.

We sit down at a table and wait for the waiters to come. I see some of the people already eating. Guess what's not on their plates? That's right… bacon.

"Dinah isn't here." I blurt out, noticing that her usual chair is empty. "Where is she?"

Ethel, Gladys and Lula give each other that secret look, the one they don't think I know about.

"She's away." Lula says. "She'll be away for a little while."

The table next to us overhears. Jenny Logan cranes her neck around. "Oh, tell her the truth, Tallulah. Dinah was taken to the General Hospital. We don't know when she's coming back."

I see Lula scowling at Jenny. Those two are like a couple of stray cats squaring off in an alley.

"Mind your own business, you insipid cow! Who asked you?" Lula hisses.

I don't know why she's so mad, but I'm glad it's not me she's after.

"It's not nice to keep the truth from her." Jenny scowls, a piece of egg flying off of her fork and landing on her pale yellow dress. "Oh! Dear!"

Lula smiles, but it's not happy. "My, I hope that doesn't stain. You would need a time machine to go back to 1942 to find another dress like that."

Jenny huffs and turns back to her meal.

Lula does too, but her sigh is much more satisfied.

So Dinah Gillespie is in hospital. I hope she's all right. If she's not going to eat her share, I'll be happy to have it. "Pass the butter, Gladdy."

Chapter Fifteen

Gladys Peachy

I am sitting in the TV room in a comfy recliner beside the white and blue paisley sofa. I need a six letter word, 13 across, possible afterlife destination. That's an easy one. Heaven!

Ethel isn't here this morning. She is doing what she has done every morning for the past two weeks; working on her new book. I wonder what she's writing about. She refuses to talk about that in case it ruins her mojo. What's a mojo? Is it like good and bad luck? I don't believe in those things. Never have. There are good times and bad times, but I don't think luck has much to do with it.

Lula and Emmett are off strolling through the gardens and Donkey is watching her latest husband on TV. Well, I assume he will be duly mourned later today. I think it's a James Dean movie. Death by car crash is my guess as to how her latest beau will meet his end.

A yawn comes over me. Why am I so tired? I slept through the night without one interruption from Donkey. I should feel fit as a fiddle, but I don't. I am thinking of abandoning this crossword puzzle and heading to my room for a little unscheduled repose.

I take one last look to make sure Donkey is all right before heading out of the activity room and down the hall toward my quarters. Just as I exit, I see Gabriel Kehoe and his big strapping boys, Connor and Tyler. How nice! Donkey is having a visit from family this morning.

"Good morning, Gladys."

"Good morning, Evangeline." I return the wide smile she offers me.

We are walking in the same direction and she passes me, seemingly in a hurry.

I hope they haven't cut back on staff again. I hate to see the attendants run ragged with barely a moment to think, let alone complete their duties. I know that these days, it's all about the bottom line and the personal touch has fallen by the wayside. How sad! This world has become as cold as the dark side of the moon.

I hear the high-pitched notes of... what song is that? It's *Oh, What a Beautiful Morning* from "Oklahoma". Guy, the whistling janitor, is collecting garbage as I pass by, oblivious to all but his job and the song that is playing in his head and from his mouth.

As I round the corner, heading for my own personal space, my heart leaps, mouth going dry. One hand darts out and grabs the wall to steady my suddenly erratic gait. I've got to stop for a minute to catch my breath. *Please, God. Say it's not true. Say she's all right.*

Biddy Finneyfrock stands rigid and erect, like a majestic, but unfeeling obelisk, tall, straight, and unflinching. Evangeline is at her side now with a clipboard and a pen. Even in death, our lives are inundated with endless forms and papers and impersonal personal duties.

"You have until month's end to collect all of her things." Bidelia says in that cold tone that always makes me cringe. "Her fee is paid up until that time."

Out of the room steps Linda... er... Lynn... Lindy! It's Lindy. Dinah's daughter, a middle-aged, modestly dressed, plain, yet well kempt woman now stands in the hallway, one of her mother's sweaters draped across her arm.

"If it's all the same..." She replies to Biddy. "...we can spend today packing everything up and have it out of here in a few hours."

Out of here? It must be true then. Dinah died. Didn't she? Did she really pass from this world and nobody had the heart to let any of us know? I know that we're just fellow residents. It's none of our business, technically, and maybe I am just being a nosy parker, but we saw her every day. We ate with her and talked with her and suffered through St. Bart's choir visits with her. She became a part of our routine as much as anything else.

Surely we deserve more than this abrupt and unannounced exit. Are we that insignificant now because we are no longer at the age where we are considered worthy of the world's attention? I am feeling cynical this morning, and maybe a little bitter. That nap might do me good.

"Of course." Biddy tries to smile, but it looks out of place, like a happy face painted onto a rock. "Take all the time you need. If you require any assistance, please let us know. I'm sorry that your mother won't be returning to us. She was a valued member of the Tranquil Meadows community."

I bite back tears.

"Look." Lindy purses her lips, which makes them almost non-existent. "I realize it was unintentional..."

"You must realize..." Biddy interrupts. "...that this facility is not a nursing home. It is a retirement villa. We keep watch over the residents as much as is reasonably possible. No one is to leave the grounds without signing out at the desk, but we don't keep people locked up here. It's not for those who are unable... or who are no longer able to..."

"I understand." Lindy nods. "I knew she was getting a little forgetful. I just didn't realize it had become that bad." She frowns.

My heart goes out to her and I wish I could give her a hug and tell her everything will be all right.

"Anyway..." Lindy recovers her composure. "We have secured a placement at The Braceridge."

Biddy's posture stiffens even more, if that were possible. "The Braceridge. Well, that is a well-managed facility. Of course, we could have transferred her across the way to Tranquil Meadows Plus where she would have had round the clock supervision and nursing care..."

Lindy folds her arms across her chest. "The Braceridge is closer to my home. It was a more workable solution."

So Dinah is not dead. Not physically anyway, but I know what going to The Braceridge means. It's the type of facility that Ethel calls 'the roach motel'. You check in, but you never check out until... you check out.

All of a sudden, I don't want to hear anything more. Not about Dinah. Not about Donkey. Not about anything. Just get me to my room and to my bed and let me rest. Let me forget this whole ugly business for a little while.

I whiz past the crew outside Dinah's former room. *Please don't take any notice of me...*

What a sigh of relief when I finally close my own door behind me. I make a pit stop in my bathroom first and then slide under the covers, pulling them almost right over my head. I feel like a foolish little girl trying to escape a storm or the dark or a monster in the closet. I am a woman of faith, aren't I? Death is not supposed to be a monster -- not for me.

Still, the tears splash freely onto my pillow and my last memory of Dinah Gillespie, even if she was a mere acquaintance, causes me to blubber like a fretful little baby.

THE GRANNY DIARIES

"Donkey… dear Donkey… we are going to lose you. How long? We can't protect you forever…"

My shoulders bob with the rhythm of the sobs until merciful sleep comes and I float into its peaceful waters, off to the land of dreams.

Ethel MacNarland

"The Granny Diaries, A Septuagenarian Adventure" by Ethel MacNarland, Chapter Four.

Life at Tranquil Meadows is about as tranquil as a stray cat convention, especially when Jenny Logan and Tallulah Pratt get into one of their infamous hissing matches."

I stare at the sentence I just wrote and frown.

What am I thinking? I can't use real names. These folks aren't fiction and I'm exposing the events of their lives for all to see. I wouldn't want everyone gawking into my private life as if I were some goldfish swimming around in a glass bowl.

Maybe I could just change the names. Instead of Tranquil Meadows, I could call it Shady Acres. No. That's too cliché. Last Train to Deadsville. Haha! That would be hilarious, but not very comforting.

Drumming the end of the pen on my desk, I think. What would be a good name for a seniors' villa? It has to sound legitimate, but the name can't be too similar. I don't want to be sued by Biddy Finneyfrock, and she would do it!

I glance mindlessly at my bed, the lamp, the window that has a view of the entrance to the gardens. I like the vibrant colours of the rose blossoms and I smile as I catch a glimpse of an acrobatic pale blue butterfly flitting up and down, making curlicues in the air.

Inspiration strikes and I pick up my pen again.

"Life at The Rose and Butterfly is about as peaceful as a stray cat convention, especially when Jenny…"

I stop writing again. I like the name Rose and Butterfly. It's elegant and memorable. It would be a better name than "Tranquil Meadows". I wrinkle my nose in disgust, wondering who came up with that one.

I can't use Jenny's name though or, God forbid, Lula's! I would never hear the end of it. Maybe I'm making a mistake trying to write about the antics that happen in my real life. What if I made something up? How about a story about two best friends who have amazing adventures until a man comes along and they fight over him and it breaks up the friendship, at least for a while? That has been done to death, I suppose. Love triangles. Silly women fighting over some charming cowboy type who isn't really worth their attention.

The women in those stories are always young and beautiful and the men constantly fall at their feet or fight over them. Their smiles and girlish figures seem to be all they have going for them. Not that there's anything wrong with being young and beautiful. It happens, but why does old age have to be boring? Why does it have to mean that you're no longer interesting or worthy to be written about?

No, I don't want to write about some young, voluptuous siren drawing the men in like flies to a spider web. I want to write about the way that life doesn't magically stop just because you hit your senior years.

We still have lives. We have fun. We fall in love. We dream. We regret. We long for our families and friends to be near us. We ache with loneliness. We hurt.

Youth is not the magic potion that makes us people. We are

all a part of this humanity. Hmm... I'm being philosophical this morning. I had better write some of these good thoughts down. I can incorporate them into my story somewhere.

Tallulah Pratt (Lula)

"I wish you had asked me first." I shouldn't be cross with Emmett.

It's such a lovely summer day, still warm, but that crazy sticky heat wave has let us go for now and a refreshing, cool breeze blows ever so gently through the garden this morning.

"I'm asking you now." Emmett smiles, his demeanor unshaken by my ireful outburst.

"I can't very well say no now, can I? It would be bad manners. What would they think of me if I declined after you already said yes? Besides, I know they won't like me."

I turn away from him and try to distract myself by focussing on a particularly perfect pink rose blossom. It seems to beckon me to smell it and relax and let go of my fretting ways, but you know, if that rose could talk, I would tell it that it's hard for an old dog to learn new tricks.

Emmett's soft laughter triggers the anger to rise within me again.

"What is so funny?" I whirl around, the fire in my bones pushing its way to the surface.

"Why can't you see the obvious?" He asks in that infuriating way that he has. "You are wonderful and my kids are going to love you. What's the harm in going to dinner with my family? They want to meet the woman who has put a spring back in my step."

I am not going to fall for that little boy face, Emmett

Muggeridge! "But... they might get the notion that our courtship is getting serious!"

"Isn't it?"

That is a question I don't feel comfortable answering right now. If I answer yes, then Emmett will strut and crow and I will never hear the end of it. If I say no, he'll be wounded. I'll feel like I just hauled off and kicked a puppy. We have only been courting for a couple of months. What is the rush?

"It's hard for kids to see their father with someone other than their mother." I attempt to divert the subject.

"They know I loved their mother, but they also know that I have been alone for over ten years now. Will smiled from ear to ear when I told him that I met someone and Connie is fine with it too." He shrugs. "This is a no risk situation. Just a simple dinner. No pressure. No reason to worry. What do you say?"

Damn your eyes, Emmett! They gleam in the sunlight like mossy green pools full of life and mystery and the will o' the wisp whizzing past quick as a flash and twice as elusive. I could get lost. I could wander into that magical forest and not ever wish to come out.

Can I trust you? You seem to be a faithful man, a loyal friend, a gentle soul with which to glide through the last miles of my life's ocean, and I like how it feels with you beside me, holding my hand, cradling my skittish heart.

"Can I think about it?" I ask. "It's not for another week, right? Can you let me consider it? I need to think it over."

"What's there to think about?"

"I don't know. Just... everything seems to be happening so fast. It's overwhelming. I need time."

Emmett's smile flees away. "I don't want you overwhelmed,

Tallulah, but I hope you realize, we're not in the springtime of life anymore."

"Oh, Emmett!"

"I am fully aware that the moments are finite at this stage of the game." He takes my hand. "I don't want to miss a single fleeting second of whatever time I can have with you, so please, take a little time, but just a little. We have a lot of living left to do and such a short window of opportunity."

Emmett's words frighten me. Am I stupid? Do I not realize that we are in our seventies and not our twenties? What is wrong with me? Only everything. I don't want Emmett to know what a screwball woman I am. I don't want this to go any further. If I go to dinner with his son and his daughter, I am opening the door to something more than I am prepared to give. I am afraid that he will ditch me like yesterday's newspaper once he finds out what a cold-hearted fool I am!

"What's wrong? You look like you just lost your best friend." Emmett touches my cheek. His hand is warm and I wish it could be like this forever.

What words could possibly convey this feeling of foreboding? "I'm all right. I just can't handle rushing into things. I know it's silly to you, but I just can't."

I turn away from those eyes of his before I blubber and cry like a child.

Carefully, with such a delicate touch, his arms slide around me from behind, his lips right next to my ear. "Tallulah..." He whispers. "...don't lock your heart up in a vault. Don't hide yourself away from me. I'm not going away. It's far too late for that."

"I don't want you to go away." I confess, a little more harshly than I mean to. "I just want a little time to decide about this cockamamie dinner!"

Emmett's soft laugh is irritating, and also intoxicating, and I am so confused.

"All right. You win. I'll wait." He lets go of me and takes my hand. "Shall we head inside? It will soon be time for lunch."

I force a smile and we stroll toward the doors, the tiniest wedge suddenly standing between us. I know that I put it there. I don't know if I should say the words that will bring it down.

As we pass the attendant's desk, I see Evangeline Martin standing there, someone's file open in front of her. Donkey's son, Gabe, is there too. They are having some kind of exchange. It looks a little heated to me and, where Donkey is concerned, I am downright nosy.

"I wonder what that's about." I say to Emmett, craning my neck to see, but not wanting to look like I'm looking.

"Beats me." Emmett shrugs.

"I'm sorry, Mr. Kehoe." Evangeline's voice carries, barely within earshot. "I can't find anything in our records to support that claim."

Gabe's voice rises in pitch. "Look harder, then! There has to be some mistake!"

I purse my lips tight, mainly to stop them from launching an irate tirade at Donkey's son. I like Evangeline. Everyone here does. She doesn't deserve to be screeched at like that!

"Perhaps we could set up an appointment and you can come in and discuss the matter with Ms. Finneyfrock."

"I don't want an appointment! I want you to look into this right now! Do you understand? I don't have time for this. You get paid good money for my mother to be here!" Gabe's face is as red as a chili pepper around the ears.

"Isn't that your friend Dawn's boy?" Emmett asks.

"Yes, and if he doesn't watch it, he'll give himself a stroke. Lordy, what a temper!"

A terrible thought comes into my mind, like a storm cloud forming over the ocean, small as a fist at first, but it is growing.

"It can't be." I say.

"It can't be what?" Emmett looks confused.

"Oh, I am so blind!"

Why didn't I see it before? Well, to be fair, Donkey can never remember where the bruises come from, so why would I think... why am I thinking it now? What kind of sick mind thinks a thing like that? Am I finally losing it?

I look up into Emmett's face, a tempest of worry swirling about in my brain and I know it will not go away until I get to the bottom of this.

"Tallulah? What is it?"

I shake my head. I dare not say it. I dare not think it. God help me... I do think it. I do!

Dawn Kehoe (Donkey)

"Ow! That hurts!" Lowell's hands were always strong, like there was metal inside them instead of bone. As his thumb and fingers bore into my wrist, it feels like sharp knives piercing me through.

"Shut up!" The edge of Lowell's voice is sharp and cruel.

How did I ever think he loved me? What a fool! My mother was right about me. I deserve her constant disappointment.

"Sign it." Lowell's command sends fear shooting through my body like a poisonous bullet.

"I don't want to." I am still stupid enough to resist him. Stubbornness runs deep.

His hand encloses mine now, so large that I can barely see my own fingers encased in his hatred. As he applies more pressure, I tremble. I feel as if my hand will be crushed to dust and I will finally disappear and that will be the end of the grand story of *Dawn Gardiner: The Invisible Woman*. My mother didn't see me. My sister didn't see me. Now, my own husband, he doesn't see me either.

"Do it. Come on!" Lowell snarls and his nostrils flare as his seething breaths go in and out.

"I thought you were dead."

"What are you talking about?"

I didn't realize I spoke that out loud. I'm going to pay for saying something like that to Lowell. I wince, waiting for the blow.

"Sign the damned thing!" Lowell slams the writing desk with his fist and I jump, heart pounding with the fright.

The door to my room swings open. Who is it? Is it one of Lowell's floozies from Marty's Bar? Is it that handsome man with the wavy hair, our next door neighbour? Is it his old drinking buddy, Harry?

Lowell takes his hands off of me. It's like he's afraid. I have never seen him fearful before.

Who just came into the house? It's… I don't know who that is… wait… I know him… I think I do…

??????????????????????????

I am singing and dancing on the stage, Miss Montgomery

smiling her approval at me.

??????????????????????????????

The nurse puts the most beautiful baby boy into my arms. I have never looked into such a wonderful face. Wrapped in a blue blanket, he is warm and fills my arms and my heart in a way that I never dreamed possible.

????????????????????????????

The China cup, it has a crack. My mother is going to kill me!

??????????????????????????????

'We've got to go, Gran."

I look up into the face of my grandson, Tyler. He is so tall now and his features remind me of my older brother, Knight, the same jet black hair and jawline. When did he get here?

"I'm taking the boys fishing this weekend. We've got to get packed up and head to the cottage." Gabe smiles. "It's been great seeing you, Mom."

"How did you get so old?" I ask.

Gabe laughs. "The same way you did. I kept having birthdays." He kisses my cheek.

I didn't realize I asked that question out loud, but I smile at my son. The grey streaks mingling with the darker strands of his hair jolt me. He is past 40 now. He is almost older than his father ever got to be.

"See you, Gran." Connor leans in to kiss my cheek.

I look into his face and I see… well, it's not his fault that he is the spitting image of his grandfather, is it? We can't help how we're born.

They walk out of my room.

HAZEL MAY LEBRUN

I sit on my bed for a minute.

"Ouch. Why does my arm hurt? Did I fall down?"

My stomach growls.

"I'm hungry. It must be time for lunch."

Chapter Sixteen

Gladys Peachy

"What is a seven letter word, 15 across; the clue is *'whodunit'*?" I scratch my itchy scalp with the eraser end of the pencil.

"Mystery." Lula's eyes peek over the edge of her open copy of *Better Homes and Gardens*, her legs stretched out, feet crossed as they lean on the coffee table that sits in front of the white sofa with the blue paisley pattern.

"Oh, of course." I smile and fill in the letters, enjoying the comfort of what I secretly call 'my recliner'.

"Speaking of mysteries…" Lula sets the magazine on her lap. "…I think I have figured out the secret to those nasty bruises Donkey keeps getting."

Well, that is not what I was expecting to talk about this morning.

"Do tell." I glance across the room at Donkey. "Look at her over there, finding a new husband to mourn."

Lula grins. "She's watching… oh, what is that?" She squints. "It's in colour."

I crane my neck to see. "Christopher Reeve. It's one of the Superman movies. I guess we'll have to rename Donkey Lois Lane."

Lula raises her eyebrows. "Christopher Reeve was quite the looker. He could have rescued me anytime."

"Yes. Well… Donkey will be mourning his death later on, so try and be sensitive."

Lula gives me a funny look, until she sees the grin on my face and then we both burst out laughing.

The laughter dies off and then, Lula says: "It's her own son." She frowns. "I'm sure of it. I mean, I haven't seen him do it, but I think Gabe is hurting Donkey."

My heart seems to skip a beat. "Lula! That is a terrible thing to say." Why am I chiding her? I have had the same awful thought myself.

She shakes her head. "I know it's terrible. Do you think I don't know that?" She huffs. "Believe me, I wish I didn't have this feeling in my bones. I just know that I know that I know that those bruises aren't silly accidents. Now, I realize that Donkey goes off with the fairies sometimes. She doesn't always know where or when or who she is, but she gets them too often, Gladdy. The bruises… I saw a fresh one on her wrist at breakfast this morning."

I nod. "I saw it too."

"Then, you know I'm right. Something is happening to our dear friend and I, for one, am not going to sit idly by and let it continue!"

"What are you going to do? We can't just waltz up to Donkey's son and tell him to stop hurting her. He'll deny the whole thing. We've got no real evidence."

"We'll have to get some." Lula folds her arms across her chest.

She has that determined look on her face; the one that means business. I wouldn't want to be the fool that gets in her way when she puts her mind to something.

"Are you suggesting that we…"

"Do some spying?" Lula shrugs. "I guess I am."

I am not comfortable with that, but then again, I always did hate a confrontation and spying is risky. I am the type of woman who even gets uncomfortable watching movies about confrontations. Lula is asking me a hard thing.

I look over at Donkey again, my dear, innocent friend. She is worth every bit of discomfort that I am going to experience on her behalf. I will go along with Lula's plan for her sake.

God, please help us. Help Donkey. I don't want her to get hurt anymore.

"Good morning, Ladies." Emmett doffs his fedora. "Mind if we sit down?"

"Be my guest." Lula smiles and Emmett sits beside her while Pete Marsden sits at the end of the sofa.

"Has Ethel gone on vacation?" Pete asks, his face looking sullen. "I hardly see her anymore."

I give him my best maternal smile. "No. She hasn't gone anywhere. She's busy these days."

"With another fella?" Pete sounds like a kid who just dropped his ice cream cone.

"No no." Lula rolls her eyes. "Lordy, she doesn't seem interested in any of the men around here."

Pete looks both relieved and forlorn at the same time.

"She's writing a book." I set down my crossword magazine. "Fancy that! Our Ethel is going to be an author."

"Gladdy!" Lula scolds. "I don't know if Ethel wants that broadcast everywhere."

"Why not?" I cock my head to one side. "I'm proud of her. How many people still chase their dreams at our age? I find it inspirational."

Emmett chimes in. "Best of luck to her. It's never too late. That's what I always say." He slides his hand over Lula's. "Carpe diem!"

Lula laughs. "Really, Emmett? We're sitting in the TV room corralled with the rest of the old herd and you want us to seize the day?"

"Absolutely!" Emmett nods. "The older I get, the clearer I see that. We may only have this day to seize. So we had best get to it and grab on as hard as we can."

"Well, aren't you the philosopher!" Lula leans her head on Emmett's arm.

"I'm a hungry philosopher." Emmett grins. "Hungry for Chez Napoleon."

"Chez Napoleon?" My mouth waters at the thought of that. "I love their rotisserie chicken. Mm… it tastes like Heaven."

"Me too." Lula's blue eyes get a dreamy look. "I can almost taste it now. For goodness sake, why did you get us started thinking about that? You know we aren't going to get anything even close to that for lunch today! It'll be something less savory, like mac and cheese casserole."

A soft chuckle escapes Emmett before he continues. "That's where my family wants to take us for dinner this weekend. How can you say no to that?"

Lula's eyes flash with that blue fire that tells me she is irate. "Oh, that is dirty pool, Emmett Muggeridge! I am craving rotisserie chicken now and I want to go, but I don't think I'm ready. How could you!"

Emmett's laugh is hearty and mischievous. I grin too, though I don't know if that will put me in Lula's line of fire or not.

"You know you want to go." Emmett manages to say amid the raucous laughing. "So just say yes and you'll be enjoying a sumptuous feast… with… with…"

"With your children gawking at me like some specimen on a microscope! No, thank you!" Lula folds her arms across her chest and turns her face away from Emmett.

"Wait a minute." I risk Lula's wrath and look into her eyes. "Are you telling me that Emmett's children want to have dinner with you?"

"Yes!" Lula exhales. "They want to meet me. I'm not comfortable with that. It's too rushed."

"You should go." I interrupt her fretful ranting.

"What? Gladdy, are you crazy? What will they think of me?"

Now, it is my hand that reaches out to touch hers. She is my friend and I love her. For all her puffed up crowing, I have discovered that Tallulah Pratt still has a little girl inside of her who needs affirmation, and she sometimes doesn't feel safe in this world.

"Dear Heart..." I pat her hand. "...they are going to think the same thing that I do."

Lula's eyes widen. "What?"

I grin. "They are going to see a strong, confident, capable woman, who makes their father happy."

"Well, I..." The imaginary peacock feathers that I picture on Lula fan out now into their full, dazzling array. "I don't know about that. I mean, what if they..."

"Lula, it will be all right." I say.

She goes quiet for a few seconds. "If you put it that way..." She turns to Emmett and smiles. "I suppose I could go with you..."

"Hot diggity dog!" Emmett's arms shoot up into the air.

"...just this once."

3 "Tallulah, you just made me a happy man!"

"But..." Lula turns to me with a steely glare. "...if it all goes horribly wrong, I am holding you personally responsible, Gladys Peachy!"

I smile and shrug my shoulders. She has already dragged me through hours of shopping mall torture. What else can she possibly do to me?

So, I quip: "Have a wonderful time and make sure you try the coconut cream pie. It's to die for."

The scowl on Lula's face as I utter those words is slightly severe, and highly entertaining.

Ethel MacNarland

I prance like a skittish deer, tapping my feet on the floor in alternating rhythm, trying to slide my pants and undergarments down before I pee all over myself. Mercy! My bladder is as impatient as a four year old at the candy store! I confess that I kept writing when the first urge to go arrived, but I didn't wait that long. Why is this damnable body of mine punishing me for wanting to be productive?

Sighing with relief, I let my tinkle run free now, grateful that I don't have to change clothes and clean up a mess. I thought wearing bladder control underwear would make my life easier. I suppose it does. It's my own foolish fault for not darting to the bathroom as soon as my bladder started calling out, 'Yoo hoo! Ethel!'

Seated back at my writing desk, I read over this morning's short entry. Why is it so short? Distraction! My mind is wandering off instead of concentrating on writing about my adventure at the spring social, the first time in my entire life that I was the object of two men's affections at once. This chapter ought to be fun and light and easy to write, but it isn't.

It's Donkey. It's the bruise I saw on Donkey. All right, it's the bruise I saw on Donkey and the accusing whisper in my ear from Lula. She believes that Gabe Kehoe is hurting his own mother. Would he really do that? I don't know him. I know what he looks like. I have seen him here with those two handsome young boys of his. I know that he sings professionally and has a reputation as a wonderful performer.

Is he putting on the performance of a lifetime and only pretending to be a loving, devoted son? I don't want to think a thing like that! But where are those bruises coming from? What is happening to our friend? She can't even tell us. Sometimes she thinks we gave them to her.

I bite my lip and think about Donkey. I can't write right now, except for the notation I made in my journal about Donkey and the mystery injuries she keeps incurring.

The sins of the father... Whoa... where did that line come from? I think it's actually a Bible verse. I don't even know which part it's from. I could ask Gladdy. She would know. She was married to a famous preacher's son and I know she reads her Bible every day. It's more than just a bunch of stories to her.

I walk over to my bed and lay down, arms folded on my stomach, listening to a happy robin cheery-upping outside the open window. Unlike some seniors' residences, we can actually slide our bedroom windows open here to get fresh air. The air conditioning makes me cold sometimes and I open that window to get warm at this time of year. Isn't that a hoot?

I think about Donkey and how much she loves her son. In a world that seemed to cheat Donkey out of so much happiness, Gabe is her one thing. She survived that beastly Lowell and I know he beat her senseless. He nearly killed her! She had

229

to struggle and strive just to keep Gabe clothed and fed. It wouldn't be a nice ending to her life story to have her son turn out to be a chip off the old block.

Still, where else could the bruises come from? She can't just fall down every time. The wounds are too frequent, too predictable too. Someone is harming her.

"Oh! I can't take it anymore!"

I get up from the bed, check out my appearance to make sure I'm still presentable and head out into the hallway. If I can't concentrate on writing today, I may as well go and see what the girls are up to.

Evangeline Martin is scribbling onto a notepad at the attendants' desk while Biddy Finneyfrock stands behind, looking over her shoulder.

"She looks like a decrepit old buzzard." I grimace.

"Good morning, Mrs. MacNarland." Evangeline manages to smile at me, quite a feat with Biddy breathing down her neck.

"Good morning." I smile back. "And may I say, Evangeline, that we all appreciate the great job you do around here."

Biddy's expression remains as blank as a piece of paper, but her brow furrows, as if one of her employees doing a good job was a shocking thing.

"Why, thank you. That's kind of you to say." Evangeline replies.

As I pass by, I can barely hear their conversation as it resumes, but I do catch the words "Mrs. Kehoe" and "discrepancies". I'm no detective, but I can tell you that writers, even aspiring ones, have inquiring minds and right now, I am more curious than a cat in an aviary. What discrepancies? What is going on with our Donkey?

I don't know what it is, but my concern is growing, and the

girls and I must get to the bottom of it all somehow, and soon.

Tallulah Pratt (Lula)

It's just as I thought. A dire-looking bowl of macaroni and cheese casserole sits in front of me, steaming and unappealing. I pick at it with my fork and think about Oliver Twist and the gruel they served him at the orphanage. *Please, Sir. Can I have some more?* Don't bother, Oliver. Here! You can have my portion of this disgusting food!

Look at Donkey stuffing her face as if she hasn't eaten in days. I think she would eat practically anything they put in front of her. I smile and wish I could take a pair of scissors to those wild tufts of white hair. It needs to be cut. She is oblivious to everything except shoveling macaroni in her mouth.

Thank goodness they served a nice salad with our entrees. I love fresh vegetables.

"How's your book coming along, Ethel?" Gladdy asks, before taking a sip of her tea.

Ethel shakes her head. "Not bad, but today wasn't a stellar writing day, I'm afraid." She glances over at Donkey. "I was a little distracted."

"You haven't told us what the story is about." I stab a cherry tomato with my fork.

"I don't want to tell you that." Ethel looks a little sheepish. "It's bad luck."

"Tsk! It is not!" I snicker. "Who told you that?"

Ethel shrugs and shoves a spoonful into her mouth. "I heard it somewhere and I believe it."

The look on her face tells me that she's feeding us a line of hooey!

I roll my eyes. "I don't understand that. I've met writers before and they're usually chomping at the bit to talk about their books."

Gladdy is Gladdy and, true to form, jumps to Ethel's defense. "Oh, come on now. If she doesn't want to talk about it, we shouldn't force her."

"I'm not!" I put on my best grin. "I'm just so curious. Aren't you, Gladdy?"

Gladdy hesitates, then nods. "Sure I am, but I don't want to pry."

"Nonsense! You just finished prying half an hour ago and convinced me to go with Emmett to have dinner with his son and daughter. Don't want to pry, my foot!"

Ethel bursts out laughing. "You didn't."

Gladdy's cheeks turn crimson. "I did."

"Would you like more tea?" One of the servers (is his name Joe?) is standing there with the tea cart.

Three of us nod yes and, even though Donkey did not nod, we indicate her cup and he refills it as well.

"Thank you." Gladdy chirps like a happy little bird.

"Thank you!" Donkey pipes in suddenly, then looking around the table at us, she blinks and adds: "What am I thanking you for, Eve? You're a big, ungrateful cow!"

Don't laugh, Tallulah! Don't! I notice that we are all struggling to hold it back. Ethel's hand is right over her mouth.

"Donkey, Dear." Gladdy notices that Donkey's bowl is empty and passes her some of her mac and cheese.

"Oh, that's why! Thank you!" Donkey smiles like a kid that just got a new puppy.

Ethel turns her face away and chortles.

Somehow, Gladdy keeps a straight face. "Donkey, can I ask you something?"

Donkey is busy chewing and doesn't seem to register that Gladdy is talking to her.

"About… about that little bruise on your arm…" Gladdy runs her fingers over the spot and Donkey winces and pulls her arm away.

"Ow! Don't do that, Eve."

Taking a deep breath, Gladdy continues prodding carefully. "Do you know where you got that bruise, Dear Heart?"

Ethel and I glance at each other and shrug, hoping for something coherent.

"I'm not supposed to tell."

My heart flutters and tears inch their way into my lower eyelids. I bite them back hard. The dining hall is crowded and I will not give them reason to gawk at me.

"Who said you can't tell?" Gladdy asks.

Donkey's mouth is full of food. "You know. It's Lowell." The words come out a little garbled as she chews.

"Lowell? But, Dear Heart, Lowell is…"

My hand darts out and touches Gladdy's. I shake my head no and whisper: "No, don't say that. Let her keep talking."

Gladdy nods. "Dear Heart, where did you see Lowell?"

I nod emphatically and Ethel sets down her teacup.

Donkey tilts her head and rolls her eyes as if we are a bunch of dunces. "You know where, Silly! At home! He wants to go drinking at Marty's Bar and I hope he never comes back."

Come on, Donkey. We can't help what happened in your past. We need to know what is happening right now! Frustration feels like lava pushing up on the volcano of emotion inside my soul.

"Well, he's not ever coming back!" Ethel says. "Don't you worry about that."

Donkey looks confused, more so than usual.

"What do you mean, Mother? He made me sign that cheque. He made me! See?" Donkey holds up her arm, bruise side out.

I have a creepy feeling right now, as if I'm watching a spooky movie or it's Hallowe'en and the streets are full of goblins and witches and darkness.

"Discrepancies! Oh God!" Ethel's hand flies to her mouth, her eyes wide, breath catching in her throat.

We all turn to look at Ethel, confusion written on Gladdy's face and, what is that on Donkey's? Disdain? Does she even do disdain?

"Don't worry, Mother." Donkey shakes her head and returns to her lunch. "It's only a hundred dollars. That's what he always says."

Dawn Kehoe (Donkey)

I fly through the air with the greatest of ease like the daring young man on the flying trapeze! Haha! Isn't that funny? I made up a poem and I wasn't even trying.

Humans don't fly, but look at me. He's got me. Clark Kent. He's Superman. He doesn't think I know it's him behind those dorky glasses, but I do, and we're flying above the clouds and everything is wonderful and I am… eating macaroni.

????????????????????

What place is this? Where is my beautiful blue dress?

????????????????????

This blouse is ugly… I think I spilled tea on it.

????????????????????

"Thank you." Eve says.

"Thank you!" I look into my sister's face. "What am I thanking you for, Eve? You're a big, ungrateful cow!"

She stole my boyfriend. She gets the handsome boys, the fancy clothes and all the love my mother can give. I'm just their third wheel.

"Ow! Don't do that, Eve!" I scowl at her. Why is she touching my arm?

"Do you know where you got that bruise, Dear Heart?" Eve is talking nicely to me. Why would she do that?

"I'm not supposed to tell."

It's true. He told me. He told me he would hurt me.

"Who said you can't tell?" Eve looks concerned.

"You know. It's Lowell." I'm surprised that she isn't telling me off for talking with my mouth full.

"Dear Heart, where did you see Lowell?"

Where else would I see him, you dopey dame? "You know where, Silly! At home! He wants to go drinking at Marty's Bar and I hope he never comes back."

"Well, he's not ever coming back! Don't you worry about that." That's what my mother says. When did she get here?

"What do you mean, Mother? He made me sign that cheque. He made me! See?" I show her my bruise.

"Discrepancies! Oh God!" My mother looks like she showed up at a party in the same dress as somebody else.

"Don't worry, Mother." I roll my eyes at her. "It's only a hundred dollars. That's what he always says."

???????????????????????????

Where is Dinah Gillespie? Did she run off and join the circus?

???????????????????????????

I don't know… I can't remember… what is this place? Where am I? Where is my baby? My baby! "Gaaaaaaabe!"

???????????????????????????

"Shhhhhh!" The hand that is patting my shoulder belongs to…

"Gladys Peachy?" I look into her friendly green eyes.

"That's right." Gladys smiles at me. "Everything is fine now. Lowell isn't here and Gabe is safe and sound at home."

"He has two sons." I say, but I'm not convinced of that.

"Yes." Lula is stirring milk into my teacup. "Two strapping teenaged boys. They certainly are handsome."

Are they handsome? What do they look like? I think… hard.

"Tyler." Thinking of him makes me feel happy. "And Connor…" Thinking of him makes me feel…

???????????????????????????

"I want dessert."

The ladies sitting with me at the table are having a good laugh. Who are they? They look familiar. Are they teachers? I don't know what they find so funny, but it doesn't matter because raspberry cobbler is sitting on a plate in front of me and until I finish eating it, the whole world can go fly a kite.

Chapter Seventeen

Gladys Peachy

I remember our humble home on Dunfield Crescent. Paul and I finally saved enough for a down payment and apartment living was over for us. He never moved again. I never moved until the upkeep of the house became too much and I sold it and relocated to Tranquil Meadows.

One Sunday afternoon after church, I was busy as a bee in my happy open kitchen. How I loved that room! Apple pie lay cooling on the window sill, the aroma of cinnamon and sugar filling the house with joyful comfort. A cut of beef sat roasting in the oven and I was on KP duty! I would make mashed potatoes and fresh yellow beans that Paul picked for me from the garden and, last but not least, Yorkshire puddings, made from a generations old recipe handed down by my father's mother's mother.

We were still relatively young then, too young to have this emptiness between us, the finality of the doctor's words, 'cannot have children'.

The hi-fi was playing a 33 rpm record, the New Life Gospel Quartet, their harmonies rich and perfectly blended, serenading Gladys the not-so-five-star chef:

We have a heavenly Father above
With eyes full of mercy and a heart full of love
He really cares when your head is bowed low
Consider the lilies and then you will know...

I felt utterly blissful in that moment, sitting there at the table with a potato peeler in my hand. I knew God loved me no matter what life held in store.

Paul picked that moment to burst through the front door. "Gladdy! Gladdy! We have company!"

That is how a new tradition began. Paul Peachy found single mothers with small children, lonely old men with no family to care for them, newly bereaved widows and even the odd teenager who had run away from home. Different people with different backgrounds and challenges became our Sunday dinner guests and I honestly never knew what would come through that door with him.

Sometimes my parents or siblings would visit with their families. On rare occasions, the Reverend John and Adelaide would visit, either with or without their other children in tow. Sunday afternoons became a cooking odyssey for me, but I never complained. I loved it! I searched recipe books for new things to try and, if it isn't boasting, in time I turned out to be a decent and respected culinary artist. Not that I felt qualified to stand beside Julia Child or anything like that, but the family, friends, neighbours and strangers who ended up at our table always seemed glad and satisfied with both the meal and the camaraderie we all shared.

That is what happens when you have an empty hole to fill. I don't just mean your stomach. The lack of children in our home felt unnatural, but we found ways to have a full and happy life nonetheless.

Paul had his classroom full of curious minds to fill. I taught Sunday School and hosted Vacation Bible School in our back yard for the neighbourhood children every summer. We took in the odd foster child for a while and helped them pick up the pieces after their lives had been shattered by abuse or bereavement.

Oh God, what a blessed life! I have nothing to whine about, and yet here I am, whining... or is it just praying? It's Donkey again. I know

I have come to you before, but my heart hurts for her. I fear for her. I am troubled. This facility is full of people and yet someone is getting away with hurting her. Please, bring dark things out into the light.

I sit on my bed, my Bible open along with the devotional book I read every day. I have been reminiscing and ruminating on scripture readings and Donkey's bruise.

A thought flutters into my head. "Haugh!" *Should I do that? Maybe I should run it by Lula first.*

I slide into my *Tender Tootsie* white summer penny loafers and head across the floor. "Owwww…" Pain shoots up across my shoulders and into my jaw. *Now what is that for?*

Aging is like a surprise box. You never know when you're going to have weird aches and pains or where they are going to be. I wait for a few seconds and the pain eases off.

Out into the hallway I go, heading toward the dining hall for breakfast. How amazing that Donkey didn't come to get me this morning! In fact, she hasn't had a midnight wander in over a week. Thank God for a good night's sleep.

Evangeline Martin stands at the attendant's desk, eyes focused on something or other in front of her.

"Good morning, Evangeline." I smile.

"Oh, good morning, Mrs. P… I mean… Gladys. I'm never going to remember that, you know."

I chuckle. "Try being 75. You won't remember much of anything."

She nods. "I'm sure I'll find out in a few years. I must say, you look lovely today. That peach colour is pretty on you."

"Thank you."

"I saw your lady friends heading toward the dining hall."

"So I'm a straggler today, the rotten egg." I guess I can take my time then. "Do you mind if I ask you something?"

Evangeline's smile fades and she sets down her pen. "Go right ahead. Is there anything I can help you with?"

I hope so and I hope I won't be causing a ruckus or making things worse. "I know you can't give out information on someone's personal file."

"No. We take confidentiality quite seriously here." Her eyes dart left and right, probably to make sure Bidelia is nowhere in sight.

"It's just that..." I hesitate, but it's too late to turn back, isn't it? Besides, if someone doesn't take the bull by the horns, we may never get to the bottom of this. "Donkey... I mean..."

Evangeline's smile returns. "Mrs. Kehoe. I know that's your nickname for her. It's so cute."

Oh? Are our affairs not as secret as we believe? "Yes, well, we have noticed some troubling injuries..."

She blanches. "Gladys, no one at Tranquil Meadows would harm a resident. Ms. Finneyfrock is adamant about respect and she screens her employees really well. I mean..." Her eyes roll. "...really really well."

I put a hand up. "No no. I don't believe that anyone here is harming Donkey. She can't... er..." *Don't say she can't remember.* "She hasn't told us what's happening, but she has said a few things that disturb me."

"Oh?"

"It seems as though... I don't mean to accuse anybody... I don't know what to do! Maybe this is all foolish and she's just falling

241

down all the time."

Evangeline scuttles out from behind the desk now. Her expression is not stern, but serious. "Gladys, if you know something, even if it's just a maybe, you can trust me. You can tell me."

Fear grips me. If they find out that Donkey isn't all there, they'll ship her off across the way and it will be my fault! *Gladys Peachy, you dimwit! What are you doing?* How will the girls ever forgive me?

I take a deep breath. *Here I go... in for a penny, in for a pound.* "I know it's none of my business, but Donkey has mentioned someone making her sign cheques by force."

The coffee cups that are Evangeline's eyes go wider, the liquid even deeper, a hand flying up to her mouth. "Are you sure about that?"

"I'm not sure about anything, Dear Heart. You're probably listening to the incoherent ramblings of some dotty old fruitcake!"

She smiles at me and pats my shoulder, almost like a mother would a child. "You've still got all your marbles, Gladys. I have no doubt about that. Now, just tell me exactly what you heard and I'll see what I can do about it."

I would have done it. I would have spilled my guts out like some lily-livered stool pigeon squealing on Al Capone, but Al Capone suddenly arrived.

"Mrs. Martin!" Biddy's voice cuts through me like a knife through cheese. "What is going on here?"

Evangeline's hands drop to her sides, the smile on her face running for dear life. "Ms. Finneyfrock, I was just…"

"We don't coddle the residents here. I have discussed that with you before." Those ice blue eyes drill through me like a flash freeze.

"She wasn't... er... she wasn't coddling me." I say. "You see, I felt a little faint as I was walking toward the dining hall..." I put on my best frail old lady tone. I even manage to crackle my voice.

Evangeline gives me a shocked look. Maybe she doesn't think I know how to fib. I don't like fibbing, but I won't let her get reprimanded by that crusty old bird on my account.

"You what?" Biddy cocks her head and looks puzzled.

I grip the edge of the nurse's desk as if I might fall dead away. "I had a spell. Oh... dear... they put me on a new blood pressure pill. The side effects say *'may cause dizziness'*. Well, that must be it then." That is not even a lie, though I don't feel dizzy at all.

"We can arrange to transport you to hospital if you require it." If Biddy is trying to sound compassionate, it isn't working.

"Oh no no, of course not." I fake trying to steady myself. "I'm sure I'll feel better after getting a little breakfast into me. I just get like this sometimes first thing in the morning."

Biddy cackles like the hen she is. "I see. Well, don't just stand there, Mrs. Martin! Help Mrs. Peachy to the dining hall!"

"Yes, Ms. Finneyfrock."

"And don't forget we have a staff meeting at 9:30!"

"Yes, Ms. Finneyfrock. Thank you." Evangeline grabs my elbow and 'helps me' down the corridor. As soon as we are out of earshot, she chides me, though not seriously. "I didn't think God-fearing women told tall tales, Gladys."

I snicker. "This one was for a good cause."

She loosens her grip on my arm. "You are perfectly fine to walk to the dining hall on your own."

"Yes." I reply. "But how else was I going to get you out of hot water?"

Evangeline laughs softly. "You really are something else!"

"I just look after the people I care about."

"Really?" Evangeline stops outside the dining hall. "You care about me? That is about the sweetest thing I ever heard."

I smile at her. "I would take you over Bidelia any day."

"Oh!" Evangeline laughs harder. "Don't let her hear you calling her that!"

"It's our secret."

"You go and enjoy your breakfast."

I hope I can do that. I hope I didn't mess things up for Donkey by confiding in Evangeline. I hope a lot of things and, you know what the book of Proverbs says: *"Hope deferred makes the heart sick..."*

Well, it's all I have to hold onto this morning, so I hope.

Ethel MacNarland

It's Sunday morning and the game is afoot. That sounds like something Sherlock Holmes would say, and he wouldn't be far off the mark.

Sunday is the day that a lot of the residents here have visitors, and here we sit, Lula, Gladys and I, in the TV room while Donkey watches *To Kill a Mockingbird* on Classic TV. Lucky girl! I would have snatched up Gregory Peck in a heartbeat. He was tall, gangly and handsome, and what girl didn't fall in love with him playing Atticus Finch?

Breakfast was uneventful, but we sit, full of nervous energy now as we wait, doing small time police surveillance. I want to laugh at that thought.

"What's so funny?" Lula scowls at me. "Don't act silly. You'll give us away."

I try to hold it back, but I feel like having a giggle fit. "Oh, come on. We look more unnatural sitting here staring and serious. Madame Tussaud's is going to come and take us away. They'll think we belong in her wax museum!"

Gladdy chuckles, but Lula stops her with one stern glance.

"I don't want to miss anything if he shows up." Lula whispers, her lips taut, the fine creases around her mouth more pronounced.

"We won't miss it." I say. "From where I'm sitting, nobody could come in here without having to pass right by. It's better if we look like we're having a pleasant conversation."

"But this is serious, Ethel! I want to catch that no good son of hers red-handed. We have to do this for Donkey!" Lula's arms are folded across her chest. "What's more, we only have so long to do it. I promised Emmett I would go out for dinner with his family this evening." She glares at Gladys again. "A decision made by coercion, I might add!"

Gladys grins and shrugs as if she has no idea what Lula is talking about.

"Sitting here griping about Gabe isn't going to make him show up any faster." I point out. "At the very least, we could enjoy each other's company while we stake out Donkey."

"Stake out…" Lula huffs and drops her jaw open. "…this is not a joke!"

"If we were a detective show, Lula would definitely be the bad cop and I would be the good cop." I chortle, which incurs even more unkind looks from Detective Tallulah Crankypants!

"Lighten up, Lula!"

"I will not lighten up! I can't bear to think of Donkey being harmed in any way. It's bad enough that I can't control what her own mind is doing to her!"

Gladdy reaches out (is she brave or daft?) and brushes Lula's hand with her own. "Dear Heart, I know it's hard. It hurts me terribly. I want our Donkey safe."

Lula says nothing.

"That is why…" Gladys purses her lips. It's like something is worrying her. She hesitates.

"That is why what?" I ask.

After a loud sigh, Gladys continues. "That is why I spoke with Evangeline Martin this morning and…"

"You what?" If Lula were a cartoon, the artist would have drawn steam shooting out her ears just now. "Gladys! This is supposed to be our secret! You know what they'll do to Donkey if they find out she's not playing with a full deck anymore!"

I feel like I'm in the middle of a Tranquil Meadows civil war.

"But Evangeline is a good woman!" Gladys says.

"I know that, but she's still a member of the staff. She still has to report to…" Lula grimaces. "…Drill Sergeant Finneyfrock."

Gladys lowers her head. "But I don't think she will. I mean, we got interrupted anyway. I didn't get to tell her everything."

"Good! Tsk!" Lula chirps. "We have got to stick together, Girls! We have got to protect our friend. It's time to circle the wagons!"

Circle the wagons? Are we in a Clint Eastwood movie? If so, can I be the sad widow this time?

"What exactly did you tell Evangeline?" I ask. I feel uneasy about that too, though not as flustered as that feisty redhead.

Gladys gives me an apologetic look. "I asked her if she had noticed anything out of place. I told her that Donkey had mentioned being forced to sign cheques. I didn't say anything about Donkey's mind wandering, just that she wouldn't tell us who it is, and that's when old Finneyfrock happened along. I clammed up and Evangeline did too."

Gladdy and Lula look worried. Do I? That is how I feel. I may not be as stern about it as Lula is, but I don't like what is happening to Donkey, both in her mind and in her life. She has been through enough trauma and it shouldn't happen to her anymore.

After a strange silence passes between us, Lula tries to smile. It's forced, but she tries. "Well, I suppose all we can do now is pray for the best and wait to see if Gabe shows up for a visit today."

I nod. "But can we please try and look a little less uptight?" I hope that doesn't ruffle Lula's already ruffled feathers.

"All right." Lula agrees. "I suppose it doesn't do any good to fret the whole day away."

"Just one thing..." Gladdy gives us a sweet and innocent grin. "...what exactly are we going to do if he does show up?"

"Why, catch him in the act, of course!" Lula slaps her knee.

I roll my eyes. "Oh boy..."

Gladys looks stunned. "Three seventy-somethings are going to shake him down? A big man like that?"

Lula grins. "Gladys Peachy, don't you ever underestimate me!"

In a match between Gabe and Lula, my money is on Lula.

Tallulah Pratt (Lula)

A big fat nothing! That is what happened this afternoon as we waited for Donkey's son to show up. He usually visits on Sundays. You can almost set your clock by it, but we watched Donkey all afternoon; never letting her out of our sight. Of all the cheek! That conniving man didn't come. I should be glad that Donkey didn't have to endure his abuse, but I'm irritated beyond belief. I wanted to catch him and put all this nonsense to an end.

I hope I look all right, for an old bird that has been attacked by the predator of time. I do have some age spots and a few lines and creases. I don't look 25 anymore or even 35 or 40! I have to face it. The years are catching up with me.

Still, I can look my best. I pulled out a delightful dress that I have not worn yet this season. It's pale green and has a spray of purple lilac blossoms part way across the top and down one side. I fell in love with it last year when my daughter, Sarah, took me on a vacation trip to Toronto. I saw the CN Tower, the Royal Ontario Museum. We shopped and shopped and, Lordy, then we shopped some more.

I smile at my own reflection. Makeup is done with a little extra panache. I switched to a small, mauve clutch with matching pearl-shaped earrings and a dainty gold necklace, also with a mauve cluster of beads sitting on a gold leaf setting. *Emmett Muggeridge, I am going to knock your socks off!*

I take a deep breath. I need to shake off this grouchy feeling and the anxiety about Donkey, just for tonight. I don't want Emmett's children to think I'm a mean old battle axe.

I feel pretty in these clothes. Slipping into a pair of shimmery ivory shoes, I head out the door of my room and down the hall toward the lobby. That is where Emmett and I are going to be picked up for dinner. I feel like I am going to face the Spanish Inquisition. I swallow past a lump in my throat. *Oh come on, Lula!* Ha! I sound like Ethel now. *It can't be that bad. You're a grown woman. You are not about to be intimidated by people who are young enough to be your own children.*

I steel myself, determined to try and take my own advice.

Emmett's grin is ear to ear, those remarkably white teeth glistening, eyes twinkling, sharp white, collared shirt and dress pants enhancing his tall frame, handsomeness radiating toward me.

"Oh my my…" He raves. "Don't you look like the cat's pajamas this evening!"

"The cat's pajamas? Well, I suppose that's better than something that the cat dragged in."

He reaches for my hand. "No no, much better than that. My darling, you are a vision… you are the picture of loveliness." He draws the hand up to his mouth and kisses it.

A giggle lurches out of me. "Oh, Mr. Muggeridge. You can pour on the sugar anytime."

"At every opportunity." He offers me an arm and I take it. "Shall we, Cinderella? Our carriage awaits."

Cinderella? At my age? Well, why not?

As we exit the building, a silver car awaits. Both front doors open and two people step out, a slender, pretty, carrot top woman with an adorable pixie cut and… oh my Lord… it's Emmett! Well, it was Emmett! He looks the spitting image of Emmett if he were younger (he looks about 40). Those good looks could knock a lady dead.

"Dad!" His smile is as flashy and handsome as his father's. "Let me get the door for you."

"Hello, Son."

"Mrs. Pratt, it's such a pleasure to finally meet you." The pixie cut woman says, extending a hand toward me.

I take it and smile back at her, suddenly understanding that the affinity for redheads has passed down the generations.

"I'm Susie Muggeridge." She says.

I pause for a second. *Susie. Just like my Susan. She was a redhead like me. Would she have looked similar to this if she had lived?* I shake the memory off. "Tallulah Pratt." I finally reply. "But please, just call me Lula. Everybody else does."

"Tallulah." Emmett is grinning so much. I wonder if his cheeks hurt. "I want you to meet…"

"You must be Will." I interrupt. "I must say, you are the spitting image of your father."

He takes my hand and kisses it. *Like father, like son!* "Thank you, Ma'am. I take that as a compliment."

"That is exactly what I meant it to be." I let him lead me to the car as he opens the back door and helps me into the seat.

"Everybody else is meeting at the restaurant." Will announces to both of us. "Reservations are for 7 o'clock."

The two men exchange strange little glances. I don't know what that means, but I know that they're up to something. That is the same look Gladys, Ethel and I give each other when we're scheming or trying to keep a secret. *I am on to you, Emmett! All is not as it appears.*

Dawn Kehoe (Donkey)

My husband is named Atticus. He was a fancy lawyer. No no no... wait... that's not true.

My husband died. His name was... Gregory. Gregory? That doesn't sound right. Do I know anybody named Gregory?

"Hello, Mother."

"Gabe! You remembered. I'm so glad you came to see me." I smile at my son and he smiles back at me.

"I'm sorry we're late." He kisses my cheek. "I can't believe my producer wanted to have a meeting on a Sunday."

"Oh, you had to work this weekend?" I don't like them working my Gabe too hard.

"Yeah." He shrugs. "No rest for the wicked, I guess. Did they feed you a nice dinner tonight? They had better. This place costs a small fortune."

I think... hard. Did we eat?

"Tsk. Why do they just let you walk around wearing part of your meal on your clothes?" Gabe touches my blouse.

I look down and see a brown stain there. "We had roast beef." At least, that's what the stain looks like, beef gravy. "And... and blueberry pie."

"Hey! Gran is watching Godzilla." Tyler laughs.

I'm so glad he's here. Tyler is a wonderful grandson.

"The new one?" Connor asks.

Connor sits beside me on the other side. His arm brushes against me. I flinch.

"Mother? What is it? Are you feeling all right?" Gabe looks concerned.

What was I thinking about before? What was I doing? How did I get in this room? Weren't we all in the dining hall just now?

I look at my son. Nothing else matters. I am so happy that he came to visit. Gabe is the best thing that ever happened to me.

Chapter Eighteen

Gladys Peachy

"Red alert, Ethel! Red alert!"

Ethel sets down her crocheting. "What on earth are you talking about?"

I try to look inconspicuous, thrusting my head sideways in the general direction of the sofa where Donkey is sitting. "Enemy at two o'clock."

Ethel laughs. "Are we characters in an Ian Fleming novel? The geese fly high at midnight…"

I think Ethel is being deliberately thick right now or perhaps I am a little cranky after listening to Lula's nonsense earlier. "Would you take a look over that way?" I am almost whispering.

Ethel's lips purse together. "Ah, our quarry has arrived late to the party."

"Yes, I'm surprised he got here so late in the day. It's going to be a pretty short visit."

A silly grin spreads over Ethel's face. "Won't Lula be a bear to live with if we apprehend the perp without her?"

"Apprehend the…? You've been watching too many police shows!"

"Just picture it." Ethel is chortling now. "Old Red will see red if we catch this guy and she wasn't even here to capital L-E-A-D the charge."

I bite my lip. "You're right, of course. She'll be hissing for days. Still, the thought of catching Gabe doing something so unpleasant to Donkey. It makes me feel…"

"I know." Ethel pats my hand. "But we can't let it go on."

A lump forms in my throat. "No, we can't, but it's going to hurt Donkey either way. That man is her pride and joy."

Ethel and I stare at each other, the burden between us weighing like an invisible anvil. I know that they say emotions are intangible, but in my chest at this moment, the pain feels as real as if somebody reached out and punched me.

"Oh dear!" Ethel exclaims. "I think we're fired!"

I turn to look and see that Donkey and her entourage have left the room while Ethel and I were distracted with worry.

"Let's go, Ethel. We've got to follow them. We shouldn't leave them alone where he can…" I don't finish that thought.

Off we go like rockets, if the rockets were old, rusty and had seen better days. Ethel and I are both quite mobile, but we are not as agile as the young ones anymore. Still, we scoot as fast as we can across the floor toward the door of the TV room.

"There!" Ethel points. "I see them."

"Let's go!" I don't want to let them out of my sight.

They go straight. We go straight. They make a left. We make a left. They pass the dining hall. We pass the dining hall.

Residents and attendants pass by us in both directions on their way to wherever. A young man pushes a cart filled with supplies, its wheel squeaking like my creaky bones do when I move. I don't know if that is poetic or insulting. I have become an old wheel that needs a squirt of oil.

"Hey there, Ethel! How about a nice cup of tea?"

"Not now, Pete!" Ethel's scolding makes Pete Marsden's face wince as if she just hit a puppy with a newspaper for peeing on the floor. He gets the message though and skulks off to lick his wounds.

Where are they taking Donkey? I wonder this as we keep tracking them and they keep on walking. How does Gabe do it? How does he get Donkey to sign those cheques? Does he corner her while she's alone somewhere? Does he force the pen into her hand? The thought of it is a torment to me now! I can't let it go on one more day.

I see him lean over and whisper something into Donkey's ear. His hand brushes across her back with what ought to be affection, but it strikes me right now as cold and calculating and I want to scream out, "How dare you! Don't give her such fake love in front of everyone and then do that to her in private!" *Forgive me, Paul. Forgive me, God. I am not thinking kind thoughts just now.*

"Wait, Gladdy." Ethel stops and puts a hand on my shoulder.

Donkey and her entourage have stopped at the main attendant's desk, the one that I pass every day when I go from my room to the dining hall and the activity rooms.

"It's Evangeline." I whisper to Ethel. "Why is she here this evening? She worked the day shift today."

"I can solve that mystery for you." Ethel replies. "I spoke with her before dinner. Somebody called in sick. She agreed to pull a double shift."

"She's going to be so tired if she has to come in early tomorrow morning. I don't like the way the staff are overworked here. Too few of them to do too many tasks."

Ethel nods. "I can't argue there, but that is a problem best left for another day. One case at a time for the Old Farts Detective Agency eh?"

"Oh! Ethel! You have such a way with words."

Ethel grabs my arm. "Oh-oh. Finneyfrock alert."

"What's she doing here at this hour?" I can't believe it. "We don't see her on Sunday nights as a rule."

Sunday is usually the day when we get a lovely roast dinner, but the rest of the staff are on skeleton crew. It's not the day when big tasks get done, when the lawns get mowed and the supplies are all stocked up. That happens on a more industrious day like Monday.

"Gabe's having quite the chat with Finneyfrock now." Ethel sighs. "Do you think we're going to look conspicuous just standing here waiting for them to start moving again?"

"We had better look like we're having a deep conversation or something."

"Well, that's what we're doing, isn't it?" Ethel's eyebrows lift. "This police surveillance stuff is harder than it looks, wouldn't you say?"

I glance over at the attendant's desk while trying not to look like I'm doing it. Nobody notices, or so I think, until Evangeline smiles and gives me a friendly wink.

"Oh!" I smile back. That isn't even fake. I hope it doesn't look strained. I send her a little wave and then turn back to my 'deep' conversation with Ethel.

"So how is Savannah doing in that summer art class you said she was taking?" I ask, not caring that much about the answer.

Ethel's face lights up. "She loves it! Marianne says that the teacher is encouraging her to enroll Savannah in a special elementary school that focusses on kids who are gifted in the arts. It's a modest school with small, personal class sizes and Savannah could get the instruction she needs to fully develop her gift."

"That sounds wonderful." I smile and nod.

"It is. You know, I wish there had been something like that for me when I was a girl. Maybe I would have pursued my dream of being a writer in my younger years instead of waiting until the last minute."

I pat her shoulder. "I'm inspired by you, Ethel. It's good that you're still pursuing a dream."

"Really?"

"Really."

"I hope you still feel that way when you find out what I'm writing." Ethel's eyes twinkle.

"What do you mean? Are you writing a tawdry romance novel?" I grin at the thought. "I do wish you would spill the beans. I can't stand the curiosity any longer."

"No. It's not a romance. I'm writing a book called… are you ready for this? *The Granny Diaries*."

"*The Granny Diaries?*"

Ethel throws her head back and laughs. "Yeah. It's about…" She hesitates. "… four friends and their adventures in a retirement villa."

A golf ball could fly into my open mouth right now and make a hole in one. "Ethel? Are you saying… are you writing about… us?"

Now she is doubled over, laughing harder. "That's exactly what I'm saying."

I don't know what to think about that. I don't know if I want my personal life splashed across the pages of some book on the shelf at *Chapters*. What is Ethel writing about? What is she writing about me? Is she telling the world that I'm a silly old woman with a wrinkly face and old fashioned values? A dinosaur who is about to go extinct?

"I shouldn't have told you." Ethel sighs as the laughter dies away. "You don't look pleased. I'm changing the names. Nobody will know it's us. They won't even know it's real."

I don't want to discourage Ethel's dream. "I'm pleased that you're writing a book. It's just… who would want to read about my boring life? All the bestsellers these days seem to be about young couples falling in or out of love or detectives investigating murders or handsome vampires that make a horrible death seem like a romantic thing instead of what it is… a horrible death."

"Look around us. Look at this place." Ethel stretches her arms out. "All of these people have interesting lives. We have lived for a lot of years and I think our adventures are as exciting and funny and engaging as anything else."

I can see the truth in what she says. Old folks, we have lived a long time and we have seen some amazing things. Maybe that is worth writing (and reading) about.

"Oh, for the love of…!"

"Ethel, what is it?"

She points toward the attendant's station. Gabe is still standing there having what looks like a rather intense conversation with Biddy and Evangeline. One of his sons is standing beside him. The problem is… where in the world did Donkey go?

Ethel MacNarland

Running is not recommended at age 72. Yet here I am, breaking out into a run… okay, a light jog… okay, maybe we are just walking really fast and heading past the main attendant's desk. Somehow, Donkey has wandered away and managed to give us the slip.

"Come on, Gladdy!" I have her arm and we are moving at a fair clip.

"Slow down, Ladies!" Biddy Finneyfrock caws as we pass by. "We don't run in the halls here!"

I respond without thinking first. "Sir, yes, Sir!" My hand flies up to my forehead in a salute.

"Ethel!" Gladys sounds alarmed. "We'll draw attention…"

"Oh, pshaw! We're having a seniors' moment." I say softly, before raising my voice and shouting: "Last one to my room is a rotten egg!" *See, Gladdy? I know how to cover our tracks!*

As we round the corner, I am distressed at what I don't see. Where is Donkey?

"We've lost her." Gladdy stops to catch her breath, her delicate green eyes misting over.

"That tricky dame!"

This corridor is long. It's part of a U-shaped section of the building that boasts all of the ladies' quarters. The men have their own section on the other side past all the activity rooms. It's all very prim and proper and kids' summer camp-ish. We are 70 plus years old and need chaperones and babysitters and camp counselors telling us what to do.

"I'm afraid for her." Gladdy moans, the tears beginning to spill over onto her cheeks now. "What is being done to her? We're so stupid! We can't even protect her!"

I rub her slight shoulders and look into her face. "Now now, Gladdy… Dear Heart… that's what you always say, but to me, that's what you are."

"Oh, Ethel... I just..."

"Hush. This isn't that complicated."

"It isn't? I'm afraid I turned out to be a pretty poor detective."

I chuckle. "It's elementary, my dear Gladys..."

"This isn't a joke!"

"Don't go all Tallulah Pratt on me." I shrug. "What is the most obvious thing to do now?"

"I'm praying."

"Okay, after that, what should we do? There really is only one logical choice. If Donkey isn't in the corridor here and she didn't double back and pass us going back the other way, there are only so many places she could go and my bets are on..."

"Oh!" Gladdy's face lights up a little. "Yes, let's do that."

Now we strut down that hallway like a couple of plucky hens. Rounding another corner, I don't see anyone familiar. Not a cleaner or a straggling resident. The coast is clear.

"Should we knock first?" Gladdy hesitates.

I shake my head. "We're going in."

"But what if she gets upset with..."

"Gladdy, how many times has that woman sleepwalked into your room?"

A wry grin comes over Gladys' face and I'm relieved to see the teardrops gone from her eyes.

I look at her and mouth: "One..." I put my hand on the knob of the door. "Two..." I grit my teeth with determination. "Three..."

CLICK! WHOOSH! BAM!

My heart lurches in my chest. "What in the blazes is going on here?"

Tallulah Pratt (Lula)

Chez Napoleon is a little gem of a restaurant in this city. It's not grand. I mean, the building is simple and elegant, not flashy and gauche. Simple grey stone frames quaint, tall windows grouped together in threes, a red awning overhanging the door.

I love the ambience as we step inside. Soft lighting spills over the lobby, frosted glass partitions hemming us in as we await an escort to our table.

"Reservations for Muggeridge." Will smiles at the waiter and it does me in to see the uncanny resemblance to his father. I don't know if I will ever get used to that.

The waiter scans his list. "Ah, yes. The rest of your party has arrived already. Follow me."

Butterflies swarm in my stomach. I shouldn't be nervous. Lordy, if the rest of Emmett's family are as lovely as his son and daughter-in-law, all my fretting has been for nothing. Isn't that the way it always is with me?

We follow the waiter past the regular dining room where at least ten tables are filled with happy customers filling their faces and chatting with each other. We go through a high, elegant archway into a section of the restaurant that I have never seen before, a room that people can book for special functions.

That makes me curious. Emmett doesn't have that many children. Why would he need to book a large room in the back? I want to ask him. The nervousness returns. *Emmett Muggeridge, what have you gotten me into? I don't care how good the food is here. I can march right back to Tranquil Meadows without you if I don't like it! I will hail a cab faster than you can say 'Hey! Where did that redhead go?'*

"Darling, are you all right?" Emmett puts on his best smile, and yes, I know he is 'putting it on', trying to fake me out, distract me from whatever shenanigans he is up to.

"I'm fine." I lie.

He cocks his head to one side. "Are you sure? You've got that face on."

"What face?" What is he talking about? I only have one face. Who does he think I am, Dr. Jekyll and Mr. Hyde?

"Nothing."

"Nothing? You can't just make a statement like that, Emmett Muggeridge, and expect me not to notice it." I remove my arm from his grip and snap it down at my side.

He sighs. "You looked a little…" He pauses. "…worried. I don't want you to feel uncomfortable, that's all."

I'm sure that is not all that he meant, but that answer will have to do. We have arrived and… what on earth is going on here?

A pretty, dark-haired, middle-aged woman jumps up from her table and rushes over to greet us, hand extended toward me. "Oh Daddy! She's as lovely as you said." She smiles and shows off a perfect row of dazzling white teeth. "Mrs. Pratt. I'm Connie Larson and these are my boys, Emmett and Daniel." She indicates two well-dressed pre-teens with the same dark hair as hers, slicked back and parted to the side like mothers do for weddings and picture day at school.

I paint on the biggest smile I can. It isn't hard to do when looking at such lovely children. "Hello." I shake her hand, but she is having none of that. She pulls me into an embrace. "Oh!" I laugh. "I'm Lula, but you already know that."

I note the absence of a husband in the picture. Emmett told me about her painful divorce. He ran off with another woman. Ha! Of course he did! Philandering jackass! I don't want to think about that subject though. This is a happy occasion and both Emmett and his son Will seem to be exceptions to that equation.

Well, now that I have met Emmett's children, perhaps now he can explain something to me. "Emmett, what in the world...? You never told me there would be... that this would be..."

He grins. "I wanted it to be a surprise."

And surprised I am!

"Hello, Mom." My son, Stephen, greets me and smiles as he comes over to hug me.

In fact, all of my children are here and they have rushed over to us.

"How did you manage this?" I ask, wanting to be irritated with Emmett for his ruse, but my heart is so happy to see all of my children together under one roof, how can I be anything but grateful right now? "I'm so glad to see all of you!" I say this to Shelley, Sam and Stephen and I sign it to my deaf daughter, Sarah.

My grandchildren are dressed up like little ladies and gentlemen. This has become quite the occasion. I have never known men to be so adept at pulling off these things, but my Emmett did it, and I didn't suspect a thing!

Hugs and smiles are all around me and I feel so happy, why I could burst into a million joyful pieces.

"Will and Susie dropped into Sarah's flower shop." Emmett explained. "They talked about it and the idea grew from there."

"Well, it was a wonderful idea." I have to admit that. Yes, I was hesitant to come, but looking over both Emmett's family and mine, it all looks so lovely. They're all beautiful and smiling and my children are greeting Emmett and seem just as taken with him as his children are with me. Who would have thought?!

"Why don't you and Emmett come and sit down, Mother?" Stephen escorts us to a place in the middle of one of the long tables that the restaurant reserved for us.

Now I have Emmett holding one arm and my oldest son holding the other. "All right." I am grinning like the Cheshire cat from "Alice in Wonderland." "I still can't believe you're all here. Lordy, I think… I think I might be speechless…"

A soft chuckle comes out of Emmett's mouth. "There's a first time for everything."

"What?" I ought to swat Emmett for a crack like that, but I can't do anything but enjoy this special moment. I am completely surrounded by people that I love. How wonderful that feels!

Dawn Kehoe (Donkey)

"No, Lowell. No. I'm not giving you one more penny." I know it's dangerous to defy him.

"Sign it! Come on! It's only a hundred dollars."

Why does it hurt? He has a hold of my arm. He is squeezing too tight.

"I earned it myself." I protest. I know he just wants to go out drinking again at Marty's Bar. "I won't give it to you. Gabe needs milk. He needs a new pair of shoes."

"Sign it!"

Lowell forces my hand down to the paper. I resist. I pull back. He is stronger than I am. Why did I ever marry him? Some mistakes aren't written in pencil. You can't just erase them.

"Stop fighting me! Do it!"

"Ow!" I wince. The pain and pressure on my wrist frightens me. What if he breaks a bone? "Ow, Lowell! All right! All right! Just don't hurt me anymore…"

I am about to sign my name when I hear a noise.

I look up.

Lowell says a bad word.

A bright light hurts my eyes.

BAM! A door swings open.

I hear a voice. Is it an angel from Heaven? Am I dead?

"What in the blazes is going on here?"

Chapter Nineteen

Gladys Peachy

I stand frozen in place; my feet glued, it seems, to the white tiled floor. My eyes see something, but my brain refuses to admit to what it is. It is too heinous, too sad, and my mind and my emotions balk like a rebellious, frightened horse at the truth that lies so blatantly before me.

"You get your hands off of her!" I hear Ethel shouting, venom-laced syllables launching like a missile.

"Shut up! I can spend time with my Gran if I want to!"

I don't know the boy... is he a boy? I don't know the young man that looms taller than any of us just now. I have seen him before, but we have never spoken. He is in the corner of the room hovering, leaning like a death-feeding vulture over Donkey while she sits, teary eyed and oblivious, pen loosely sitting in one hand.

"We know what you've been doing!" Ethel snarls. I never knew she could be so stern. I would have believed it about Lula in a heartbeat, but Ethel is the one who is always laughing, always joking, though right now, she is anything but jovial.

"I'm visiting with Gran!" The boy-man chides. "So if you don't mind, you're interrupting. Go back to your knitting, or whatever you old ladies do."

I fight the desire to run out of here as fast as I can go. I hate confrontations. Didn't I say that before? I hate them so much. They turn my insides to water, but there is something else I hate, even more than that. I hate seeing my dear dear Donkey sitting there, obviously fearful, pitifully powerless.

"Donkey, are you all right?" I ask, rushing toward her.

Her grandson steps between us, his expression threatening and dripping with malice. "You leave us alone! This is a family thing."

He could hurt me. A fear bullet hits me and I shiver without meaning to. "You must be... Tyler? Connor? Which one of Donkey's grandsons are you?"

His leer cows me, but I refuse to back off, wobbly as I feel.

"Connor. That's right." He says. "You two can visit with Gran later. We were having our special time together, weren't we, Gran?" He tosses a glance back at her.

Donkey doesn't seem to register that any of us are even here.

"Lowell..." That is the only word I can discern from her senseless rambling.

Ethel is right behind me now. "Don't you hurt her." She wags a finger toward his face.

"I'm not going to hurt anyone." Connor laughs. "What is with you ladies? Do you even know what day it is? Are you going to tell me that Pierre Trudeau is still the prime minister?"

He thinks we're dotty! What a rude boy...

"We've got all our marbles, Sonny." Ethel folds her arms across her chest. "And you ought to have a little respect."

Connor turns his nasty attention toward Ethel for a second, which gives me the opportunity to slip past him and get to Donkey. What I see, to my horror, is a partially filled out cheque on her desk, a pen sitting not so much in, but against, her hand and a welt on her arm that, no doubt, will become an unsightly bruise later on.

"Hey!" Connor whirls around as I reach out to hug Donkey. He grabs me by the arm and the pain shoots into my flesh from the tips of his strong fingers. He's a formidable young man, physically at least. No wonder Donkey couldn't resist him.

"You let her go!" Ethel orders.

He does not comply.

"You ought to be ashamed of yourself." Ethel hisses.

"That's right." I add. "What kind of a person robs his own grandmother?"

"I'm not robbing anybody. She gives me gifts sometimes."

"Gifts?" Ethel snickers. "Is that what you call it?"

Connor's grip on my arm tightens. I wince.

Ethel grabs his elbow, trying to pull him away from me, but she doesn't have the strength to do it.

Oh... it feels like the bone will bend and break beneath the pressure.

Ow... I feel a sudden sharp pain in my chest.

God? This isn't something I ever expected to face in my life. This violence is foreign to me. It shouldn't happen to anyone. Please... help me... he must... he must... "Let go..." I whisper. "Oh... Paul..." I am going to fall... a fuzzy feeling spreads through my head... everything takes on a whitish aura.

"Who's Paul? This one doesn't know me either." Connor starts walking me toward the door. "It's time for you to go now and find Paul."

I stumble like a drunkard beside him, feet barely finding their way one in front of the other.

"Let go!" Ethel yells.

"Connor!"

The sternness of the voice causes Connor Kehoe to loosen his grip on my arm, but the throbbing remains as if he were still squeezing me, hurting me... I grab the wall to steady myself.

Ethel is beside me all of a sudden, her arm reaching out to me. I hope I don't take her down to the floor with me if I fall.

"Tyler." Connor smiles in that same slick way that a used car salesman does. "Is Dad ready to go?"

Tyler sees Ethel struggling to help me and puts an arm around my waist, leading me to the edge of Donkey's bed.

"Are you okay?" He asks, concern written on his nearly cherubic face.

I nod. Ethel sits down beside me, rubbing my back with her hand. I let myself lean into her, waiting for my equilibrium to return.

"Dad is still chatting with the administrator." Tyler purses his lips tight, blanching as his eyes land on Donkey. "What are you doing to her? Gran?"

Connor laughs softly. "What do you think? Gran was tired. I brought her here so she could sit down."

I am about to protest, but I don't get the chance.

"Like hell!" Tyler strides across the floor of Donkey's private room.

Connor intercepts him. "What's wrong, Little Bro? Don't believe me? Think I would lie?" He grabs Tyler by the arm and I see the same pained expression that must have just been on my own face.

Tyler can't hold Connor's gaze. He looks at the floor. He seems to be just as cowed as Donkey is, and who can blame him? Connor is bigger, older, and likely the one he has looked up to all his life. We can't expect him to resolve this, but I am grateful that he came and interrupted what was happening to me.

Apparently, Ethel is intimidated too. I watch as she rises from where she was sitting next to me, rushes toward the door and opens it, taking flight into the hallway. Who can blame her? Neither of us anticipated such a terrible thing. Detective work is harder than it looks on TV. I have decided that it isn't for me.

Ethel MacNarland

"Mr. Kehoe! Mr. Kehoe!" I am cawing at the top of my lungs like some maniacal crow, my voice crackling and strained. "Please, Mr. Kehoe! Come quickly!"

As I round the corner, I find Gabriel Kehoe still chatting, rather heatedly it appears, with Biddy Finneyfrock and Evangeline Martin. Evangeline is marking something down on a clipboard. Normally, I wouldn't interrupt, but there is nothing normal about these circumstances.

"Mr. Kehoe! Hurry!" I nearly trip over my own feet.

"Mrs. MacNarland!" Evangeline drops the clipboard and it slams down on the floor as she rushes to keep me up on my feet. "You shouldn't run like that!"

I open my mouth to talk and find myself out of breath. "Oh, but..." I gasp. "...it's Dawn. There's been trouble... her grandson... I..." I don't know how to break this to Donkey's son, but one of his children is a conniving little monster! I guess there's no easy way to relay that kind of news.

"Trouble?" Gabe Kehoe turns to face me. "Is my mother all right? Where is she?" He looks around. "Where are the boys? They were right here."

"No, they weren't." I say, more sternly than I intended. "What I mean is... they haven't been for a while. I... oh! I can't explain now! Follow me!"

And that is how I started a parade at Tranquil Meadows Seniors Villa. Off I marched. Evangeline followed, still trying to keep hold of my arm. *Well, step it up, Woman, or I'll leave you in the dust!*

Then came Mr. Kehoe and the ever militaristic Biddy Finneyfrock, looking every bit the cold piece of work that she is. We are in fine form, causing the eyes of some cart-pushing orderly type to turn and gawk as we go by, me full of purpose. I don't know what they're full of... probably wondering if it's time to ship me off across the way. They likely think I'm off my nut!

Oh, you stupid bladder! You have picked an inconvenient time to send me a signal to find the bathroom. Too bad! I'm not doing that until Donkey and Gladdy are safely away from Connor Kehoe! If that means I tinkle a bit, then so be it. I've got my big girl potty training pants on!

Evangeline gets to Donkey's door slightly ahead of me and opens it.

"Ow! Let go of me!"

I hear Donkey's other grandson. Poor Tyler! He's on the floor, the older boy having just pushed him there.

"I told you not to interfere!" Connor snarls.

"I'm not letting you do this anymore!" Tyler's words sound so brave, but they are quivering with emotion and I see a tear streaming down one cheek.

"Oh, dear God!" Evangeline's hand flies up to her mouth.

"What is going on here?" Gabe Kehoe's voice oozes strength and shock. "Connor! What are you doing to your brother? Where is your grandmother?"

Gladys points behind Connor to the desk and Donkey sitting on the chair behind it. Then, she quickly pulls her arm back, fear evident on her face as she notices Biddy standing behind Gabe, eyes fiery and curious. Gladdy tosses me a sad look.

I agree with what she's not saying in words. It looks like Donkey's boat may be sunk. The secret about her ever-increasing dementia will be out.

"We were just playing, Dad." Connor puts on his best angelic face. It comes across to me as smug.

"We were not!" Tyler begins to protest, but Connor shoots him a severe look that shuts him up as fast as if he had slugged the kid in the jaw.

"Gladdy, are you all right?" I scuttle over to her, still seated on the bed and rubbing the spot on her arm where Connor grabbed her just moments ago.

"I'm fine." She nods, but she looks like she might throw up.

"Mother!" Gabe flies past his sons and everyone else and reaches her side. "What happened?"

Discouragement drops like an anvil on top of my emotions. One mention of Lowell or Cary Grant or whomever Donkey was married to on TV this morning and I know she will be sentenced to Tranquil Meadows Plus, the stinking roach motel. What can I do? There's no way to create a diversion to cover for our friend. I could just cry.

I look over and see that Gladys already has a tear inching down one cheek.

Donkey looks up slowly. She doesn't notice me or Biddy or Connor or Tyler, but wow! Her face lights up like a Christmas tree when she looks into the face of her son.

"Gabe!" Donkey smiles. "You're here!"

Gabe Kehoe gently caresses his mother's cheek. I feel guilty for thinking he was hurting Donkey just a short while ago. What made me think that?

"I'm here. I'm always going to be here for you." He kisses the top of her head. "It's been you and me for a long long time."

Donkey leans her head against him and I hear a sigh of utter relief pour out of her.

"What's this?" Gabe notices what is on the desk in front of Donkey. "Mother, what have you been doing?"

Donkey gets a serious look on her face.

I hope she doesn't blow it.

I notice Gladdy mouthing words. I know her. She's praying.

"It's him." Donkey points toward Connor. "He should be a good boy."

Connor's face sinks and I see the first crack in his stern, mean resolve. "No. Gran..."

Gabriel's expression turns dark. "This is a cheque! It's..." He looks at his eldest son. "...what have you done? I was blaming the staff here for taking my mother's money, but..." Steam isn't literally coming out Gabe's ears, but it should be. "...what would possess you to do something like that?"

"Dad! I didn't do anything..." Connor's lies are flimsy little scraps of paper blowing in the wind.

"I apologize to both of you." Gabe says to Evangeline and Biddy. "Don't worry. I'll deal with my son..."

Connor squeals like a scared pig as his father advances and grabs him by the shirt collar. "No... no!"

"Dad?" Tyler hangs his head.

"Tyler, can you look after your grandmother for a few moments while your brother and I go and deal with these things? Ms. Finneyfrock, can we discuss this in your office?"

"Absolutely." As if this day hadn't been shocking enough, here is where I saw Biddy Finneyfrock smile, and it was genuine. "I'm relieved to resolve this issue, Mr. Kehoe. I don't want anyone harmed or taken advantage of. Not on my watch!"

With that, Biddy, Evangeline, Gabe and a reluctant Connor leave the room and Gladys, Tyler, Donkey and I are left alone.

"Are you okay, Gran?" Tyler slips his arms around Donkey from behind, resting his head on top of hers, a tear streaming down his face. "I'm not going to let Connor hurt you ever again."

Donkey smiles and pats his hand. "You're a good boy, Gabe. You saved me."

Tyler grins. "Gabe?"

I chime in. "Just go with it."

Tyler laughs. "Yeah, I know." He kisses Donkey's head. "I love you, Gran."

"Are you all right?" I rub Gladdy's back. "I'm sorry that brute hurt you."

Gladdy shrugs. "I'm all right, Dear Heart." She turns her attention toward Tyler. "Tyler, Donk... I mean... Dawn told us that you sing in the Glee Club at your school."

How sweet Gladys is, I think, to try and divert Tyler's attention away from the nasty events that have just unfolded.

"Yeah." He replies. "We came in first at the regional competition last spring, but we lost at nationals. Next year, we're going to get 'em. We'll practise harder!"

Gladys gives him her sweetest grandmotherly smile. I think what a good grandma she would have been if only she had been able to have children.

"Does your Glee Club sometimes perform in public?"

Where is Gladdy going with that?

"I mean..." She continues. "...would you ever consider coming here to perform for us at Tranquil Meadows?"

Tyler's mouth opens as if he's going to sing an aria. "Here?! Yeah! I'm sure that could be arranged, and then I could show Gran. I know Gran used to be an amazing entertainer. Dad told me."

"Did he?" Gladdy's smile is a mile wide. "Well, we have an opening in our activities calendar and we would love to have you come."

"I'll talk to our director about it. That would be awesome!" Tyler takes Donkey's hand. "Would you like that, Gran? Would you like it if I came here to sing for you?"

Donkey nods. "You can sing for me anytime, Gabe."

I look at Gladys. "Who told you we have an opening in our activities calendar?"

Gladys shakes her head. "A little bird told me. The Glee Club could come in on Tuesdays once a month, right in that slot that used to belong to St. Barts."

I double over laughing. "Yes, that's perfect!"

Now we just need to convince the administration to allow it. We'll get Lula right on that.

Speaking of Lula..."Oh boy, imagine Lula's reaction when she gets back and we tell her what went on today."

Gladys puts a hand over her mouth. "We are going to be in big big trouble, Ethel!"

Tallulah Pratt (Lula)

Oh my! It has been a long time since I sipped a glass of champagne. I think the last time may have been... Lordy, I don't remember the last time. Does that mean I am getting as forgetful as Donkey?

If I keep smiling like this, my face is going to freeze this way. There I will be with a perpetual grin, always looking happy as a clam, even if I'm ticked off at somebody. I should give my face a rest and stop this, but I simply can't!

My children are sitting in the same room with me. Then, there is Emmett's son, the spitting image of him. There is his daughter, who seems so lovely and accepting. I don't know why I was worried about what they would think. Look at them! They're not put off by me. If they are, they should get Academy Awards for the performance of a lifetime.

Emmett signals for the waiter to pour more champagne into the elegant crystal flute in front of me.

"I shouldn't, Emmett. What will they say back at Tranquil Meadows if we both stumble in like a pair of winos?" I giggle a little at that. My hand clamps over my mouth to stop it. I sound like a silly teenager.

Emmett chuckles too. "We should sneak some of this stuff into Ms. Finneyfrock's coffee mug." The waiter tops up his glass too. "She could use a little help loosening up, don't you think?"

I don't know why that makes me burst out cackling like a crazy hen. "Imagine that old battle axe with a few drinks in her. That would be such fun!"

The whole evening has been like this... like I am on the most exhilarating ride at the amusement park. I feel thrilled and joyful and childish. No. Not childish... childlike. This may be the first time in my 72-year-old life that I understand the difference between those two words.

"It's wonderful to hear you laugh, Tallulah." Emmett looks deep into my eyes and my breath seems to catch in my throat. "You have the most beautiful laugh."

Beautiful is not a word I ever expected to hear at my age. We women tend to fall off the romance radar once we're not perky and young and gullible anymore. Is this a dream? Am I going to wake up to find I imagined it all? Am I foolish for trusting that this isn't all going to blow up in my face?

Emmett's hazel eyes twinkle with merriment and sentiment and I do love to stare into them. It isn't hard to return his smile or the affection he so freely offers me. "Emmett, I am having an unbelievably lovely time tonight. Thank you for arranging all of this."

We have enjoyed food and conversation and I know it has to end soon, but what a precious memory this will be.

Clink clink clink clink clink...

Emmett bangs on the side of his glass with a spoon.

"And now, if I might have your attention." Emmett announces.

I turn to watch and wait and listen. This evening has been perfect. What on earth is that man up to now?

With a sly smirk, Emmett reaches a hand into his pants pocket and pulls out a folded piece of paper, opening it with meticulous care and shielding it from my inquiring eyes.

He clears his throat.

"As you all know, Tallulah and I have been courting these past few months and may I say…" He bites his bottom lip. "…I am happier than I have been in a very long time. I only hope the feeling is mutual."

Every pair of hands except Emmett's and mine are clapping now and the room is full of smiling faces. I feel a little embarrassed… or maybe that's the wrong word… self-conscious… don't I enjoy being the center of attention? Aren't I the venerable peacock fanning out my proverbial feathers for all to see? Why do I suddenly feel squirmy? I am a strong, determined woman. I am not a mouse!

Emmett continues. "I wrote a little something to express my…" He hesitates. "…my appreciation for the fine lady sitting beside me this evening."

Okay, now I am smiling and enjoying this. Emmett called me a fine lady. I could get used to that!

"And so…" Emmett goes on. "…please indulge an old… well, an older man for a moment while I read these lines from the heart."

The room goes quiet enough to hear a fly cough.

My heart flutters like a timid butterfly perched on a flower.

Emmett's words flow as gentle and clean as a crystalline mountain stream.

"My heart has wings
It leaps and sings
Every hour you are by my side

It will stay that way
If you agree today
To be my beautiful blushing bride…"

As Emmett's poem finishes, my daughter Sarah, excellent lip

reader that she is, pulls a rose from somewhere... where was she hiding that? She reaches out with the rose in her hand and Emmett takes the lovely red blossom and offers it to me.

I am trembling and glued in place... too stunned to move... and I watch as Will, Emmett's son, hands Emmett a dainty box coloured midnight blue. I know what it must contain. I don't know what to say or think or do.

Emmett takes the box and opens it, revealing the sparkling diamond inside... hidden within the velvety softness. He slides the ring onto the third finger of my left hand, making me really thankful that I didn't decide to be a martyr and keep Tom's rings on forever.

"Listen to me." Emmett says. "Diamonds spend a lot of time hidden in the deep dark depths, embedded in the dirt and filth where nobody can see them shine. That is who you are to me, Tallulah. You are a diamond, hidden too long by the hurts and circumstances of life. I want to walk with you, side by side... savour whatever time we have here. What do you say? Can you see yourself in a pretty dress in front of a preacher... one more time?"

Silence follows those heartfelt and pretty words.

I love you, Emmett. I can't deny that it's true.

I want to scream yes yes yes!

I hurt Tom. I was a bad wife. I don't want to do that again!

"I..." My throat is as dry as the Sahara. "I..."

Tears threaten to spill over onto my cheeks. I want to run from this room like a frightened child.

"Tallulah?" Emmett's earnest, expectant eyes bear down on me.

He needs an answer. He deserves one.

Lordy, but I am afraid to let go and let love overtake me.

I am about to fail the most loving man I have ever met.

I feel a sharp slap on my arm.

I turn to see Sarah, eyes flashing, hands flying in sign, which I understand perfectly, but Emmett does not.

"What is wrong, Mother? I know that you love Emmett." She forces a smile, but I can tell that she is upset with me.

"I'm afraid." I sign to her.

"Don't be scared." She signs. "Tell Emmett yes. Yes, you will marry him."

I want to, but...

"Tell him yes! It's what you want to do!" Sarah gestures toward her siblings before signing again. "We love you. Shelley, Stephen, Sam and me. We want you to be happy."

That is the wisdom of my dear deaf daughter. She always makes things so simple. I am the one who complicates life and overthinks everything.

Her smile gives me a courage that I didn't know I had.

I turn back to Emmett, grinning like a child. "Emmett Muggeridge..." I say with conviction. "...I would be honoured to be your wife."

The ring feels as light as a feather. It's not a solitaire, but two smaller diamonds surrounded by a lovely setting. I sigh with a relieved happiness that I pray will last till death do us part.

"You had me worried there for a minute." Emmett lifts my hand up to his mouth and kisses it.

"Well, it is a woman's prerogative to keep a man waiting, isn't it?" I quip.

With that, the whole room erupts with laughter.

Dawn Kehoe (Donkey)

"Ding dong! The witch is dead!" I am singing and dancing in my room all by myself.

I am supposed to be sleeping. If Jean Montgomery finds out that I am up after lights out, she won't be too pleased with me.

For some reason, I feel happy.

I open the door to my closet.

"The monster is gone." I shut the door again.

I bend down down down and look under the bed.

"Ha! The monster isn't there either."

Lowell is dead. He's not coming back anymore. My Gabriel is safe! He's a good boy! A good boy!

I don't know why the Jean Montgomery School of Music makes me go to bed so early... and where is the other bed? It's two students to a room!

I got the lead in the new concert. I get to sing and dance in front of a whole room full of people. I'm going to make Eve so jealous! For a change, all the eyes will be on me... Dawn Gardiner... talented singer and dancer extraordinaire!

Hurry hurry hurry! Get your tickets! Opening night is coming soon.

Chapter Twenty

Gladys Peachy

I have always been confident of this truth. The Lord in Heaven is so kind. His love reaches down to the lowest of valleys and up to the highest of mountains. I can't remember a time when I didn't know that. It seems just as real and poignant today as it did when I was a child.

Donkey is safe. Her grandson won't be visiting here anymore. Her son isn't the cad we thought he was and that is good for Donkey. Despite the rather large deep blue map of Texas that was on my arm this morning when I awoke, there is a smile on my face as I sit in the recliner beside the white and blue paisley sofa in the activity room. The bruise (and a couple of other smaller marks beside it) smarts a bit, but it won't last long, so I won't complain.

"9 across. What's an eight letter word, the clue is wedding?" I stare at the crossword puzzle on my lap, brow furrowing.

"Marriage." Emmett says, tossing a mischievous grin at Lula who is seated on the sofa beside him.

Lula rolls her eyes, but she smiles too.

"Uh uh." I shake my head. "Right number of letters, but it doesn't match with the letters I already have filled in for 6 and 8 down."

Emmett shrugs.

"I still can't believe you and Ethel solved the mystery of Donkey's bruises without me." Lula huffs. "That's a nasty injury he gave you, Gladdy!"

I look at my arm. "I think I'll leave the detective work to

Sherlock Holmes from now on. That's too much adventure for me."

"I'd like to give that no good delinquent a piece of my mind!" Lula's blue eyes flash with sternness. "Hurting our Donkey and then attacking you too? It's unconscionable!"

"Ethel overheard Evangeline Martin talking about it. Apparently, young Connor got in with the wrong crowd and he's been doing drugs or some such thing. I guess habits like that are expensive and he was stealing money to pay for it." I frown. How thankful I feel that I never got involved in things like that! How different might my life story be?

"Well, I'm just grateful that you're all right!" Lula reaches over to pat my good arm.

"Nuptials!" Emmett pipes in all of a sudden.

Both Lula and I turn to give him funny looks.

"The crossword." He chuckles. "Have you forgotten already? An eight letter word for wedding."

I burst out laughing. "Oh! I guess I did!" My cheeks turn red.

"You've got weddings on the brain." Lula swats him, but her smile tells me that her ire is as fake as a three-dollar bill.

I note that nuptials fits perfectly and fill in the letters.

"You should have weddings on the brain too." Emmett grabs Lula's hand and kisses it fondly. "If you don't start thinking about it, I'll pick the wrong colours for everything. I guarantee I will!"

"Oh! Emmett!"

"I'm telling you. We'd better pick a date fast. I'm going to put… the… I'm going to… well, I will sure enough have one of them blue polyester suits with the… you know… the ones with the frilly dress shirts like they wore in the 1970s…"

"Emmett! Those were an abomination to all things fashionable!" Lula's mouth is wide open now, even though Emmett is obviously pulling her leg.

He laughs and slaps his knee in amusement. "I might wear a sparkly silver suit jacket and a matching fedora."

"You will do no such thing!"

"I'll find a replica of John Travolta's Saturday Night Fever outfit cuz we should celebrate stayin' alive, shouldn't we?"

"Emmett! Really!"

I grin at the two of them. Aren't they lovely? I thanked God profusely at the breakfast table this morning when Lula broke the news and showed off that ring as if it were a gift from King Solomon himself. You should have seen her. She made sure Jenny Logan got a good look too! That naughty redhead!

"Well, have you actually thought about it yet?" I interrupt.

They both stop their bantering and look at me.

"When is the big day going to be? And where are you going to have it? Lula, Emmett is right. There is an awful lot of work to do if… well… if I know you, you're going to want a fancy do with everything matching just so and I'm willing to help out if I can." I give her my best radiant smile.

Lula looks a little bit cross. What reason could there be for that? Her lips are pursed in a straight line across her face and that is not a good look for her. It emphasizes the fine age lines around her mouth.

"Well, tsk! Why don't you two discuss it?" Lula chirps. "Since you're both in such a doggone rush!"

I shrug. Emmett shrugs.

"We just got engaged last night." Lula continues. "I would like to get used to that idea for a little while. You know, I was a widow for a long time and it's overwhelming and I don't want to rush into planning our..." She rolls her eyes and points toward my forgotten crossword puzzle. "...nuptials!"

I try to hold back a grin. "For a woman who is so overwhelmed, you sure did show every person in sight that ring of yours this morning..." I giggle. "...twice... three times, if you count Evangeline."

Lula's unseen, but implied, peacock feathers ruffle. "Oh, but..." She looks down at her finger (again!) and her face relaxes and the lovely smile returns. "It is a beautiful ring. Emmett, you have excellent taste in jewellery."

"M'hm..." Emmett pats her hand. "I do know something fine when I lay eyes on it."

I watch Lula melt right there in front of my eyes. Emmett does know how to turn a phrase with the lady he loves.

"Emmett..." She blushes a bit. "We will plan this wedding. Of course, we will." She leans into his shoulder. "Just let me catch my breath for a few days. You have swept me off of my feet and I need you to give me a little time."

He has the patience of Job, I note, as Emmett nods and acquiesces to Lula's words. They are a beautiful couple. They are a symbol of hope to me. Life is not over when the young ones tell you it is. God's kindness radiates to everyone and just when you thought he was finished with you... bam! He throws in the most delightful surprise.

Ethel MacNarland

The Granny Diaries seems like a cute name for this book. I wonder if anyone will read it. I suppose it doesn't matter. I am going to write it whether a million people read it or it collects dust and nobody does.

I am grinning. I can't help it. You would think that life at a seniors' villa would be mundane, boring even. You would think I would be writing about endless days spent staring at the same dull scenery, counting the time until the Grim Reaper comes to collect us.

Not so! Life can be vibrant and exciting anywhere! I have a real romance to write about!

Lula and Emmett are making my job easy. People say you should write what you know and this story has been dropped right into my lap. I suppose I'll have to change their names. Lula would have my head on a spike if I didn't.

She's going to be upset with me if I choose the wrong name too! It can't be something drab... like Ethel, for example. Ha! I can't call her Mildred. Picture that! Tallulah Pratt, soon to be Muggeridge, reading about her own story and seeing the name Mildred there instead of her own. I'm starting to laugh at the thought of that. Now I have to pee!

I stumble across the room to the bathroom, laughing all the way and trying not to leak. Mildred! She would murder me... twice! Imagine picking a name for her like Gerty... or Bessie... or Hilda. Hahaha... no! What name should I actually use? It has to be elegant... different, but not too much so. It has to accurately give the readers a picture of our lovely, precocious Tallulah.

I sit on the porcelain throne and think.

Nothing comes to mind. All the possibilities seem either laughable or beneath her. I don't want to inadvertently insult her. Lula and Emmett are one of the focal points of my story.

I wash my hands, head back to my desk and stop to look out the window at the grounds outside.

"There she is." I whisper, a gratified smile expanding across my face. "There is Tallulah right there. I wonder who planted those magnificent roses. Whoever it was, thank you."

Never mind that I don't have an alternate name for Emmett yet. Rose, no Rosa, no... Rosemary is a beautiful pseudonym for Queen Tallulah of the Kingdom of Tranquil Meadows.

Tallulah Pratt (Lula)

Lordy, what is the rush? I just got engaged last night! I have been asked at least a dozen times today when the wedding day is. Newsflash! I don't know when it is. Maybe we won't get married until next year. Maybe it will be the year after that! Does it matter? Emmett and I have made a commitment to be faithful to each other. That ought to be enough.

Cold feet. That's what Gladdy said I have when I talked to her about it in private. I certainly didn't want to talk about it in front of Emmett. He would be all down in the mouth and take it personally.

Well, I do love you, Emmett! I surely do, but the whole idea of wedded bliss and sharing a bed and being under someone's thumb scares me to pieces! You may be a wonderful man. No, correct that. You are a wonderful man. I know that, and I know you wouldn't try to be a bad husband like I wouldn't try to be a bad wife, but I was a bad wife. Emmett, it was all romance and sweetness at that dinner, but what if you find out who I really am? I would disappoint you. I couldn't bear that!

"Penny for your thoughts?"

I look over at Emmett. When did he get here? After supper,

I decided to take a walk in the garden alone to collect my thoughts. The roses smell as beautiful as they look out here. I am enraptured by the artistry of their pink and red blossoms. They have a white rosebush in the garden too. That may not be as bright a colour as some of the others, but it takes my breath away nonetheless.

"Emmett." I slip my arm around his elbow and rest my head against his shoulder. "Are you sure you want me? Do you know what a wretched woman I can be?"

He laughs. Imagine that! I am pouring my utmost fear out to him and he thinks it's funny!

"Don't!" I bite back tears. "I mean it! You deserve much better!"

He pecks the top of my head. "Why are you saying such things? I don't know what is going on in that lively mind of yours."

I try to catch my breath and stop the tears from spilling out.

"I was…" I can't believe I'm going to tell him this. "I was… the walking Frigidaire!"

"The what? Tallulah, what in the world…?"

I drop my hands to my sides. There's no use in pretending anymore. The only way to show this man that he doesn't want to marry me after all is to let him see me… warts and all!

"That's what Tom called me sometimes." I shake my head. "The walking Frigidaire! You know… a fridge… as cold as an Arctic wind… frigid! I loved him. I truly did. I just… there was… I didn't know how… he didn't understand… how could he? I wouldn't tell him about Uncle Wally."

Emmett's face looks bewildered just now. Who can blame him? I'm talking like the Riddler in that old Batman series. Nothing makes sense… to either of us.

Emmett's arms are around me as gently as a mother's. The

warmth makes me want to lean in and tuck myself away like a caterpillar crawling inside a cocoon.

"I love you, Tallulah. It's that simple." He caresses my hair.

"I know that, but..." I am frustrated by my own struggle for words. "...you don't know how... how I can be. How I can... pull away. I can pull away from... from a man... and it wasn't his fault and it won't be your fault it will be all my fault my fault oh but it will be my fault and you will be unhappy and I will feel like a failure and you won't want me anymore..."

I finally stop to take a breath before I faint.

"Stop... stop it... okay..." Emmett coos. "I know I'm not a scientist or a revered academic, but..." He pulls me a little closer. "... I sure enough knew the first time I laid eyes on you that you were a bird with a wound on your wing."

"What? You... knew?"

"Well, I don't know all the details, but yes. Your eyes tell me everything."

I pull back a little, but not out of fear. I want to look into the face of this amazing man. "Emmett, I don't understand. I was married to Tom Pratt for years and he never... I mean..."

Emmett shakes his head. "Didn't he ever ask what was eating at you? Didn't he ever wonder?"

I shrug. "I don't know if he did. Well, he would ask... Tallulah, what in the hell is wrong with you?"

Emmett's eyes soften even more if that were possible. His smile is a bowed little lifeboat and I could get in it and sail safely away from the shipwreck that was my first marriage. His love and insight is something I thought only existed in the silly fairy tale dreams of little girls.

"That is not how you ask a woman a question if you want an

honest answer." He says. "Maybe he wasn't that interested in an answer."

"You think...?"

"I know. I know that if I wanted a scared little mouse to come out of its hole in the wall, I wouldn't shout and berate it." He wipes the tear from my face. "I would set down a little piece of cheese and wait."

That sounds sweet and sentimental, and also somehow infuriating! "What? Am I a scared little mouse? Emmett Muggeridge!"

My rant is cut short.

I see Emmett's smile disappear.

"Emmett?"

"Oh..." He groans. "I feel..."

He falls to one knee.

"Emmett?!" My hands fly to my face. "What's wrong?"

His eyes go back into his head before they close altogether and I watch his body collapse on the newly mown grass.

"Emmett?!" My voice is screaming now. "Emmett?!" I fall to the ground, my arm grabbing for him, shaking him. "Wake up! Oh my God! No!"

There is no response.

My eyes scan the garden, the walkway, the trellis... "Where is everybody?!"

Tears and snot and sweat stream all over me as I run. Yes! Tallulah Pratt! 72 years old! I run toward the building shouting for help at the top of my lungs.

"Help me! Help! God, please! Not now! Don't take him from me now! God! Pleaaase!!"

Dawn Kehoe (Donkey)

I buried you in the cold, hungry ground.

A strange quietness came to my heart.

You are gone. You are gone. You are gone. You are gone. You are...

??????????????????????????????????????

Where am I?

I don't know this place.

??????????????????????????????????????

Is this Heaven?

That lady has a long white coat. That's a little bit like I always pictured angels wearing. I thought the material would be shinier.

Where is the music? I always wanted to play the piano.

"Hello Mrs. Kehoe."

Someone is calling my name. Who is that?

She is a beautiful lady with rich, dark skin and a lovely smile.

Oh, I know! I remember her! Her name is... her name is...

???????????????????????????????

"Can you sing for me?" I ask her.

"Sing for you?" The woman laughs.

Why is that funny? Isn't that Gladys Knight?

"Gladys?" I wonder where her band is. Did they leave already?

"Gladys is over there." The woman points across the room to an old lady in a chair.

That's not Gladys Knight.

"That's Gladys Peachy." That makes me smile. Gladys is my very best friend.

"Would you like to go and sit with her?" Gladys Knight, minus her band, is helping me across the floor to a white and blue sofa.

"Hello Donkey." Gladys says, setting down whatever she was reading.

I see a big bruise on her arm. Wait a minute. I look at my arm. There's a bruise there too.

"Gladys? Did you… how did you get a bruise that matches mine?"

"It wasn't easy." She replies.

Gladys Knight smiles at us and walks away without even singing 'Midnight Train to Georgia'. Oh well. Maybe next time.

I hear a loud noise. What is that?

????????????????????????????????

It's a siren. Are the police here?

"Oh dear." Gladys looks worried. "That's an ambulance. I wonder what they're doing here."

Gladys is looking out the window. I look too and that's when I see the red light flashing.

"They're not here for me." I say. "Lowell is gone. He's dead. I won't be seeing him anymore."

Chapter Twenty-One

Gladys Peachy

"God? It's me, Gladys. Of course, you know that. I can't sleep. You know why I'm awake at this hour. It's poor Emmett and Lula.

Emmett collapsed in the garden last evening. My dear Lula had to run for help The attendant called an ambulance and they took Emmett away on a stretcher. I thought Lula was going to cry herself sick. I know how she feels. I remember those scared hours sitting by Paul's bedside and then... and then... when his end came."

I feel tears rising up in my lower eyelids. It's been a long time. I grieved for Paul so long ago now, but I guess watching them take Emmett away brought the memories back and I find myself still missing my husband as if a part of my insides is gone and I am not as complete as I was when he was here.

"God, sometimes... well, I am grateful for everything. I have had a wonderful and blessed life. There is nothing to complain about, but sometimes I miss Paul so much and I wish I could tell him all about my day, but I can't. There is a hole in my heart that will never be filled this side of Heaven."

And what about Lula? Here I am selfishly thinking about Paul, but Lula and Emmett have only just found each other. They haven't had a lifetime of happy moments. That's not fair.

"God, please don't let Emmett die now." I fold my hands across my chest as I sit up in bed. I want God to know I mean business! "Please reach down with your healing touch and fix whatever is wrong with him. I know you can. Jesus did that when he was here and the Bible says that you never change. You are the same yesterday, today and forever."

A sigh seems to take these burdens out of my soul with it as it escapes my mouth and floats up into the air.

"I know you're going to look after everything. I just need to trust you."

I lay back down and sleep comes to claim me even as my lips keep mumbling… rambling… half-praying… "…and look after Donkey… Donkey… please… Donkey…"

Ethel MacNarland

I can't sleep. For one thing, they served chicken cacciatore for dinner and it has come back to haunt me. If it isn't my bladder making me crazy, it's my digestive system growling, whining and sending the food back up for a second round. Nobody told me getting old would be like this.

I'm a little miffed too. It's silly and it's selfish and I don't know if being a writer is all it's cracked up to be. I mean, sure, I could spend my time writing fluffy bunny stories that don't mean anything. I could write 'Once upon a time there was a fairy princess who was kidnapped and locked in a tower and then came a handsome prince with a dimple on his chin to save her…"

I could do that, but it's not what I want. I am invested in this story now. I am excited about giving people my age a vibrant story, making their lives leap off the page. I want people to pick up this book and not be able to stop reading until the story is over and they're out of breath and sorry to say goodbye to the characters inside it.

I'm a moron. Lula is worried sick over Emmett. Who can blame her? He was taken away in an ambulance, and what am I worried about? I'm thinking about the romance I have been writing in my book. I'm thinking that if something happens to

Emmett, that's not a nice ending, is it? I want to marry them off and have them live happily ever after, however long or short that may be.

My concerns are purely self-serving and I don't know if I like knowing that about myself. Not that I don't care about Lula's heartache. I do! She's my friend! The first thought I had though when she came running in from the garden, screaming for help after Emmett collapsed was... there goes my novel. See? I'm a selfish jerk!

I may as well get up. Sleep isn't coming! What a cranky dame I'm going to be in the morning if this insomnia doesn't soon let up! Still, if there's one thing I hate, it's lying in bed trying to sleep, but not being able to. You can only count ceiling tiles so many times. In case anybody wonders, there are 82 of them in here.

I answer the 'call of the bladder' and then head over to my writing desk.

"Dear Diary:

Ethel MacNarland here. It took me 72 years to discover that I am a selfish jerk. Maybe it's not too late to change. I might feel better if I was Gladys Peachy. I know what she's doing, praying her heart out for Lula and Emmett."

I should try that. Will it make me feel better? I'm not a prayer. It's not something I have ever done on a regular basis. I can recite prayers... the ones I knew as a child. "God is great. God is good. Let us thank him for our food." That won't cut it dealing with Emmett in the hospital.

I shrug and resolve to leave the praying to Gladys for now.

Tallulah Pratt (Lula)

"Tallulah?"

I am sitting on an uncomfortable chair at Emmett's bedside holding his hand in both of mine, lips pressed to the knuckles, praying like the dickens.

"Yes, it's me." I reply as Emmett's hazel eyes finally flutter open. "You gave me the scare of a lifetime! I don't know if I can ever forgive you!"

He smiles. The past few hours of my life have been a nightmare.

"Is that Will?" Emmett's eyes look past me.

"Hi Dad." Will's voice crackles slightly as he approaches the bed in the small cubicle where the ICU staff have monitored Emmett's vital signs since he came in here.

"I don't remember…" Emmett's eyebrows lower, furrows on his forehead deepening. "Wait. I was in the garden." He pauses. "I was with you, Tallulah."

"Yes." I nod. "And then you fainted dead away. Scared me senseless! I thought… well, I thought…" I don't even want to say those words.

"So what happened? This isn't Heaven, so I'm obviously still here." Emmett tries to sit up, but Will puts a hand out to stop him.

"Wait." He urges. "I can put the head of the bed up a bit for you." He adjusts the hospital bed and now Emmett can see this drab little room.

I ponder that some people spend their last moments in a dungeon like this with horrible colours, machines beeping and nothing beautiful to look at… just gadgets and contraptions with company names, weird words, charts depicting body parts.

"Your blood pressure. It went low." Will says. "Has it done that before?"

Emmett shakes his head. "No. Not that I can recall. In fact, I thought they put me on a medication because it was a wee bit high." He grins at me. "I took my pill yesterday. I keep my meds in one of those little plastic things that shows you Monday through Sunday, morning and evening."

"M'hm." Will gets a funny look on his face. "And I looked in that plastic thing, Dad, and you accidentally took two days' worth on the same day."

"I what?"

"Oh, Emmett! No wonder the pressure went low."

Emmett bites his lower lip. "How did that happen? I'm not usually that forgetful." He glances over at me. "See, Woman? I need a wife to help me get that stuff straight. I can't even remember what day of the week it is."

I swat him. "We are getting married, you dotty old fart! You can count on that… and sooner rather than later! I should think next month would be enough time to plan a little do, don't you?"

Emmett's eyes light up. "You mean it? We can get married next month? Hot dog! Tallulah! I should faint more often if it gets me what I want!"

That's infuriating. If Emmett wasn't lying here hooked up to all those blipping bleeping wires, I would tear a strip off of him right now!

"We are getting married as soon as possible" I continue. "because I had to wait until Will and Connie arrived here before they would even let me in to see you."

"Really?" Emmett shrugs.

"Really." I huff. "I told them that we were engaged. I showed them the ring and everything, but I couldn't come in to the ICU because…" I do the quotes sign in mid-air. "I'm sorry, Mrs. Pratt, but only family is allowed to see Mr. Muggeridge. Hmph! Imagine! They wouldn't let your own fiancée come in."

Emmett caresses my arm. "But here you are now."

"Yes." I smile. "But you're only allowed two visitors at a time, so I am going to have to go and let Connie come back in here soon. I suppose I can't hog you forever." The smile turns to a frown. "Though I would if I could. I don't want to ever leave your side."

"Well now…" Emmett pats my hand over and over again. "…that's more like it. It's awfully tiring having to chase you down. I'm glad you're going to stay right by my side."

I could slap that smug grin off of his face! Of all the cheek! But I can't really, can I? Just last night I thought I might never see that grin again. This insufferable man is going to get away with murder after his shenanigans! I'll never live it down.

"I'll tell you what." Will pats me on the shoulder. "I'm going to go and get a cup of coffee because I need one." He chuckles. "You sure had us hopping."

"I'm sorry, Son." Emmett reaches his other hand out to Will, the one with the IV still sticking out of it. "I didn't mean to frighten you."

"I'm going to send Connie in, okay? That way, you two can still spend time with each other."

"Oh, but I don't want to deprive you of time with your father." I protest, even though I absolutely do want to do that… that is, I don't want to give up my staked out spot right beside the man I love. It feels foreign to me now to be without him.

"Really, it's okay. I could use a jolt of caffeine right about now.

I'll be back after Connie has a visit with you."

I could hug Emmett's son right now. The thought comes to me suddenly that he is about to become my son too. Wow! I am not just marrying a man. I am acquiring a whole new family.

"Next month. That doesn't leave much time to pick out matching napkins and tableware for dinner." Emmett teases. "And I guess you'll have to wear out your friends again on a big shopping trip for a fancy dress."

The thought of shopping for a new dress excites me. "Don't you worry about that. Once I set my mind to something, I can get it done in no time."

He laughs. "I'm counting on it."

I am about to get infuriated again, but his charming smile disarms me and I am so happy to see the sparkle returning to those eyes.

"Hurry, Tallulah." His hand reaches to brush my cheek. "I don't want to spend one more day without you."

Dawn Kehoe (Donkey)

It's almost time... opening night! The costumes are stunning. I will be wearing a shimmery and dazzling golden gown that makes me feel like Lena Horne taking the stage in front of an adoring audience. I understand why some of those songstresses wear such fancy dresses. It transforms you from a scared little urchin trying to sing for a few bucks into a powerful, capable woman who is ready to make everybody fall at your feet and give you the accolades that your gift deserves!

I am going to feel that way when the curtain goes up and the audience is staring at me, little Dawn Gardiner, the girl with perfect pitch!.Every eye will be on me and, sweetest of all, no eyes will be on Eve!

I can't believe that it's almost time. I've been rehearsing for what seems like an eternity.

Look out, World. Here I come!

??

"Donkey?"

I jump. Where did these people come from? Where am I?

"It's your turn, Dear Heart." Gladys smiles at me in that friendly way she always does.

I look down and see the cards in my hand.

"Oh, so it is." I laugh. "Do you have any fives?"

"Not a one." Gladys replies. "Go and fish."

Chapter Twenty-Two

Gladys Peachy

I took two Tylenol this morning. I am wearing my most comfortable pair of shoes. Sneakers, no less! When do I wear sneakers? I bought them on a lark last year and discovered why the young ones like them so much. They're comfortable!

As I board the mini bus that we take on field trips, I am confident that my footwear will hold up under the stress. We are having a big shopping day today. We're going all the way to the Rideau Centre to shop. That's not our usual stop, but Lula is over the moon about it.

Apparently, there are some stores in there where she can try on or order a fancy dress to wear to get married in a few short weeks.

Here we are: Ethel, Lula, Donkey and me. I've got a track suit on, royal blue Adidas with a white stripe down the side and my amazing Reebok shoes. We are all aboard this morning and we can shop till we drop, have a bite of lunch at the food court, and then shop some more before the bus comes back around 3 o'clock. I'm sure we'll all be exhausted tonight.

"You look ready for our safari today." Ethel laughs at me, pointing at the little sun visor I am wearing on my head. "Where did you get that? They went out years ago."

"And I was alive years ago." I quip. "I have had this old visor since Paul was still alive and I like it. It will keep my hair out of my face and the sun out of my eyes." I jerk my head to one side, indicating Lula across the way. "You know we're going to be dragged all over creation, don't you? We'll see every store in that place… some of them twice! The quest for the dress is on!"

"And the shoes and the purse and the jewelry. I know I know... and I don't want to miss any of it." Ethel opens her purse and pulls out a small notebook. "I've got to get it all recorded, if you know what I mean."

My mouth drops open. "You don't mean... are you still writing about all of us?"

"Sure. Why not?" Ethel chuckles. "And this shopping trip is going to be one of the best chapters in the whole book. I'm so glad Emmett is all right. That would have made a terrible plot twist... having one of the best characters in the whole book pass away so suddenly. How awful!"

I nod. "That would have been terrible. I couldn't sleep a wink the night it happened."

"Me neither."

"I prayed and prayed for them. When my feet are sore later and I get cross, remind me that I got what I prayed for, will you?"

"I sure will, Gladdy." Ethel pats my arm. "You know, I knew that's what you were doing."

"Huh?"

"I knew you would be praying up a storm for Emmett and Lula. I admire that about you, you loving old gal!"

I don't know if being called an old gal is so much fun, but Ethel is smiling as she says it. It is nice to be called loving. That is what I always prayed I would be. I hope that when people look back on my long life that they say I succeeded at becoming a loving woman. Maybe some folks want to accomplish great things: build skyscrapers or change the world. I just wanted to learn how to really love. In the end, did I do that?

I'll have to think about that later. Here comes Benny the driver. We are on our way.

Ethel MacNarland

I am lounging on a big leather-covered chair beside Gladys and Donkey at C'est La Vie. It's a high end fashion boutique in which I would never be caught dead shopping. For one thing, I refuse to pay three times what a dress is actually worth. For another, I was never fond of the fancier things. I like to dress well. My clothes are clean and well made, but I was never what anyone would consider posh.

Lula is oohing and ahhing over sequins, lace and frills. She has tried on at least a dozen outfits in here. C'est La Vie is not a bridal shop per se, but for a second wedding, a woman often opts for a fancy dress, but not the classic white bridal gown with a train or meringue.

"Come on, Woman. Are you going to keep us waiting out here forever?" I huff, sounding more miffed than I feel. I'm just hungry and ready for lunch.

"One second." Lula's muffled voice replies from behind the curtained booth where she is grunting and struggling to get into the latest potential dress auditioning for a part in her wedding.

"I'm hungry."

I can't complain that Donkey is saying that for the fourth time in the last five minutes. My own stomach is growling like a ravenous lion.

"Soon, Donkey. Soon." Gladdy pats her hand. "We're going to go grab a bite as soon as Lula is finished trying on wedding dresses. Isn't it exciting? She's getting married and we're all invited! Won't that be fun?"

Donkey tilts her head to one side. "It will be way more fun after

I have something to eat."

"Of course it will." Gladdy chuckles. "What kind of food are you in the mood for? They have lots of choices at the food court.

"McDonalds. I'm in the mood for a cheeseburger… with bacon!" Donkey claps her hands like a giddy child.

"Shhh!" Gladdy puts a finger to her lips. "Let's use our indoor voices, Dear Heart."

"McDonalds?" I grimace. "They have way better selection here than that! They've got Chinese, Thai, Indian food, a vegetarian place and Wowzaburger if you want a better bacon cheeseburger than that."

"Can I get anything for you ladies?" The perpetually pursed lips of the anal retentive sales associate strike me as funny, but maybe laughing would get us thrown out of this fancy joint.

"No. We're fine." I say. "We're waiting for our friend. She's still trying on dresses."

"I see." The associate looks down on us as if we were vermin. She's got one of those petite figures that makes me wonder if she eats at all. She's not just thin… she's skeletal, the designer label suit jacket and skirt she's wearing hanging off of her in a way that isn't flattering, in my opinion. "Well, let me know if I can be of assistance." She turns her attention back to Lula. "Can I get you anything in there? How are we managing?"

Swoop!

The curtain pulls back, revealing Lula in a stunning off white, elegant, mid-length dress with sparkly sequins across both shoulders, slightly puffed sleeves and a bit of a plunging neckline with more sparkles in a diamond shape at the waistline. It hugs Lula's curves and shows off the formidable figure that she still has at her age.

I see the sales associate blanch… and she should, I note, with a satisfied grin. At 72, Tallulah Pratt, soon to be Muggeridge, looks more stunning than that skinny young thing that only eats salads and breadsticks.

"Wow!" Donkey almost shouts. "You look ready to knock 'em dead on stage!"

Lula bursts out laughing. "Oh, Donkey! How sweet!"

"It looks… good." The associate forces a smile. "I have to admit that this is the first time I have seen that particular dress on a more…" She hesitates. "…on a more…"

"A more what?" Lula asks.

"A more mature person." The associate has chosen her words carefully, but not carefully enough.

"Oh." The smile flees from Lula's face. "I thought you were going to say…" Lula stares down the stick woman. "…on someone who actually has curves."

The cat fight is on, if not physically, definitely in words. My money is on Lula.

"What do you think, Girls? Is this the one or what?" Lula does a little dance and whirls around to show us the back.

"I love it." Gladdy says. "But the question is, do you?"

Lula throws her head back and laughs. "Oh, I'll say I do! It's light and airy and I feel gorgeous in it! This is perfect!"

"Okay then." I jump up from the chair where I have been sitting bored stiff for an hour. "Let's buy that sucker and head off to the food court!"

"Not so fast." Lula says. "I want to think about it… and maybe check out a few other stores."

305

"Ohhhhh…" Donkey groans. "I'm so hungry."

My heart sinks too. Just when I thought I saw a light at the end of the shopping tunnel… I find out that it was an oncoming train.

Tallulah Pratt (Lula)

"Wow! This butter chicken is fantastic!" I can't believe it's a fast food menu item. We've come a long way from burgers, fries and deep fried chicken. These days, there are so many choices.

Having said that, Donkey is chowing down on a Wowzaburger with double the bacon. We couldn't convince her to try something more adventurous. Despite the napkins we tucked into the neck, I know that her pale yellow blouse is going to be splattered with mustard and ketchup before the meal is through.

We are sitting in hard red chairs around a stark white table, the drone of the many voices around us sounding like a giant flock of hummingbirds. It makes it a challenge to hear the conversation, but we are making do.

"I'm loving the honey garlic ribs." Ethel says. "Since they renovated this food court, the menu choices have seriously improved."

"I agree." Gladys scoops some chicken fried rice into her mouth. "I wonder when the other renovations will be finished."

"I don't know." Emmett crosses my mind. He wanted to come today, but he stayed behind to let me do my wedding shopping without snooping. It's bad luck for a groom to see what his bride is going to be wearing. "Oh girls, I can't believe that I'm going to be married in less than three weeks! I never thought I would do that again."

"Do what again? I can't hear you!" Ethel wrinkles her forehead.

"Getting married!" I shout talk at her.

"Oh! I know I won't be doing it again." Ethel quips, a sour expression appearing, then disappearing as quickly as it came. "I want to focus on writing now. I can't believe how rejuvenated I feel actually pursuing a dream that I thought had passed me by long ago."

"Excuse me." Donkey interjects. "I've got to go to the ladies room. I'll be right back."

"Okay, Donkey." I pat her arm. "Now you be careful and don't get lost."

"Oh, Lula! Don't be silly. I'm not a baby." Donkey's scolding is endearing to me and I don't mean to treat her like a child. I still watch like a hawk as she makes her way through the rows upon rows of tables toward the ladies room.

"How is your book coming along?" I turn my attention to Ethel, moving my chair closer to make it easier to converse.

"Well..." Ethel tosses Gladdy a funny look. It's sheepish, even. "...it's coming along very well and... uh..." She giggles. "...it'll be finished really soon."

"Really?" That idea delights me. I want Ethel to succeed. "Ethel, I couldn't be prouder if I tried."

Ethel nods. "I hope you are proud, Lula. I really do."

"Of course I'm proud of you." I brush her hand. "It's a wonderful thing. You're pursuing a dream and I want it to come true."

Ethel bursts out laughing.

"Lordy, Ethel, are you losing your marbles?" I wait for her

giggle fit to subside.

"Not quite her marbles." Gladdy says. "She's worried about what you're going to think of her book."

I don't understand that. "But why? I'm your friend. I would only ever wish good things for you."

"It's not that." Ethel shakes her head, still half laughing. "It's just… I should have told you before I was near the end of the book…"

"Told me what?" I have butterflies flitting about in my stomach now. What am I missing and why do I feel like a bomb is about to drop in my lap?

"Well…" Ethel pauses. "I changed all the names, so don't worry about that…"

"Changed all the names to what?" I'm still clueless… until a lightning bolt hits me and I get a frightful thought. "Oh my word, Ethel! You didn't!"

"I did!"

"You wrote about… about…"

"All of us… our adventures…" Ethel is about to start laughing again.

She might start crying if I start swatting her! "All of us? You wrote about the four of us? Oh Ethel… why would anyone want to know about us?"

She gives me an apologetic shrug. "For starters, your life does have a lovely romance in it."

I finally get the whole picture. My first reaction is fury. "Ethel MacNarland, how could you?! I feel so violated! Now I know we joked about it, but I never thought you would actually do it!"

Ethel shakes her head. "Don't you see? Your story is beautiful."

I stop mid-rant. "It's what?"

"She's right about that, Dear Heart." Gladdy gives me her most angelic smile. "You and Emmett have a beautiful love story, as romantic as anything they write in those best-selling books."

"Others will be inspired by it." Ethel continues. "I won't divulge who you really are or where you're from, but I hope you'll forgive me. I think it should be told."

I take a deep breath. "Well…" The storm inside me subsides. "…I suppose it's kind of flattering, in a way. Tallulah Pratt, sexy 72-year-old siren and star of a romance novel." I start to giggle.

"You make a better leading lady than that stick woman from C'est La Vie." Ethel raises her eyebrows. "Don't you think so?"

I raise my glass of Sprite and mock toast toward Ethel. "Absolutely, but we'd better not tell Emmett."

Ethel's jaw drops open. "Oh no! Do you think he'll be angry about it?"

I think about it and I am sure of the answer. "No. He'll strut and crow about it and that would be impossible to bear."

That comment gets us all laughing.

It comes to an abrupt halt.

"Lula, it's been…" Gladdy looks at her watch.

"Too long." Ethel adds.

I look toward the women's restroom. I see a group of overdressed teenagers walking in, probably to take endless selfies and make those strange-looking poses, the ones they call duck faces. I wonder why they call it that; maybe because they're all quacks for doing it.

"She could just be dawdling." I say, but my stomach has a pit inside it just now.

We're finished eating, but Donkey is not.

"Stay here, Girls." I get up from my seat. "I'll check to see if she's still in there. I'll be right back."

Past hungry people eating burgers or salads or Chinese noodles I go, weaving through the food court as fast as I can. With a crowd like they've got today, that isn't easy.

"Excuse me..." I accidentally bump somebody. "I'm so sorry..." Somebody accidentally bumps me. "...Oh! Look out!" I narrowly miss a head on collision with a bunch of older kids who are not teenagers yet, but want to appear as though they are. They're not fooling anyone with that high-pitched squealing and arguing and singing along badly with some awful thing they call a song.

I break free of the madness and find my way to the corridor where the restrooms are. There is no door; just a curved pathway with a picture of a stick woman with a skirt on the wall, Braille dots underneath the image. I follow the round pathway until I see a row of sinks, a hand dryer and two long rows of stalls, three of which are closed and locked, so one of them must be Donkey.

"Donkey, Dear." I call out. "Are you in here? It's me, Lula."

No one answers. I get strange looks from the gaggle of teenagers who are in here applying makeup and texting each other on cell phones, even though they are standing together in the same room. Lordy, I am thankful right now that I was not born in this decade! How will this world survive?

I realize how ridiculous it must sound hearing someone call out for a donkey. I change my strategy. "Dawn? Dawn, are you here? The girls are waiting for you back at our table."

There is still no response. My heart lurches into my throat as one of the stall doors opens and a middle aged woman in a loud floral summer dress steps out, salt and pepper hair screaming out for a dye job.

I wait, breath catching as another stall opens and a child, looking 9 or 10 years old, comes out, a long, ginger braid down her back. She could be Anne of Green Gables, the look and colouring is that similar and I smile at her as she timidly sticks her hands beneath the tap.

One more stall remains. Any of the others that are occupied now became that way after I came in. I feel guilty for letting Donkey go to the bathroom by herself. I know she does that when we're back at Tranquil Meadows, but this is a whole other ballgame. We should have kept a closer eye.

The last stall opens and a fast food worker still wearing her uniform walks out, dashing any hopes I had that Donkey was just a restroom dawdler. There is no time to waste.

I dash out of there, taking a moment to look around the food court and down the one corridor that I can see from here. I don't see Donkey in this mob; that telltale disheveled mop of white hair, the pale yellow blouse, the brown pants. Where is she?

A terrifying thought comes to mind. If she wandered out to do some shopping, mall security could likely locate her easily enough, but what if something else happened? If Donkey's mind has gone off with the pixies, she could end up in real danger. Some of the mall is sectioned off right now while the building is being overhauled and renovated. Higher end stores are coming in.

I am going to scurry back to our table, but Gladys and Ethel catch my eye from across the room. Seeing me empty-handed and shaking my head, I see them hastily gather up purses and whatnot and make a beeline toward me. Lordy, I'm glad I didn't buy the dress yet. I wouldn't want to cart shopping bags around with me while hunting for our dotty escapee.

Dawn Kehoe (Donkey)

Opening night is here. I have to get to my dressing room. It's almost time for the curtain to go up. *Break a leg, Dawn!* That's what they always say before I go on stage. They don't really want me to break a bone. It means good luck!

Where am I? We rented a big auditorium and the backstage area is messy and dirty. There is debris everywhere. Can't they afford a janitor?

Look at all the dust! Boards are everywhere along with strange signs that say, "Keep out." and "Danger". What am I in danger of? Forgetting the lyrics?

I can't find the stage. I know it's around here someplace. I have been walking for quite some time. "Oh!" I almost scream. There's a big hole! I could have fallen right in there! I'm going to tell the others to be careful back here. The last thing we need is to have the performers injured. Maybe they should think twice about renting this place again.

"Ma'am?" A voice is calling out to somebody. I wonder who he's looking for. It can't be me. I'm not even 18 yet. Nobody calls me Ma'am.

"Ma'am?" I hear him again. Maybe I should stop and help him find whoever he's looking for. What if he wants to talk to Jean Montgomery?

"You're not supposed to be 'ere. It's hoff limits." Now somebody with a French Canadian accent has me by the arm.

"Oh!" I turn and look into the face of a man who could be my brother Knight. He resembles him a little. "Hello. Can I help you?" I offer him the best smile I can. "I'm looking for the stage entrance."

The man tilts his head to one side. "Stage entrance? Dare are no stages 'ere."

I look around, but all I see is random junk. "I'm supposed to be singing today."

The man smiles back at me. "You must want da concert hall. You def-hinitely took a wrong turn." His dark eyes narrow and the creases at the corners of his eyes are inviting and let me know that he's my friend.

"Yes." I reply. "I guess I did get a little lost. Can you help me?"

"Let's get you out of dis place and on to your performance." The man offers me his arm, and I take it. What a gentleman! It's a pity he came to a gala dressed in a hard hat.

"What's your name?" I ask him, happy to be getting attention from a man instead of Eve for a change.

"It's Don." He says.

My jaw gapes open. "Don? Why, that's my name too!"

He laughs softly. "Dat is a co-hincidence. Here we are, Dawn. It's hokay if I let you out on Rideau Street? Dis will be a lot safer for you. You take care now."

I follow him outside a door and onto the sidewalk. He leaves me before I can even say goodbye. He must be one of those reclusive celebrities.

"Now where is that stage? I'm on in 10 minutes."

I need to find it soon. I feel anxious if I'm not on time.

Chapter Twenty-Three

Gladys Peachy

Headless chickens! That's what the three of us look like rushing around this food court looking for Donkey. She is obviously not here, but where did she go?

"Girls! Follow me!" Lula sounds like a drill sergeant just now, but that's all right. This isn't the time for diplomacy.

We gather outside the corridor where the restrooms are.

"All right. Listen!" Lula says. "She couldn't have gone right past us. We would have noticed that."

I could cry right now, but I can't allow myself to fall to pieces.

"Where could she be? God? I'm frightened for Donkey. We need your help right now!" I don't care that my prayer isn't formal and I don't give a hoot if the whole mall knows I'm praying. "Send us help. Take care of her!"

Ethel slides an arm around me and rubs my shoulder. "Now now, it's going to be all right. We're going to find her."

"In this crowd?" I gesture outward toward the food court. "Every tourist and citizen in Ottawa seems to be in the mood for shopping today!"

"Quiet!" Lula claps her hands sharply. "We've got to focus! Now, she didn't go back toward the food court and she had to go somewhere from this very spot. So, think! Which way could she have gone from here?"

"What in the world would entice that dame not to come back to her lunch? She likes to eat!" Ethel almost laughs, but Lula glares at her and she stops.

I look around and see that there are only two choices, the one leading back to our table and the one leading toward Special T, a teashop that has a beautiful display of fancy pots, porcelain cups and tea boxes in the window.

"She might have gone there." I point to the teashop. "Donkey loves tea."

"Well, that's as good a place as any to start." Lula agrees. "Keep your eyes open! She could be wandering down the hallways. Check every direction!"

We move forward like one person, the Donkey Defenders on a quest to find our dear wandering soul.

I see mothers pushing baby strollers, a boy flirting with a girl, gaggles of giggly teenagers and bedraggled couples, usually with a husband unenthusiastically in tow. There are some white heads like mine, but none of them look familiar. None of them belong to the dearest little lady in the world and I feel like my heart is beating at the bottom of my shoes.

"Yes, may I help you?" An overly friendly young woman asks, though she is much sweeter in demeanor than that cranky sales associate at C'est La Vie. "We have a sale on raspberry green tea today. Would you like to try a sample?"

"Not today." Lula gives her a friendly, but no nonsense tone. "Perhaps you can help us though. Our friend got lost and she may have wandered in here."

The woman's smile fades. "We have had a lot of customers today. There's a festival on in the Byward Market across the way and a lot of attendees have come into the mall to escape the heat."

That explains the overcrowded mall, but not the location of Donkey.

"I see." Lula purses her lips. "She was wearing a pale yellow blouse, brown slacks with white, short hair that is not perfectly combed. Lordy, I've been meaning to make her get to the salon."

The woman's brow furrows. "Oh... uh... was she recently widowed?"

Lula, Ethel and I smile at each other, me secretly thanking God for Cary Grant, Jimmy Stewart, Gregory Peck and every husband that Donkey has never had.

"That's her!" Lula blurts. "I'm so glad you remembered."

The woman grins. "She was very sweet." She indicates a row of dainty cups with Japanese cherry blossoms sprayed across the white porcelain. "She said she was buying one of these cups to replace one that she broke... she was going to give it as a gift before the concert tonight."

Now we are looking at each other with worry again. *Oh God, Donkey has gone off on a mind excursion. She doesn't even know what year it is!*

"Thank you." Lula says. "You didn't happen to see which way she went?"

"Yes!" The clerk says emphatically. "Only because... well... I called out to her that she was going the wrong way." She points down a hallway that leads off toward what used to be the Goth Garb store, but there is construction going on there right now. "I told her that the shops are over that way."

"And did she turn around?" I ask, fear leaping into my brain like a crazy kangaroo. I try to hush it, but it is persistent. "Oh God! She didn't go down that way!"

The clerk shrugs. "I'm not sure. I'm sorry. Someone asked me a question and when I turned back around again..." She shakes her head. "She wasn't there, so I just assumed…"

I feel like an anvil just landed on my chest. I can barely breathe.

"Thank you." Lula forces a smile. "You've been so helpful."

"I hope you find your friend. I hope she's all right." The woman sounds genuine when she says this. She has lost her 'sales pitch' voice.

A large rectangular white sign with red block letters tells us to "STOP! DO NOT ENTER! CONTRUCTION AREA!" Normally, I would obey a sign like that, but right now, I am trying desperately to trust God and not imagine Donkey lying on the concrete with a big pile of cement or wood or something on top of her head. A terrible picture of her at the bottom of a deep, dark hole seizes me.

I know that I am supposed to have faith. I thought I did. Don't I? I'm just fretful, anxious, and feeling more than a little guilty for not paying close enough attention. Would Donkey be in this mess at all if I had just followed her to the bathroom? Hindsight is 20/20… and it is beating me to a pulp. I should have known better!

"Maybe we should go find a security guard." Ethel says, her voice oozing with trepidation. "We're not exactly dressed for a construction site. They don't make steel toe penny loafers."

"Oh Donkey! What have you done to us?" I say.

"Calm yourselves." Lula snaps us to attention. "Let's have a quick look around and then get out of there if we don't see her right away. If we wait, she'll get farther away from us or…" She stops herself.

"Or what?" Ethel asks.

I don't need to hear the answer to that. My mind is already playing it out. "Or something worse!" I add. "Come on. Lula's right! If there was ever a time to break the rules, this is it."

Ethel MacNarland

Opening the temporary door that was installed in the drywall, we enter the forbidden zone. I breathe in sawdust, drywall, paint and a host of other smelly things that I don't want to know about.

I cough. "How do any of the workmen get around in here?" It's not a building site. Not to me. It reminds me of one of those mazes for lab rats.

"Do you see anything?" Lula holds a hand over her eyes and blinks repeatedly.

That's what we're all doing. It's broad daylight, but there are dust particles everywhere.

"Not a thing." I reply. "See? We need security. We can give them a description and look for her."

"Where is everybody?" Gladys asks. "If it's a work site, shouldn't they be here working?"

I check my watch. "It's Friday afternoon. They all clocked off for an early weekend."

I step around scaffolds, ladders, random debris. I'm not sure what this part of the mall is going to be, but right now, it just looks like a big, half-built nothing. Are there going to be windows or will it be one of those cages? I would hate the idea of working in a shop with no windows showing me the outside world. The very thought makes me claustrophobic and the closed-in nature of this room, spacious as it seems without any shelves or racks or fixtures in it, causes sweat beads to break out on my forehead.

"I don't see her." Gladys laments. "She gave us the slip, Girls, but good! When Bidelia finds out, Donkey's goose is cooked."

Lula's striking blue eyes narrow. "I am not giving that pompous battle axe the satisfaction of taking our friend down without a fight." She walks forward. "Donkey didn't have that much of a head start on us. We're going to find her!"

"Look out!" I grab Gladys' arm, pulling her away from a sizeable hole in the floor. I don't know what the hole is for. Getting rid of employees who forget their name tags? That would be funny, but my heart is pounding a hundred miles an hour thinking about Gladys falling down that hole.

Gladys begins to sob. "Oh God... no..."

Lula and I exchange worried glances.

"Lordy, what is it?" Lula asks. "Are you hurt?"

Gladys shakes her head and points to the hole. "Donkey... what if she's... in there?"

That thought is terrifying. I might cry too.

"Stop it!" Lula snaps. "We can't give up and we can't let fear of what might have happened stop us. We keep going. Got it?"

I nod. Gladdy does too.

"Good. Now, I can't see over that way. Let's see if we can find Donkey and get out of here. If she came in here, there's no time to lose and..." Lula frowns. "...we can't leave her in here to... to possibly fall."

"Dawn?" Gladys calls out. "Dawn? Are you there?"

That's a good idea. If Donkey is having one of her episodes, she might not remember her more modern nickname.

I join in. "Dawn? Dawn, we're looking for you! Are you here?"

Slowly, carefully, hand in hand, we advance as if we are one being and not three.

"Dawn?" Gladys shouts again. "Come out come out wherever you are."

Silence.

Lula sighs and raises her voice to a shout. "Dawn! Stop hiding and come out of there! Right now! Dawn?!"

More silence.

A rustling noise follows.

"Yes. I'm here." Comes a voice. "Dis is Don."

It's a male voice and a young smiling man with a hardhat and steel toe work boots comes around a corner to meet us.

My jaw falls open.

Gladys groans.

"I..." Lula stammers. "I... you're not the Dawn we're looking for."

He shrugs his broad shoulders. He's a scruffy but handsome man. "Well, what can hi say? My colleagues are on break and I only got back a few minutes hago." His French Canadian accent is thick.

Gladys, Lula and I huddle together like a herd of scared sheep.

"You know dat dis area is hoff limits." He continues. "May hi escort you back to da main mall? Really, dis is not a safe area for a group of nice ladies like yourselves."

His smile clinches the deal. This guy could be on the cover of a fabulous romance novel. I resolve to remember his face for future reference. I feel guilty about that... I mean, about thinking about that while our dear friend Donkey is still missing and possibly in trouble.

Don walks us toward the door that we just entered, carefully leading us past the junk and the hole and the other miscellaneous construction type stuff. Doesn't that sound technical? I just betrayed the fact that I know as much about a construction site as I do about brain surgery... absolutely nothing!

"Funny ting." Don shakes his head. "You're not da first people to accidentally hend up in 'ere today. I guess dat sign outside isn't big enough." He laughs.

"Wait a second." Lula stops dead in her tracks. "Are you telling me you've seen other people in here this afternoon?"

"Yes, Madame." He is reaching for the door knob now. "Dare was ha little lady, maybe your age or older, hand she said she was late for da concert. Do you know... it was funny too. 'er and me, we had da same name."

Gladys jumps up and down.

I sigh with relief.

"Which way did she go?" Lula demands. "Please, Don. She's our friend. She's got dementia and... we've got to find her before something terrible happens."

The young man's smile drops into a frown. "Mon Dieu. I'm sorry. She sounded so coherent. She said she was going to da big concert and dat somebody special was going to be dare."

Gladys' hand flies in front of her mouth.

"Did she say where she was going? I mean, where did you leave her?" Lula's confident tone turns slightly panicky. "We've got to get to her now!"

Don turns around and leads us back through the construction junk, carefully making sure we don't trip or step into anything dangerous. "I left da sweet lady 'ere on Rideau." Don says, opening another door which leads out to the street. He points.

"I know she crossed da street 'ere and was going into da Byward Market toward da festival. I thought she was going to dat. I 'ope she's hall right."

"Thank you." Lula pats his arm and we're off like a flock of wild... old people.

I hope we find Donkey soon. How far could she get in such a short time? She's 78 years old!

"Gladdy! Ethel!" Lula says. "Do you have any pictures of Donkey? Is there anything in your purse?"

I think. Yes, there should be. I undo the clasp on my big white everything holder and rummage through it.

"Here!" I smile, opening my wallet and finding a small 4 by 6 shot of the four of us, taken by Evangeline Martin at last year's Christmas party.

"This will have to do." Lula looks unsure. "It's not the clearest shot, but hopefully, somebody has seen her. Come on! Let's go find our girl!"

Tallulah Pratt (Lula)

Lordy, I would love shopping in the Byward Market if we were here on a happier occasion. Just look at it! Outdoor vendors' stalls line the sidewalks, selling locally made or grown produce, crafts and flowers. Cafes, restaurants and tourist shops surround the square and the line-up of customers waiting to buy a treat at the Beaver Tails pastry take out window stretches part way around the block.

"Free sample?" Asks a young, dark-haired girl with a slight overbite. "It's a crepe made with sorghum flour." The white sign on her stall reads, in green block letters: 'Demo Corner: Free Samples'.

I smile at her, hoping it doesn't look as strained as I feel. "No, thank you, Dear, but it smells lovely."

We move on, Gladys stopping to drop a dollar coin into the container of a busker who is playing Bach quite beautifully on a flute.

"Look, Ethel! They have an author's corner. You could rent a stall here and sell your books!" Gladys giggles.

"Really, Gladdy!" I chide her, but instantly feel guilty for doing it. "Let's not get distracted. We're here to find Donkey!"

"I'm sorry. You're right, of course," Gladys shrugs. "It's just… such a busy place. So much to look at."

"Look at all the people." Ethel remarks. "How will we find Donkey in the midst of all this? She could be anywhere! Lula, we had better spill the beans and get security or a police officer to help."

Ethel! I can't believe you would give up so easily. I don't say that. I maintain courtesy, though I feel like biting somebody's head off. "Not yet. Let's see if anyone has seen her."

We start with the girl demonstrating the sorghum flour creations.

"No, I'm sorry." She shakes her head. "I've seen a lot of people today. I don't recognize your friend."

My heart sinks, but I know that if we tell the mini bus driver that one of our party has gone AWOL, Donkey will be turfed from Tranquil Meadows and sent to Tranquil Meadows Plus as fast as you please.

Nobody in the Beaver Tails line saw Donkey either.

She wasn't seen by the woman who runs the stall selling bouquets of roses, lilies and carnations.

I told Gladys not to get distracted, but had to resist the urge to buy a beautiful potted gerbera flower from another vendor who hasn't seen Donkey.

"Yes, I remember her." The flute busker says, smiling. "She tried to sing along to *Greensleeves.* Can you imagine?"

I grin. Yes, I can imagine that.

"You know, she had a pretty good singing voice." He continues. "She told me that she's performing today, so I assumed she was part of the festival."

Finally, Donkey's wandering is starting to make sense to me. The pieces of the puzzle are coming together.

"Whereabouts is the festival?" I ask. *And please say it's close by.*

He points down William Street. "That way. If you keep going and then turn right, you'll come to a group of pubs and restaurants. There are performers off and on all day. It's going to continue on through the weekend. I don't know which one she might go to, but you'll find her if you keep going that way."

"Thank you, young man." I put five dollars in his container.

"Young? I'm over 50." He chuckles.

"Sir, I am 72." I reply. "Everybody is young to me."

Off we trot, Gladys and Ethel trying to keep up with me as my feet fly down the sidewalk, carefully avoiding shoppers and dawdlers and a couple of brazen panhandlers that I could smell before we passed them.

Turning right at the end of the block, a cacophony of clashing music notes greets my ears. That is because these pubs and restaurants have their doors wide open, so the music going on inside is spilling out onto York Street and the tunes are colliding with each other, crashing and burning... at least that's how it sounds to my sensitive ears.

I wince. "What a racket! I wonder if she's actually inside one of these buildings."

There are buildings all along this street, all with outdoor patios, more vendors on the sidewalks in front of them and, of course, today's something or other festival, which draws in tourists and regular patrons and I can't tell which is which.

We peer in the door of the Hard Rock Café and I see a young woman sitting on a stool playing an acoustic guitar and singing "What if God was one of us… just a slob like one of us… just a stranger on the bus trying to make his way home…"

"No Donkey." I sigh. "Let's try the next one, Girls."

As we leave, I notice Gladys turning back to smile at the woman. I didn't know she liked folk rock.

"Let's try this place." Ethel suggests. "The music definitely sounds louder."

No kidding. As we walk in to the… what's the name of it again? As we walk into this no-name place, I see men at the bar, barmaids weaving through the crowd with pitchers, bottles and glasses of beer. A band is playing on the stage and I see a sign advertising the various musicians who will be performing today.

What I don't see is… you guessed it… Donkey.

"Another dead end." Ethel complains as we exit. "I'm telling you. This is too hard! We need to recruit help."

"Let's just try these places first." I urge, then blanch as we stand outside the next establishment.

Gladys, Ethel and I exchange worried looks as our eyes land on the row of motorcycles parked outside. Names like Harley Davidson and Yamaha advertise to me from the sides of these contraptions. If the riders of these machines are inside this place, maybe we should skip it. Would Donkey ever go into such a place?

"There's a sign." Gladys points.

So there is. It may not be from God, but it does list the festival performers.

"Hmm…" I shrug. "Whatever. We've lived this long. If they kill us, at least we're old."

With that, we head inside to look for Donkey among the Hell's Angels.

As soon as we step inside, I have to blink over and over again. The sun was bright outside today and it isn't that bright in here, so my eyes need to adjust. I notice Gladys and Lula groping along, trying to find their way.

"Hold on." I say. "The spots will be gone in a minute."

"Ladies and Gentlemen." A smooth-talking man who sounds like a radio announcer speaks into a microphone. "We have a surprise for you today. She just wandered in and introduced herself to the house band and… well… now we're introducing her to you. Please give a warm welcome to… Miss Dawn Gardiner!"

Applause erupts as the first notes of a song begin.

Ethel pokes me. "Dawn Gardiner! She doesn't even remember she was married."

"Her husband isn't dead now." I quip. "He never existed. That is a suitable punishment for Lowell."

Gladys grabs my arm. "Should we rush up to the stage and get her?"

I look around at the burly men (and women!) sitting there, eyes glued to the stage. To be totally honest, it surprises me. There are bald ones, bearded ones who look like ZZ Top, big sailor types, some covered in tattoos, chains and leather. These big tough guys are suddenly smiling as if they were looking at the most wonderful thing in the world.

I shake my head in disbelief. They are smiling at the disheveled little figure on stage before them... our own beloved Donkey... Dawn Kehoe, that is... though she has decided to be Dawn Gardiner today.

"I hope they don't laugh her off the stage." Ethel says.

We're about to find out.

In the background, the band plays a series of smooth, pleasing notes and the performance begins.

I hold my breath.

Donkey opens her mouth.

"Somewhere over the rainbow way up high
There's a land that I dreamed of once in a lullaby
Somewhere over the rainbow skies are blue
And the dreams that you dream of, dreams really do come true..."

Her voice comes out clear and strong. Donkey really can sing! I mean, I heard her at Tranquil Meadows and I knew she could, but she is taking it to a whole new level right now. Donkey is on stage... I don't know if she realizes that she is on stage in a biker bar in Ottawa. She may be at Massey Hall right now... or she could think she's really starring as Judy Garland in *"The Wizard of Oz."* It might be a command performance for The Queen or a special number on The Grammy Awards.

Her mind wanders off to places unknown and I know that we can't protect her much longer, but right now, I am biting back tears. In fact, unabashedly, I decide to let them fall. To hell with appearances!

Look at our Donkey… she's absolutely beautiful, disheveled hair and all. What is even more extraordinary is watching the effect she is having on the people in this place. Every person has stopped moving, drinking, talking or otherwise carrying on. That never happens in a bar. Singers have to sing over top of the constant din.

Donkey has captivated her audience and I see some wiping their eyes with napkins… big, burly bikers brought to tears by a sweet little old woman. She may have led us on a wild goose chase, but watching what is undoubtedly Donkey's last big public performance before the dementia steals her away from the world, I feel happy for her… and sad for those of us who are going to miss her so.

World, her name was Dawn Gardiner and she deserved so much better than the wretched hand you dealt her. I am thankful right now though for the incredible blaze of glory that she is riding out of whatever spotlight she commanded.

Dawn Kehoe (Donkey)

"If happy little bluebirds fly
Above the rainbow why oh why… can't… I…"

I did my very best, Mother. Are you proud of me?

Chapter Twenty-Four

Gladys Peachy

"That was beautiful, Donkey." I hug her, the love in my heart shooting through my body like some kind of drugged euphoria. I could hold her forever, this dotty little lady. "You know you scared us silly. We couldn't find you for quite some time."

"What do you mean, Eve? You were looking for me?" Donkey's eyes light up. "You've never looked for me before."

I toss Ethel and Lula a worried look. "Donkey, it's me, Gladys Peachy. Don't you know me?"

"I know that you were finally jealous of me for a change. Weren't you? I finally got my day in the sun." She giggles. "You can't steal this from me… the power of my moment on stage. I shone and you couldn't take that away."

I hold back the tears that want to storm out of my lower eyelids. I look deep into her eyes. "Yes, Donkey. You shone and I'm so proud of you."

"Ma'am. That was so beautiful. Can I buy you a drink?" A burly man with a stubbly head and bushy brown beard leans in to kiss Donkey on the cheek.

"Oh, thank you." Donkey responds before I can intercept and protect her. "You're very sweet, but my mother says I'm not allowed to drink alcohol.'

The man's smile is electric. He doesn't even seem shaken by the fact that Donkey is obviously at an age where she doesn't have to ask her mother about anything… though in her mind, it seems, she is not aware of that.

"I can get you a root beer or a Coke if you prefer that." He says. "Or even a cup of tea." His voice raises a little. "Hey, Murty! You got any tea back there?"

The barkeep shakes his head. It's not surprising. This doesn't seem like an establishment where people ask for tea often.

Donkey slips her arm around his. "You're very kind, but don't go to any trouble on my account."

The big guy pulls out a chair and offers Donkey a seat. "For you? It's no trouble at all. You just took me back to when I was a little boy and my mom used to sing that for me when I couldn't sleep."

Donkey sits down. I see that a crowd is around her, eager fans wanting to talk to her, compliment and fawn over her. I wonder what Dawn Gardiner might have been if she had never met Lowell Kehoe. I know that there is no use in fretting over should have, would have or could have, but I feel a pang of regret.

A cup of tea suddenly appears in front of Donkey and she cocks her head to one side.

"It's okay." Says another stocky man with so much hair, he could be a male Rapunzel. He has a large tattoo along his forearm that reads "Live to ride; ride to live". "I ran over to Moulin de Provence and grabbed one. Murty won't mind me bringing in outside drinks... not on this special occasion."

As I watch this entourage of burly, bushy, tattooed, pierced, leather clad, boot wearing, drinking and otherwise gruff looking people all smiling and wanting to tell Donkey how wonderful she is, I realize something about myself. I am more judgmental than I want to be. These people aren't trying to harm Donkey at all. They may look rough and tumble, but somewhere in their hearts is a soft, mushy marshmallow and

I quietly ask God to forgive me for my prejudice. I really didn't see it until now.

Ethel MacNarland

A bar full of big brutish bikers! I have hit the writer's jackpot! This will make an awesome entry into my novel. Wow! What a plot twist!

The only downside I can see right now is... Donkey doesn't seem to be teetering between fantasy and reality today. She seems to have taken a one-way trip to Narnia and we can't find the wardrobe door to get her back to reality.

"Donkey, you sounded even better than Judy Garland up there." I say. "Everybody loved hearing you sing."

She shrugs. "I'm a professional. That's what we do."

I could laugh right now. Maybe I had better not. I don't want to jolt Donkey or incur the wrath of her newfound fan club.

"When can we put the next act on?" Asks a whiny bald man in a ratty tee shirt and jeans, who strikes me as a man who is trying to look as tough as the rest of them, but he doesn't quite measure up. "Can we put the background music on at least?"

I hear the sound of chair legs scraping wood. The tallest man in the bar, looking as broad in the shoulder as a Roman gladiator, approaches the whiner and stands toe to toe, but not eye to eye. He looks down at his quarry and says, almost in a growl. "We'll get back to business as usual when the lady is finished here."

That is all he says. I can see the unspoken conversation going on right now between the big guy and the smaller wannabe. It doesn't matter what anybody else wants. Mr. Big Fella likes Donkey and until we're ready to vamoose out of here, things are going to remain quiet, civil and as innocent as a song and dance from "*The Wizard of Oz.*"

Tallulah Pratt (Lula)

"Thank you for being so nice to our friend." I give these sizeable men my best smile, all the while thanking Heaven for my clean cut, handsome Emmett. "She is having the time of her life right now." *And it's never going to happen for her again.*

"She's my Nana." Says the man with the dark bushy beard, the same one who arranged for the cup of tea. He pats Donkey's hand, eyes sparkling, grin ear to ear.

"She's my Nana too." Says another big boy, one whose bared biceps look more like the trunk of a tree in their girth.

Donkey has stolen the hearts and attention of most of these patrons. Their softness toward her makes me swell with emotion... a much better feeling than the dread I had when we first entered this establishment expecting danger and madness.

"Do you want to sing again?" Somebody asks. I can't even tell who.

"Oh, you want an encore?" Donkey's face lights up.

"But..." Gladys pipes up, checking her wrist watch. "I guess it doesn't much matter anymore. We have missed the bus back to Tranquil Meadows."

Fear grips me. "How in the dickens are we going to get back?"

Mr. Brown Beard (it's as good a name as any... I don't know his name!) shrugs and says: "Don't you worry, Ladies. You're from Tranquil Meadows? I know where that is. We'll get you back safe and sound."

Gladys, Ethel and I exchange worried glances.

Donkey is already being helped back up onto the stage.

I watch her whisper something into the ear of one of the band members.

"I guess we're stuck here." Ethel says. "She's going for it again."

I look at Donkey up there, beaming with pride and accomplishment. "It's all right, Girls." I grab each of them by the hand. "This is her last hurrah. You know that. We've got to give it to her. She deserves that much."

And as the band starts to play, Donkey's whole demeanor changes. She is not a little old lady who lost touch with reality. She is a professional performer and her shoulders go back, her head snaps up, and her face has an almost enchanting glow. Never mind that this isn't the style of music that they usually play, the band members seem just as thrilled with Donkey as the people sitting at the tables giving her their undivided attention.

"We'll meet again, don't know where, don't know when
But I know we'll meet again some sunny day…"

I don't know how that country rock band pulled that song out of their hats, but they are backing Donkey up for her finale. I could hug them for it! I could slug them for it! I feel joy and also an incredibly sharp pain in my heart. No, I'm not having a heart attack! I just feel like I'm saying goodbye to a dear old friend. It's a good way to do it, but it breaks me apart to know that we can't save her anymore.

We can't… can we?

Maybe she'll snap out of this when we get back to Tranquil Meadows and her familiar surroundings.

We're late. We missed the bus.

Can we sneak in somehow and act as if nothing is amiss?

"We've got to try and sneak past the attendants' desk." I say as quietly as I can to Ethel and Gladys. "If we can get Donkey back to her room, maybe we can smooth this over and she'll be her old self again after a little rest."

Gladys and Ethel are looking at me as if I've lost my mind too. Well, maybe I have.

"It's worth a shot, isn't it?" I ask with all the earnestness I can muster.

"All right." Gladys agrees. "We'll do our best."

I look back toward the stage at our dotty songbird. "Lordy, I hope she comes back to us soon."

"We'll meet again, don't know where, don't know when..." Now half the bar is singing along with Donkey. They're hooking arms, clinking glasses, holding up lit lighters and waving them in the air. Whatever is happening here, for good or ill, Donkey has mesmerized every motorbike-loving hombre in the city!

As the song ends and applause and cheers erupt, Mr. Brown Beard sets a hand on my shoulder, which makes me shudder despite his friendliness, and says: "I spoke with my friends here." He gestures toward three large, imposing men; two with beards, two with hair on top of their heads, one with a bald head and all with tattoos and chains and likely rap sheets at the police station. "This is Curly." May I point out... Curly is the one with no hair. "This is Larry." Larry has no beard.

I wait for him to say 'Moe' as the name for the third man. "This is Cody." Then, he points to himself. "And I'm Rob." I want to ask, *'Is your last names Banks?'* I realize that is judgmental, for one thing, and probably insulting, for another.

"Thank you for offering us a lift." I force a smile. *And dear God, I know Gladys prays more than me. In case she isn't praying right*

THE GRANNY DIARIES

now, could you get us all back to Tranquil Meadows in one piece?

"You don't have to worry, Ma'am." Curly says. "We don't drink and drive."

I am relieved to hear that.

"Hey Murty!" Mr. Brown Beard, now known as Rob, yells. "Hold our tabs. I'm just leaving everything here. We'll be back as soon as we get these ladies home." He looks at us. "Ladies, if you'll follow me." He smiles at Donkey. "It's hard for me to get you away from your fan club."

Donkey laughs. "Yes, it seems so. What an exciting day! I only wish…" She frowns for a second. "Well, my mother was never big on compliments, so…"

Rob's head snaps back. "Are you kidding me? With a voice like that, you should be famous."

The beaming smile returns to Donkey's face. I don't know what these big fellas do in their spare time, if they're honest and good or rowdy and rotten, but I do know that they all have a soft spot for their nanas… and Donkey fits that bill today.

We step outside, preparing for our trip back to the seniors' villa. My heart leaps into my throat. I suppose I didn't follow through and think about this thoroughly. To be truthful, I don't know if I can do this! *Donkey, it's a good thing you're worth it!*

Dawn Kehoe (Donkey)

I am on stage in front of an adoring audience. I just sang 'Over the Rainbow'. Where is my mother? Where? Didn't she come? Couldn't she interrupt her busy schedule to fit me in? Maybe I don't want to know. Maybe I don't want to see her scowling at me.

??

What kind of a place is this? Did they invite the circus to come and watch?

Well, they paid for their tickets and a show is what they're going to get!

"We'll meet again, don't know where, don't know when…"

??

Where are we going?

Who are these people?

Am I under arrest?

I won't tell them the truth. I can't tell them! I know that Gabe pulled the trigger of the gun! I know it now, but… I'll never tell. Never never never! I'll take the rap. I'll say it was me!

???

Why is my skin so spotted and wrinkly? That can't be me.

I know that lady. Don't I know her?

"These nice gentlemen are going to take us home." A nice lady says.

"Are you coming home with me?" I ask her.

She grins. She has the prettiest blue eyes. "Yes. I guess I am. We're…" She pauses. "…very close neighbours."

I don't see how that can be true. My neighbour is Mr. Winslow. He was there the night Lowell tried to kill me. He took the gun from Gabe's hand. I know you can't be his girlfriend. I think Mr. Winslow preferred… well… he never had girlfriends. Never!

"Oh!" I am being lifted onto the back of a… oh my! What is

happening to me?

Chapter Twenty-Five

Gladys Peachy

Cue the song 'Born to Be Wild'. I am on the back of a motorcycle with a big bald man named Curly, holding on to him for dear life and closing my eyes.

"Relax." Curly says, chuckling. "We haven't even left the Byward Market yet."

Vroom! The engine revs and I am moving forward with no car frame or bus surrounding me for safety. All I've got on is the spare helmet that Curly had. It has a picture of a snarling wild cat on it.

God? I hope you're watching right now... and if you are... help meeeeeeeeeeee!

Ethel MacNarIand

I'm wearing Depends! I'm wearing Depends! I'm wearing Depends!

Varrrooom! The engine roars and I can feel the vibration of it between the legs that are apart behind Larry's giant frame. I can't squeeze them together to stop the pee from flowing. If my adult diapers hold up under these conditions, I am going to write the company and suggest this for their next commercial. Never mind the old farts dancing... film me freaking out on the back of a motorcycle, pee running as freely as we are down the roadway.

"Hang on, Nana!" Larry says. "Everything's okay. I'm not going that fast."

I beg to differ as we hit the onramp for the Queensway.

I'm suffering for my art! I'm suffering for my art! I am determined to remember every terrified, traumatic second of my first (and last!) motorcycle ride. It is going to be in my novel… there is no way I'm going to go through an ordeal like this and leave it out.

"Lean in to the turn…" He says.

He doesn't have to say anything. I feel the bike tilt to the right, his foot grazing the pavement as he gets us moving forward again.

I hope the other girls are all right… and this helmet is too big! I can barely see a thing!

Tallulah Pratt (Lula)

"Hang on, Red." Cody says.

This isn't so bad. We rode through the Byward Market nice and slow, and I took in the sights and didn't even mind the feel of the wind on my face. The helmet makes me feel a little claustrophobic, but I think I'll be all right.

"We're heading onto the highway." Cody glances back and smiles. "Don't let go!"

Zzzzooooooom!!! The bike lurches forward as Cody leans on the throttle.

"Aieeeeeeeeeeeeeeeeeeeeeeeeeeeeeeeeeeeeeeeeeeeee!!!!!!!!"
Screams of terror erupt from my mouth as our slow scenic tour of the Byward Market gives way to full speed ahead, wind whipping into me with fury and other cars and things passing by like a movie on fast forward.

Lord, if I survive, I'll never get angry with Emmett again! I'll be the best wife in the world! Get me home! Get me off of this thing!

"I don't want to dieeeeeeeeeeeeeeeeeeeeeeeeeeeee!"

Dawn Kehoe (Donkey)

"Whoooopeeeeeeeeeeeeeeeee!!!"

"Hold on, Nana!"

I don't think I'm this big fella's Nana, but I'm not going to tell him. I'm having too much fun!

"Wheeeeeeeeeeeeeeeeeeeeeeeeeeeeeeeeeeeeeeeeeeeeeeeee!!!"

Chapter Twenty-Six

Gladys Peachy

Rubber! That's what my legs feel like as Curly helps me off of his motorcycle. Despite the horror I just experienced, I know that he was trying to be kind. So I put a smile on my face. I am determined that this man will not experience one more second of prejudice than he likely has already faced in his life. It is not going to come from me, whatever his future may hold.

"Thank you, My Dear." I reach up and he receives my embrace, returning it with a gentleness that puts me in mind of my father. There is no physical resemblance, but I recognize a kind spirit when I meet one. "God bless you."

"It's no trouble." Curly blushes a little. "I wouldn't want my nan to be stuck downtown without a way home."

"She's blessed to have such a caring grandson." I say, noting that Curly seems to be not used to compliments. I hope the best for him. I resolve to pray to that end.

I meet Ethel, Lula and Donkey outside the main entrance with its inviting, happy signage and ample lighting, wondering what kind of 'music' we are going to face when we go inside. There's not much they can really do to us. We pay a lot of money to be here and it's not a lockdown facility, but if they know that Donkey's dementia led to us missing the ride back, that could pose a problem.

"Donkey." Lula says as the biker boys drive away back to their very different world.

"Heehaw!" Donkey replies. "Here I am."

Lula and I smile with relief. Ethel just looks... well, I don't know what she looks like. She looks uncomfortable, as if someone just goosed her.

"Do you know who I am?" Lula's hands are on her hips. "One of three women who would willingly go AWOL for you."

Donkey cocks her head. "Don't you know who you are, Lula?"

Lula huffs at that. I find it funny. Ethel, as I was saying, looks miserable.

"I'm hungry." Donkey says as we stand around trying to figure out how to arrive without looking like anything is amiss.

"No wonder." Ethel quips, her lips scrunched together, eyebrows lowered. "You didn't finish your lunch today."

"I didn't?" Donkey doesn't look convinced. "You're right. I didn't eat today at all."

I roll my eyes. "You ate today, Dear Heart. But it is almost dinnertime."

"Yes, it is." Ethel sighs. "So let's get in there and get it over with. Just make up something. Tell them we lost track of time shopping or… we wandered to the Byward Market to shop and forgot about the time."

"Do you think they'll buy that?" Lula checks her wrist watch. "We've got about an hour till dinner. It's a good thing we didn't miss the whole thing."

"Let's just apologize for not keeping better track of our times. What are they going to do? Give us detention?" Ethel sounds grumpy.

"No." Lula shuffles a foot. "But they could give Donkey plenty of trouble if they find out… well…"

"Find out what?" Donkey asks.

"You don't remember singing and dancing in a bar?" Lula asks, dryly.

"I sang and danced in bars lots of times."

"I give up." Ethel heads toward the door. "I'm tired and soaked and crabby now. I just want to freshen up and eat dinner and go to bed early. Come on, Girls!"

Like good little sheep, we follow Ethel toward the... wait a minute! Did she say soaked? No wonder she's feeling cranky.

Ethel MacNarland

Sneaking past the attendants' desk isn't easy. We are trying to look inconspicuous, but I find that that usually makes a person look as guilty as sin.

"Good afternoon, Ladies."

If that voice belonged to Evangeline Martin or any of the other attendants, my heart wouldn't be dancing the jitterbug right now. Why oh why did it have to be Biddy Finneyfrock standing at the attendants' desk, looking every bit like an annoyed mother whose daughter stayed out past curfew?

I don't feel like talking. I want to get these soggy underpants off and rinse off in the shower before dinner. I don't know if I can keep up my pleasant demeanor. I want to yell at her: *"Hey! Leave us alone! Hells Angels and pee! That's all I have to say!"*

Three of us are faking smiles right now. Donkey's is real... and puts me in mind of Howdy Doody.

"Hello." Gladys says. "And how are you today, Ms. Finneyfrock? That's a lovely pin you're wearing."

It's a silver cat pin. I'm certain that Lula hates it.

Biddy's smile is as fake as ours, but less benevolent.

"Did you ladies forget something?" She asks in a strained,

trying hard to stay professional tone. "Do you know you gave Benny our driver reason to worry? If you weren't going to come back with the rest of the shoppers, you should have informed him. In fact, you should have said so before the bus left today."

The silence right now is telling on us. We had better come up with something fast.

In one unisonous burst, we all decide to confess at the same time.

"I got distracted and wandered into the Byward Market." Gladys says.

"There was a festival on and we lost track of time." I explain.

"It's all my fault. I couldn't decide on anything for my wedding." Lula frets.

"I got hungry." Donkey says last, looking sheepishly at the rest of us, probably wondering why we're having to give account for our whereabouts.

I give an awkward shrug as we all stop talking at the same time.

"I see." Biddy raises an eyebrow. "It seems you all have very good reasons for missing the ride back." She purses her lips, then makes that weird duck face thing that the young ones are always doing. "All very different reasons and yet… you arrived back here together."

We all hesitate to talk now, not wanting to speak over each other or say the wrong thing.

"Well…" Lula puts on her authoritative, don't mess with me voice. "It's just that… the ladies are trying to cover up…"

Gladys and I toss Lula menacing looks.

"Now now, Ladies." Lula puts up her hands. "There's no use in pretending. It's time to tell Ms. Finneyfrock the truth."

"Please…" She says, leaning an elbow on the desk. "I'm all ears."

Lula winks at me and grins before going on. "You see, it really is my fault. I have been so excited about marrying Emmett in a few weeks that I… well…" She holds out her left hand and admires the ring. "I confess that I dragged my friends here away from the mall and into the Byward Market. I thought I might find some interesting things to wear on my wedding day. It's coming up really fast, you know. There's not much time."

"No, there isn't." Biddy nods. "So you went outside the mall and… couldn't find your way back?"

"Oh!" Lula huffs. "We most certainly knew our way back. I just lost track of time. We had quite the odyssey this afternoon. I'm sorry. It won't happen again. It was terribly irresponsible of me and… and I will most definitely apologize to Benny in person. I'm so sorry that we worried him…" She catches herself. "…and others."

Biddy has a look on her face that says, "I don't believe a word you're saying", but Lula's story is plausible. She can only cite us for not informing them about our excursion.

"Please see that it doesn't happen again." Biddy relents.

We're home free… in the clear!

I spoke too soon.

"I rode on a motorcycle!" Donkey announces excitedly. "Me! Dawn Gardiner!"

"Donkey!" Gladys pipes up. "Let's not bother Ms. Finneyfrock with that story." She half smiles. "You've been telling it to us all day…" Gladys looks at me desperately. "…hasn't she, Girls?"

Donkey's hand comes out and slaps Gladys in the face.

All of us jump.

"Dawn!" Gladys grabs Donkey's hand before she can do it again. "We're not playing that game anymore. Come on. Let's go and get ready for dinner."

"A game?" Biddy's face looks paler than usual, if that is even possible. "You ladies play a game that involves striking each other?"

"Yes." Gladys lies (and I know she'll be repenting to God for it later). "Dawn is a little too enthusiastic today though. It's usually just light taps… you know, like… yellow punch buggy! No punch back!" She punches Donkey lightly in the arm.

Biddy shakes her head. I think we are going to get away with this… until…

"Ow! Eve! That wasn't very nice!" Donkey shouts. "You're mean and you steal my boyfriends all the time!"

"No… No, Donkey… I mean… Dawn…" Gladys' desperate voice is as heartbreaking as watching Donkey seal her own fate in front of the heartless administrator of Tranquil Meadows.

I see a tear making its way down Lula's cheek.

"She calls me Eve sometimes." Gladys tries to explain.

"Stop, Gladdy. Stop." Lula sets a hand on her shoulder.

"No, but she…" Gladdy shakes her head. "She does, doesn't she?"

She calls me Eve too. Seriously, she doesn't know any of us for more than a few minutes at a time anymore. I am like Lula. I am hoisting a big white flag.

"It's time to…" Lula's voice cracks. "We can't cover for her anymore."

Tallulah Pratt (Lula)

I'm a heel. A traitorous witch! Lordy, I'm the worst friend anybody could ask for!

"Lula?" Gladys hands me a tissue. "Here, Dear Heart. You mustn't blame yourself."

The three of us are hiding out in Gladdy's room. If I sulk anymore, my face is going to stay that way forever. I just can't help it!

"What are they going to do to her?" I shake my head in dismay. "The thought of her living across the way in that... that..."

"Roach motel." Ethel's dry delivery matches how we all feel.

"Ethel!" Gladys scolds.

"Sorry, Girls." Ethel sighs. "I just hate that we got defeated in the end."

"Me too." Gladdy opens the drawer to her night stand. "Here. I was saving these for a special occasion."

She produces three packets of Lindt chocolate balls. They are like eating a slice of Heaven, I admit, but right now, they're like a prescription for the blues. I don't know if it will work, but it's worth a shot.

"Hand over the chocolate and nobody gets hurt!" I growl.

Gladys grins and for a few seconds, all that can be heard is the collective crinkling of wrappers. I glance over as Gladys shuts the drawer and I notice that she had a fourth packet of the Lindt balls, but that's not going to matter now, is it?

"Gabe arrived half an hour ago." Ethel says. "I saw him with one of his sons... not the nasty one. I guess... he and Biddy are going to discuss Donkey's options. They won't let her stay here if she's that far gone."

I feel sobs pushing up my windpipe and more water welling up in my eyes. "I can't believe it! We almost had the old warhorse convinced that it was me that held us up! Lordy, maybe chocolate won't be enough. Maybe I need a stiff drink!" I reach for the tissue box that Gladys put on the bed when we all plunked down on it to lick our wounds and mourn our loss.

"She was so far gone today." Ethel grabs a tissue too. "It's like... she is finally crossing over and leaving the real world behind."

"It's beyond sad." Gladys rests her head on my arm and we all sit in silence, contemplating life without Donkey, me wondering what more we could have done... how could I have prevented this? If only she hadn't opened her mouth at the end, we wouldn't be sitting here now, awaiting news of what her life sentence is going to be... Tranquil Meadows Plus? The Braceridge? Take her for a walk in the woods as if she were the family dog and... kablam? That's morbid. I know it. I just... it feels like we sentenced her to die.

I run a hand over the pretty peach-coloured fabric of Gladdy's quilt. Peachy. Just like her name... just like she is... a peachy kind of friend.

"We should remember her at her best." Gladys says, reaching for the photo of the four of us that we showed people in the Byward Market earlier today. She smiles as she looks at the snapshot.

"That was such a happy day." I recall. "And Donkey wasn't so... well... she was more herself."

Ethel tosses the empty chocolate wrappers in the trash can. "You're right, Gladdy. We need to remember Donkey before her mind stole her away... think of her at her best. That's just what I'm going to do."

I pat Ethel's hand. "Me too."

Gladdy puts her hand on top of both of ours. "It's settled then... we're going to try our hardest to forget the bad things. We had more than two years with her and I want to treasure those memories."

"Yeah." It feels like a huge burden is rolling off of my shoulders. I feel grief, yes, but something is lifting off of me.

"We should resolve to do the same for each other." Ethel proposes. "To always think of each other and remember our best times... when we were our true selves. I mean, I don't intend to 'leave the planet' mentally anytime soon, but... if I do..."

"It's a deal." Gladdy agrees. "If anything should happen to one of us, let's promise to hold on to the good memories and not think about anything else. I can't think of a better way to honour Donkey."

A thought comes to me. "Is that how you remember Paul?"

Gladdy smiles. "Yes. I think of all our best times, our laughs and our good moments. I was truly blessed to have him in my life... and that's how I feel about Donkey too... and you, Lula... and Ethel. I have been so very very blessed to know you and call you my dear friends. What more could a girl ask for in life? I can't think of a blooming thing."

"Except maybe more Lindt chocolate." Ethel quips, giggling. "And a bladder that doesn't work so hard." She slides off the bed faster than an old woman should and rushes to the bathroom.

I am sitting here thinking about what Gladys just said. If she can think about the good times she had with Paul and with Donkey, maybe I can do that too. Maybe, instead of focusing on Tom's philandering, I can remember what a good father he was, how in the end, he chose his marriage over his affair. He

wasn't a perfect man. Lordy, no he wasn't! But I wasn't perfect either. And maybe that's all right. Maybe it's time to just…
"Haugh!" I gasp. Let it go…

"Lula? Are you all right?" Gladdy wiggles over closer to me. "You're not going to cry again, are you?"

I slide my arm around her and give her a squeeze. "Absolutely not! I'm going to miss Donkey like the dickens. I know we all are, but… Gladys Peachy, do you know what? You are such a good friend. I could just hug you to bits! I love you! Don't you ever forget that!"

I hear a soft chuckle. Ethel is back from the restroom.

"Bonzai!" She hollers and jumps on the bed on the other side of Gladys, skooching up close and putting her arm around her, so now Ethel and I are the bread on either side of a Gladys sandwich.

"Ditto, Gladdy!" Ethel says. "I love you too! You're a fantastic friend and… well… I've never been much of a pray-er, but if I was, I would be thanking God above for letting me be alive at the same time as you."

We all fall back onto the bed and laugh.

"You girls are bananas!" Gladdy replies. "But I love you and we're going to get through this thing together."

"Like the three musketeers?" Ethel asks.

"Sure." Gladdy lifts her arms in the air and we shout together.

"All for one and one for all!"

Everything goes quiet. I hear the tick… tick… tick… of Gladdy's bedside clock, the beginning of the cricket's song telling me that dusk is on its way.

"Girls?" Gladdy finally speaks. "If it's all right with you, can we say a prayer for Donkey? I want her to be looked after right… I don't want her going someplace where they'll shove her in the corner and forget about her."

Fear tries to seize my heart. In my mind, I push it back.

"Sure." Ethel agrees. "Lula?"

"Of course."

We all sit up again and Heaven hears the collective request of The Donkey Defenders.

Dawn Kehoe (Donkey)

There's that lady again, the nutty blond one with the cat pin. I think she stole it. Did she? Did it belong to me?

"Mother."

I look into the face of a smiling man. He looks familiar. What's his name? It's… it's… it's…

??

"I'm afraid of the attic."

"I know." The man puts an arm around me. "You never have to go to that attic again."

"I don't?" I smile back at him. "Am I going back to the Montgomery Institute?"

The man and the cat pin lady exchange funny looks.

"They have a piano there, Mother." The man says.

Why does he keep calling me Mother?

I like pianos.

I can play a piano fairly well.

I have perfect pitch.

I'm sure that cat pin is mine.

"Don't do that." The man grabs my hand.

What was I doing?

I was trying to grab the pin.

Well, it's mine! She should get her own stuff!

Who cut her hair? An army barber?

???????????????????????????????????

Where am I?

What is this place?

???????????????????????????????????

Who am I?

Who?

Who?

An owl?

Hahaha… no, not an owl.

I am a donkey. Yes, that's it. I am a little donkey.

Some people told me that.

I don't remember who they were.

Chapter Twenty-Seven

Gladys Peachy

What a long day it has been! So much excitement... happy, sad, frightened, disappointed... and now I am exhausted.

Slipping my nightie over my head and onto my arms feels so good. Whoa... goodness me! I sit back down on the bed. "Oh! I feel winded! I changed clothes. I didn't run a marathon!" I chuckle... shake my head. I feel a little like I could float... or sink... or I am joining Donkey on Fantasy Island. I know my name and who my husband was... that can't be it.

"God. Forgive me if my prayers are a little shorter tonight." I smile as I slide this achy bag of bones under the covers. "Sleep is going to feel really good. I can't believe I waited until I turned 75 to join a motorcycle gang." What a funny thought that is! "Oh... Curly. God, would you look after that nice young man? He's had a lot of rejection in his life. Send him some good friends and maybe a wife... and let him know that you love him whether he's dressed in leather or a fancy suit. It's all the same to you."

I sigh, grab the glass of water on my night table and pull it toward my lips.

"And Donkey..." I add. "Dear, dear Donkey..."

My hand shakes a little. How silly is that! Oh! Some of the water is spilling... spilling all over...

"Gladdy."

That voice... as familiar to me as my own... yet I have not heard it in more years than I want to count. A dream... I am dreaming... but...

"How are you feeling?"

That's a weird question coming from a person who hasn't spoken to me this decade. Weirder still is the ease with which I answer and the sudden realization. "I feel fine." I smile. "I don't feel tired at all… but it's bedtime and… Paul?"

"Yes, Gladdy."

"I spilled water all over the bed."

"It doesn't matter now."

"Doesn't it?"

"No."

I look into his face, almost afraid that if I dare, he will dissipate like a vapour into thin air. But he doesn't.

He looks as handsome as the day I met him. In fact, didn't he almost look just like that? Waves of brown hair and eyes as blue as a peaceful lagoon.

He laughs. "Are you ready?"

His hand reaches out in invitation.

"I don't understand." Even so, my hand automatically extends out to meet his and now, his fingers slide over mine and it is like I have slipped on a most cherished and comfortable garment.

"It's better than we ever dreamed." He says.

"Is it?"

"You'll see."

As we walk together, the back wall seems to disappear and I see what I can only describe as a cable car with no line at the top sitting there, door open and waiting.

For a brief second, I think of Ethel and Lula and Donkey… I turn to wave, but I know they don't see me.

"Oh!" I notice the smoothness of my own skin and reach up a hand to feel my face, my hair, the peripheral vision catching a glimpse of dark brown curls.

Somewhere, and my mind is quickly forgetting, my former shell lies… like the hollowed out remains of an old, shrivelled snake skin that I won't be needing anymore.

Chapter Twenty-Eight

Ethel MacNarland

Sitting on my bed, my hand trembles as I hold the letter in my hand.

It has been several weeks since Donkey went to live at the Braceridge and Gladdy… my breath catches at the thought of her. When they found her, she looked as peaceful as a sleeping baby, Evangeline said. She just turned the page from one chapter to the next, it seems. I know that none of us are spring chickens around here, but the whole place was shocked.

I caught Evangeline Martin crying in the ladies' room. I promised never to tell. I know Biddy would never approve of her staff getting attached to the residents. Well, what does that old crow expect? Compassion is what makes Evangeline so good at her job. Ah well, there's no use in trying to explain it. Biddy would actually need to have a heart to understand and she's colder than Antarctica.

She was annoyed when Gabe chose to take Donkey to the Braceridge. It's a roach motel too, but from what I've heard, it's friendlier, brighter, cleaner and better run than Alcatraz… I mean… Tranquil Meadows Plus. I wonder if Dinah Gillespie and Donkey even remember each other. I frown at the thought of them staring at each other in the dining room and not having the foggiest notion that they have ever met.

I turn my attention back to the letter in my hand.

"Dear Mrs. MacNarland,

Your son, Tim, forwarded a copy of the first draft of your novel, "The Granny Diaries" to my company, Late Bloom Publishing, and I would like to meet with you to discuss options. Please contact my secretary and we can arrange to have lunch sometime soon.

Kind regards,

A.J. Bloom"

Tim was true to his word. I didn't think he would do it... or at least, I thought he was exaggerating about his connections in the publishing world. I am also happy to report that, so far, things are looking good between him and Sylvia. That's one worry off of my mind.

I grin. I picture a book with a fancy cover and my name as the author sitting in the window at the book store. Even as I was writing it, I doubted it was possible. Today, I feel optimistic about my prospects.

And now, I'd better hurry up and get dressed. It's not every day that a friend gets married and when it comes to Tallulah Pratt, soon to be Muggeridge, being late is not an option.

I pull out the new dress that Lula made me buy. She insisted that no maid of honour of hers was going to be caught dead in anything but the best. I have to admit, the old broad has good taste! I take the sunny peach dress from the hanger and begin dressing myself.

"Nice touch, Lula." I say, though she isn't here.

She made the colour scheme of the décor and the maid of honour and flower girl dresses peach... to honour one of the dear friends who won't be attending today. For all her haughty drama, Lula is one fine, caring woman. She can fan out those peacock feathers all she likes. She's not fooling me.

"Well, let's get this show on the road. Hey God... um... give Gladdy my regards and... maybe I'll talk to you later?" I take a deep breath and carry on.

Tallulah Pratt (Lula)

I hear the strains of the music being played on an electronic piano.

A flock of butterflies mounted on Roman candles seem to be flying and exploding in my stomach right now.

It's going to be perfect! I am waiting behind a hedge with Ethel and both Emmett's and my granddaughters. They are dressed in lovely peach dresses, in memory of the dearest heart I have ever known… our beloved Gladdy, who is watching over me today, reunited with her Paul and her son.

My dress is not peach. It isn't pure white either. I opted for off white… an ivory colour… and since, for my second wedding, I am not an almost broke youngster just trying to make do with whatever my parents can afford, I went all out. I bought something beautiful… not from C'est La Vie. That snooty salesclerk looked at my friends as if they were lower than she is. I will never shop there again.

The dress is satiny. It shimmers and hugs me in all the right places. It has a stunning short lacy jacket that goes with it and I fell in love with it on sight.

My hair is done up, matching earrings and necklace on, and I feel as beautiful as I did when an entire lifetime lay before me and a younger woman spoke the vows that I am about to say. Well, these words will also be for a lifetime… I pray that lifetime is years and years long.

Gabe Kehoe (yes, Donkey is here… I hope she knows me!) steps up to a microphone in the gardens at Tranquil Meadows and begins singing the song that will guide our little procession down the aisle.

"There were birds in the sky
But I never heard them singing

No, I never heard them at all
Til there was you..."

Donkey was right. He sings like an angel... at least as well as she does. If only she were well enough to sing here today. I would have given that job to her gladly. Still, she is here. Gabe was kind enough to arrange it and to offer his formidable talent to us. I purposely put bacon and tomato sandwiches on the menu for afterwards to make Donkey happy.

Ethel has made it to the front and has taken her place. And now... it is my turn.

Emmett is standing on one side of the lovely trellis that the staff at Tranquil Meadows erected for this occasion... at the behest of Bidelia Finneyfrock no less! With a shock like that, it's a wonder Ethel and I didn't follow Gladdy to Heaven.

Rows of chairs are set up with beautiful roses and bows. Bouquets of flowers line the aisle and the front area. That and the flowers that already surround us in this garden are enough to take my breath away... though my eyes right now are riveted on, as Ethel would say, a hot man in a fedora... without his fedora. He is, however, in a pretty spiffy off-white tuxedo jacket with contrasting black trim and pants.

Time freezes.

I take slow, even steps down the aisle, knowing how to pace, knowing how to keep everything in place... everything, that is, except the raw emotion that crescendoes within my heart. Oh... how could I have ever hesitated to be with this man? He is who I want to spend the rest of my life beside.

His smile sends electricity coursing through me, waves of gratitude and wonder and the desire to be so close to him that it becomes impossible to tell where Emmett ends and Tallulah begins.

As I stand beside Emmett and the minister begins the ceremony, his hazel eyes draw me into their inviting pools and the happy people watching us exchange our vows seem to fade away as if Emmett and I have been transported to some ethereal plane somewhere between the earth and the heavens.

"I do." I say, as Reverend Whats-his-name (he told me three times, but I can't remember) asks me to vow to be with Emmett for the rest of my life. I would like to add, "I really really really do", but that would not be fitting. I would sound like my darling dotty Donkey.

"I do." Emmett smiles and I see his eyes glistening with tears.

It's an odd and empowering thing, being loved despite who you are. If you are wondering, I highly recommend it.

"And now..." The Reverend says. "The groom has prepared a little something special for his bride."

My heart leaps as Emmett's son scurries to the platform and hands Emmett a piece of paper.

"If you'll pardon me..." Emmett grins. "I'm not as young as I used to be, so... I don't memorize things so easily."

Nobody minds. I notice the audience for a few seconds and I try not to giggle at the sight of four motorcycle enthusiasts dressed in their Sunday best instead of chains and leather. Curly cried like a baby when I told him about Gladdy, but there he is. I'm so glad they came.

Emmett clears his throat.

"I will never grow tired of seeing your face
Of the way that you walk with such elegant grace
Of the laugh that reminds me of angels in song
Of the scolding you give me when you think I'm wrong

I will never grow tired of walking with you

With your hand in my hand as we travel on through
You can have all the love that I hold in my heart
Please believe me when I vow, till death to us part."

It's not Keats. It's not even Hallmark, but it was written just for me by the most wonderful soul. We are going to be all right, Emmett and me.

Things are changing as surely as the season is about to move into autumn, but I can face these things because I am no longer alone. Lordy, I didn't think I deserved this, but maybe I was wrong. Maybe second chances are God's way of saying, "It's okay, Kid. Let's try this again, shall we?"

"I now pronounce you husband and wife. You may kiss the bride." Reverend Thingamabob says.

He doesn't have to tell Emmett twice.

He doesn't have to tell me either.

"May I introduce Emmett and Tallulah Muggeridge."

Tallulah Muggeridge. It has a nice ring to it. Euphoria surges through me like the arrival of high tide.

Emmett grabs my hand and we head back down the aisle to the pianist's rendition of the traditional end of wedding song.

Bidelia said no confetti on the grounds. I notice it flying through the air anyway. Oops! Lordy, she can just get over it.

I shout: "Ethel! Catch!"

I hurl the bouquet right at her and… ha! She caught it!

Her face says I'm in trouble.

Pete Marsden's face just lit up like a Christmas tree.

Dawn Kehoe (Donkey)

I smooth out the skirt of my short-sleeved, light blue dress. It has little white flowers across the top. I don't remember putting this on. I don't remember coming here, but I'm sure I've been here before. I can't think what for.

Everybody is dressed up. It's quite a shindig. I'm hungry. I hope they feed us soon.

"The bride is wearing satin and lace." I point. "See? And the flower girls are wearing peachy dresses."

I think... hard.

"Peachy... that's like your last name."

My friend smiles at me. She has beautiful brown curls and green eyes. I never noticed that before. I don't know why.

I get up from my seat.

"I know they have sandwiches around here somewhere." I gesture for my friend to follow. "Let's go rustle some up. I don't feel like waiting anymore. I haven't eaten in days. I'm staying at a fancy hotel, but they only feed me once a week."

We walk through a crowd of strangers. No. Wait... I know some of them. Don't I?

"Come on. They've got tables set up. We can sneak some food. Nobody will know." I laugh. "I bet they won't have ba..." My eyes and mouth both go wide. "Is it? It is! I see..." I throw my hands in the air. "...bacon!"

My friend nods as I grab a sandwich. I know the way even though I have never been here before.

"Did you ever have a déjà vu feeling? I'm having that now." I say. "It's like... I've lived this before somehow. Isn't that strange? My sister Eve always talks about spooky stuff like that. I think she just does it to scare me."

I see that the bride and her maid of honour have finally entered the room with all the food. They must be hungry too.

"I hope they don't mind that I started eating without them."

My friend looks over at the wedding party. Do they know each other?

"I think I know them." I say.

"Mother!"

I turn with a start! "Gabe, you sang a beautiful song." I am so proud of him.

He smiles, but not as big a smile as mine.

"Who are you talking to?" He asks.

"What? Isn't it obvious? I'm talking to my friend."

He sighs... then pecks me on the cheek and walks to the buffet table to get some food. "You and your imaginary friend again." He mutters as he goes.

I look at my friend and motion for her to come and sit at a table with me.

"Come on, Gladdy. To make you happy, I'll even wear a bib this time."

HAZEL MAY LEBRUN

ABOUT THE AUTHOR

Hazel May Lebrun

Hazel May Lebrun is a Metis mother and grandmother originally from Braeside, Ontario, now residing in Ottawa, Canada's capital city. In addition to writing novels, short stories and plays, she is also an accomplished songwriter and poet, having written Christmas pageants and songs for various occasions, playing in folk venues and festivals in the Ottawa and Ottawa Valley region for more than 40 years. She loves torturing people with pictures of her grandchildren, animals and treasure hunting at estate sales like a pirate.

THE GRANNY DIARIES

AFTERWORD

I thought that some would wonder after reading this book, was Donkey seeing a ghost? Was Gladys Peachy a ghost? Didn't you write that she went to Heaven? Yes, that is correct. I didn't see Gladys as a ghost. The way I saw it, Donkey's dementia had put her perpetually in that mysterious place between this world and the next, where she was simply seeing a little peek into that place as she herself inches closer towards it. In her Donkey-esque way, she simply assumed Gladys was there along with everyone else and spoke to her accordingly. I hope that clears up any questions before they begin.

ACKNOWLEDGEMENT

The author would like to thank family members, friends and acquaintances for many encouragements, pep talks, wise words of advice and for their patience during this writing process. Thank you specifically goes out to her sister, Norma, to Kathy for encouraging me to write, to Courtney, Roxanne, Stephanie and Judy, the members of P.O.D. (Publish or Die) for hours of read throughs, edits, go girl go and... the most important part (wink)... snacks.

Manufactured by Amazon.ca
Bolton, ON